Front Page News

Sadie Gordon Richmond

Book cover design by RockingBookCovers.com

Also by this author

Sins of Silence
Sticks and Stones
Shadow Lines
One in a Million
I Have Never
The Ties That Bind

For Mum & Dad

Prologue

Lucian drew his fingers up his brow towards his crown, dragging his sodden hair back from his forehead in an attempt to stem the flow of rainwater into his smarting eyes. He passed Hampstead Heath Station and a train home reluctantly, throwing the waterlogged remains of his cigarette into the gutter and reaching into his jacket pocket for another. Pausing briefly to light up, he flicked his eyes left, then right, before jaywalking through two anti-parallel lines of near-stationary rush hour traffic.

Ahead, more cars crawled in single file up Pond Street, commuters drumming their fingers in impatience at the delay, muttering under their breath and making calls on mobile phones. Heading home to wives, husbands, partners, children, friends, houses, mortgages, flat shares – warmth and security which, at that moment, seemed accessible to all but Lucian. Thinking bitterly that being caught in traffic served every one of them right for driving a car, he kicked a mangled Coke can in the general direction of his destination, now in sight.

Struggling in vain to concoct a plausible excuse not to make the daily trip to the hospital, he had lingered so long on Parliament Hill that visiting hours were now all but over, and he half hoped he would be refused access. Even at the best of times he scarcely needed reminding of his mother's imminent demise, and the increasingly frequent hospital admissions were starting to bring home to him the fact he was likely to be spending his next Christmas alone. Today was certainly not the best of times, and with the pressure of A-level exams hanging over the next twenty-four hours of his life he felt unable to cope with anything at all.

Having woven through the traffic at the zebra crossing, he paused at the hospital steps to finish his cigarette, wondering whether to risk having one more before heading inside. Reluctantly, he decided against it, tossing the butt to the ground and turning to climb the steps up from the road. Twenty minutes, he told himself. Just twenty minutes, and today's ordeal would be over.

'Lucian,' Dr Klein began, as he joined Lucian in the corridor, his tone and expression one of mandatory impassivity that served only to heighten Lucian's anxiety. Standing, Lucian ran an uneasy hand through his hair, sending water running down his arm and the back of his neck.

'How's Mum?'

'We have the pneumonia under control,' Dr Klein informed him, concluding the statement with a hesitancy that suggested he hadn't finished and that what remained to be said wasn't encouraging. 'But unfortunately the cancer has spread.'

Lucian didn't reply immediately, absorbing this information. 'What happens next?' He asked, at length.

'To be honest, we don't really know. These things aren't easy to predict, and the underlying condition only makes it more difficult. At the moment we're monitoring the situation closely, and we're keeping her as comfortable as possible.'

'How about treatment?'

'We've increased the painkillers – I'm afraid there are too many complications for us to be able to do anything more at this stage.'

'But surely there must be –'

'We're doing our best, but you have to understand that there are limits to what we can achieve.'

'Yes, but –'

'We're doing our best,' Dr Klein repeated firmly.

Lucian bowed his head, biting into his lower lip and fighting to retain his composure. 'When do you think she'll be well enough to come home?' He managed, as he looked back up, his voice wavering slightly.

'Lucian, she isn't going home again. I'm sorry.'

Lucian stared at the man. 'But – I mean –'

'I'm sorry, but there's really nothing more we can do.'

Lucian remained standing for a moment, desperately trying to think of something to say or do. Shaking, he sank down onto the bench that he had occupied only moments earlier, reaching instinctively for his cigarettes before remembering where he was. Resting his forearms across slightly parted thighs, hands between his knees, he stared down at the polished floor for an indefinable period of time before the doctor spoke again.

'Lucian, are you all right?'

He nodded mechanically, thinking, meanwhile, that it was a stupid question to ask. How was anybody expected to be *all right*

10

when the only family they had ever known was about to be snatched away? Defiantly, he blinked back the tears, swallowing hard. He couldn't cry now. He *couldn't*. Repeating this thought as he forced himself back onto his feet, he drew a deep breath, raising his head.

'I'd like to see her, please.'

Lucian observed his mother from the doorway of her isolation room, where she lay propped up in bed, an oxygen mask over her mouth and nose, and a drip running into her wasted left arm. Now pallid and skeletally thin, with cold sores clustered around her lips, she seemed to have aged by twenty years in just a few months. From where Lucian stood, her hair looked damp, although he supposed it could just be in need of a wash, preferring that possibility to the more likely explanation that she was running a temperature. When she didn't immediately react to his arrival, he wondered whether she might be sleeping, suddenly hoping that she were. He wasn't sure he felt ready to face her so soon after the exchange with Dr Klein, and hesitated before taking a step into the room.

'Luke?' She turned her head slightly, and, on seeing him, held out a hand. 'How did the exam go, love?'

'Fine,' Lucian lied, taking her hand and forcing a smile. It was easy to lie now, knowing she wouldn't live to see his results.

'I told you not to get so worked up,' she whispered, giving his fingers a weak squeeze. 'Is tomorrow the last one?'

'Yes.'

'I wasn't sure whether I'd see you tonight. I thought you might have too much on.'

'Of course not.'

'You –' she broke off, coughing painfully. Lucian thrust his free hand into his pocket, desperate for a cigarette.

'You look tired, Luke.'

He shrugged. 'It's been a long day, I guess.'

'I suppose so.'

Lucian opened his mouth to speak, closed it, and then tried again, coming out with little more than 'Uh –'

'What is it?'

'Uh – I –' he pulled his hand from his pocket and raked it through his hair, searching for the words he'd nailed down just hours earlier. He had intended to confer to her how important

11

the answer to this question was to him, hoping that by phrasing it carefully and eloquently she might understand that he had given the matter appropriate thought and consideration. As it was, he stumbled through several disjointed syllables before blurting, 'I need a name.' Then, when she didn't respond, 'Please. Just give me that much.'

The pause before she answered was almost unbearable. Eventually, she nodded slightly, whispering, 'If that's what you really want.'

'It is,' Lucian replied, as firmly as his rather unsteady voice would allow. 'Before it's too late.'

One

Rebecca was caught in that semiconscious limbo between asleep and awake where dreams merge with reality and render the two almost inseparable on waking. Too hot to sleep comfortably, yet too drowsy to realise there might be some way to remedy the situation, she drifted, confused, through imaginary encounters and buried anxieties. Surfacing momentarily on occasions that felt, according to the luminous figures of her digital alarm clock, deceptively distant, she was never sufficiently alert to do more than register that she hadn't yet overslept. She might have floated uneasily in this manner, from one doze to another, until morning, had she not been suddenly and violently jolted awake by what sounded and felt alarmingly like an explosion.

'Uh? What?' She exclaimed, sitting up almost before she awoke. The noise and vibrations continued for several seconds before quiet resumed, and, when it did, Rebecca stayed where she was in bed, trying to gather her thoughts and get her bearings. Shortly, she leaned towards the window and pulled the curtain back to peer at what she could see of the street outside. The houses were all still there, nothing was on fire, and she could see nobody, perhaps unsurprisingly, given that it was ten past four on a Friday morning. Moments later, a bright flash of lightning, accompanied by an almost instantaneous crack of thunder, answered the question of what had disturbed her. She could only assume, from the intensity of the previous crash, that the lightning had struck something.

Relieved that nothing serious was amiss, she released the curtain and relaxed back against the bed's headboard, waiting for her heart rate to return to normal and hoping it wouldn't take her too long to get back to sleep. She had worked late all week, partly in an effort to clear some of the paperwork that had been breeding at the side of her desk for far too long, and partly because, with Elliot, her fiancé, away, the alternative was long evenings alone in the flat with little more than the television and Facebook for company.

Climbing out of bed to open a window, she fervently wished she wasn't working that day, as the combination of long hours and paperwork, which she found tedious and difficult, had left her feeling drained. During her three years working in CID at Scotland Yard she had rarely found herself watching the clock, but the previous day had been particularly monotonous, and the thought of another day trapped at her desk was less than appealing. The only possible respite would be a new investigation, which would eat into the weekend she had planned to spend with friends in Brighton.

Returning to bed, she slid down onto her back. The curtains were now slightly parted, allowing an anaemic yellow light to permeate the room, fanning out across the ceiling and illuminating the wall opposite the window. This was hung with a selection of framed promotional band photographs, and, casting her eyes over them, Rebecca idly wondered what Elliot might be doing at that moment. The singer and songwriter of a band named Astatine, he had been away on tour for the last fortnight, and wasn't due back for another ten days. The band had released their first album three months earlier, and since that time Elliot had barely been home, touring Britain, North America and Europe for weeks at a time. He was currently in the north of England, after which he would be heading up to Scotland before returning south to perform at the Glastonbury festival over the last weekend in June.

Rebecca was looking forward to July, when she and Elliot would be taking a short holiday, although she also felt slightly apprehensive about the break. They had agreed to spend a long weekend with her parents in Norwich, and, although Elliot had met them on several occasions, Rebecca knew the prospect of spending three days with them was a daunting one for him. She was also well aware that her parents were more than a little sceptical about her engagement to Elliot. He wasn't the first unconventional boyfriend she'd had, but Rebecca suspected her parents had dismissed her penchant for what her father called 'creative types' as *a phase*, and had never imagined she might actually settle down with one of them.

Not that Rebecca had initially envisaged becoming so deeply involved with Elliot herself. In all honesty, she hadn't expected a charming and very pretty rock musician to *want* much more than a fling. On occasion, she found herself questioning what the future might hold for their relationship, given that they were pursuing such different and, in some ways, conflicting careers. The music industry's long history of decadent, licentious and often unlawful behaviour was hardly compatible with Rebecca's profession, and she had no idea which way she would jump if forced to choose between the two. As far as her parents were concerned, Rebecca hoped they might change their tune once they had had the opportunity to get to know Elliot properly. Half the problem was her mother's enduring fondness for Rebecca's previous boyfriend, Miles, whom she had been convinced was going to be *the one*. Rebecca had thought otherwise, and had ended their eighteen-month relationship only weeks before meeting Elliot. Her mother, she was sure, suspected that the two events had happened in the reverse order, which didn't help matters at all. With a sigh, she turned her back on the glowing crack in the curtains and closed her eyes. Whilst her parents never said as much, Rebecca sensed that they disliked Lewis, her twin sister Angela's husband, and she didn't want this going the same way. Although, whatever happened, they would have to accept the situation, because, in her mind, Elliot was there to stay.

'Good of you to drop in,' Detective Chief Inspector Lawrence Forrester, Rebecca's immediate superior, greeted cheerfully as she hurried into his office twenty minutes late, apologising profusely. A pragmatic and dedicated detective in his late thirties, he was held in high regard by many at Scotland Yard, including Rebecca, who had worked closely with him for well over a year. Tall and robust, with dark hair, distinctive features and clear hazel eyes, he was currently leaning against the edge of his desk, dressed in a grey pinstripe suit and blue shirt, his loosely crossed legs extending into the room. Given his normally tough stance on tardiness, he looked surprisingly relaxed – roughly the antithesis of Rebecca's feelings at that moment. Her journey from Highgate to Embankment had been little short of unbearable, packed into an overcrowded and inadequately ventilated underground train that had been sultry and odiferous with sweat before it even reached Camden Town. The experience had left her feeling hot, sticky and distinctly irritable at the start of what was evidently going to be another blistering June day.

'Sorry,' Rebecca repeated. 'Northern Line.'

'If you ever move onto another line, you're going to be in trouble,' Lawrence teased, leaning backwards slightly before pushing himself away from the desk and up into a standing position.

'Apparently the trains were running late due to a *delay*,' Rebecca replied, scathingly. 'Anyone would think they'd not had time to come up with one or two decent excuses – next time around I'm expecting them to claim the dog ate the timetable!'

Lawrence laughed, turning towards his desk to reach for his car keys and a large brown envelope on which they lay.

Rebecca frowned. 'Don't tell me we have a case.'

Lawrence raised his eyebrows, holding his hands out rather helplessly. 'We have a case,' he said, with an apologetic smile. 'Crime scene pics,' he added, proferring the envelope and starting towards the door.

Rebecca took the envelope with a rather bad grace and followed Lawrence from the room. 'So much for my weekend.'

'Sorry.'

'What have we got?'

'Nineteen-year-old model raped, strangled and mutilated in her flat in Golders Green. Presumably by somebody she knew, or at least granted entry to the flat, given that there appears to be no sign of forced entry. Time of death was probably in the early hours of yesterday morning – her boyfriend found the body last night.'

'How did *he* get into the flat? Assuming he doesn't live there.'

'Good question. As yet unanswered.'

'Where are we heading first?'

'I think we ought to start with her parents – they live in Hampstead – after that we'll have a chat with the boyfriend and see where that takes us.' Lawrence pressed the *down* key to summon the lift. 'How late were you here last night?'

'Half ten,' Rebecca replied, ruefully.

'Not much of a way to spend your evening. Did nobody tell you Thursday night is the new Friday night?'

'Elliot did observe that there was little point wasting a Saturday recovering from a hangover when you could do it at work on a Friday instead, yes.' Rebecca stepped into the lift and selected *ground*. 'But since I don't have a strictly Monday to Friday job and am incapable of working with a raging hangover, I vetoed the idea.'

'Elliot doesn't work Monday to Friday either.'

'He also has the advantage of being able to drink *while* working, which tends to help cure the hangover, much as it may not be a wise way to do so.'

Lawrence nodded.

'So what did you get up to last night that was so exciting?'

'Not a lot. I seemed to spend most of the evening clearing up after the kids.'

'Ah,' Rebecca raised her eyebrows knowingly. Lawrence was the father of two, a rather unruly twelve-year-old boy named Jimmy, and a lively daughter, aged nine, called Elise. Lawrence and his wife, Katie, had a holiday in France booked for August, but the school term was due to finish some weeks ahead of that, and Rebecca guessed Lawrence now regarded the impending commencement of the summer holidays with some trepidation.

'My paper had already been destroyed by the time I arrived home,' he sighed as they departed the lift on the ground floor. 'We have a garage so full of old papers that I can barely squeeze the car in, and Elise picks yesterday's *Times*.'

'Perhaps it might be time to invest in an iPad and an online subscription?'

'You assume I'd ever see the thing. I imagine I'd just spend my time trying to pry it out of the kids' hands rather than cleaning up papier-mâché.'

'Less messy, though.'

Lawrence smiled. 'True.'

'So what was Elise making?'

'A large cardboard pig.'

Rebecca laughed. 'Is that a comment on your profession?'

'An extension of some activity from Brownies, apparently,' Lawrence responded, with a slight shake of his head. 'The most ironic part of the whole affair is that that pig is going to be my Christmas present. And she's going to paint it in a realistic green, too.'

'I'm very envious,' Rebecca giggled.

'Naturally.'

'Although I can't believe we're talking about Christmas. I've not even come up with a birthday present for Elliot yet.'

'When's his birthday?'

'August.'

'Is it a big one?'

'No. Twenty-nine.'

'And does that make you feel *really* old?' Lawrence baited, well aware that Rebecca was already thirty-one.

'Well –' Rebecca wrinkled her nose, pretending to ponder the suggestion for a moment before concluding, 'No, not really.' She allowed a moment to pass in silence before she added, with a triumphant smile, 'But it does make me realise just how ancient some of my colleagues are.'

The image was nauseating. Afraid to close his eyes and visualise the snapshot memory again, yet desperate for sleep to grant some respite from the hell of the past forty-eight hours, Pete reached for the bottle at his bedside. It was close to empty, and he downed what remained, coughing as the neat vodka burned his throat. He held the bottle upturned for far longer than was necessary to drain the last of its contents, listening to the steady ticking of his bedside alarm clock and staring up at the poster directly over his head.

Despair giving way to fury, he hurled the empty bottle across the room, watching as it shattered against the partially open kitchen door and the shards rained down in what seemed like slow motion. For a time he lay motionless, one arm flung over the edge of the bed, head tipped to one side, eyes on the framed photograph on his shelf. The picture rested just inches from his fingers, and he felt torn between the need to hold it close, as he had done the night before, and a sudden urge to grind the glass into the photograph with the heel of his boot.

She had teased him. Tormented him. Cheated, manipulated and used him, and now he had nothing, nothing but guilt, regret and one last, horrific memory. Reaching out, he lifted the frame from the shelf and held it directly in front of his face. Hating her might have made his anguish more bearable, crushing the glass into her face would perhaps have eased the pain – but not necessarily for the right reasons. In truth, he wanted to hate her only to disguise the contempt he felt for himself. He had *allowed* her to use him; been willingly manipulated; permitted her to make a fool of him by ignoring her disloyalties – and her final, acrimonious words to him had conveyed nothing but pity and total disrespect. His retaliation had been as inadequate as she had painted him to be, and his actions might have been forgivable should his frustrations not have been directed elsewhere.

Once he had not doubted that he loved her; now, he wondered whether his feelings had spoken more of obsession. Addicted to the *je ne sais quoi* that had first made her so irresistible, and consumed by the high of having what he had previously only imagined, he had revelled in being the man on her arm, had felt some prestige by association. He had thought himself on a par with her peers and colleagues, and now supposed that they, too, had jeered and laughed when his back was turned. For so long he had believed she loved him; recently he had started to realise he had been her safety net. Dependable and compliant, she had toyed with him when it suited her, and forgotten him when to do so was convenient. Whether she had felt anything at all for him, he would never now know.

Rolling into a sitting position, he replaced the frame on the shelf and reached for his slippers, mindful of the broken glass on the carpet. Standing slightly unsteadily, he walked the few paces to the kitchen, stepping over what remained of the vodka bottle. Opening the fridge, he gazed disconsolately at its contents, a bottle of tonic water and a lemon – originally intended as accompaniment to the gin he had consumed after Wednesday's row – and half a chicken pie, now out of date. He kicked the door closed, turning back towards his bed and reaching for the pair of jeans that lay splayed out across the sofa. He stopped neither to wash, nor to change the shorts and t-shirt that he had worn for close to three days, but pulled on the jeans, fastened his boots, and departed the flat for the off licence.

The girl in the photograph was stunning. Tall and svelte, she stood erect, her long dark hair spilling over her shoulders and diffusing across her modest breasts. She was posing at an angle to the camera, her head slightly turned, steel blue eyes gazing directly into the lens. The rims of her eyes were licked with black, and her delicate cheekbones were sufficiently prominent to enhance the configuration of her face without according her the gaunt appearance so prevalent among catwalk models. Her features were relaxed, lips parted marginally and disclosing no sign of a smile. The thumb of her right hand was hooked loosely into the waistband of a red leather skirt, her left arm free at her side.

This was Zoë Mitchell at a fashion shoot less than two months previously. Lawrence turned to the next page of the portfolio, glancing curiously at Dr Gavin Mitchell, who sat across the table from him and Rebecca. A tall, sinewy man, his physique suggested that he devoted a considerable amount of his time to exercising, while his tan implied that he was either no stranger to outdoor life or had access to a sun bed. Immaculately attired in well-pressed black trousers and a silk shirt, his grey hair brushed carefully across his crown from a side parting, he waited patiently, arms resting along the edge of the table. His expression was impassive, and he appeared so composed that it was almost impossible to imagine he had just lost a daughter.

'When did you last see Zoë?' Lawrence asked, leaning back in his chair.

'Last weekend. She popped in on Saturday afternoon to collect something from her bedroom here.'

'And did you hear from her at all after that?'

'No. She led a rather hectic life – both in terms of her job and her social whirl – and my wife and I are also very busy. Getting hold of Zoë was never easy.'

'What is it that you do?'

'I'm a cardiologist.'

A very affluent one, Lawrence surmised from what he had seen of the Mitchells' home, wondering whether Gavin had made the money himself. Aside from its immensity, the house was unremarkable from without, disguising an almost palatial interior. The drawing room in which they now sat was decorated in a deep jade green and rich fuchsia; the elaborate, ornate wallpaper was crowned by an intricate white cornice, and puddle curtains cascaded either side of a twelve-foot-high window. A sizeable chandelier was suspended from the ceiling, and the fireplace and mantelpiece were quite breathtaking.

The mahogany furniture was undoubtedly antique, although every piece in the room appeared to match, and all looked to be in almost perfect condition. Lawrence guessed that many, disparaging in their envy, might describe this room, and what he had seen of the hallway and dining room, as ostentatious. In truth, they were simply beautiful.

'Did Zoë seem herself on Saturday?' Lawrence continued.

Gavin didn't seem to require any time to think this over. 'She seemed to be, although she didn't stay long. Her main topic of conversation was a catwalk show she'd been asked to participate in in Milan.'

'Do you think she would have told you if she was worried about something?'

'I suppose it would have depended what the problem was. She did come to me when she was having trouble with her landlord a couple of months ago, but I doubt she would ever have discussed any concerns relating to her personal life. That was her mother's department. Zoë generally looked to me for practical help.'

'What was the problem with her landlord?'

'He threatened to evict Zoë from the flat – I'm not really sure why, because I didn't believe he was being entirely truthful when he gave me his reasons, but we did succeed in smoothing everything over in the end.'

'What reasons did he give you?'

'He claimed to have had complaints about Zoë from the other tenant in the building.'

'Did you think that very unlikely?'

'Not at all, it was more the man's demeanour that made me doubt him.'

Lawrence nodded, threading his fingers loosely together. 'I'm sorry to have to ask, but do you think Zoë might have taken somebody she didn't know, or didn't know well, back to the flat, and perhaps let them stay the night?'

'In her bed, you mean,' Gavin interpreted.

'Yes.'

'It wouldn't surprise me,' he sighed. 'Zoë was never one to advocate fidelity. She was a very pretty girl who loved male attention, and generally got what she wanted.'

'Did that not worry you?'

'She was nineteen – I couldn't exactly send her to bed without any supper,' Gavin remarked, before adding, as if the thought had only just occurred to him, 'Besides, that would have been totally hypocritical. I was hardly a choirboy in my youth.'

Lawrence felt rather taken aback by this disclosure, and a moment passed before he continued. 'Who did she usually socialise with?'

'I'm afraid I've no idea. I expect it varied according to her boyfriend of the moment and what invitations she received. Her job was fairly erratic too – sometimes she was exhausted because she'd worked so many hours, and in weeks like those I don't suppose she socialised much at all.'

'Are there any names you can give us?'

'She's been seeing a lad called Pete Morgan – he's been around for a while – other than that, all I can suggest is that you try her modelling agency. I suspect she spent more time around work associates than anybody else.'

'Do you think your wife might be able to provide us with a few more names?'

'Probably. She was always closer to Zoë than I was. I suppose you'll be wanting to speak to her as well?'

'I'm afraid so. Is she likely to be home soon?'

'I don't even know that she'll be back today. Her mother's been very ill, and she wanted to break the news about Zoë in person. My brother-in-law collected her first thing this morning to drive her down to Cornwall.'

'I see,' Lawrence nodded, finding himself increasingly irritated with the man's matter-of-fact manner. His daughter was dead, and the tenor of the interview was growing so prosaic that they might have been discussing the previous evening's television viewing. Lawrence couldn't help wondering what sort of home life Zoë had known, and, taking in his immediate surroundings as discretely as possible, it occurred to him that from where he sat he couldn't see a single photograph. He could think of at least five pictures of Jimmy and Elise that populated his own home, and from what he had seen of Zoë's portfolio there was certainly no shortage of material. With this in mind, he posed another question.

'Do you have any other children?'

Gavin nodded. 'Zoë was a twin. My other daughter – Christia – still lives at home.'

'What's she doing at the moment?'

'She's just finished college – in a few months she'll be off to university. She's not home at the moment, but she should be back in half an hour or so, if you'd like a word with her?'

Lawrence confirmed that he would, curious to see how she had taken her sister's death and hoping she might be able to shed more light on Zoë's social life. His sister had certainly known far more about his activities at nineteen than had his parents, although in retrospect he wasn't sure the same had been true in reverse. Whatever the case, Christia must surely be able to tell them more than her father appeared – or purported – to know.

Ian leaned against the wall of the toilet cubicle, tipping his head back. 'My life is saved,' he breathed, passing Elliot the small straw fashioned from a ten pound note. Elliot took it, and rolled it carefully between finger and thumb to tighten the coil, coughing badly.

'I think I'm getting 'flu,' he complained, rubbing his chest with his fingers.

'Bollocks. You smoke too much.'

'I can't believe we didn't get to bed.'

Closing his eyes and simultaneously raising his eyebrows, Ian grunted incoherent agreement.

Holding the makeshift straw in his right hand and pinching one nostril shut with his left, Elliot leaned over the toilet cistern to snort the hastily prepared line of cocaine. Straightening up, he began coughing again.

'I'm definitely coming down with something.'

'It's called a cocaine habit, Elliot.'

'Funny,' Elliot retorted, sarcastically.

'I'm not joking. You want to be careful Becks doesn't find out.'

Elliot turned on his friend. 'You tell her and I'll fucking kill you.'

'Like she's going to need me to tell her.'

Elliot frowned. 'Explain.'

'You've been away two weeks and you look like you've dropped about ten pounds. Much more and she's going to start asking questions. There's a limit to what you can blame on irregular meals and lack of sleep.'

'I'll think of something,' Elliot shrugged, unconcerned. 'Anyway, quit worrying about me. Do we have time for another line?'

Ian glanced at his watch. 'No,' he grinned, moving to ready one regardless.

'So what happened with that girl last night?'

'Girl?' Ian echoed, feigning innocence.

'One minute you were virtually shagging her on the dance floor, the next time I see you, she's vanished. What happened?'

Ian didn't reply, his back to Elliot and eyes on the task in hand.

'You're going to tell me sooner or later,' Elliot continued, cheerily. 'Especially given that if this situation were reversed you would beat, bribe or otherwise extort a confession out of me.'

'If this situation *were* reversed, you'd be in *big* trouble with your lovely fiancée.'

23

'So you did screw her.'

Ian turned around, shaking his head and rolling his eyes in mock disbelief. 'Well *obviously*. Are you suggesting for one moment that I might have lost my touch?'

'What touch?' Elliot quipped, losing interest in Ian and leaning to finish the job of chopping out the cocaine.

'If you didn't currently have control over a highly expensive substance, paid for by me, I'd give you a good kicking,' Ian replied, amicably. 'But as things stand, I'll kick you later.'

'I'll look forward to it.'

'Can you fucking hurry up? We're going to be late for this interview.'

'Well that's your fault. You're the one with the watch.' Elliot hurriedly rolled the ten pound note back into a straw and disposed of his share of the cocaine before handing the note to Ian, who did likewise. Running a quick finger over the cistern, Elliot gathered the last of the cocaine, and, disregarding hygiene, rubbed it into his gums. He reached to unlock the cubicle door, opened it and moved towards the basin.

'I need a tab,' he muttered, peering at his reflection in the mirror from beneath his long fringe and dusting the remnants of the cocaine from around his nostrils. There were dark shadows beneath his brown eyes, which were faintly bloodshot, and his skin was almost colourless. 'It's a fucking good job this is a radio interview,' he observed, teasing his bleached hair to create a ruffled appearance. 'I look like something out of a vampire film.'

Ian grinned. 'You always look fucking awful, Elliot, I'm sure nobody's going to notice any difference one all-nighter and a couple of grams of Charlie might have made.'

'You're right, of course, it could be worse,' Elliot remarked as he turned to leave the room. 'I could look as bad as you.' He opened the door onto the corridor.

'Or Damian.'

Elliot sniggered. 'I don't think I've seen anybody looking that rough since New Year.' He reached into his pocket for his Marlboros. 'Do you think I'll be all right to smoke in here?'

'Oh, sure, Elliot, if you want a shower. Mind you, I don't suppose you've had one all week.'

'What?'

Looking exasperated, Ian indicated the sprinkler system in the ceiling above their heads.

'Sodding typical,' Elliot muttered.

'I suppose y–'

Ian was interrupted by a shout, and Elliot turned to see Jeff Silvers, their tour manager, striding down the hallway towards them. 'Where the hell have you been?' He demanded, clearly furious.

'Uh – we –' Ian began.

'As if I needed to ask!' Jeff continued, clearly struggling to keep his temper under reasonable control. 'Touring with you two is like running around after a couple of kids! The purpose of this tour, in case you need reminding, is to promote *your* album and *your* band! You aren't big rock stars yet, and if you really want to do more than release one album before fading into total obscurity, you need to stop pissing about and take this seriously! All right?'

'Yeah yeah,' Ian retorted, sounding bored.

Jeff looked to Elliot, who glared back petulantly, his geniality abruptly evaporating.

'Right! Now get into the studio! You're on air in less than two minutes, and please at least *try* to sound like you haven't just snorted half of Colombia!'

Pushing his cigarettes back into his pocket with an unnecessarily pointed sigh, Elliot followed Jeff back down the corridor he had travelled along a few minutes earlier. Playing in a band was becoming far too much like a job for his liking, and the continual touring was really starting to irk. Whilst he was generally fairly gregarious, he found coping with other people every hour of the day exceedingly difficult, and in recent weeks had been granted little respite from incessant human company. Denied adequate time to himself, he felt suffocated, and was growing increasingly tense and oversensitive. The fact that he and Jeff had never really seen eye to eye wasn't helping matters, and the discord had reached a point where Elliot found everything Jeff did or said unjustifiably irritating. He was doubtful they would make it through the final ten days of the tour without altercation, although what the consequences of that might be, he wasn't sure. Currently, he was almost past caring.

Two

Whilst the word *twin* hadn't automatically evoked the image of a carbon copy, Lawrence had expected Christia Mitchell to bear some resemblance to the nineteen-year-old model whose portfolio he had browsed through less than an hour earlier. As it happened, the two were startlingly different, and, had he not known, Lawrence wouldn't even have put them at the same age.

Christia was several inches shorter than her sister had been, and much heavier. Approximately five foot six in height, Lawrence guessed she probably weighed in at about sixteen stone, a dramatic contrast to Zoë's sylphic size eight. She looked older than nineteen, albeit less sophisticated than her twin, her hair shorter and several shades lighter. She was pretty, although her facial features lacked definition as a result of her weight, and her skin was flushed with the heat, perspiration beading on her forehead.

Sitting heavily on the sofa and simultaneously looking up at Lawrence, she asked, 'What do you want to know?'

'I just have a few questions about Zoë. I'm sorry to have to go through this so soon after –'

'Don't be,' Christia interrupted. 'She made my life hell.'

Lawrence felt startled by this revelation, more on account of Christia's readiness to admit it than anything else. His expression evidently betrayed something of that surprise, because Christia frowned and snapped, 'What? Just because we were twins doesn't mean we were soul mates!'

'Of course not, it's just that people tend not to share that sort of information so freely when I'm investigating a murder.'

'Well, there's no point my pretending we were best friends, because anybody else you talk to will only tell you otherwise. Is it not better that I tell you the truth myself?'

'Yes, it is,' Lawrence said. 'Would you mind telling me how she made your life so difficult?'

'Is it not obvious?' Christia asked, raising her eyebrows. When Lawrence made no reply, she continued, 'Zoë was gorgeous, and she knew it – she also knew that I wasn't happy with my weight, and she enjoyed making fun of me and putting me down. I get enough comments on the street and at college – I didn't need it from my sister as well.'

Lawrence nodded. 'Did she do anything else to upset you?'

'She tried it on with my boyfriend.'

'When was that?'

'All the time. She was always after him.'

'I was under the impression she had a boyfriend of her own.'

'She didn't want to go out with him, she just wanted to take him off *me*.'

'And how did your boyfriend respond to that?'

'He generally ignored her advances. At least, he did when I was there.'

'So you didn't entirely trust him when you weren't,' Lawrence concluded.

'I trust Lucian, I just didn't trust Zoë. She was incredibly manipulative. She would have loved to screw him just to see the look on my face when she told me.'

'Do you know whether anything did happen between them?'

'No. Zoë would have told me, first chance she got.'

Unless she died first, Lawrence thought to himself.

'When did you last see Zoë?'

Christia appeared to consider her answer before saying, 'I couldn't tell you, exactly. Not for several weeks.'

'Did you not see her when she visited on Saturday?'

'I was out.'

'Would I be correct in assuming you didn't see much of one another?'

'You would.'

'Do you have any idea who she did spend time with?'

'No. Aside from Pete. Try asking my mother. She probably has every detail of Zoë's life on record.'

Lawrence didn't miss the resentment in Christia's tone, and wondered what that stemmed from. 'Doting mother, eh?' He remarked, lightly, hoping to encourage further comment. He wasn't disappointed.

Christia made a sound somewhere between an exclamation and a sardonic laugh before saying, 'As far as Zoë was concerned. In my case I don't suppose she even knows which A-levels I'm taking.'

'Do you not get on?'

'She's ashamed of me,' Christia shrugged, adding, after a moment, 'Because I'm fat.'

Lawrence drew breath to continue, but Christia evidently anticipated his offering some placatory argument, and jumped in ahead with, 'And I know that, because she told me.'

Thinking that the Mitchell family appeared more dysfunctional with each new fact that he gleaned, and unsure quite how to respond, Lawrence switched to a different subject. 'Could you give me an account of where you were on Wednesday night, please?'

'I was here.'

'Doing what?'

'Not much. Watching TV, mainly. I was supposed to see Lucian, but –' she stopped short.

'But?'

Christia sighed. 'He sent me a text – said he wasn't feeling well – so we didn't meet up. I was home all evening. Mum and Dad were here too.'

Lawrence nodded. 'How long have you been seeing Lucian?'

'Eight months. We met at college.'

'And for how much of that time had Zoë been chasing him?'

'I don't know – probably since the first day she met him.'

'Had she made a play for your boyfriends before?'

Christia averted her eyes. A couple of seconds passed before she admitted, in a small voice, 'I've not *had* a boyfriend before.'

'Do you know whether she ever behaved similarly towards other couples?'

'All the time. Zoë loved splitting people up. It was a game to her.'

'Did she often succeed?'

'You've seen her picture, haven't you? What do you think?'

'Is that a yes?'

'She had an eerie power over men. Most that met her were either falling over themselves to get her into bed, or else so tongue-tied and flustered they could barely make conversation.'

'So where did Pete fit into the picture?'

'God knows. The guy was either so stupidly naive that he never noticed what was going on under his nose, or pathetic enough that he allowed it to continue.' Christia paused. 'Zoë obviously had some use for him, but I've no idea what. He was most probably besotted with her, but I don't suppose she gave a monkeys for him.'

* * * * *

Having had to make seven telephone calls to trace Pete Morgan's whereabouts, Rebecca finally arrived in a rather dilapidated back street ten minutes walk from Seven Sisters Road at a quarter to twelve. Cursing the waste of a morning, she made her way to number sixteen. The building looked to be in a similar state of decay to its neighbours, with lichen thick on the window frames, the paint dirty and peeling, and the front steps chipped and cracked. Once, no doubt, this had been a respectable Victorian terrace; now it was crumbling quietly into dereliction, overlooked by the council and unseen by the capital's tourists.

Reaching the front door of number sixteen, Rebecca peered through the filthy plastic protecting the row of doorbells and communal intercom from the elements. These were labelled with no more information than 'FLAT 1' up to 'FLAT 4', and Rebecca checked her notes before trying the bell of flat 3. When this drew no response, she tried again, wondering whether the bell even worked. There was still no answer, and she gave the door a firm push on the off-chance it wasn't secured. To her surprise, it swung open, striking the internal wall behind it and revealing a dingy passageway that led up to a narrow flight of stairs. Entering the building, she made her way along the corridor and up the stairs, locating flat 3 on a landing four steps up from the first floor. Knocking sharply, she took a step back, crumpling the A5 page of directions into her jacket pocket.

'Yeah?' A voice snapped almost before the door opened, revealing an unshaven young man clad only in a dirty t-shirt and boxer shorts. His mousy hair looked in desperate need of a wash and his eyes, in the dim light an indistinguishable colour somewhere between green and grey, were bloodshot and slightly puffy. Tall and broad, he leaned heavily on the door frame, accompanied by the rank odour of unwashed flesh combined with alcohol. He was clearly intoxicated.

'Pete Morgan?'

He scowled. 'What's it to you?'

'I'm Detective Sergeant Palmer,' Rebecca displayed her warrant card, thinking she might be better off returning at another time in the hope of finding him at least half sober. His response forced her to reconsider, as she wondered what truths he might let slip while under the influence.

'Is this about my headfuck girlfriend?' He slurred, bitterly.

'I'd like to talk to you about Zoë Mitchell.'

'She screwed around once too often and got what she fucking deserved!' Pete returned, almost spitting the words out.

'Perhaps you could explain exactly what you mean by that.'

'Maybe,' Pete muttered, without enthusiasm. After a short pause he added, rather grudgingly, 'I s'pose you'd better come in,' before turning and moving unsteadily away from the door. Taking a deep breath, Rebecca followed.

The main room of the studio flat in which she now stood was fairly spacious, and in considerably better repair than the exterior of the building. Unfortunately, it was also a pigsty, and the fetid combination of summer heat, unopened windows and the ammoniacal stench of stale urine almost made her retch. A considerable number of beer tins were scattered about the unmade bed, the sheets of which were visibly soiled, and a three-quarters-empty whisky bottle sat on a shelf nearby. Towards the other side of the room, the carpet was strewn with broken glass, the shards sparkling in the sunlight that passed from the kitchen window through the open doorway between the two rooms. The remainder of the floor was littered with torn newspapers, dirty clothes, adult magazines, empty pizza delivery boxes and other miscellaneous rubbish. Rebecca had never been particularly houseproud, but she couldn't begin to imagine how anybody could live in such disgusting conditions.

Pete dropped onto the bed, where he leaned back against the wall, tipping his head to one side. Rebecca looked about herself for somewhere to sit before perching on the sofa that crouched in the corner closest to the door, serving, so the number of clothes heaped upon it seemed to indicate, the function of a secondary wardrobe. Inhaling only through her mouth, she reached for her notebook, hoping to keep the interview brief.

'I understand you were dating Zoë.'

'Me and half a million others.'

'Are you saying she was unfaithful?'

'If we were *in* a relationship,' Pete shrugged, reaching for the whisky.

'If?'

'She didn't want a boyfriend. She wanted a reliable escort and a fuck on tap for the occasions she couldn't get one elsewhere.' Pete fumbled with the cap of the bottle.

'When did you come to that conclusion?'

'I pretended it wasn't happening for months. I loved her enough to – to – and now – I –' he broke off, shaking his head.

'I'm sorry to have to bring it up, because I know it must have been very traumatic, but I understand you found the body.'

Pete nodded. 'How could anybody do that to her?' He managed, his voice choked. 'To anyone – I mean – I – it was horrible –' he swallowed hard, tears in his eyes.

Having seen the crime scene photographs, Rebecca could understand his distress. Zoë's thorax had been viciously and repeatedly slashed, leaving her breasts and bed sheets caked with blood. The extent of the blood loss, although insufficient to have caused death, left no doubt that the damage had been done while Zoë was still alive.

'I'm sorry to have to ask, but how did you come to find her?'

'She wasn't answering my calls.' Pete blinked, tears escaping his eyes as he did so. 'We'd had an argument – the day before – so I thought she was just angry with me. I went round – with some flowers – but – but –' he shrugged, stifling a sob.

'How did you get into the flat?'

'I have a key. Zoë had it cut for me a couple of months ago.' Pete took a mouthful of whisky. 'She was often held up – with photo shoots – or plane flights – or whatever – so –' he gulped. 'She thought it would make life easier for both of us.'

'Do you know whether anybody else had a copy?'

'I'd like to think I was the only one, but I'd probably be kidding myself.'

'So not as far as you know.'

'No.'

'You mentioned that the two of you had an argument on Wednesday. What was that about?'

'None of your business!' Pete snapped, rudely.

'Can you think of anybody who might have borne a grudge against Zoë, or wanted her out of the way?'

'Who wouldn't might be quicker.'

'Does anyone in particular come to mind?'

'No,' Pete responded sullenly, taking another mouthful of whisky.

Rebecca sighed, guessing she was unlikely to get much of any value out of Pete in his current state. Reluctant to spend any longer than necessary in the flat, she decided to call it a day and stood to leave. Perhaps Lawrence could conduct the second interview.

* * * * *

31

Lucian Price was not at all what Lawrence had been expecting. Looks might be merely skin deep, but Lawrence was well aware that in the eyes of adolescents they tended to be of disproportionate significance, and, although he didn't like to admit it to himself, he wouldn't have thought an attractive young man would have looked twice at Christia. Lucian was more than simply attractive, he was incredibly striking. Tall and slender, he had untidy dark hair, prominent cheekbones and a sharply defined jaw. His eyes were a very pale aqua, surrounded by remarkably long lashes, and, as he hovered uneasily in the doorway of his council flat, caught in an anxious frown.

'Hello?'

'Lucian Price?'

He nodded.

'I'm DCI Forrester. I'd like a few minutes of your time. Could I come in, please?'

'Um – I guess –' Lucian stepped back from the doorway, allowing Lawrence to join him in the hallway, before closing the door and turning towards the living room. Lawrence followed. The room was small and rather dark, and the air was heavy with cigarette smoke. Lucian took up residence in an armchair, reached for a packet of Berkeley menthols that lay on the armrest and tapped one out. Lawrence noticed his hands were shaking. Lighting the cigarette, he looked up. 'Please – sit down.'

Lawrence did so, settling himself on the sofa. 'I have a few questions about Zoë Mitchell.'

'I figured.'

'I know you and Christia are dating – did you know Zoë well?'

'Not really.' He took a nervous pull on the cigarette.

'She and Christia didn't see much of one another?'

'Not when I was there.'

'Did you ever see Zoë when Christia wasn't around?'

'No, I didn't.'

'Did you like her?'

'Not especially, no.' He inhaled deeply.

'So you knew her well enough to form that opinion.'

'I knew a lot about her from Chris, but I rarely saw her, because she and Chris didn't get on.'

'What was it that you disliked about Zoë?'

'She devoted much of the time she spent with Chris to putting her down and making hurtful remarks. I don't like to see anybody treated like that, especially not by their own twin sister.'

'What sort of remarks did Zoë make?'

'She commented incessantly on Chris's weight, and –' he paused for a quick pull on the cigarette. 'She flirted with me whenever she had the chance.' He returned the cigarette to his lips. He was still shaking, and Lawrence wondered why he was so anxious.

'Was that simply because you were Christia's boyfriend?'

Lucian's eyebrows contracted into a frown. 'Why else would she have done it?'

'I'm trying to determine whether she was doing it out of malice or whether she wanted you for herself.'

'You're suggesting she actually fancied me?' Lucian exclaimed, sounding incredulous. 'That's absurd! She was a model! What would she have wanted with me?'

Lawrence felt unconvinced, doubting Lucian could be oblivious to his own physical allure. 'Is the possibility so inconceivable?'

'She didn't fancy *me*!'

'Were you attracted to her?'

'She was a bitch,' Lucian returned, shortly, his hand shaking even more violently. Lawrence noticed that he never held the cigarette more than six inches from his mouth, drawing deeply on it at every opportunity.

'You haven't answered the question.'

'She was model – of course she was attractive. That doesn't mean I *fancied* her!'

'That's still not an answer. *Did* you fancy her?'

'No,' Lucian snapped, stubbing out the cigarette and reaching for another. 'Nothing happened between Zoë and I.'

'Where were you on Wednesday night?' Lawrence asked, as Lucian turned his attention to lighting up.

Lucian dropped his hands, staring at him in disbelief. 'You think that *I* –'

'It's a question I'm obliged to ask everybody,' Lawrence replied, wearily. 'I'm aware you were supposed to be spending the evening with Chistia, and that you cancelled the date at the last minute. I'd like to know why.'

'I wasn't feeling well. I spent the evening here.'

'Alone?'

'Yes.'

'What was wrong?'

33

Lucian sighed. 'I had a really tough day – I was upset and I felt sick. I needed some time to myself, and I couldn't face eating out.'

'Why were you upset?'

'How is that your business?'

'I don't know whether it's my business or not, until you tell me.'

Lucian returned his attention to his cigarette. Several seconds passed before he responded. Closing his eyes momentarily, he took a deep breath. 'I – I went to – the hospital – my mother's there – she has –' he paused for a long, shaky pull on the cigarette. 'She's terminally ill,' he revealed, very quickly. 'The – her doctor – he – uh – he told me –' Another pause, another pull on the cigarette. 'Basically, she's about to die!' Swallowing hard, Lucian met Lawrence's gaze. 'Will that do? Or do I have to go into further detail?'

'No,' Lawrence replied. 'I'm sorry, this must be a very difficult time for you to have to cope with this.'

Lucian shrugged, casting his eyes down and clearly struggling to control his emotions.

'Maybe we've done enough for now.'

'Could you – leave me – please?' Lucian asked, his voice wavering.

'Of course. I'll see myself out. Will you be all right on your own?'

'Yuh.'

'Ok.'

Lawrence stood and left the room. At the front door he paused to glance back. Lucian had buried his face in his hands, the cigarette still gripped between his slender fingers, his thin shoulders shaking as he sobbed. Reluctant to leave him alone, but respecting his request, Lawrence departed the flat, closing the door softly behind himself and turning his mind to how he might validate Lucian's account. It seemed inappropriate to ask the boy where his mother was receiving treatment. He guessed Christia or Gavin Mitchell would probably be able to answer that question for him. They might, he hoped, also be able to tell him whether Lucian was always so highly strung.

Zoë Mitchell's flat had once formed the first floor of a fair-sized detached house, which was now divided into two apartments. There were no signs of damage to the front door, and, on inspection, Rebecca concluded there would be no easy way to open it without a key; a narrow ridge protected the lock from the outside world, negating any possibility that a credit card might have been used to gain entry. Inside, a small hallway opened onto the living room, which was furnished with a two-piece suite, a large coffee table and a modest set of shelves. This stood adjacent to a television and DVD player, and was predominantly occupied by DVDs, save for one shelf, which housed a telephone.

Off the living room was a dinette, containing a folding table and, rather unusually, three chairs. The table was folded against the wall and the collection of belongings scattered upon it and stacked on the chairs suggested that the room had rarely been used. It was only partly segregated from the kitchen, which was quite large in comparison, equipped with a separate refrigerator and freezer, as well as a washing machine, microwave oven and cooker. Cupboard space was plentiful, and Rebecca found more than half of it to be unused. A quick search of the room turned up nothing of any significance – kitchen utensils, cleaning products and a motley selection of food stuffs – and Rebecca wasted little time in moving back to the dinette.

One of the chairs was piled with haphazardly folded sheets and towels, and Rebecca relegated these to the floor in order to sit down, turning her attention to the table. This would have benefitted from a letter rack, as the limited surface space was all but buried beneath a sea of leaflets and letters. Most, but not all, of the latter had been opened. Many had been roughly returned to their envelopes, and, from the postmarks, Rebecca was able to arrange them in chronological order. Few turned out to be of much significance. Several hailed from Zoë's grandfather, who addressed Zoë as *my little princess* but whose style of writing was otherwise strangely formal, considering his relationship to Zoë. One had been sent by a friend in Edinburgh, and made reference to the old photograph she had enclosed of herself and Zoë as children, and two others turned out to be party invitations, one of which was already past.

The remaining seven letters were all penned in the same hand, and four of them were unopened. Rebecca made a start on the first to find it wasn't so much a letter as it was poetry, and badly written poetry at that. Initially, it seemed to be little more than a love letter, but as Rebecca read on, the subject degenerated to a point at which it bordered on pornographic. It was signed simply with the letter *L*, and there was no return address on the envelope. Rebecca worked her way through the letters one by one, finding that they varied little from the first – beginning with declarations of love and ending with graphic descriptions of one sexual act after another.

Slipping them into a separate evidence bag from the rest of Zoë's personal correspondence, Rebecca set them aside and stood to take a look at the items on the room's two other chairs. One held a number of catalogues, with the cover of the topmost one featuring Zoë in a bikini; the other an out-of-date TV guide and, hanging from the back of the chair, a handbag.

Emptying the contents onto the table, Rebecca sifted through them, finding nothing more than she would have expected – a purse, Oyster card, several items of make-up, a pair of nail clippers, a pocket pack of tissues, a couple of pens, a handful of tampons and a squashed box of cigarettes. The clasp of the purse strained with the quantity of cards that had been forced into it, along with almost one hundred pounds in cash. Evidently Zoë's attacker had not been motivated by any thought of financial gain, and Rebecca turned towards the living room. With any luck she might find something more there, and, she hoped, a means of identifying the nameless letter writer.

'Hello again,' Gavin Mitchell greeted, with something approaching a frown, on finding Lawrence on his doorstep for a second time that day.

'Hello. Might I come in for a few minutes?'

'Oh – yes, certainly,' Gavin nodded, stepping back from the door but making no move to leave the hallway, apparently keen to keep this meeting as brief as possible. Lawrence closed the front door behind himself before posing his question.

'Would I be right in assuming you know Lucian Price?'

'Yes, of course, he's Chris's boyfriend. Why?'

'He told me his mother is terminally ill in hospital, and I didn't feel I could ask for more information. I wondered whether you might be able to tell me which hospital she's at?'

'The Royal Free.'

'You don't happen to know her first name, do you?'

'Maria.'

'How well do you know Lucian?'

Gavin appeared to consider his answer before saying, carefully, 'I see quite a bit of him. That's not to say I know a lot about him.'

'When I visited him earlier he seemed extremely on edge.'

'I'm not really surprised. He suffers from an anxiety disorder. He's generally quite overwrought, and your reason for being there would hardly have helped matters.'

'He was shaking.'

'He often does. He worries about things that seem silly to most of us – he has panic attacks over things like his college deadlines quite frequently, despite the fact he has plenty of time to meet them.'

'Has that been officially diagnosed?'

'I diagnosed it.'

Lawrence's eyebrows rose. 'Are you his doctor?'

'That would hardly be appropriate, would it?' Gavin returned. 'But I do see quite a lot of him, so it wasn't something I could miss. I suggested he see his GP, because he isn't my patient, so I couldn't treat him.'

'And did he?'

'As I understand it, yes, but he hasn't responded particularly well to treatment.'

'Any reason why not?'

Gavin shook his head slightly. 'Some people respond better than others.'

'Does his involvement with Christia worry you?'

The man frowned. 'No. Should it?'

'I don't know, you know more about his condition than I. Do you like him?'

Gavin's frown deepened. 'I really don't see how that's relevant. How does my opinion of Lucian have any bearing on what happened to Zoë?'

'Could you just answer the question, please?'

Gavin looked and sounded irritated as he said, 'For what it's worth, yes, I do like him.'

Lawrence gave a perfunctory nod before turning for the door. 'Thank you for your time. I'll be back tomorrow to speak to your wife.'

'Right.'

'Goodbye for now.'

'Goodbye,' Gavin replied, smiling rather forcedly as he moved to close the front door. Lawrence set off down the path, reflecting on Gavin's reluctance to discuss his feelings about Lucian. His reticence might have no bearing on Zoë's death, but, from experience, Lawrence suspected he was holding back more than just an opinion.

Three

Zoë's bedroom held a double bed, which had been stripped of its sheets by the scenes of crime officers, a narrow set of shelves, a wardrobe and a dressing table. A chair was positioned in front of the last of these, with several items of clothing heaped over its back, including a lilac basque and a black velvet mini dress. Central to the dressing table was a large rectangular mirror, its left corner draped with a colourful silk scarf that, judging by its dusty appearance, hadn't been worn in some time.

The surface of the dressing table was littered with jewellery, make-up and associated paraphernalia: eye shadows, mascaras, eyeliners, lip liners, lipsticks, nail polish, foundation, cleansers, toners, moisturisers, hair spray, deodorant, perfume, cotton wool buds – some of them used – and, amidst the chaos, a mobile phone. From the remaining residue, it was clear this had already been dusted for fingerprints, and Rebecca felt surprised it hadn't been bagged up by one of the scenes of crime officers. Switching it on, she was pleased to find the battery active. Touchscreen technology made scrolling through the menus in latex gloves no easy task, but with a little perseverance she succeeded in accessing the contacts library and counted seventy-three, a potentially very useful source of Zoë's acquaintances. Opening the text messages, Rebecca worked her way down the list, stopping at one sent the previous Wednesday afternoon.

'Hi sex kitten,' the brief communication read. 'Whatcha up to tonight?'

If Zoë had made any reply, it had since been deleted. There were no clues to the sender's identity; no name was associated with the message, so the number it had hailed from evidently wasn't among Zoë's contacts. And it seemed unlikely it had been a wrong number, as two other messages sent from the same number on Tuesday evening hadn't gone unanswered. Zoë had responded to the words 'Thanx 4 last nite, I love u baby xx' with a heart emoji, and followed up the second message, 'Fred's in town again. Wanna meet up B4 Fri?' with a thumbs up.

Wondering who Fred was, Rebecca perched on the end of the bed and trawled through the electronic address book again.

Several of the numbers were, to all intents and purposes, duplicates – Pete mobile, Pete work, Theo office, Theo site – but Fred's name didn't feature. She copied out the unidentified number and the associated text messages before switching the phone off and consigning it to an evidence bag.

Moving to sit at the dressing table, she began a search of the drawers to her left. The first contained a limited selection of make-up, but little else, and she guessed it was where a considerable number of the items scattered atop the dressing table belonged. The second drawer was stuffed with official letters and bills, none of which seemed to have gone unpaid, and having uncovered nothing of consequence, Rebecca proceeded to the third drawer. At a glance, all this appeared to hold was a collection of expensive and rather risqué lingerie, but, having removed and examined the items one by one, Rebecca came across a small ring box hidden at the rear of the drawer. Inside it, an engraved silver ring with an unusually concave surface was slotted into a black velvet cushion. Her curiosity aroused by the fact that a heart crossed with two arrows had been cut into the face of the ring, Rebecca pulled it free to inspect the engraving, but was left none the wiser: the inscription was not in English. Turning her attention to the ring box, Rebecca noticed that the name of the company responsible for the ring's manufacture was printed inside the lid, and she noted this down, hoping that if they couldn't tell her the meaning behind the words they might at least be able to point her in the direction of someone who could.

Replacing the ring in its box, she set it beside the mobile on the dressing table top, turning to explore the drawers to her right. The top drawer contained a myriad of belongings, none of which had anything much in common, and Rebecca guessed it was where Zoë had thrown anything for which she had no proper place. A thorough search turned up nothing significant, and Rebecca checked the final two drawers, but was disappointed to find that they held nothing more than a selection of women's magazines not dissimilar to those she herself had amassed on the coffee table at home.

Leaving the dressing table, Rebecca moved to the wardrobe. Both doors were wedged open by the excess of clothing that had been packed inside. Rummaging through this and the assortment of shoes and bags on the wardrobe floor, Rebecca noticed nothing unremarkable, aside from the fact Zoë had apparently owned a considerable amount of designer clothing – hardly surprisingly, given her occupation. Closing the doors as far as she was able, Rebecca turned last to the set of shelves that stood adjacent to Zoë's bed. The top shelf was scattered with candles, some of which had never been lit, and a porcelain oil burner. A small stereo, accompanied by two equally small speakers, sat on the shelf below, a lead running from it into an MP3 player. This, Rebecca discovered, held a rather eclectic selection of albums and compilations. Beside it, a photograph frame leaned drunkenly against the side of the shelf unit, its subject Zoë and an older, equally sophisticated-looking woman. Rebecca noticed with interest that whilst two of the lower shelves also bore photograph frames, none of the pictures featured Zoë's father, or, from the fact that in all but the first Zoë was accompanied by attractive young men, her twin sister.

Perhaps even more curiously, Pete didn't appear in any of the four that featured male companions, and Rebecca wondered who the men were. By the time she had gathered up the frames, all that remained on the lower shelves were a few small cuddly toys, a row of books and a tissue box. A glance under the bed satisfied Rebecca that the scenes of crime officers had missed nothing there, and, straightening up, she decided to conclude the search. Collecting a handful of items that she had left on the dressing table, she made for the living room, glancing at her watch. It was after four, and, thinking she ought to give her superior a call, she pulled her mobile from her handbag only to find the battery was flat. She had only charged it the night before. With a sigh, she turned to use Zoë's landline, lifted the receiver and jumped as the coil connecting it to the telephone swung towards her. Looking down, the reason why was immediately apparent. The line had been cut.

'I'd like to speak to Dr Klein,' Lawrence announced, presenting his warrant card to the woman at the front desk of the department he had been directed to by the hospital's main reception. She frowned up at him over her spectacles, then turned her attention to his identification. Apparently satisfied, she looked back to Lawrence.

'He's on rounds at the moment – I can't say how long he'll be. You might be better off coming back later.'

'I'll wait. Could you let him know I'm here, please?'

'But I –'

'I'll *wait*,' Lawrence repeated, firmly, turning from the desk and making his way to a nearby bench. As he sat, a notice above the desk caught his eye. A picture of a mobile phone with a bold red line scored through it was accompanied by the words *PLEASE TURN YOURS OFF*. Pulling his from his pocket, he did as directed.

'Excuse me, you can't use that in here.'

Lawrence glanced up to find the receptionist leaning across her desk, glowering at him.

'I was just switching it off, actually,' he replied, pleasantly, indicating the sign above her head. 'Following instructions.'

'Well if you want to use it you'll have to go outside,' came the tart response.

Lawrence raised his eyebrows, returning the mobile to his pocket and looking about himself. It had been hot enough outside, but the air inside the hospital was stifling, and his throat was beginning to feel uncomfortably dry. Failing to locate a drinks machine in the immediate vicinity, he considered asking the receptionist where he might find one, but by this time she was on the telephone, and from her animated tone he suspected the call was a personal one. With a sigh, he leaned back against the wall, reaching into his pocket for his notebook and a pen. He suspected he might be in for a long wait.

Rebecca knocked on the front door of the ground floor flat beneath Zoë's. Shortly, it was opened by an elderly lady who looked to be in her late seventies, if not older. Shrunken and stooping, she leaned heavily on the door handle, slowly raising her head to look up. She wore old-fashioned spectacles that magnified her watery brown eyes and pinched the bridge of her nose, and her white hair was tinged blue. She regarded Rebecca keenly before frowning and saying, 'Yes?'

'Mrs Hazell?'

'Yes.'

'I'm Detective Sergeant Palmer. I'd like to have a word with you about Zoë Mitchell.'

'What?' The woman cupped her free hand behind her ear, leaning forwards.

Rebecca sighed. It seemed unlikely that Mrs Hazell was going to be much help to them as far as Wednesday night went. She repeated herself loudly.

'Oh, certainly,' Mrs Hazell nodded, standing back from the door and looking excited. 'Come in, dear, come in.'

Rebecca followed her through to a cramped living room; cramped more because too much had been crowded into it than because of its size, which was fair. Mrs Hazell sat herself down in a high-backed armchair, gesturing Rebecca towards the sofa. Rebecca sat, pulling her notebook from her handbag.

'I tried to warn her,' Mrs Hazell said, earnestly. 'I tried, but she wouldn't listen.'

'You tried to warn her?' Rebecca echoed, puzzled.

'Oh yes,' Mrs Hazell nodded, enthusiastically, before Rebecca could enquire further. 'Of course, I had my own interests in mind also – it's hardly the sort of thing one wants on one's doorstep, is it?'

'What exactly are you referring to?'

'Prostitution, Sergeant.'

Rebecca felt her eyebrows rise. 'You think Zoë was a prostitute?'

'I assumed you knew *that.*'

'What gave you that impression?'

'You can't miss something like that when it's going on under your nose!' Mrs Hazell exclaimed, sounding affronted. 'Her clothes looked more like underwear, and she had a different man back every night!' The woman leaned in, holding onto the armrest. 'I warned her. I remember the days of Peter Sutcliffe, and I told her it was only a matter of time before another like him stalked the streets.'

Rebecca sighed. 'Did you see or hear anything on Wednesday night?'

'Nothing out of the ordinary. The first I knew about it was when that young man came hammering on my door on Thursday evening.'

'Oh?'

'Ever so upset, he was.'

'You don't remember his name, do you?'

'Um –' Mrs Hazell frowned. 'No, no I don't –'

'Could you describe him for me?'

'Tall.'

Rebecca felt inclined to point out that almost everybody would seem tall when you measured little more than five foot, but instead forced a smile and asked, 'Could you give me a little more?'

'Said he was her boyfriend. I doubt that will help you narrow it down much.'

'Pete?'

'What's that?' Mrs Hazell turned her head slightly, leaning towards Rebecca.

'Was his name Pete?' Rebecca asked, enunciating her words slowly and clearly.

There was a momentary pause before Mrs Hazell smiled and nodded. 'That's right.'

'Could you tell me what he said?'

'He didn't say much at all – he was gasping and crying – all he really managed was *Zoë* and *police*.'

'What happened next?'

'I made him a cup of tea. Poor lad was shaking, and –'

'Did you call the police?' Rebecca interrupted, rather impatiently.

'Well of course I did. The landlord, too.'

'Would you mind giving me his name?'

'Dr van Prior,' Mrs Hazell replied, barely pausing before continuing, 'He's been trying to evict her for weeks, you know. I wrote to him detailing my concerns regarding Zoë's lifestyle. I think he's had some trouble getting her out, because he recently suggested that I might want to move somewhere else myself. Not that I had any intention of being pushed out by some cheap tart.'

Rebecca noted this detail with interest, thinking it sounded more like the landlord was trying to clear the building.

'Do you have his address to hand?'

'Certainly,' Mrs Hazell nodded, struggling to her feet and looking pleased that she had been able to be of such assistance. 'Can I make you a cup of tea as well, dear?'

'No, thank you,' Rebecca forced another smile. 'If you could just find me the address, then I'll be on my way.'

'Can I help?' A voice behind Lawrence enquired. The words sounded hurried, as if their owner didn't really have the time to be saying them at all. Lawrence turned from the noticeboard he had been perusing to find a heavily built man of about fifty hovering behind him, a pristine white coat thrown over his shirt and tie.

'DCI Forrester,' Lawrence afforded the man a glimpse of his warrant card. 'I'm hoping you can help me. I understand you're treating a Maria Price here.'

'Yes.'

'Might I have a quick word with her?'

'I'm afraid not.'

'It is very important –'

'That's as may be, but you're not going to get any sense out of her. She's not awake, and I think it's unlikely she'll fully regain consciousness.'

'What's wrong with her?'

'You know that's confidential. Look, I'm really very busy – is there anything more I can help you with, or will that be it?'

Irritated by the man's abrupt manner, Lawrence felt inclined to hold him up for as long as possible. 'Do you see her son here often?'

Dr Klein sighed. 'Yes, I do.'

'Was he here on Wednesday afternoon?'

'Er – yes, yes I think I did see him on Wednesday. I had a brief chat with him before he went in to see her.'

'What did you discuss?'

'His mother's condition. What else would we have talked about?'

'If I knew I wouldn't need to ask.'

'I had to be rather blunt with him, because he didn't seem to have much grasp of how serious the situation was. I haven't seen him since.'

'What did you say to him?'

'I –' Dr Klein stopped, frowning. 'What is all this about?'

'Murder,' Lawrence replied, his tone deliberately casual, anticipating the predictable change in the man's expression. He wasn't disappointed.

'*What?*' Dr Klein exclaimed, looking shocked. 'Uh – wh – I mean – has – has something happened to Lucian?'

'No.' Lawrence dug his hands into his pockets. 'I'm just checking out what he told me of his activities on Wednesday evening.'

'You think *Lucian* –' Dr Klein snorted disbelievingly, shaking his head. 'Chief Inspector, that bundle of nerves couldn't kill a houseplant!'

'You could well be right.'

'Oh come on, the kid virtually needs tranquillizers to visit his mother!'

'I never assume anything,' Lawrence replied, coolly. 'Now, could you please tell me what you said to Lucian on Wednesday evening?'

'He asked when his mother would be well enough to return home. I told him that wasn't going to happen.'

'How did he take the news?'

'He was rather shaken. I don't think he'd really managed to face up to how serious her condition was.'

Lawrence nodded. He couldn't help thinking Dr Klein didn't seem very sympathetic to Lucian or his mother, and wondered what his manner had been on Wednesday evening. Given that he had no further questions, he terminated the interview, thanking the man for his time. He sincerely hoped it wouldn't be necessary to speak to Dr Klein again.

By the time Rebecca returned to the office, Lawrence was seated at his desk, poring over the crime scene photographs. Totally absorbed in this activity, he clearly failed to notice Rebecca approaching, and jumped as she deposited the photograph frames collected from Zoë's bedroom in his uppermost filing tray.

'More pictures that might be of interest,' she offered, by way of explanation.

'Oh?'

'Zoë had five photos on display in her bedroom – none of which included her father, sister or boyfriend. Rather weird, don't you think?'

'To be honest, the whole family strikes me as rather weird.'

'Do expand,' Rebecca invited, pulling a chair up to his desk and making herself comfortable before reaching for one of the crime scene photos.

'Did Gavin Mitchell's behaviour this morning not strike you as a little odd?'

Rebecca shrugged. 'I don't know. He did seem to treat the situation rather casually, but who are we to say what his reaction to Zoë's death ought to be? When my grandfather was dying I couldn't understand how my father could be so matter-of-fact about the whole affair, but looking back I think that was probably just his way of coping with it all.'

'Maybe,' Lawrence nodded. 'But I went back to see him again this afternoon to ask him a couple of questions about Christia's boyfriend, and he seemed quite on edge.'

'This can't be an easy time for him to answer questions.'

'There's more than one reason why that might be.'

'Do you think he was responsible for Zoë's death?'

'Well I'm certainly not going to rule him out simply on the basis of his daughter's testimony that he was in all night.'

'What else did she have to say?'

'She stopped short of telling me she was glad Zoë was dead, but only just.'

'Oh?'

'It seems Zoë went out of her way to make Christia's life as miserable as possible. I always thought twins were supposed to have some sort of special bond.'

'Whatever gave you that idea?' Rebecca responded, flippantly. Lawrence raised his eyebrows, clearly not missing the slight bitterness in her tone.

'I thought you and Angela were close?'

Rebecca sighed. 'We were.'

'What happened?'

'Elliot happened,' Rebecca replied, sadly. 'And she hates him.'

'Why?'

'I don't think she knows. I don't even think it's Elliot she has a problem with. I think it's me. She's very possessive, and she's very competitive. I think the idea that not only could I be closer to somebody else than I am – or was – to her, but that I might also be happier with him than she is with her husband poses a big threat.'

'But you've had boyfriends before.'

'I know.' Rebecca reached for the stress toy on the edge of Lawrence's desk and squeezed it hard. 'But I think Angie recognised quite early on that I had something more with Elliot than I did with the others. Plus I met Elliot at about the time the honeymoon period began to wear off for her and Lewis. I get the impression they aren't particularly happy together, which is probably what's at the root of it all, but I don't know, because we don't really talk any more. We meet up, we get through the usual niceties, and then, sooner or later, it somehow degenerates into an argument.' Rebecca shrugged. 'I think unless you're an identical twin whatever bond you do or don't have depends on the two different personalities involved.'

'Do you think she wants to be one up on you at all times?'

Rebecca thought this over before saying, 'Yes, to a degree I think she does.'

'Why do you suppose that is?'

'Insecurity?' Rebecca suggested, before shaking her head. 'How did we get onto this? Sorry, I've digressed.'

'Don't apologise, I was the one who nudged you off course. I wanted your take on the twin subject. It seems Zoë spent most of the time she was around Christia trying to score points or put her down. Perhaps that isn't so strange after all.'

Rebecca shrugged. 'In different families sibling rivalry reaches different heights.'

'Yes, it does,' Lawrence agreed, standing and moving towards the printer by the window, where he began sifting through the heap of paper that had accumulated in its receptacle. 'Did you find anything else of interest in Zoë's flat?'

'Some bizarre letters signed only with a single initial, most of which were unopened, a mobile phone containing a couple of rather interesting text messages and –'

'What was the initial?'

'L.'

Lawrence looked around sharply. 'L? That's Christia's boyfriend's first initial. What was bizarre about the letters?'

'They start out as poorly written Shakespearean sonnets and then degenerate into something more reminiscent of a substandard Marquis de Sade,' she reached into her handbag for her notebook. 'Although saying that, I might just have made them sound a lot less boring than they actually were.'

Lawrence smiled.

'I also turned up a ring with a heart cut into it.'

'What's so strange about that?'

'It was in a box, hidden at the back of a drawer.'

Lawrence returned to his desk, a printout in hand. 'That still doesn't strike me as particularly unusual.'

'The rest of her jewellery was scattered across the dressing table, and the ring is inscribed, although I don't know what it says, because it isn't written in English.'

'Any idea what language it is?'

'Not really. Maybe Latin?' Rebecca leafed through her notebook for the relevant page, then presented it to Lawrence, pointing to four incomprehensible words.

Lawrence scanned them quickly before shaking his head. 'That's not Latin. Aside from possibly the DV, which is a common abbreviation of *Deo volente*.'

'And what does that mean?'

'God willing.'

Rebecca lifted her eyebrows in response, but didn't comment. 'I'll try running it through Google Translate in a minute.' Lawrence set the notebook aside, returning his attention to the recently collected printout.

'What's that?' Rebecca enquired.

'I spoke to someone at Zoë's modelling agency and asked them to send over the names and addresses of any colleagues who might be able to fill in some blanks about Zoë.'

'Do you want to make a start on that now?' Rebecca asked, without much enthusiasm.

Glancing at his watch, Lawrence shook his head. 'I think we're unlikely to find many people in on a Friday evening. We'd probably be better off leaving that until tomorrow, and concentrating what's left of today on going over what we have so far.' He slid the printout into his middle filing tray. 'But before we go any further, I'm going to order pizza. I'm ravenous.'

The discordant refrain of Rebecca's mobile ringtone penetrated the not-quite-but-almost asleep phase that she had reached. Jolted awake, she fumbled to answer it, knocking over the glass of water at her bedside as she did so.

'Hello?'

'You called.'

'What?' Rebecca managed, reaching to retrieve the glass and switching the light on to inspect the damage. Her notebook was soaked, although the digital clock had, thankfully, escaped unharmed, and told her that it was now five to two. She sighed. 'Three hours ago, Elliot.'

'Oh. Sorry. Did I wake you?'

'Yes. Where are you?'

'Hotel in Nottingham. We stayed on for the club after the gig.'

'How did it go?'

'The set went fine.'

'What didn't?' Rebecca asked, guessing from his tone that something was amiss.

'Jeff is driving me insane.'

49

'Why?'

'Because he's a tosser,' Elliot replied, laconically.

'You mean the two of you are rubbing one another up the wrong way,' Rebecca interpreted.

'Yeah,' came the honest answer. 'I'm sick of being stuck with the same people twenty-four hours a day as it is, and it really doesn't help having him watching my every move!'

'I can understand that,' Rebecca responded, trying to *sound* understanding. She wasn't at all surprised that the touring was getting Elliot down – it invariably did. He had always required a certain degree of personal space, and that was a luxury touring simply didn't afford. Sooner or later, Rebecca inevitably found herself having the same conversation with him, and had recently felt inclined to ask why he put himself through repeated touring when he clearly found the experience so trying. Bearing in mind that it was a Friday night and Elliot had apparently just returned from the club, she was surprised his words sounded so lucid.

'I'm sorry,' he spoke, after a brief pause. Then, as if he had read her thoughts, 'You must wonder why I do this at all.'

'Sometimes I do.'

'So do I.'

Unable to gauge the tenor of this statement over the telephone, Rebecca struggled to know how to respond. 'What do you mean?' She asked, at length.

'Oh I dunno,' Elliot returned, dismissively. 'I love the band, and I love *playing* in the band – it's just all the other crap that comes with it that I hate.' He sighed. 'I'm sorry, you've heard this a hundred times before. How are you, anyway?'

'Tired.'

'Tell me about it. Ian and I didn't get to bed at all last night. Still, at least you've the weekend now. You're off to Brighton in the morning, aren't you?'

'I'm afraid not.'

'Work?'

'Yes.'

'That sucks. Anything interesting?'

'Murdered model.'

'Wow. That'll make the papers.'

'I know. By morning we'll no doubt have the media all over us.' Rebecca yawned.

'I'm sorry I woke you,' Elliot offered, slightly awkwardly. 'I guess I should let you get some sleep.'

'I'll give you a ring tomorrow.'

'Yeah, ok. Sleep well.'

'You too. Good night.'

'Night. I love you.'

Rebecca tapped the *end call* icon and moved to switch the light back off, wishing Elliot could occupy the same time frame as the majority of the population. An idea struck her almost as she was thinking this, and she released the cord of the bedside light, reaching instead for her notebook. Carefully peeling the sodden pages away from one another, she located the unidentified mobile number responsible for the text messages that had caught her attention that afternoon. She climbed out of bed and padded through to the hallway, where she set her notebook down on the shelf beside the landline phone. Lifting the receiver, she dialled the number, prefixed with 141, on the off-chance she might get a personalised voicemail, and perhaps even gather sufficient information to trace the phone's owner. She was more than a little surprised when, after a single ring, a female voice spoke.

'Hi, this is Candela, leave a message.'

Rebecca hung up, still rather nonplussed. Looking back at the list of phone numbers she had made from Zoë's mobile memory, she ran her eyes down the associated names, stopping at 'Candie home'. That the number was a central London one was clear from the STD code; further than that there was little Rebecca would learn without the help of British Telecom. Returning the notebook to the shelf to dry, she headed towards the kitchen for cloth to mop up the spillage in the bedroom. Physically she felt fatigued, but the surprise of the mobile's ownership had filled her mind with new questions, and she suspected sleep would not now come easily.

Four

'Candela,' Rebecca announced, tossing her notebook onto Lawrence's desk and dropping into a nearby chair.

'Unit of lux,' Lawrence replied. 'What of it?'

'It's a girl's name.'

'Is it?'

'Yes. And she appears to be the owner of a mobile that was used to send three rather interesting text messages to Zoë. One of which refers to Wednesday evening.'

'What's her surname?'

'I don't know yet,' Rebecca admitted. 'I tried to trace her through the phone companies, but it's an unregistered pay-as-you-go.'

'So how did you find out who she is?'

'I called the number at two this morning when I guessed it would probably be switched off. Went straight through to voicemail.'

'What were you doing up at that hour?'

Rebecca smiled ruefully. 'Elliot.'

'Ah. How is he?'

'Rather overwrought. He doesn't really enjoy touring, and he and his tour manager seem to be on a bit of a collision course.'

'Oh dear,' Lawrence remarked, with an expressive lift of his eyebrows. 'So. What was so interesting about these text messages? Other than that they refer to Wednesday night, that is.'

'Take a look.' Rebecca retrieved her notebook and flicked to the relevant page before handing it to him.

'Leave it out in the rain, did you?' Lawrence joked, as he took hold of the crinkled pages. A couple of seconds passed as he presumably scanned the sentences Rebecca had indicated before he looked up expectantly. 'What are you suggesting? That the two of them were in a relationship of some kind?'

'That's what I assumed, until I found out the messages were sent by a woman and not a man.'

'It's still not inconceivable.'

'I know, but the possible meaning of these messages sent girl to girl is rather more ambiguous than it would be sent boy to girl.'

'True enough,' Lawrence said. 'But I certainly think we need to find the girl in question – especially as she may have seen Zoë on Wednesday night.'

'There's a landline number in Zoë's mobile for someone named Candie – ten to one it's the same person. I've managed to trace the number to an address in Battersea, but it's registered under another name. Do you want me to knock on the door?'

'Definitely,' Lawrence nodded. 'We'll start with Mrs Mitchell this morning – I think it's best if we both speak to her – after that you can try to track this girl down while I visit the landlord. Once that's done we can make a start on Zoë's modelling friends. And at some point I'm hoping the scientists might pitch up and join the party – all I've heard so far is that there was no sign of forced entry at the flat. I've tried calling Leighton to see what he got from the postmortem, but he's not picking up. Have you heard from him this morning?'

Rebecca shook her head and Lawrence glanced irritably at his watch.

'It is Saturday,' Rebecca defended her friend.

'That's as may be, but as you pointed out yesterday, we don't work strictly Monday to Friday, and neither does Leighton.'

Rebecca made no reply, and after a moment Lawrence continued. 'Besides, we ought to have had a report on the postmortem by close of play *yesterday*. Goodness knows what he was doing all day!'

'Give him a break – he was up most of Thursday night at the crime scene.'

Lawrence sighed. 'I suppose we'll have to pop back to meet with him later. I can only hope it'll be worth the effort.' He paused. 'In the meantime, given that there was no sign of forced entry, the obvious assumption is that either her killer came through the door invited, or else he has a key.'

'Pete,' Rebecca submitted.

'Or,' Lawrence replied, lifting his eyebrows for emphasis, 'The landlord.'

Rebecca identified Carrina Mitchell immediately as the woman in the photograph she had taken from Zoë's bedroom the previous afternoon, and calculated that she was probably in her forties, although she looked younger. Like Zoë, she was tall and slender, elegantly dressed in a long floral skirt and a tailored white blouse.

Her dark hair was swept back from her face, lacking any hint of grey, and Rebecca guessed the colour was artificially maintained. Carrina's make-up was impeccable, but her pale eyes looked tired, and she appeared considerably less composed than her husband had done the previous day, her expression anxious and hands clasped tightly in her lap.

'I'm sorry to have to put you through this, I understand you and Zoë were very close,' Lawrence began, nodding his thanks to Gavin Mitchell as he set a mug of coffee down on the table between them.

'Yes,' Carrina confirmed, her tone rather subdued.

'When did you and she last speak?'

'Early Wednesday evening.'

'Did you talk for long?'

'No. She was about to go out. She just called to see if there had been any post for her.'

'Was she expecting any?'

'I don't know. We quite often redirected things – she never got around to informing many people that she'd moved out.'

'You said she was about to go out when she called – did she say where to?'

Carrina seemed to think this over for a moment before answering. 'I think she said something about a wine bar in Soho.'

'Do you know whether she was going with anybody?'

'Just that she was meeting a friend.'

'She didn't give a name?'

'No. She rarely did unless it was somebody we knew.'

'Did she generally go into much detail about her social life?'

'I don't know, really – I'd like to think so – but while she did tell me a lot, I don't know how much she may have omitted. I think there are always certain things children keep from their parents.'

'Was she happy?'

Carrina twisted her wedding ring around her finger. 'She certainly seemed it.'

'Can you think of anybody who might have wanted some harm to come to her?'

'No,' Carrina replied, her voice wavering. She swallowed. 'No. Nobody.'

When Lawrence didn't immediately pose another question, Rebecca asked, 'Did Zoë talk much about Pete?'

'Not really. I don't think she was particularly serious about him. She always said she was too young to be tied down to one man.'

'Do you know whether she dated anybody else while she was seeing him?'

'There were certainly other men on the scene.'

'Did that concern you?'

'Why should it have done? She was old enough to make her own decisions. Besides, she always gave me the impression that her relationship with Pete was fairly casual.'

'Do you have any idea how Pete viewed the situation?' Rebecca enquired, reaching for her coffee.

'None at all. I don't know him that well – we've only met on a few occasions.'

'Did you like him?'

'I didn't dislike him.'

'Were you in on Wednesday evening?' Lawrence asked, as Rebecca sipped her coffee.

Carrina nodded. 'I arrived home shortly before seven. I didn't leave the house again until Thursday morning, when I went to work.'

'And your husband?'

'He was here,' Carrina confirmed, rubbing her forehead. Rebecca didn't miss the fact that this action served to obscure her eyes from theirs.

'Do you have a spare key to Zoë's flat?'

'Yes.'

'Would that have been easily accessible to visitors?'

'Not unless they knew where it was kept. We don't leave keys lying about the house.'

'Where do you keep them?'

'We keep all spare keys – both ours and other people's – in a drawer in my husband's study.'

'Would you mind checking that Zoë's key is still there?'

'Of course not.' Carrina stood up. 'I'll do that now.'

'Thank you,' Lawrence nodded, as she left the room. He glanced to Rebecca, eyebrows raised. She guessed what he was thinking. It was unlikely that many outside the family knew the whereabouts of the box of keys, and even those that did would doubtless have had difficulty identifying Zoë's from the others of which Carrina had spoken. Had that key led directly to Zoë's death, her killer was chillingly close to home.

*****

Gavin's study was the only room in the house still furnished with a view of the abandoned summerhouse, now secluded by tall conifers that had been little more than seedlings only fifteen years earlier. At the time they had been features of the garden that Gavin had planted for Zoë and Christia outside the summerhouse, but they had long since taken over, dwarfing the surrounding miniature picket fence, which had, at Gavin's request, been removed by the gardener. The near side of the summerhouse roof was trapped permanently in the shadow of the house, and over time the asphalt had been colonised by thick, dark moss, while the wire mesh bird feeder hanging from the eaves, devoid of nuts for nearly a decade, had rusted almost beyond recognition. The once green paint of the shutters now blistered grey, and, where one was missing altogether, the faded, rotten curtains were just visible through the filthy glass.

It was a far cry from the days when Zoë and Christia had played house inside, held secret meetings and given tea parties for their friends, and, on rare occasions, for Carrina and Gavin. Carrina had watched their games from the kitchen window, had played the part of next-door neighbour, shop keeper, policewoman and numerous other characters as her two young daughters came and went from house to summerhouse and back again. It had been months since she had given it a second thought, for, like so many aspects of their family life, it had become a case of *out of sight, out of mind*, and, gazing out at what now looked to be nothing more than a derelict garden shed, Carrina tried to pinpoint just where it had all started to go wrong.

The slow decay of the summerhouse now seemed something of a metaphor for the happiness and security that Carrina had once embraced. Overlooked and undervalued, her relationships with those closest to her had atrophied unnoticed through her own selfishness and neglect. Whether her husband's duplicity had been the source of the deterioration or merely a symptom she didn't know, but the betrayal of the past few days had brought home to her the fact that there was little, if anything, left to salvage. She had concealed the truth not through loyalty but fear; fear borne of the knowledge that while she had already lost so much, there was still more to lose. One wrong word and she would be alone. By comparison, justice seemed almost immaterial.

Sinking down onto the chair at Gavin's desk, she moved to open the drawer in which she knew Zoë's key should lie, at the last moment changing her mind and impulsively reaching for the drawer below. The contents had changed little, if at all, since her previous foray into her husband's most personal and private mementoes. There were photographs, drawings, poems, birthday cards, letters and postcards – pictures, handwritings and illustrations all so familiar that Carrina barely glanced at them as she drew out the faded blue envelope concealed beneath the collection. Sliding the single remaining content of the envelope from its sleeve, Carrina wished everything could be as black and white as the photograph now grasped between her shaking fingers. Turning it over, she stared down at the thick lines of indelible marker that obliterated whatever inscription had originally appeared on the reverse. Tears stung her eyes as she returned her attention to the infant subject of the photograph, reflecting on what might have been. One picture, one moment, one memory. The son Gavin had always wanted, and never known.

Hearing footsteps on the landing, Carrina hurriedly slipped the photograph back into its envelope and replaced this where it belonged. Closing the drawer as she simultaneously opened the one above, she reached for the sturdy cardboard box that had originally contained golf balls. Lifting the lid, she rifled through the contents, aware now of a presence behind her. Desperately seeking the reassurance she craved, she allowed some moments to pass before she finally turned. Gavin stood motionless in the doorway, and as their eyes met, Carrina prayed that with a few well chosen words he might somehow absolve her of any responsibility. As they looked silently upon one another, she tried in vain to read his expression. The atmosphere between them was close to unbearable by the time he spoke. Holding up a small, translucent blue plastic pig, from whose tail dangled a silver yale key, he said, almost casually, 'Looking for this?'

It was quite a walk from the nearest station to the Battersea address Rebecca had obtained that morning in connection with the telephone number 'Candie home', and when she arrived she had to ring the bell twice before she drew any response. The door was eventually opened by a young man, clearly not long awake, clad only in boxer shorts. Holding the door open with one hand, he smoothed his short dark hair with the other.

'Yes?' He snapped.

'Good morning. Is Candela in?'

'She's asleep.'

Rebecca felt the surge of excitement that always accompanied a hunch proving correct. 'I'm Detective Sergeant Palmer,' she revealed, displaying her warrant card. 'I'd like a word with her, please.'

'For Christ's sake, it's Saturday morning!'

'I'm sorry about that, but it is very important.'

'It'd better be,' the young man grumbled, stepping backwards. 'You'd best come in.' He turned from the door. 'Grab a seat in the kitchen and I'll wake Candie for you.'

Rebecca thanked him with deliberate courtesy as she entered the flat.

The kitchen was the first room off the hallway, and Rebecca perched on one of the Formica-covered chairs, looking around herself and reaching into her bag for her notebook. She was joined surprisingly quickly by a petite, pretty redhead wrapped in an overlarge green-and-black-striped man's dressing gown.

'Hi,' the woman greeted, hovering anxiously in the doorway.

'Candela?'

She nodded.

'I'd like to ask you a few questions about Zoë Mitchell.'

'Zoë?' The redhead's expression registered both surprise and relief, leading Rebecca to suspect she had been anticipating a visit from the police for some other reason. 'Why?'

'I'm sorry to have to tell you, but Zoë was found dead on Thursday,' Rebecca informed her, as Candela sat on a chair just inside the door.

'What?' Candela exclaimed, her eyes widening. 'How?'

'I'm afraid she was murdered.'

Candela swallowed hard, clearly shaken. 'God.'

'I thought you might have known by now.'

Candela shook her head. 'No – I've not really been in touch with her this week.'

'You sent her a text message on Wednesday afternoon.'

'How do you know that?' Candela asked, sharply, looking alarmed.

Rebecca ignored the question. 'You asked what she was doing that night. Were you hoping to meet up with her?'

'No,' Candela responded, defensively. 'I just wondered what she was doing.'

'And what was she doing?'

'Meeting someone.'

'Who?'

'I don't know. Some guy.'

'I assume it wasn't her boyfriend, if you don't know?'

'You mean Pete?' Candela half smiled. 'No, she wasn't seeing him.'

'What was your relationship with Zoë?'

Candela shrugged. 'We were friends.'

'Just friends?'

'Zoë wasn't bisexual.'

'Are you?'

'Does it matter?'

'I'm just curious. You sent her a text message early in the week that said something along the lines of *thanks for last night, I love you*. What did that relate to?'

'What's so weird about telling a girlfriend you love her? Have you never done it?'

'So you were close.'

Candela sighed. 'Yeah. She was a good friend.'

'In which case, why was your mobile number not listed in her phone's contacts?'

'I – uh – only bought it a couple of weeks ago. Maybe she hadn't found time to update it.'

Rebecca sensed the girl was lying, but there was no way of disproving the statement, so she moved on.

'In one of the messages you sent, you asked if she wanted to meet up with Fred. Who is Fred?'

Candela hesitated, licking her lips nervously. 'Private joke.'

'Oh?'

'One of those silly things that comes about from a drunken night out, that's all. Fred doesn't actually exist.'

From Candela's body language it was clear there was more to it, but Rebecca didn't push the girl, asking instead whether Zoë had ever mentioned the bombardment of love letters stacked on her dining table. Candela's blank expression indicated she was telling the truth when she denied any knowledge.

'Did she have any particularly persistent admirers?'

'Several,' Candela replied, with an expressive lift of her eyebrows. 'Men loved her. And then there was her stalker.'

'Stalker?' Rebecca echoed, wondering why nobody else had mentioned him.

'That's what she used to call him, but she never seemed all that concerned about it, I think she viewed him as a cross between an irritation and a joke.'

'Do you know his name?'

'No. We referred to him as the two-tone twat.'

'Why?'

'Because of the awful dye job he did on his hair.'

'Any idea where he lives?'

'No, but I can tell you where you're likely to find him.'

'Where?'

'A club in Soho. It's called The Velvet Lounge – it's off Dean Street – and there's a night called Whipped Up on Saturdays. He's there every week. Someone on the door's sure to be able to point him out to you.'

Rebecca noted this down. She was about to move on to her next question when Candela asked, rather hesitantly, 'What happened to her?'

'I can't give you any details at present. But it happened in her flat, which is why I'm keen to trace whoever she was seeing that evening.'

Candela nodded. There was a pause before she said, 'It doesn't feel real.'

'I'm sorry, I know it must be a shock.'

The girl nodded again.

'Do you know her boyfriend, Pete Morgan, well?'

'I don't really know him at all. Zoë rarely brought him along when she was seeing us.'

'Us?'

'Me and Darren – that's my boyfriend – and – um – his friends.'

'Why not?'

'He didn't really fit in,' Candela replied, mysteriously.

'And how about Lucian Price? Do you know him?'

'Lucian?' Candela's eyebrows rose, her expression answering Rebecca's question before she did. 'Oh yes. I know Lucian.'

Michael van Prior lived in a modest detached house in a suburb of Birmingham. He was a slight man in his early fifties with a hooked nose and a beard that was considerably more voluminous than the hair on his head. The waistband of his green trousers was slightly over-generous, which, in the absence of a belt, looked rather odd, and, teamed eccentrically with a sky blue shirt, stranger still.

'This is about the girl from Grosvenor Street, I assume,' he surmised, showing Lawrence into a spacious and tidy living room.

'Zoë Mitchell, yes.'

'Please – sit down,' Michael invited, closing the door to the room and moving towards an armchair by the window.

Lawrence did so, and, when his host had done likewise, asked, 'How long had Zoë been a tenant of yours?'

'A little over six months.'

'I understand you threatened her with eviction a couple of months ago.'

Michael nodded. 'Yes.'

'Would you mind telling me why?'

'Not at all. It was really quite simple. The contract made it very clear that she wasn't to keep pets of any sort in the flat. After moving in, she acquired a kitten, and I told her she had two options – move out or get rid of the cat.'

'And did she?'

'I believe so.'

'How did you find out about the cat in the first place?'

'One of the window catches in the flat was broken, and Zoë asked me to have it repaired. I decided to do the job myself one evening when I was passing through London – Zoë wasn't expecting me, and when she opened the door, the cat ran past.'

'Zoë's father seems to be under the impression you wanted her out as a result of complaints from another tenant,' Lawrence replied. 'Is there any truth in that?'

'That is what I told him, if that's what you're asking.'

'Why tell him that? If, as you say, Zoë was breaching the terms of her contract, surely you were in the right?'

The man sighed. 'Dr Mitchell and I had something of a disagreement. He was getting nasty, and I threw that at him as a means of winning the argument.' There was a pause before he added, 'Rather childish of me, I admit.'

'So that wasn't true?'

'Well, I have had endless letters of complaint from the building's other tenant, but she's clearly completely batty, so I had no intention of acting on her grievances.'

'What were they?'

'Oh, she got it into her head that Zoë was a prostitute.'

'That didn't concern you?'

'No. I doubt it was true, and even if it were, to be quite frank I don't give a damn what my tenants do with their lives so long as they pay the rent on time and take reasonable care of my property.'

'When did you last see Zoë?'

Michael paused for thought before saying, 'Five or six weeks ago, I suppose.'

'Could you tell me where you were on Wednesday night?'

'I was here.'

'Can anybody confirm that?'

'Several people. My wife and I had friends staying – we were up until about two.'

'Rather late,' Lawrence observed.

'We hadn't seen them in some time – they live overseas, and they only arrived on Wednesday evening, so we had a good deal of catching up to do.'

'I see.'

'And if you need to know where I was after two, the burglar alarm went off shortly after three, so both my wife and our visitors would be able to verify that I was here then.'

'What set it off?'

'We forgot to mention that we set the alarm at night,' Michael admitted, rather sheepishly. 'And one of our guests ventured downstairs for a glass of water.'

'Are your guests still here?'

'Yes – they're in the garden with my wife.'

Lawrence nodded, concluding that Michael van Prior was unlikely to be of further assistance, and voicing his desire for a quick word with the man's wife and guests. Unless this turned up anything unexpected, he would waste little time in returning to London.

Five

Having expected Candela to have little knowledge of Lucian – beyond perhaps a vague awareness of his involvement with Zoë's sister – Rebecca felt startled by the girl's response to his name. The answer to the question of how she knew him came as an even greater surprise. Running a hand through her thick red bob and around the side of her neck rather seductively, Candela revealed, 'He's my ex-boyfriend.'

'Ex-boyfriend?' Rebecca exclaimed.

'Yeah,' Candela smiled, looking amused by Rebecca's response to this revelation. She didn't seem nearly as distressed as Rebecca would have expected in the circumstances, leading her to wonder how long Candela and Zoë had known one another, and how deep the friendship had really run.

'When was it that you dated him?'

'A couple of years ago. Before he cracked up.'

'Did that happen while you were still together?'

Candela nodded. 'He became someone else. I hardly knew him anymore.'

'What changed?'

'He used to be really fun. One of those people everybody likes. He had so many friends I rarely had him to myself.' Candela cast her eyes down. 'He seemed to withdraw almost overnight. Never wanted to go out, never wanted to see anybody – including me, a lot of the time. He just sat at home chain smoking.' She shrugged. 'In the end, he reached a point where I was scared to be alone with him.'

'Why?'

'I never knew what was going to happen next,' Candela admitted, raising her gaze. 'I was eighteen, and I had no idea how to deal with him when he freaked out. There was rarely any warning – it could happen anywhere – any time –' she shook her head. 'I wasn't going through the easiest time myself, and I needed somebody who could look after me, not the other way around.'

'What did you mean when you said he *freaked out*?'

'He used to have panic attacks, and nightmares – sometimes I think he was even hallucinating, although he always denied it.' Candela sighed. 'Seeing him like that terrified me.'

'Had they diagnosed his illness by then?'

Candela frowned. 'Illness?'

'As I understand it he suffers from an anxiety disorder.'

Candela raised one eyebrow. 'Is that what they call it?' She asked, sounding almost amused.

Rebecca felt taken aback by this reaction. 'What would you call it?'

'Cannabis psychosis.'

Rebecca blinked. 'Is that your way of saying that Lucian used cannabis heavily in the past?'

'For all I know he still uses it now.'

'You haven't seen him recently, then.'

'I see him every now and then. We didn't part on bad terms, and for a while we did remain friends, but –' she swallowed. 'It's hard spending time with somebody you still love when you can't have anything more.'

'So where did Zoë fit into the picture?'

'Zoë?'

'She knew Lucian.'

'Yeah, she knew him.'

'Was that through you, or her sister?'

'I don't know.'

'Was she ever involved with him?'

'Not as far as I know – but –' Candela hesitated.

'But?'

'I doubt she would have told me if she were.'

'I thought you said she was a close friend?'

'She was.'

'That being the case, why would she not have told you?'

'Because she knew I still had feelings for him, and she would have been sensitive enough not to throw it in my face if she had been seeing him.'

'From what I've heard, Zoë doesn't seem to have had many qualms about other people's feelings when it came to getting what she wanted.'

'Not where those she was close to were concerned.'

'Apparently that didn't apply to her twin sister.'

'They weren't close. They barely spoke.'

'Do you know why that was?'

'Zoë never really said,' Candela responded, uncomfortably. 'I think it had something to do with their parents.'

Rebecca suspected the girl knew far more than she was letting on, but decided not to press her, saying instead, 'Do you think Zoë would have wanted a relationship with Lucian? If he's as erratic as you say.'

'Zoë wasn't like me. Some women can enjoy a one-night stand for what it is without wanting or expecting anything more. I'm not one of them.'

'And Zoë was?'

'Yes.'

Rebecca nodded thoughtfully. 'You said earlier that towards the end of your relationship with Lucian, you were scared to be alone with him. Did he ever hurt you?'

'No.'

'Were you ever afraid he might?'

'No,' Candela repeated, shaking her head. Her expression changing abruptly, she said, 'You're not suggesting that *Lucian* –' she shook her head again, more vehemently this time. 'No! No, he wouldn't have done that to her! No way!'

'What makes you so certain?'

'He wouldn't *hurt* anybody!' Candela exclaimed, visibly distressed. 'He freaks out now and then, but he'd never do something like *that*!'

Rebecca raised her eyebrows, leaning forwards. 'If you're so sure of that, why were you sufficiently afraid to walk away from a man you loved?'

The question was met with silence; it seemed Candela had no answer. Rebecca suspected that was an answer in itself.

'This might interest you,' Rebecca announced, looking up from her desk as Lawrence approached his office.

'Oh?'

'A request for planning permission. One Michael van Prior. He wants to build two houses in place of the one he's renting out.'

'It would interest me more if his alibi didn't check out,' Lawrence replied, leaning a forearm on the divider that separated her desk from the one opposite.

'He's a businessman – he's unlikely to get his own hands dirty, is he?'

'True, but I can't really see it. It's not that hard to get the average tenant out.'

'Do you want me to look into it anyway?'

Lawrence considered the matter for a moment before shaking his head. 'No. Not yet. I don't think he's our man. Yes, it's possible he may have wanted her out of the flat, but I really don't think he, or his associates, would have gone to the trouble of raping her and slashing what basically amounts to a macabre work of art into her chest, do you?'

Rebecca wordlessly conceded the point with a change in facial expression.

'Whoever was responsible inflicted a lot of damage. They didn't just want her dead, they wanted her defiled. It doesn't exactly smack of contract killing. I think we're looking for someone closer to home.'

'So who's top of your list at this stage?'

'Pete. Or Lucian, maybe. If there was something going on between him and Zoë.'

'I'd have thought Pete would have been more likely to go for Lucian.'

'Who knows? If Christia's to be believed, Lucian would have been far from an isolated conquest for Zoë. Perhaps it was a case of *if I can't have her, no one can.*'

Rebecca nodded.

'I can't help wondering how many couples Zoë has come between in her time. It sounds as though she enjoyed breaking relationships far more than having them. There could be any number of people who would have liked to see her safely out of the way. Although Lucian probably has a stronger motive than most.'

'Do you think he could have killed Zoë? If he's as anxious as you say, it seems unlikely he'd have the nerve.'

'Presumably anxiety would only have been a major impediment if the attack was premeditated. If you act on the spur of the moment, panic tends to kick in after the event.'

'I suppose so.'

'And I'm not convinced by his *what would a model want with me* line. I don't believe he really sees himself as nothing special – he could probably pass for a model himself.' Lawrence paused. 'Plus, I'm suspicious about his motives as far as Christia goes.'

'Oh?'

'He's very attractive – I should think he could have almost any girl he wanted – yet he picks Christia. She's big, and I don't just mean plump.'

'Love isn't just about appearances.'

'No, but for teenage boys it frequently is,' Lawrence observed, bluntly. 'He's going out with Christia. He lives in a council flat, and she lives in a mansion. Her parents must be loaded. I see a motive there.'

'He'd have to marry Christia to stand any chance of inheriting.'

'Which wouldn't happen if she found out he'd had a fling with her sister.'

'Presumably Zoë also stood to inherit. Do you think Christia and Lucian might have been in it together?'

'That's not beyond the realms of possibility,' Lawrence acknowledged. 'There certainly doesn't seem to have been any love lost between the two sisters.' He paused. 'How did you get on with your search for Candela?'

'Finding her was easy enough. And she didn't only know Zoë; it turns out she's also Lucian's ex-girlfriend.'

'Really?' Lawrence's eyebrows climbed. 'How about Fred? Where does he fit into the picture?'

'She claims Fred doesn't exist, and was simply part of a private joke between herself and Zoë, although I'm disinclined to believe her.'

Lawrence nodded.

'She also mentioned that Zoë had what she referred to as a *stalker*, although it didn't sound as if Zoë found him particularly threatening. But then it's not unusual for stalkers to start out as tiresome but seemingly harmless, only for their behaviour to grow more sinister as time goes by.'

'Do we have a name?'

'Candela couldn't give me one, but she did give me the name of a club in Soho where she thought he was more than likely to be tonight. Apparently the staff should know who he is. I thought perhaps we could drop in there later.'

'I can see I'd blend in well at a nightclub,' Lawrence joked, gesturing to his suit and tie.

'It's all right, Sir, if anybody asks I'll tell them you're my father.'

Lawrence smiled, shaking his head. Then, his thoughts moving on, he asked, 'Have you had a chance to catch up with Leighton since you've been back?'

'He thought you might want to be around to hear what he had to say.'

'You mean he was running late,' Lawrence surmised, irritably. 'Well, he'd better be ready now – let's pop into the pathology unit on our way to –'

'I think he's gone for lunch.'

'Good God, does he think we have all day?' Lawrence exclaimed, pulling his mobile from his pocket. 'He can get right back here now! We don't have time for him to swan off to the pub, and neither does he!'

'Hullo,' Leighton greeted, affably, as he entered Lawrence's office, apparently unconcerned by the rather rude interruption to his lunch break. A cheerful, laid-back young man in his early thirties, he had joined the pathology unit some six months previously, and had already attained a reputation at Scotland Yard, both for his brilliance as a forensic scientist and for his seemingly non-stop social life. Stocky and of median height, he had a soft, rounded face, which took some years off his age, and long dark hair, kept almost permanently fastened away from his face. He was dressed casually in jeans and a black t-shirt, and carried nothing with him, presumably owing to the fact he had just returned from the pub.

'Sorry I wasn't about earlier, I –'

'I'm not interested in excuses, Leighton, I'd rather you just got on with doing your job,' Lawrence snapped, impatiently. 'Where are you at?'

Looking not in the least put out by Lawrence's sharp tone, Leighton leaned against the back of a chair and raised a hand to clear a few wayward hairs away from his face. 'Ok – well, as I think one of the SOC guys already told you, there didn't seem to be any signs of forced entry to the flat – all the windows were securely locked, there are no scratch marks or wood chips around any of the window frames, and no fingerprints anywhere to be seen.' Leighton absentmindedly reached for the biro wedged behind his ear and twisted it around the fingers of his right hand. 'As to the body, I can't definitively say the sex wasn't consensual, but if it was it must have been pretty rough, because there's a degree of bruising to the tissues. And it looks like her assailant wore a condom, because there are no traces of seminal fluid.

'Death as you know was by strangulation, and there are fingernail marks about the girl's throat, which tells you how that was accomplished, and which indicate her attacker was right-handed. There's more than one set of marks, which isn't uncommon, because people are apt to struggle. But what is interesting is that some of the finger marks show considerably more bruising than others.'

'What does that mean?' Lawrence asked.

'I can't be certain, but I'd guess there was a time lapse between the two. If she'd died straight away, there would have been little immediate bruising to speak of.'

'You mean she was strangled on more than one occasion, and the first didn't actually kill her?'

'Yep.'

'Have you any idea what sort of time lapse we're talking about?'

'No, not really – minutes rather than hours is probably about as specific as I can be.'

Lawrence nodded. 'Is it possible that she was first rendered unconscious, then raped?'

'And mutilated.'

'Poor girl,' Rebecca murmured.

'I doubt she would have known much about it – it's very unlikely she was conscious at the time. The cuts aren't just random slashes – there's a clear design to them, and I can't see anybody managing to successfully complete something like that if their victim was free to move about.'

'Do you have any idea what might have been used to make the cuts?' Lawrence asked.

'No,' Leighton replied, apologetically. 'There was no sign of whatever it was at the scene. All I can really tell you is that it had a very sharp blade. Sorry.'

'How about the man responsible? What do you have on him?'

'I retrieved traces of tissue from under Zoë's fingernails, and I also combed out a few pubic hairs – I'm still waiting on the lab for DNA results, but from the pigments in the tissue it's likely you're looking for a Caucasian. Preliminary chemical analyses turned up traces of tetrachloroethylene – that's commonly used as a dry cleaning fluid. It's also used in metal degreasing, which may be relevant to a few tiny metal filings I picked up from the bedclothes. I've not yet had time to analyse those, but they might give you a clue to your killer's occupation.'

'So in all likelihood we're looking for a right-handed Caucasian who probably uses a dry cleaners,' Lawrence observed, with a sigh. 'That narrows it down.'

'Yeah, I know. Sorry.'

Lawrence shook his head. 'Hardly your fault.'

'I'll let you know if I find anything else. And when I hear back about the DNA results, although that'll be Monday at the earliest.'

'Thanks.'

'Have you made much headway?'

'Not really,' Lawrence admitted, resting his elbows on his desk. 'Zoë's parents have a key to the flat, as does her boyfriend, and we'll be having another chat with him this afternoon. Whether there are any other key holders remains an open question.'

'Ah well, good luck.' Leighton pushed off from the chair and made for the door. 'I'll be around for the rest of the afternoon, and if you need me after that you can get me on my mobile.' He turned in the doorway with a grin. 'But I'd prefer it if homicides could be scheduled either this side of midnight or after nine tomorrow morning. Could you pass that on to any potential killers?'

'That guy is like the Cheshire cat,' Lawrence observed, after Leighton had departed. 'He disappears, but the grin stays with me.'

Rebecca laughed. 'Are you frightened of getting to know him in case you find that you actually like him?'

'It's not that I dislike him, Becky – it's his lackadaisical attitude to his work that I find infuriating.'

'That's not fair, he's very good at what he does.'

'Yes, he is – *when* he gets around to actually *doing* it.' Lawrence moved to stand. 'Speaking of which, we should get moving. It's nearly three, and we've four corners of London to cover before everybody, including us, hits the clubs for Saturday night.'

Tossing her mobile onto the sofa and parting the curtains at her living room window, Olivia Hunter wondered whether she was the only person on Earth who truly detested summer. Outside, the sky was blue, the Sun was shining and the temperature in the shade was creeping past twenty-nine degrees. Across the road, the park was heaving with bare-chested men and scantily clad women enjoying the hottest weather yet that year, and Olivia could think of nothing she would have liked to do less than join them. How anybody could call this weather glorious, she simply couldn't imagine. Hot and sticky, she felt too lethargic to contemplate going anywhere or doing anything, and at the same time unbearably bored, trapped indoors with nothing to do. It seemed impossible to believe she could ever feel cold again, and, were it not for the conviction that she could never happily live anywhere but London, she would seriously have considered moving to cooler climes.

Turning from the window, she headed for her bedroom, peeling her pink camisole off as she did so and flinging it in the general direction of the laundry basket. Slipping out of her skirt, she reached for her dressing gown, feeling guilty for declining Claudia's invitation to meet for a drink. A friend from her school days, there had once been a time when the two of them had been out every Saturday of the summer until the early hours of Sunday morning, drinking their way through the afternoon and evening in their local pub before adjourning to one club or another to dance, quite often for two or three hours straight. How she had done so, Olivia now had no idea. In recent months, she had barely seen Claudia, so caught up had she been with her work and its associated social demands, and she felt bad that not only had she refused to meet her friend, but that her excuse for doing so had also been untrue.

Entering the bathroom, she turned the shower on, adjusting the thermostat and feeling the water, aiming to get it as close to cold as she could bear. She had told herself the weather was a justifiable reason for not meeting up with Claudia, but she knew that was as much making excuses to herself as Zoë's death had been to her friend. She had first noticed they were growing apart when she realised that their most animated conversations began with the words *do you remember when.* For a time the reminiscences had proved entertaining, but lately they seemed to have little, if anything, to talk about, and Olivia couldn't face the thought of sitting opposite Claudia for the rest of the afternoon, smoking and drinking in the near silence that had plagued their previous meeting. With a sigh, she fitted the shower head into the holder on the wall and stepped into the bath, at which moment the doorbell rang.

* * * * *

71

From the look of the Kensington Georgian terrace in which she lived, Rebecca guessed Olivia Hunter was further up the ladder of the modelling world than Zoë Mitchell had been. When, moments later, Olivia answered the door, this was confirmed by the fact Rebecca recognised her. Tall and almost unnaturally thin, with ash blonde hair that fell to within inches of her waist, soft blue eyes and perfectly formed lips, Rebecca placed her immediately as the girl featured in the perfume advert on the back cover of one of the glossy magazines lying on the coffee table at home. She appeared to be almost posing where she stood, lips slightly parted to display flawless white teeth and fingers tracing the neckline of her mint green satin dressing gown.

'Olivia Hunter?'

'Yes.'

Lawrence displayed his identification and introduced himself and Rebecca before asking whether she would mind answering some questions.

In a barely discernible movement, Olivia caught her lower lip with her teeth before she replied. 'About Zoë.'

'Yes.'

Olivia nodded. 'Come in.'

Lawrence and Rebecca followed her across the hallway into the living room. The room was shrouded in semi-darkness, the curtains tightly drawn, and Olivia moved to open them. Light flooded in, illuminating a modern, minimalist decor not entirely in keeping with the high, cornice-bound ceiling. The walls were a pale cream, almost white, as were the cushions of the sofa and armchairs, which had solid wooden frames in a contrasting rich, dark mahogany. This matched the nest of tables beneath the window, and the shapely legs of the glass-topped coffee table central to the room. The walls were hung with a collection of rather anaemic watercolours, and a vase of white lilies sat atop one of two glass corner shelves, the lower of which housed a framed photograph. A dish of glass sweets on the coffee table was the only item of colour in the room, and the almond carpet looked so impossibly clean that Rebecca had to consciously refrain from checking the soles of her shoes as she entered.

'Would you like a drink?' Olivia asked, turning from the window.

Lawrence declined, perching on the sofa. Olivia sat in the armchair closest to where she had been standing, drawing her feet up and tucking them into one armrest, her knees pressed against the other. Running her forefinger along her leg, she tipped her head to one side. 'What do you want to know?'

'I understand you and Zoë worked together.'

'Some of the time.'

'Meaning what?'

'It depended on what we were doing. I have a contract with one of the big fashion houses – that wasn't something Zoë was involved in – and she had commitments of her own too. We did some catwalk shows together, but they tended to be rather sporadic.'

'Did you see anything of her away from work?'

'We were friends,' Olivia replied, simply. 'I saw far more of her socially than I ever did through work.'

'How long had you known her?'

'A couple of years. We met at a fashion show when she was just starting out.'

'I imagine you know some of her other friends, then.'

'Yes.'

'Do you know her boyfriend?'

'Which one?'

'How many were there?'

'It varied.'

'So Pete Morgan wasn't the only one.'

'I think Pete considered himself her boyfriend more than she did.'

'Do you know him well?'

'Not really. I've met him quite a few times, but only because he was out with Zoë.'

'How about Lucian Price?'

Olivia frowned in thought. 'Lucian. I know the name, but –' she paused, shaking her head slightly. 'I can't think where from.'

'He's dating Zoë's sister.'

'Oh, right, yes.'

'Have you met him?'

'No. Zoë mentioned him a few times, but that was all.'

'What did she say?'

'Nothing much – just the odd comment about him and Chris.'

'She wasn't involved with him herself, then?'

Olivia shrugged. 'Who knows. Zoë seemed to be involved with almost every man she met. She didn't go around bragging about it. I think people only do that when they're insecure and want attention.'

73

'And do you know Candela Jackson?' Rebecca put in, mindful of the other link they had to Lucian.

'I know who she is. I've never spent much time with her.'

'Do you not get on?'

Olivia looked uncomfortable. 'It's not that we don't get on, exactly – it's just that she's –' she stopped, colour rising in her cheeks. 'I'm not into – kinky stuff.'

'Do you think you could explain what you mean by that?'

Olivia dropped her eyes to her lap, evidently embarrassed. 'Sex. I only – I've only been with people I've loved – I'm not into deviant or – group – acts.'

'And Candela is?'

'Yes.'

'Such as what?'

'Bondage, S and M – that sort of thing.' Olivia's distaste was evident in her expression as she spoke.

'Do you know whether Zoë was involved in that at all?'

Olivia nodded. 'She respected the fact that I didn't – wasn't –' Olivia broke off, apparently at a loss to know how to complete the sentence. 'But she seemed to get off on it. I suppose you must do, if you're choosing to do it. Candela used to hold sex parties. I guess she probably still does.'

Remembering what Candela had said about Pete, Rebecca asked, 'Did Pete participate in that with her?'

'I seriously doubt it. He was so possessive he barely let anybody else hug Zoë – I hardly think he'd have sat on the sidelines while she had sex with other men.'

There was an awkward silence before Lawrence returned to his original vein. 'Can you name any other men Zoë was involved with?'

'Yes. One of them was a model signed to our agency.'

'Was that a long-term relationship?'

'Not at all. He was engaged at the time.'

'Is he still?'

'No. His fiancée found out about his affair with Zoë and finished with him.'

'How did he take that?'

'Badly. He was under the impression that Zoë told Grace – that was his fiancée – about the affair.'

'Did she?'

'She said not. It wasn't as if they were very discreet, I expect a lot of people knew.'

'Could you give me the man's name?'

'Dayv Roberts.'

Rebecca scribbled this down. 'Do you think he might have been inclined to seek revenge of some sort?'

'Possibly. He already sent Zoë a wreath.'

'He did *what*?' Lawrence exclaimed. 'What was Zoë's reaction to that?'

'She just laughed at him,' Olivia smiled sadly. 'It took a lot to upset Zoë. I'm not sure she'd ever been in love, and I don't think she realised how much some of what she did hurt the people around her.' Olivia paused, running her right forefinger rather absently along her collar bone, before adding, almost to herself, 'At least, I hope not. Otherwise, she just didn't care.'

Six

Victoria Shelley was dressed in an embroidered ivory gown and matching bolero jacket, her strawberry blonde hair swept back from her face and fastened with an oval mother-of-pearl clip. Her long fingernails had been painted to match, her eyelids touched with soft, neutral shades that enhanced her turquoise eyes, and iridescent beige expertly applied to her lips. Clad in delicate, high-heeled sandals, she stood over six foot tall, which served to make her look even slimmer than she actually was. Clearly about to go out, she had stopped short on finding Rebecca and Lawrence on her doorstep, having evidently been expecting somebody else.

'I can't talk for long – my boyfriend's picking me up in about ten minutes,' she explained as she showed them into her living room. 'We're going to a film premiere, so I really can't be late.' Taking a seat, she gestured for Lawrence and Rebecca to do likewise.

'What does your boyfriend do?' Lawrence asked, sitting opposite her.

'He's an actor,' Victoria replied, as if that much should by now have been obvious.

'And the film?'

'Everlong.'

'Ah,' Lawrence nodded. He had seen several recent advertisements for it, the British film industry's latest high-profile attempt to rival Hollywood. 'What's your boyfriend's name?'

'Tim Whitman.'

While Lawrence couldn't put a face to the name, he recognised it, and guessed Zoë had probably known exactly who he was.

'I understand you and Zoë Mitchell shared the same booking agent.'

Victoria nodded.

'Did you see much of one another?'

'Not if I could help it.'

Lawrence raised his eyebrows. 'Would you mind telling me why not?'

'If you've spoken to anybody else you must have some idea of her reputation with men,' Victoria replied, coolly. 'If a man was single, she wasn't very interested, as a rule, but if he was somebody else's boyfriend, husband –' she paused, holding out her hands long enough for Lawrence to notice that she wore an engagement ring. 'And, if they were famous to boot, that made them really hot property.'

'Were you afraid she might make a play for Tim?'

'She *did*.'

'How did you feel about that?'

Victoria wrinkled her nose. 'I wasn't threatened by it – girls throw themselves at Timmy all the time, and I think he finds that flattering, but he's never given me reason not to trust him. It's not as if I don't get my fair share of unwanted male attention. But that didn't make her behaviour any less unacceptable.'

'Can you give us any other examples of relationships she interfered with?'

'She had a fling with my friend Janice's boyfriend – although I don't think he was ever really the monogamous type – I also heard she'd been messing about with one of the guys at work. Apparently his fiancée dumped him and Zoë finished with him almost immediately. As I said, if a man was single, she wasn't very interested. I don't know – most of what I know stems from rumours, but I saw what she could be like, and I don't doubt most of the stories are true.'

'Is your friend Janice also a model?'

'No, she's a make-up artist.'

'How did she react when she found out Zoë had been involved with her boyfriend?'

'She was devastated. It's tough working in the fashion industry if you're not –' Victoria hesitated, her cheeks colouring slightly. 'God, this sounds so arrogant –' she reached for a tube of moisturiser that lay on the shelf near where she sat. 'There are a lot of very beautiful people in the fashion world. It's hard enough being surrounded by that if you're something of a plain Jane, but if you're overweight as well –' Victoria shrugged, unscrewing the cap of the moisturiser. 'Janice didn't have much self-esteem, and when she started dating Stuart she grew in confidence. Zoë destroyed that.'

'Did Janice finish the relationship?'

'No,' Victoria sighed. 'She wanted Stu so much I think she would have forgiven him anything, but he told her it was over the same day she learned he'd been unfaithful. He thought something might come of their affair, but, as you can probably guess, Zoë wanted nothing more to do with him.'

'You mentioned that Zoë was also involved with a man at work. Could you give me his name?'

'Dayv Roberts.' Victoria squeezed a blob of moisturiser out into the palm of her left hand before setting the tube down on the armrest of her chair and rubbing her hands together. 'He's a model. I don't know if he's still with Electra, because I haven't seen him in a while – he was involved in a fight at some party, I think, so I guess they might have terminated his contract. I don't know.'

'Do you think any of those you've mentioned might have disliked Zoë enough to want her dead?'

Victoria shook her head slightly. 'I really don't know. Perhaps.'

'Can you think of anybody else who might have felt threatened by Zoë?'

'I can't name names, but I expect there's a long list. Modelling isn't a particularly secure profession, and for a lot of people that insecurity carries through into their personal lives. Zoë's behaviour was hardly going to ease that.'

Lawrence nodded. 'How about your agent, Den? Was he ever involved with Zoë?'

Victoria smirked. 'In his dreams. He was a puppet on her strings.'

'Could you expand on that?'

'Zoë flirted with him because it afforded her a level of control over him. He laboured under the illusion that he might one day have something more than a professional relationship with her. As a result Zoë tended to get her own way on just about everything.'

'And what's your relationship with him like?'

'He made a pass at me in my first week with Electra. I made my feelings very clear, and he's kept his hands to himself since. He's all right, but I think he'd be better off devoting more attention to his work and less to the girls working for him. Have you spoken to him yet?'

'I understand he's out of the country this weekend, but –'

Lawrence was interrupted by the doorbell, and Victoria moved to stand. 'That'll be Timmy. Is there anything else you need to ask me?'

'I think that'll do for now, but if you think of anything that might be relevant, please let me know.' Lawrence stood, handing her his card.

'I will,' Victoria smiled politely, turning to show them out. Privately, Lawrence wasn't convinced she would, given her clear animosity towards Zoë. Following Rebecca from the flat, he glanced at the young man standing on the doorstep, and was rather disappointed to find he didn't recognise him. From Rebecca's expression, he guessed she did.

Climbing into the car, his thoughts turned to the evening ahead.

'I wonder whether there's any way of tracing Zoë's stalker other than by turning up at the club tonight?' He mused, as Rebecca fastened her seatbelt. 'It doesn't seem the ideal setting for an interview.'

Rebecca paused for thought. 'They might have a mailing list,' she suggested, after a moment.

'Do you think that's likely?'

'Elliot used to get flyers posted to him from a couple of venues, but these days most communication is via email or social media. It only takes two minutes to bash a few lines out on a computer, and there are no associated postage costs.'

'That being the case, I imagine we could be talking about hundreds of names.'

'I suppose it depends what sort of club it is. Where did you say it's based?'

'Off Dean Street somewhere.'

'I'm not aware of any big venues on Dean Street.'

Lawrence nodded. 'It's worth a shot,' he decided, starting the ignition. 'Next stop, Soho.'

The Velvet Lounge had seemingly been deserted when Rebecca and Lawrence arrived, so, having decided to return later, Lawrence had dropped Rebecca off at the Mitchells' house to have a chat with Christia before setting off to make a start on tracing Dayv Roberts. Christia was alone in her bedroom, watching a film from the comfort of her bed and working her way through a giant bag of microwave popcorn. On seeing Rebecca, she flicked the television to standby and moved so that she was facing into the room. Rebecca took a seat at the desk by the window, setting her notebook down beside her.

'You like Quixotic Dystopia,' she observed, noticing the plethora of posters that all but wallpapered the room.

'Yeah,' Christia nodded.

'Have you seen them play?'

'Loads of times. I went to some of the really early gigs – before they got signed. And I've met them a few times. They've not played for ages, though – Justin's been ill. He's the lead singer.'

'I know. He has schizophrenia.'

Christia was clearly surprised that Rebecca knew this. 'Do you like music?'

Rebecca nodded. 'My fiancé plays in a band.'

'What band?'

'Astatine.'

'Really?' Christia looked impressed. 'I've seen them play too. They toured with QD last year.'

'That's right.'

'So do you know Justin?'

'Yes.'

'How is he?'

'He's still quite fragile, but he's out of hospital now.'

Christia nodded, saying nothing.

'I understand your boyfriend isn't too well either,' Rebecca continued, hoping to make the transition to interview as casual as possible.

'He has an anxiety disorder.'

'Is that difficult for you?'

'Sometimes. He doesn't like going out much.'

'Why's that?'

'He's scared of having panic attacks in public.'

'Does he ever have them when you're with him?'

'Quite often.'

'Do you find it frightening?'

Christia wrinkled her nose. 'I did to begin with, but I'm pretty used to it now. It's a lot more frightening for him than it is for me.'

'So you aren't afraid to be alone with him.'

Christia's eyebrows contracted into a frown. 'No. Why would I be?'

Not wanting to put Christia off side by connecting her interest in Lucian's illness to Zoë's death, Rebecca chose to link her answer to their earlier topic of conversation. 'Well, I know Justin's behaviour can be very erratic, and it's not easy spending time with someone when you've no idea what might happen next.'

'I hardly think the two are comparable.'

'I expect you know more about it than I do,' Rebecca conceded. Christia shrugged.

'Has he ever written you letters, or poems?'

This question appeared to throw Christia, but she nevertheless provided an answer. 'He's sent me a few cards, but he's never written a lot in them. And certainly not poetry.' She paused, then added, seemingly as the thought occurred to her, 'He likes the gloomy stuff, like the War poets. That isn't exactly romantic.'

'So he does have an interest in poetry.'

'We're studying English – it's part of the course.'

Rebecca nodded. 'Does the name Candela mean anything to you?'

'She's Lucian's ex.'

'Have you ever met her?'

'No.'

'Do you know whether Lucian is still in touch with her?'

'I don't think so.'

'Were you aware that Candela was a friend of Zoë's?'

Christia was visibly shocked by this revelation. 'No, I wasn't,' she replied, at length.

'I understand you and Zoë didn't get on.'

'No.'

'Were you sad about that?'

'Should I have been?'

'I don't know. I haven't been getting on well with my sister recently, and I'm finding that hard, because we used to be very close.'

'Like you'd ever understand how Zoë made me feel.'

'What makes you say that?'

'You're the sort of girl who probably looks great in old jeans and a t-shirt!' Christia responded, contemptuously. 'You've no idea how it feels to look the way I do!'

'Maybe not, but I do understand how it feels to have a twin sister who's intent on criticising almost every aspect of your life.'

Christia's eyebrows rose. 'You have a twin sister? Really?'

Rebecca nodded.

'Why don't you get on?'

'She doesn't like Elliot. That's my fiancé.'

Christia didn't immediately reply, eventually admitting, 'Zoë and I haven't been close since we were little.'

'Why do you think that was?'

Christia shook her head. 'I don't really know. We didn't get on badly until we started secondary school.'

'Do you think it had anything to do with her friends?'

The girl shrugged. 'Maybe.'

'Did you know many of them?'

'I didn't really *know* them – I knew who most of them were because we were at the same school, but they were never friends of mine.'

'How about her friends in the modelling world?'

'She rarely brought any of them home.'

'Did she ever mention somebody called Fred?'

'Fred who?'

'We don't have a surname. Presumably he isn't based in London, though, because one of Zoë's friends sent her a text message last week to let her know Fred was in town if she wanted to meet up with him.'

'Oh, right, *that* Fred,' Christia smirked.

'So you do know Fred.'

'Not exactly, no.'

Rebecca frowned. 'Surely you either know him or you don't?'

'What the message was actually asking was whether Zoë wanted any drugs for the weekend.'

'Is Fred a dealer, then?'

Christia shook her head, looking faintly amused. 'Fred *is* the drugs,' she revealed, with a lift of her eyebrows. 'And I imagine whoever sent the message is the dealer.'

Obtaining an address for Dayv Roberts on a Saturday afternoon had not proved an easy task, but Lawrence had persevered, and eventually tracked him down to a modern apartment block in Southwark. Looking about himself as he waited for a response to the doorbell, he noticed that from where he stood he could see the blue dome of St Paul's, and wondered what a view of the cathedral might add to property prices. Shortly, the intercom crackled and a voice spoke.

'Hello?'

'Good evening. I'm looking for Dayv Roberts.'

After a moment's hesitation, the voice replied. 'Who is it?'

'I'm Detective Chief Inspector Forrester. Could I please have a few minutes of your time?'

'Uh – oh – ok.'

Moments later, a soft click announced the activation of the front door's lock release, and Lawrence pushed it open. Inside lay a smart, well-maintained marble lobby, complete with pot plants and a small water feature, which bubbled and gurgled softly like an indoor stream. There was a lift, but since Dayv's flat was number three, Lawrence opted for the stairs, soon to realise that this had been a mistake. Contrary to convention, the apartments had been numbered from the top down, rather than the bottom up, and, as a result, flat three lay on the sixth floor.

Dayv was hovering at his front door when Lawrence eventually arrived, visibly anxious. So skeletal that he resembled a heroin addict, Lawrence wondered how the fashion industry's penchant for the abnormally thin had come about. While Olivia and Victoria had both looked undernourished, Dayv was little short of emaciated, with razor sharp cheekbones protruding above hollow cheeks and elbows that looked disproportionately large in comparison to his wasted arms. His dark hair was cut rather unevenly, and his eyes were bloodshot, presumably, given that his eyelashes were stuck together in clumps, because he had been crying. Were he not so pale and gaunt, Lawrence could see he might have been very attractive; as it was, he looked seriously ill.

'Hello,' Lawrence began, slightly breathless after six flights of stairs. 'Odd numbering system you have here.'

'Yeah.'

'Sorry to disturb you on a Saturday evening – I won't take up much of your time.'

'I guess you should come in.' Dayv stepped back into his flat, permitting Lawrence to enter. Closing the front door, he asked, 'What's this about?'

'I'd like to ask you some questions about Zoë Mitchell.'

Dayv frowned. 'Zoë? Why?'

'I'm afraid she was found dead on Thursday evening.'

'*What?*' Dayv exclaimed, staring at Lawrence in seemingly genuine shock. 'How?'

'She was murdered.'

'Christ,' Dayv breathed, looking shaken.

'I'm sorry, I thought you might have heard by now. It has been in the news.'

Dayv shook his head, swallowing hard. 'I – uh –' he stopped. 'I have to sit down.' Turning, he made his way along a narrow L-shaped corridor that led onto a large living room. Sinking down onto the sofa, he leaned forwards, folding his arms across his knees and resting his head on them.

'Are you all right?'

'Yeah, I'm ok,' Dayv replied, his words muffled by his arms.

'Can I get you anything?'

'No. Thanks.'

Lawrence sat in an armchair, looking around the room. To his left was a wide-screen television, a window furnished with a panoramic view across the Thames to North London and, in the far corner, a tropical fish tank that looked in need of a good clean. On his right, the living room adjoined the kitchen, which was visible, the dividing wall reaching only to waist height. Both rooms were rather untidy, with unwashed dishes stacked on the kitchen surfaces, and magazines and empty cigarette packets scattered about the living room floor.

'Sorry,' Dayv offered, slowly raising his head. His face looked almost grey.

'I'm sorry to have given you such a shock.'

'No, it's not that. I've not been well – I guess I –' he shook his head, lowering it back down onto his arms.

Thinking that perhaps explained why Dayv looked so awful, Lawrence wondered whether he ought to return at another time. 'Do you feel up to answering questions?'

'I'll give it a shot,' Dayv responded, rearranging himself on the sofa so that he lay on his side, head resting on the armrest.

'When did you last see Zoë?'

'A few months ago.'

'Did you not see her through your work?'

'If I'd been working I probably would have done.'

'How long have you been off work?'

'Eleven – twelve weeks? Something like that.' Dayv raised a hand to his forehead, closing his eyes momentarily. 'I did go along to the agency a few weeks back, but by the time I got there I didn't feel well enough to do anything, so I came back home.'

'I understand you were involved with Zoë earlier in the year.'

'Briefly, yes.'

'I've also heard you held her responsible for telling your fiancée about the relationship.'

Dayv sighed. 'Yeah. I was rather out of order, but then you never want to take responsibility for your own mistakes, do you? It's easier if you can find someone else to blame.'

'And blaming Zoë included sending her a wreath, is that correct?'

Dayv nodded wordlessly.

'What exactly did you mean by that?'

'God, I don't know. I wasn't really thinking straight at the time – Grace had just walked out on me –' he paused. 'I said a lot of things I didn't mean. I had feelings for Zoë, and when Grace left, Zoë didn't seem to want to know anymore. It was as if she'd been playing with me.'

'How do you feel about that now?'

'I don't know. I think Zoë's indifference hurt more than losing Grace. Perhaps that's why I reacted the way I did.'

'Did you ever meet any of her friends?'

'Several of them.'

'How about her boyfriend?'

'Pete? Yeah, once. He almost killed me.'

'Literally?'

Dayv nodded. 'We were at a cocktail party in March, and someone made a comment about Zoë and I – he completely lost it.'

'Is he responsible for the shape you're in now?'

'Yeah. I had a brain haemorrhage.'

'Has Pete been charged?'

'Uh-huh. It hasn't come to court yet – my solicitor did tell me why, but I was feeling pretty rough at the time so I didn't take much in.'

'Did you see Zoë again after Pete attacked you?'

'Once. She came to visit me in hospital. I hoped she might come again, but she never did.'

Realising that the question was unlikely to yield anything unexpected, Lawrence asked, 'Where were you last Wednesday night?'

'I was here.'

'Alone?'

'Yes. Well, no – not all night. I had a splitting headache, and by four in the morning I felt so ill that I called my mother in tears begging her to come over.'

'And did she?'

Dayv smiled weakly. 'I think by that time I'd lost all sense of perspective. She lives in Dublin.'

'But you weren't alone all night?'

'Mum called the doctor and then contacted my grandmother – she lives in Tooting, and she came straight round.'

'How about the doctor?'

'He arrived about five. Gave me something for the pain – I think that must have knocked me out, because the next thing I knew, three hours had passed.'

'Could you give me your grandmother's address and the doctor's number?'

'Sure.' Dayv sat up slowly, wincing as he did so.

'I'm sorry to have to ask,' Lawrence remarked, as Dayv stood and went to the cabinet beneath the fish tank.

'It's ok.' Dayv turned, one hand resting on the open door of the cabinet. 'You've a job to do – I'm not going to impede that.' He dug his free hand into his pocket. 'Besides, I'm probably as keen as you are to know what happened. I never realised how much Zoë meant to me until I'd lost her, and now –' he shrugged. 'Now it's too late for me to tell her.'

'Hiya,' Rebecca smiled, climbing into the passenger seat of Lawrence's car. 'I have a positive ID on Fred – or, at least, as positive an identification as one can get for anything inanimate.'

'Pardon?'

'Fred isn't a person, Fred is a drug – or, rather, a term for drugs in general.'

'Well that's one I haven't come across before,' Lawrence admitted.

'I didn't get the impression from Christia that it was widespread street slang.'

'What else did she say?'

'I didn't tell her who sent the text message in question, but I did ask her if she knew anything about its meaning, and she suggested that whoever sent it was probably Zoë's dealer.'

'Candela.'

'Yes. It wouldn't surprise me – she certainly wasn't too happy to have me turn up on her doorstep.'

'That's as may be, but it doesn't take us any closer to what happened to Zoë.'

'No, but it does mean we can eliminate Fred from our list of suspects,' Rebecca pointed out. 'How did you get on?'

'Would you like to hazard a guess at who on that list has recently been charged with GBH?'

Rebecca raised her eyebrows.

'Pete Morgan. Good of everybody not to mention that.'

'Do tell.'

He attacked Dayv Roberts at a party in March. I thought he must be on drugs until he mentioned he'd been ill.'

'Where was he on Wednesday night?'

'He claims to have been at home with a blinding headache.'

'Claims?' Rebecca repeated, sensing a flicker of scepticism in her superior's tone.

'I doubt he was responsible for Zoë's death – he looks dreadful, and he seemed suitably shocked when I told him what had happened, but I'm not ruling him out.' Lawrence reached for the tin of mints on the dashboard. 'He says he felt so ill that he called the doctor out at about four on Thursday morning, and although I think it would have been quite possible for him to have made it home from Zoë's by that time, it does give him something approaching an alibi. A headache isn't something a doctor can definitively disprove, and I suspect not a complaint that any doctor is going to question when dealing with a patient who has recently suffered a brain haemorrhage.' Lawrence offered the mints to Rebecca. 'He's probably telling the truth, but I've met exceptionally good actors before now in this job, and I'm not going to make the mistake of assuming anything.'

'Have you had a chance to check out what he told you about Pete yet?'

'I called Jamie and he dug out the details for me. It's not the first time Pete's been in trouble with the law, either, he was fined last year for being drunk and disorderly.'

'That I can believe from the state of inebriation in which I found him yesterday.'

'Well, we're going to pay him a visit right now.' Lawrence turned the key in the ignition. 'With any luck, he might even be sober.'

Whilst Rebecca couldn't be sure Pete was entirely sober, he was certainly nowhere near as intoxicated as he had been the previous day, although no less belligerent. He made no secret of his displeasure at finding Lawrence and Rebecca on his doorstep, and bluntly observed that he had already answered several of Lawrence's opening questions during Rebecca's visit the previous day; questions Lawrence had presumably repeated on the off-chance Pete might not remember his original responses. Abandoning the ploy, Lawrence moved on.

'I assume the name Dayv Roberts is familiar to you?'

'Yes.'

'According to our records, you assaulted him in March. Could you tell me what that was about?'

'No.'

'No?'

'He's lying.'

'Is he?'

'He was drunk, and he fell down some stairs. I just happened to be there at the time.'

'So the two witnesses who claim you attacked him and then *pushed* him down the stairs are also lying, are they?'

'It was dark. I guess maybe they didn't see what happened.'

'Dark?' Lawrence echoed, disbelievingly. 'In a hotel corridor?'

'It wasn't well lit,' Pete snapped, sullenly.

'I find it rather hard to believe that two people would substantiate Dayv's version of events if they weren't fairly clear about what had occurred,' Lawrence replied, evenly. 'Especially considering that one of them was *your* girlfriend.'

Rebecca started. Lawrence hadn't previously mentioned this fact.

'Yeah, well she was shagging him, wasn't she?' Pete retorted, angrily.

'Do you have proof of that?'

'Zoë admitted it.'

'How could you be sure she was telling the truth?'

Pete frowned. 'Why would she lie?'

'I don't know, but according to you she lied about the events of March the fourteenth.'

'I never said that. I said she didn't see what happened.'

'Given that she was not only unfaithful, but also believed that you were capable of assault, why did you continue with the relationship?'

Pete shrugged, casting his eyes down. 'I loved her.'

'It's rather convenient for you that she won't now be able to give evidence against you in court next month, isn't it?'

Pete looked up sharply. 'I didn't kill her!'

'Who said you did?'

'What?'

'I didn't accuse you of anything. I simply made a casual observation, and you jumped to the defensive.'

'You're manipulating me!' Pete reproached, heatedly. 'You're trying to twist the facts to make me admit to something I didn't do!'

'I don't want you to admit to anything that you *didn't* do,' Lawrence countered, calmly.

Pete scowled at him, but made no reply.

'I understand you have a key to Zoë's flat.'

'So?'

'Did you often have cause to use it?'

'It varied.'

'According to what?'

'Whether or not she was in when I went round,' Pete replied, witheringly.

'Did you ever go to her flat knowing she would be out?'

'Why?'

'Answer the question.'

'Once or twice,' Pete admitted, at length.

'For what purpose?'

'To surprise her.'

'Did you ever catch her with another man?'

'No.'

'Ever go through her personal correspondence?'

'No,' Pete repeated, frowning suspiciously.

'Yesterday you told my colleague that Zoë regularly cheated on you. Since you apparently didn't catch her in the act of doing so, how did you draw that conclusion?'

'She didn't make a secret of it.'

'You mean she told you?'

'Not explicitly.'

Lawrence waited expectantly for further information. After a tense pause, Pete added, 'She inferred it.'

'That's all the evidence you have?'

'Everybody knew!' Pete exploded. 'I wasn't being paranoid!'

'Everybody? Was that not humiliating?'

'Of course it bloody was!' Pete returned, wildly. 'I hated her for it, and I hated myself even more for standing by and letting it happen!'

'And Zoë's affair with Dayv was the final straw?'

'He deserved everything he got!' Pete yelled, uncontrollably. Seeming to realise what Lawrence had baited him into saying, he froze. Some moments passed before he continued, this time in a completely different tone. 'But I never hurt Zoë. I loved her.' Tears pooled in his grey eyes, and he shook his head slightly. 'I never hurt her,' he repeated, his voice breaking. '*Never.*'

The door to The Velvet Lounge was still closed when Lawrence arrived at ten past nine, but was now framed by a crack of light, indicating that the building was no longer deserted. He knocked sharply, and, when this drew no response, tried again. Shortly, the door was opened by a petite peroxide blonde clad in a tiny grey pleated skirt, black fishnet tights and a tight white shirt sufficiently unbuttoned to display a black PVC bra. A red-and-black-striped tie had been looped around her neck, the knot hanging just below her cleavage, her long hair was fastened into two plaits and her lips were painted scarlet.

'We're not open yet,' she informed Lawrence curtly, looking him up and down before adding, 'And there's a strict dress code.'

What that might be was anybody's guess, Lawrence thought, given her choice of attire. Presenting his warrant card, he introduced himself before asking whether he might speak to the club's manager. He was apparently absent, and the girl hurried away to fetch somebody else who might be able to be of assistance. Lawrence was left standing in the brightly lit foyer, from which he could see little of the dimly lit club, but for a young man heaving crates of bottles from one stack to another. After several minutes, he was joined by a man of forty-something dressed in black PVC trousers and a tight black t-shirt. He had short dark hair, neatly plucked eyebrows and a nose ring, and introduced himself as Paul, the assistant manager. Explaining that the club's office was on the first floor, he turned to ascend a narrow flight of stairs that led directly off the foyer.

The office was a modest room containing two desks, a filing cabinet and some cheap shelving, and was unremarkable but for the selection of framed photographs and posters that dominated the walls. These depicted men and women in a variety of outfits ranging from the bizarre to the erotic. Some of the images bordered on pornographic. Corsetry appeared to be popular, as did PVC and leather clothing, and underwear, which was often worn with little, if anything, else. In some of the photographs themes were evident, uniforms seemingly a favourite; in others clothing was absent altogether. A poster titled *Whipped Up* was illustrated with a picture of a scantily clad woman brandishing a whip, while another headed with the words *Back to School* was accompanied by a photograph of a girl wearing the bare essentials of school uniform. What Olivia had said about Candela took on a whole new meaning. This was no ordinary club.

'Please – have a seat,' Paul gestured to some chairs, perching on the windowsill.

'No, I won't stay long,' Lawrence replied, tearing his eyes away from the walls. 'I'm trying to trace someone, and I understand he's a regular here – do you have any means of contacting your patrons?'

'That depends.'

'What does that mean?'

'We have an e-list, but the only postal addresses we hold are those of our members, and there's a limited number of them.'

'Could I have a copy of that list, please?'

Paul frowned. 'What do you want it for?' He asked, suspiciously.

'I'm trying to track down a man who I've been told is a frequent visitor to your club, but I'd prefer not to have to interview him in the venue, and I presumed that feeling would be mutual,' Lawrence informed him. 'But if you'd rather, I can come back in a couple of hours' time with some uniformed colleagues.'

'I'm sure that won't be necessary,' Paul replied, stiffly. 'Do you have a name?'

'I'm afraid not, just a vague description and the nickname two-tone twat.'

'That doesn't ring any bells with me, but I'll call Daisy up – she may well have more idea of who he is.' Paul stood and made for the door.

'Thank you.'

Alone in the office, Lawrence embarked on a cursory study of the photographs and posters that adorned the walls. He had almost completed a circuit of the room when one caught his eye: an image of two young women, completely naked but for a covering of silver body paint and a blood-red feather boa. One girl held her arms around the other's waist, and they had been captured on camera in the midst of a passionate kiss, eyes closed, seemingly oblivious to everything but each other. The girl on the left, Lawrence realised with a start, was Zoë Mitchell. He wondered who the other one was. Hearing a sound behind him, he turned to see Paul in the doorway, now accompanied by the girl Lawrence had met at the front door some minutes earlier.

'This is Daisy,' Paul offered, unnecessarily.

Daisy forced a smile, clearly nervous.

'Have you worked here long?' Lawrence enquired, perching on a nearby chair so as not to tower over her.

'Almost a year.'

'I imagine you know some of the regulars quite well, then?'

'I suppose.'

'We're trying to identify a man who at least some of your patrons have nicknamed the two-tone twat. Does that mean anything to you?'

'Oh God *him*. He's *horrible*,' Daisy exclaimed, her face twisted in disgust.

Paul frowned. 'Who?'

'That weirdo with the stripy head who skulks about watching people and taking photographs.'

'What sort of photographs?' Lawrence asked.

'Just of people in the club – but he takes them without them knowing – and of people he doesn't know. It's creepy.'

'Do you know his name?'

'No. Just the nickname. He has his hair dyed in black and white stripes.'

'Any idea where he lives?'

'I know it's north of here, because I've seen him waiting for the night bus on Tottenham Court Road. That's all I know, really – I've never seen him *talk*. He just loiters in dark corners of the club and follows some of the girls around like a shadow.'

Lawrence nodded, and Paul dismissed the girl. She hurried for the door, then stopped in her tracks. 'Actually,' she said, turning to look back and meeting Lawrence's eyes. 'There is one other thing.'

'What's that?'

'I do know his membership number.'

'How'd it go?' Rebecca asked, glancing up from the news story she'd been scrolling through on her mobile as Lawrence returned to the car.

'It wasn't exactly what I was expecting,' he admitted.

92

'Oh?'

'It's a fetish club.'

'Ah,' Rebecca smiled. 'Bit of a shock, was it?'

'Certainly an eye-opener.'

'Did you manage to identify our stalker?'

'I think so. The girl who works the door couldn't give me a name, but she was able to provide a membership number.'

'Strange thing to remember.'

'I was surprised too, until she told me what it was.'

Rebecca raised her eyebrows expectantly.

'Sixty-nine.'

''Nuff said.'

'The member in question is one Lars Pedersen, so we may also have found our letter writer. He lives in Walthamstow. And his wasn't the only interesting address on the membership database, they also had Zoë's.'

'So anyone working there could have been able to access that.'

'Presumably.' Lawrence slipped a hand into his jacket pocket and drew out his mobile. 'There was something odd about the place, although I couldn't put my finger on what. I'm going to drop you home before I go to visit Lars, and I want you to get yourself ready to go back there for the club. I'll give Jamie a call and ask him to do the same. The theme tonight is uniforms, and I'm sure you can both come up with something suitable.'

'I think I've a nurse's uniform somewhere,' Rebecca replied. 'Elliot and I went to a fancy dress party last year.'

'Sounds perfect,' Lawrence responded. 'Just make sure it's low cut with a very short skirt. You'll blend right in.'

Seven

The moment the front door opened, Lawrence guessed he was looking at Lars and not a friend or flatmate. His head, as Daisy had said, was stripy – uneven black and blonde streaks ran through his short hair, which was either horribly greasy or badly slicked back with hair gel. He struck Lawrence immediately as something of a misfit; perhaps on account of his awkward posture, or maybe owing to his simple lack of any real physical presence. Tall and lanky, with lips that looked effeminate, his dark eyes flickered incessantly like those of a curious rodent, lending something rather sinister to his appearance. Clad in leather trousers and a black t-shirt, he held a pair of plastic tongs in his left hand, the nails of which were painted black. That most of his letters to Zoë had been left unopened came as little surprise to Lawrence; the man was playing way out of his league.

'Hello?'

'Lars Pedersen?'

'Yes,' he confirmed, warily.

'I'm DCI Forrester. Could I come in for a few minutes, please?'

'Uh –' Lars swallowed hard before nodding. Backing away down the hallway, he reached to close the door to a room immediately inside the basement flat. Noticing the speed with which he did so, Lawrence tried to catch a glimpse of the room, but Lars moved too quickly.

'Come through,' the man invited, turning into the next room and setting his tongs down on the narrow mantelpiece. Lawrence took in the room, which evidently served as a living area, at a glance. It contained an old sofa, a couple of bean bags, a stained coffee table and a standard lamp, which did little to illuminate its surroundings. The single window lacked curtains, and the wall around it looked damp. Perhaps unsurprisingly, the room smelled musty.

Lars kicked a torn newspaper under the table, perching on the sofa. Lawrence chose to remain standing.

'I believe you know Zoë Mitchell,' he began, glancing out of the window, which overlooked a lightwell littered with rubbish.

'Zoë? Yes.'

'When did you see her last?'

'Last weekend.'

'Where was that?'

'At a club.'

'Did you speak to her?'

Lars shook his head.

'Do you see her often?'

'Fairly.'

'Ever been to her home?'

'Yes.'

'Were you there on Wednesday evening?'

Lars frowned. 'No, I already told you –' he broke off. 'What's she said?'

'She's said nothing. She's dead.'

Lars blinked. 'What?'

'She was found dead on Thursday.'

'Dead?' Lars stared at Lawrence. He opened his mouth as if to speak again, then stopped.

'I understand you wrote her a number of letters.'

Lars nodded dumbly.

'Why write to her if you saw her often?'

Lars gulped. 'I love her.' He lowered his eyes. 'Loved her,' he corrected.

'How did she feel about that?'

'She wouldn't admit the way she felt,' Lars responded. 'Some people are like that. I just wanted to look after her. If she'd let me, this wouldn't have happened. I'd never have let anyone hurt her.'

'How do you know anybody hurt her?'

'Well – I mean – you – the police – if she'd just died you wouldn't be involved –'

'Not necessarily.'

'I just assumed –'

'Did you?' Lawrence raised his eyebrows. 'How interesting.'

'I didn't hurt her! I loved her!'

'Who's saying you hurt her?'

Lars' consternation turned to confusion. 'I thought –' he stopped. 'What happened to her?'

'Where were you on Wednesday night?'

'I – I went to a club. Then I came back here. Developed some photographs.'

'Which club?'

'A night called Spiral.'

'How did you get home?'

'By bus.'

'Which one?'

'Seventy-three.'

'Was there anything memorable about your journey?'

'No.'

'Anybody who can confirm your whereabouts after you left the club?'

'No,' Lars' voice was little more than a whisper.

'Right,' Lawrence nodded. 'I think that's all I need to know for now. Thank you for your time – I'll show myself out.'

'No, it's ok.' Lars jumped up and almost ran ahead of Lawrence to the hallway, positioning himself in front of the door that he had hurried to close a few minutes earlier. Lawrence bade him goodnight and opened the front door, wondering what Lars was so keen to conceal. With any luck, he thought as he climbed the steps to street level, by the next day he might have sufficient grounds for a search warrant.

The Velvet Lounge lived up to its name. The seats in the bar were upholstered in plush purple velvet, and panels of the same were fitted into the walls, interspersed at regular intervals by floor-to-ceiling mirrors. The bar itself was black with an intricate chrome surround, above which pink light bulbs hung beneath mushroom-shaped shades. Rebecca looked about herself as Jamie ordered drinks. To the right was a rectangular dance floor, with wrought-iron cages at either end. Inside the nearer one, a voluptuous blonde in a corset was dancing, while the other was occupied by two people, a young man in PVC trousers, who was handcuffed to the cage, and a girl, who looked to be scarcely eighteen, wearing a maid's uniform and brandishing a whip. Loud industrial music blared from the speakers and the dance floor was heaving with revellers clad in a variety of outfits bearing some semblance of uniforms.

'Interesting place,' Jamie remarked, handing Rebecca a glass of Coke. 'This the sort of club you and Elliot frequent, then?'

'Absolutely,' Rebecca returned, sarcastically. 'We met when I was moonlighting as a topless lap dancer, actually.' She took a sip of her drink. 'Jay, there's vodka in this!'

'So?'

'We're supposed to be working.'

'Don't be such a killjoy, one drink can't hurt.' Jamie raised his free hand to unbutton the collar of his impromptu costume, which consisted of a tight shirt and black jeans combined with the bare basics of police uniform.

'I dare you to turn up to work like that,' Rebecca teased.

'Oh yeah, bring a whole new meaning to the phrase *bent copper*, wouldn't it?' Jamie grumbled. 'I look like a fucking queer!'

'Your secret's safe with me.'

Jamie made no reply, but the withering look he shot her indicated that he wasn't amused.

'Well,' Rebecca turned. 'I suppose we ought to get on with it.'

'Where are you going?' Jamie asked, glancing nervously in the direction of the dance floor, where two young men were dancing provocatively.

'To the premiere club gossip exchange.'

'Eh?'

Rebecca laughed at his expression. 'The little girl's room, sweetie.'

There was a long queue for the toilets, and Rebecca was pleased to have an excuse to loiter. Leaning back against the tiled wall she sighed, hoping to blend in and eavesdrop on a few conversations.

'How fucking long do you need to take your drugs?' The girl immediately ahead of her in the queue shouted, after a moment. 'Fucking hurry up!' Turning to Rebecca she shook her head. 'I tell you, if I had nicer legs I'd be using the sink.'

Rebecca smiled. 'I've never been brazen enough to try it.'

'Me either.' The girl returned the smile, flicking her choppy dark hair out of her eyes. She was a little taller than Rebecca, probably about five foot seven, with brown eyes and a slight moustache that Rebecca would have opted to wax. Her choice of attire, a short, tight black PVC dress, did little for her rather dumpy figure, and Rebecca wondered how it complied with the uniform theme. 'I'm Nicki,' the woman offered, reaching into her handbag.

'Becky.'

'Where you from?'

'London.'

The girl looked surprised. 'Really? Rare breed in this place these days. I've not seen you around – have you been down here before?'

'My boyfriend took some persuading,' Rebecca shrugged. 'In the end I said I was coming with or without him – that made his mind up fairly quickly.' She lifted her eyebrows mischievously.

Nicki shook her head again. 'Men,' she remarked, derisively.

'Well, I've not seen my mate Zoë for ages, and I was hoping to catch up with her tonight, but I've yet to find her.'

'Zoë? You mean model Zoë?'

Rebecca nodded. 'Do you know her?'

'Who does not?' Nicki replied, her tone indicating that she and Zoë had not been friends.

Rebecca tried to sound casual as she said, 'True.'

'So, are you model too?'

Rebecca almost laughed. 'No.'

'No?' Nicki raised her eyebrows. 'I bet you feature in Old Three Eyes' wall of fame, though.'

'You what?'

'The weirdo with the camera. Rumour has it he decorates his walls with photo collages of pretty girls he sees around clubs and stalks around London. Your male equivalent of a bunny boiler.'

'Oh, yeah, I know who you mean.' Rebecca sighed inwardly. This conversation was going nowhere, and she didn't want to waste the next fifteen minutes going over old ground. Having peered around the corner to see exactly how many people there were in the queue, she looked back to Nicki. 'Fuck this, I'm not that desperate.' She turned to go. 'See you later.'

'Later.'

On exiting the toilets, Rebecca spotted Jamie chatting to – or, more likely, she suspected, chatting *up* – an attractive blonde in a minuscule *Bat Girl* costume. Thinking it best not to interrupt in case he was on the brink of learning something useful, she made her way to the bar and perched on a bar stool. She hadn't long been there when she was approached by a balding forty-something man clad in leather trousers and a shiny red shirt. He stood over six foot tall, the buttons of his shirt straining slightly across his protruding belly, his face flushed with the heat. Leaning one arm on the bar, he smiled at her, revealing very straight but rather yellow teeth. 'Hello.'

'Hi.'

'Nice outfit,' he remarked, brushing his fingers accidentally-on-purpose along Rebecca's thigh. Fighting the urge to slap his hand away, she gave him a coy smile.

'Thank you. What's yours supposed to be?'

'Oh, I'm not in uniform tonight.'

'No?' Rebecca lifted her eyebrows flirtatiously. 'Is that allowed?'

'It is when you're the manager.'

Rebecca tried to look appropriately impressed by this snippet of information.

'Marcus,' he introduced himself.

'Rebecca.' She shook his outstretched hand.

'First time here?'

Rebecca grimaced playfully. 'How can you tell?'

'If I'd come across you before I'm quite sure I'd remember.'

She smiled.

'Can I buy you a drink, Rebecca?'

'Thank you. I'll have a vodka tonic.'

Marcus leaned across the bar to place his order. The speed with which he was served indicated that he was telling the truth about being the manager.

'So, Rebecca,' Marcus passed her a glass. 'You already know what I do. How about yourself?'

'I'm a PA,' Rebecca lied.

'Ah,' Marcus nodded. 'Now in my experience, that's code for jumped-up secretary.'

Rebecca giggled girlishly. 'If you like.'

'That seems a terrible waste, if you don't mind my saying so.'

'Oh?'

'Pretty girl like you –' Marcus sighed, running a finger down Rebecca's arm.

Rebecca ducked her head, doing her best to look abashed.

'Do you live in London?'

'Tooting,' Rebecca lied again. 'I share a flat with a girlfriend.'

'That's a bit out of the way.'

'Yeah,' Rebecca shrugged. 'I'd really like to live in Angel, but it's rather beyond my budget.'

'Well it would certainly be a fitting address for you!' Marcus laughed at his own joke. Resting a hand on her knee, he leaned forwards. 'If you're after some extra cash, I could help you out with that.'

Rebecca raised her eyebrows innocently. 'Really?'

'How would you like to work for me, Rebecca?'

'Work for you?'

Marcus nodded, inching his fingers up Rebecca's leg. 'The thing is, Rebecca, I have friends who come down here from time to time, and they enjoy the company of a young lady, if you get my drift?'

Rebecca got it only too well, but feigned shocked confusion. 'You want – you think – you mean a *prostitute?'*

'No, no, no,' Marcus shook his head. 'I'm talking escort. It's an entirely different ball park.'

Like hell, Rebecca thought to herself. 'So I wouldn't – you know –'

'No, not at all,' Marcus smiled insincerely. 'But of course, there's a limit to what a man will pay for conversation.'

'I guess so.'

'Have a think about it, Rebecca. I'll be around for the rest of the night.' He winked, turning to go. 'You let me know what you decide.'

Lawrence was engrossed in a book when Rebecca arrived back at his car shortly after two. He didn't notice her approaching, and jumped when she tapped on the window. Winding it down he said, in a faux accent, 'Minicab?' before moving to disable the car's central-locking system. As Rebecca climbed in he commented, 'Until this evening I had no idea how many pirate cabs there were in these parts.'

'I know.' Rebecca settled herself into the passenger seat. 'They say *minicab?* and then when you say no they say *taxi?* like it's an entirely different question!'

'Where's Jamie?'

'I don't know. I lost track of him.'

'Did you look for him?'

'If I'd searched any harder I'd have found Lord Lucan.'

Lawrence frowned in irritation. 'I'll try his mobile,' he said, reaching for his own. 'How did it go?'

'It would seem the club's manager is running an escort service.'

'Really?'

'Yep. He asked if I'd like to work for him.'

'What did you say to that?'

'Oh, I played the naive innocent girl and pretended to be shocked. He assured me that it was nothing like prostitution, but then made it pretty clear I wasn't going to get very far without sleeping with the clients.'

'How scrupulous of him,' Lawrence remarked, sardonically. 'And how about Zoë?'

'As in do I think she might have been involved?'

'I suppose it's possible, but that wasn't actually what I meant. What I was asking was whether you learned anything more about her while you were there.'

'No, not really. Several people I spoke to knew her, but they didn't tell me much I didn't already know. I did wonder whether she might have worked as an escort, but –' Rebecca stopped.

'It might be worth looking into.' Lawrence dialled Jamie's number. 'After all, she was a pretty girl who, by all accounts, liked men and enjoyed sex, and she seems to have had precious few morals.' He yawned, raising his mobile to his ear. 'I'll see if I can track Jamie down, and then I'll drop you home.'

'I need my duvet,' Rebecca responded, closing her eyes and sliding down in the seat.

There was brief silence before Lawrence suddenly added, 'Oh, did you spot anybody of Lars' description down there?'

'Nope, but a girl I met in the toilets described him as a male bunny boiler, and according to rumour he has photographs of girls from London's clubs all over his walls.'

'That might explain what he was trying to hide earlier. I meant to leave his letters to Zoë with Leighton for salivary analysis, but I forgot,' Lawrence sighed, abandoning the phone call. 'No answer. Let's go. I'll catch up with Jamie tomorrow. He can find his own way home.'

Eight

Lawrence looked into the kitchen on Sunday morning to find Elise and Katie sitting at the table, Elise keeping very still while her mother painted her fingernails. Neither of them noticed his arrival in the doorway, and he remained where he was momentarily, watching them fondly.

He and Katie had met at university, where she had been studying sports science, and she had gone on to work as a fitness instructor for an up-market gym. After Elise started school she had returned to work part time, and as a result had remained very slim in comparison to a good many of her friends. She took great care over her appearance, styling her naturally wavy dark hair on a daily basis, and Lawrence only ever saw her scruffily dressed when she was working in the garden. This morning she was clad in a mid-calf-length peach skirt and a white cotton blouse, the gold chain around her neck recognisable as that which Lawrence had given her on their fifteenth wedding anniversary the previous year.

Rather oddly, Elise was wearing the pink leotard she normally wore for her gymnastics class and a pink skirt that looked to be made from netting. Her long blonde hair was held back from her face by a matching pink Alice band decorated with bees and dragonflies fashioned from fine pipe cleaners. Her pale eyes were surrounded with glitter, and bright pink lipstick had been rather inexpertly applied to her lips. She was sitting cross legged on her chair, one hand flat on the table, fingers spread wide apart, her expression one of intense concentration.

Lawrence waited until Katie had finished the nail-painting process before saying, 'Morning.'

'Daddy!' Elise jumped up from the table and ran towards him. 'Do you like my fairy costume?'

'You look lovely, Pumpkin.'

'It's for Stephanie's birthday party.'

'Ah.'

'It's fancy dress,' Elise added, unnecessarily.

'I'd never have guessed,' Lawrence smiled. 'I do like this hair band – did you make it yourself?'

Elise nodded proudly.

'Do twenty-first century fairies not have wings?'

'Mummy wouldn't let me keep them on in case they got broken.' She looked around at Katie. 'Can I put them on to show Daddy?'

'Just be careful you don't get nail polish on your clothes,' Katie advised. Elise scurried from the room, and, moments later, her footsteps could be heard running up the stairs.

'Sorry I was so late last night,' Lawrence offered, joining his wife at the table.

'Late?' Katie echoed. 'You didn't get in until quarter past *three*! What on *earth* were you doing?'

'I did leave a message to say I'd be working late. What did you think I was doing?'

Katie shook her head, saying nothing.

'I'm sorry, Kate, it's my job.'

'Oh, of course! I'm just your wife, after all!'

Lawrence sighed. 'Kate –'

'I've barely seen you in weeks! The kids often don't see you for days at a time! You didn't even manage to make it to their parents' evenings!'

'I know, but –'

'We were supposed to be going out for dinner last night. I suppose *that* slipped your mind?'

Lawrence closed his eyes, mentally cursing himself. Katie was ordinarily very tolerant of the long hours his job demanded, and he had guessed there was probably something specific behind her outburst. 'I'm sorry, I completely forgot.'

'Evidently.'

'I'm sorry, Katie.'

'Are you working today?'

Lawrence nodded.

'Fine,' she snapped, in a tone that told him it certainly wasn't.

'It obviously isn't.'

'Well, I had arranged to meet Marcia for lunch, since Elise is going to be at the party and you agreed to take Jimmy swimming, but I guess I'll just have to cancel that.'

'I'm *sorry*. What do you want me to do?'

Katie shook her head, standing and turning her back to him.

'I will do my best not to be home late.'

'What difference does it make?' Katie replied, without turning around. 'You'll doubtless disappear into the garden until after dark! Sometimes I think your lupins see more of you than I do!'

'Katie, come on, that's not fair.'

Katie looked around angrily. 'And having to constantly rearrange all of our lives around your job is, is it?'

'Look, I know I've been very busy lately, but I am due some time off in lieu and –'

'You've been saying that for months!' Katie returned, making for the door. Turning in the doorway, she added, 'I'll see you the next time you decide to drop in. Do let me know whether you'll be coming to France with us *before* I've done the packing, won't you?'

Rebecca looked into the pathology unit's main office at ten-thirty on Sunday morning to find Leighton lounging in the chair at his desk, his feet resting on the edge of his waste-paper bin. He glanced up from the lab report that lay in his lap as she eased the door open.

'Hey Becks,' he greeted, with a smile.

'Am I disturbing you?'

'Absolutely, spectroscopy makes for fascinating reading, I'm not sure I can tear myself away.' He tossed the report aside. 'Roddy dumped it on me first thing. He's in Hampshire on a triple murder. Jammy git.'

'Oh?'

'I don't know the details – all the info I got was a Post-it note on my desk.' He rubbed the back of his neck. 'Get up to much last night?'

'Working. You?'

'Just down my local. Ended up round at a mate's messing about on his PlayStation 'til the small hours. A large fry-up would go down nicely this morning.' He removed his feet from the bin and straightened up. 'Can I tempt you with a trip to the caf? Spike makes the most beautiful bacon sandwiches in the known world. I would have popped in on my way past this morning, but I was already running late and nobody had the courtesy to inform me this place was going to be like a morgue all day,' he paused for effect before adding, 'Oh, hang on a minute –' and trailing off as if perplexed.

Rebecca smiled in response to the joke.

'I'm going to head down there now if you're up for it?' He continued.

'I don't have time for breakfast, I'm afraid, I just came to throw more work your way.'

'No rest for the wicked, eh?' Leighton narrowed his eyes. 'And let me tell you, I can be very, *very* wicked.' He regarded her seriously for a moment before breaking into a grin. 'So. What can I do for you?'

'Could you see if you can get some DNA from the saliva on these?' Rebecca proffered the clear plastic bag containing Lars' letters to Zoë.

'Sure,' Leighton nodded, reaching to take it. 'And just so's I know, what time is your guv likely to be kicking my arse if they haven't been done?'

Rebecca couldn't suppress a smile. 'I think you've most of the day, we're off out on house to house.'

'Lucky you,' Leighton responded, sarcastically. Glancing at his watch, he added, 'Starting a bit late, aren't we?'

'We were working into the early hours last night.'

'It must have been pretty late considering that I made it in before either you *or* Forrester.'

'I didn't get to bed until nearly three.'

Leighton looked surprised. 'What *were* you doing?'

'We were at a fetish club.'

'Really? I didn't peg Forrester as the type,' Leighton grinned, standing and shoving his wallet into one pocket and his mobile phone into the other. 'As for you, well, that's quite a different matter.' He turned towards the door onto the corridor. 'If you ever tire of glamorous rock star types and fancy setting up shop with one of us ordinary mortals, you let me know girl!'

Knocking on yet another door, Lawrence sighed. The morning had been wasted on fruitless house-to-house enquires, which, taking into account the fact most people had been asleep in the early hours of Thursday morning, was hardly surprising. Stepping back from the door, he glanced at Rebecca, raising his eyebrows and pursing his lips to convey his frustration.

Shortly, the door was opened by a young woman somewhere between her late teens and early twenties, small and slight, dark roots beginning to grow through her bleached hair. Her heart-shaped face was tanned and possessed of rather elfin features, her close-set eyes a rich chocolate brown. Clad in a flowing floral skirt and a frilly pink off-the-shoulder blouse, she looked every inch the stereotypical gypsy girl. Resting a hand on the door frame, she raised her eyes to meet Lawrence's with the wary expression of one who had not been expecting to find strangers on the doorstep. 'Yes?'

'Good afternoon,' Lawrence began, reaching into his pocket for his warrant card. 'I'm DCI Forrester, this is DS Palmer – would you mind answering a few questions for us?'

'Is this about –' the girl trailed off, nodding in the direction of Zoë's flat.

'Zoë Mitchell. Yes.'

Rather unusually, the girl's expression changed to something approaching relief. 'Sure,' she nodded. 'Come in.'

'Thank you,' Lawrence smiled, stepping into the hallway as she turned from the door towards the kitchen, leaving Rebecca to close the door behind herself.

'Could we take your name, please?' Lawrence asked, perching uninvited on the small sofa sandwiched between the washing machine and the window.

'Antonia Villar.' She leaned against the work surface as Rebecca joined Lawrence on the sofa.

'You're obviously aware of what's happened – what we need to know is whether you can tell us anything – however small – that might be relevant to Zoë's death.'

Antonia shifted her stance uneasily. 'I – um – I did see someone, on Wednesday night. Well, Thursday morning, really.'

'At what time?'

'About three.'

'Where were you at the time?'

'Sitting on the steps outside. I saw someone go in the front door.'

'What were you doing sitting on the steps at that hour?'

'Smoking.'

'Do you normally smoke outside?'

'Yes. My flatmate doesn't like me doing it in here.'

'Did you know that Zoë lived alone?'

'Not until I read it in the paper.'

Lawrence frowned. 'So what was noticeable about someone going in the door? Did you not simply assume that whoever it was lived there?'

'He never turned the lights on. When he went in.'

'Are you sure?'

'Yes. There's a glass panel above the door. Normally, when somebody arrives home at night, the first thing they do is switch the lights on – I mean, when you're watching a film, for example, you see a character walk up their path and unlock the door. Next thing you know, the lights in the house come on.'

Lawrence nodded. It was a good point, although he could think of other reasons for leaving the lights off at that hour. When he and Katie had first moved in together, it had been to a flat featuring a mezzanine-level bedroom, and he had often ended up creeping around in the dark after arriving home from a late shift to avoid waking her. After one too many stubbed toes, they had opted to move.

'Are you sure it was Zoë's door?'

Antonia nodded.

'Why were you paying such close attention?'

'I wasn't. Well – no more than usual.'

Lawrence raised his eyebrows. 'Surely you don't scrutinise the activities of every stranger who walks down your street?'

Looking rather embarrassed, Antonia went to answer, then paused. Eventually, she admitted, 'Actually, I do.'

'Do you mind my asking why?'

'I write,' Antonia replied, her colour deepening. 'Books. You know, novels. I watch people for –' she hesitated. 'For ideas, I suppose.'

'Is that your sole source of income?'

'It isn't a source of income at all, at the moment. I haven't had anything published.'

'Do you have another job, then?'

'I'm a student.'

'How about your flatmate?'

'He works in management consultancy.'

'Was he around last Wednesday night?'

'No. I think he was in Bristol.'

Lawrence nodded. 'Do you know whether he knew Zoë?'

Antonia shrugged. 'I've no idea. I don't see much of him, he works away a lot.'

'Is he home?'

'No – he's taken his girlfriend to Paris for the weekend.'

'Would you be able to give us a description of the person you saw enter Zoë's flat?'

'Not a particularly good one.'

'Even some idea of height and build could be enormously helpful,' Lawrence offered, hoping to encourage her.

Antonia nodded.

'From what you said earlier I get the impression it was man.'

'Yes, I think so. I couldn't say one hundred per cent, though.'

'What do you remember about him?'

'He was tall. Fairly thin. Well – maybe not thin, exactly – but not broad.'

'Any idea of hair colour? Length?'

'I don't know about the colour – it was the middle of the night, and everything looks different under street lights. It wasn't noticeably long, but he wasn't a skinhead either.'

'What was he wearing?'

Antonia considered her answer. 'Uh – he had a jacket. That was quite long – it reached about halfway down his thighs. I don't know what colour it was, but it was darkish.'

'What sort of jacket?'

Antonia shook her head. 'I don't know. An anorak, or a waterproof of some sort –' she gave Lawrence an apologetic look. 'I'm sorry, I don't think I can be more specific than that.'

'Was there anything else about him that caught your attention?'

'No.'

'All right,' Lawrence concluded. 'Well, thank you very much for you time – you've been extremely helpful. If anything else comes to mind, give me a call.' He stood up, handing Antonia his card. 'Anything at all.'

'That description fits at least three people I can think of,' Lawrence observed, as he and Rebecca made their way down the steps outside Antonia's flat.

'And it certainly doesn't fit Pete.'

Lawrence looked around. 'You don't think so?'

'I'd put him firmly in the category of broad. He's not overweight, but he's a big man.'

'True. Although things often look different in the dark – shadows can be deceptive. Still, I suppose it might help narrow things down a little. It certainly doesn't rule Lars, Lucian or Dayv out.' Lawrence paused at the bottom of the steps. 'Or,' he added, 'Gavin Mitchell.'

'Is it worth running Antonia's description past the Mitchells to see whether they can give us any other names?' Rebecca suggested.

Lawrence didn't immediately reply. 'Yes, I think it probably is,' he decided eventually, with a perfunctory nod. 'Good idea. I'll drive over there now – do you mind finishing up here?'

'No,' Rebecca replied, forcing a smile and wishing she could say that she *did* mind. She was unlikely to find anybody else in the street who could give them half as much as Antonia had done, and felt rather disheartened at the thought of spending the rest of her day trawling the neighbourhood for what would probably amount to nothing. 'I might grab a sandwich first, though, if you don't mind.'

'That sounds like an even better idea,' Lawrence agreed. 'I tell you what, let's find a pub, or a café, and take another look at what we have so far over lunch. Then we can –'

The electronic tone of his mobile phone interrupted, and he drew it from his trouser pocket. Catching his thumb on a loose thread, he lost his grip, and the phone dropped to the ground. Rebecca bent to retrieve it, and immediately answered before the caller had a chance to hang up.

'Hello?' She opened, as she straightened up.

'Morning sister,' Jamie greeted, cheerily, clearly referencing the nurse's outfit she had been wearing the night before.

'Hi Jay,' Rebecca replied, resisting the temptation to ask where he'd got to in Lawrence's presence.

'Is Forrester there?'

'Yep, hang on,' she offered the phone to her superior.

Lawrence took it. 'Hello. What the hell happened to you last night?'

There was a long pause and Rebecca watched as Lawrence's expression changed to one of concern. 'Oh Lord,' he muttered. 'Poor kid. How is he? ... Do they know what happened?' Another long pause. 'Is there no CCTV? ... yes ... ok, I'll see you later. Thanks.' Terminating the call, he looked to Rebecca. 'Apparently Dayv Roberts was attacked last night – he's critically ill in hospital.'

'God.'

'The hospital found my card in his pocket – Jamie just spoke to them.'

'Do they have any idea what happened?'

'Not really, other than that he sustained another head injury. He was found lying in the street by a passer by, but until he regains consciousness – if he does at all – there's little information about who might have been responsible.'

'What time did that happen?'

'Shortly after one in the morning. I wonder where Pete Morgan was at the time?' Lawrence rubbed his chin. 'More to the point, I'd like to know what Dayv was doing out at that hour, if he really was as ill as he made out yesterday.'

'It sounds like you're going to have to wait for an answer to that one. Did Jamie say anything else?'

'Only that he'll keep us up to date on Dayv's condition.' Lawrence paused for thought. 'I think we'll have to ditch the pub. You grab yourself a bite somewhere and keep going here – I want to speak to Pete as soon as possible. I'll visit the Mitchells afterwards.'

'I could see to Pete if you like,' Rebecca offered, hopefully.

'I don't think that's a good idea. We've already identified him as violent, and he's twice your size. Besides, we still need to finish this job. I'll call you later.'

'Ok,' Rebecca sighed, remaining where she stood as Lawrence walked briskly in the direction of his car. Tired after her late night, and rather peeved at the possibility of missing out on some action, she kicked the raised edge of a badly laid paving stone in frustration, achieving nothing but a new scuff mark on her shoe. Turning to cross the road, she wondered where the nearest café might be. She needed coffee.

Dispensing with niceties altogether on arrival at Pete's flat, Lawrence announced, 'I'd like another word with you about Dayv Roberts,' as soon as Pete opened the door.

'What about him?' Pete snapped. He looked sleepy, and Lawrence guessed the insistent knocking on the door had woken him, despite the fact it was quarter to three in the afternoon.

'He was viciously attacked last night.'

'I'm sure he deserved it,' Pete returned, nastily.

'Do you know anything about it?'

Pete responded with a question of his own. 'Are you accusing me?'

'Mind if we continue this inside?' Lawrence asked, stepping uninvited into the flat, whose state hadn't improved since his previous visit. Closing the door behind himself, he leaned against it. 'Could you tell me where you were between midnight and two o'clock this morning?'

'I was here.'

'Doing what?'

'Drinking.'

'Did you see anybody? Speak to anybody?'

'No.' Pete turned and walked towards his bed. Sitting on the edge, he lay back so that Lawrence was no longer able to see his face. Moving further into the room to resolve this, Lawrence continued.

'When did you last leave this flat?'

'What are you asking me for? You won't believe a word I say!'

'When did you last leave this flat?' Lawrence repeated, impatiently.

'Whenever you say,' came the insolent response.

'Given the circumstances, it would be in your interests to be a little more co-operative,' Lawrence warned him.

'You reckon?'

'You have a key to Zoë's flat, you're already facing charges over a previous assault on Dayv, and you're unaccounted for at the times of both Zoë's murder and the recent attack on Dayv. That makes you a prime suspect.'

'Prove it,' Pete retorted, rudely.

Lawrence thrust his hands into his pockets, drawing a deep breath before continuing. 'Look, I'm not trying to victimise you here, all I want is a few answers. But if you're not minded to cooperate I'm quite prepared to haul you in for questioning and, potentially, charge you with obstruction. Understood?'

Pete held out his hands. 'I didn't go anywhere! What more do you want me to say?'

'I want an account of exactly what you did after I left here at eight-thirty last night!'

Several seconds passed before Pete spoke. 'I had some drinks,' he revealed, just as Lawrence was beginning to think he might have to make good on his threat.

'What were you drinking?'

'Jim Beam.'

'And what did you do while you were drinking?'

'Ordered a pizza. Watched TV.'

'Which firm did you order pizza from?'

'Dominos.'

Lawrence noted this down. 'What time?'

Pete shrugged. 'I dunno. Half eleven? Twelve, maybe.'

'And what did you watch on television?'

'Um –' Pete frowned. 'Point Break? Point Blank? I dunno – whichever one Keanu Reeves is in.'

'And after that?'

Pete paused for thought. 'I kinda flicked – watched some American chat show – and music TV –'

'Do you remember what channels you were watching?'

Pete shook his head. 'I have cable – I just hopped around to see what was on.'

'Anything else?'

'I –' Pete blushed.

'You what?'

'I made a phone call.'

'Who to?'

'I don't know exactly – one of those numbers – you know, to – to talk to girls.' By this time, his cheeks were scarlet.

'A sex chat line?'

'Yeah.'

'How long were you on the phone for?'

'I dunno – a while.'

'Which provider is your phone contract with?'

'Virgin. I get cable through them as well.'

'Ok,' Lawrence scribbled down this detail. 'What happened after that?'

Pete shrugged. 'I fell asleep, I think.'

'All right,' Lawrence snapped his notebook shut. 'Well, thank you for your time, I'll get back to you if there's anything else I need to know.' He turned to leave. 'In future, you might make things easier for yourself if you just tell the truth rather than jumping to the defensive.' He paused in the doorway. 'Contrary to what you seem to think, I'm keen to establish what actually happened. I'm not just looking for an easy collar.'

Nine

Lawrence had miraculously found a parking spot directly outside the Mitchells' home, and was just locking up when a voice behind him took him by surprise.

'Excuse me?'

He turned to see a young man approaching from across the street. Tall and athletic, with short sandy hair and glasses, he wore cycling shorts, trainers and a loose white t-shirt. His thin face was flushed, and Lawrence guessed he had just finished exercising. It was several days since Lawrence had had the time to do as much himself, and he doubted today would be any different.

'Yes?'

'Are you with the police?'

Lawrence confirmed that he was, pulling his warrant card from his pocket to verify this.

'I live across the street. I don't know if I really ought to be talking to you – I mean, it could be nothing –'

'What could be nothing?'

The young man shifted his weight uneasily from one foot to the other. 'It's just – I heard about what happened – to Zoë –'

'And?'

'On Wednesday night – well, Thursday morning, really – I was on my way home and I saw Dr Mitchell heading off out somewhere.'

'When was this?'

'About two-fifteen. I'd been out clubbing.'

'And you're sure it was him?'

'Positive.'

'Did you speak to him?'

'No – I was walking up the road and I saw him drive off. I didn't think anything of it at the time – I mean, he's a doctor, he works odd hours anyway. It probably isn't important, but I thought I should mention it.'

'Do you know him well?'

'No, but I went to school with Zo. She was a good friend of mine back then, and I figured I owed it to her to say something – just in case.'

Lawrence nodded. 'Thank you. What's your name?'

'Corin. I live at number seventy-two.'

'Did you stay in touch with Zoë after you left school?'

'For a while – before she moved out – but I've not seen much of her since. I've been away at university this last year, so I've not been around much myself.'

'Were you in Zoë's year at school?'

Corin nodded.

Lawrence frowned. 'So, if you've been at university for a year, how is it that Christia's still taking her A-levels?'

'She deferred her GCSEs by a year.'

'Why was that?'

The question clearly made Corin uncomfortable, but he answered willingly enough. 'She was bullied a lot at school. To begin with because she was a bit on the chubby side, but then –' he trailed off.

'Then?' Lawrence prompted.

Corin hesitated. 'I don't know quite how to explain what I'm trying to say,' he paused. 'I suppose because she was teased and ridiculed so much she became something of an outsider – and –' he broke off again. 'Somehow that made her even more of a target.'

'And do you think that affected her school work?'

'She missed more school in the fifth form than she attended. She just ballooned that year – I think food was probably her only friend by that point. In the end she took an overdose – sleeping pills I think – and after that Dr Mitchell refused to send her back to school. She did the year again at college.'

'Zoë certainly doesn't seem to have done much to help her.'

'No,' Corin acknowledged. 'There was a time when Zo would stick up for Chris. Some of the other kids made it clear she couldn't be on both sides. It was a case of bully your sister or we'll bully you.'

'And how do you know that?'

Corin dropped his eyes to the tarmac before admitting, 'Because I was one of them.'

Lawrence nodded.

'I wish I could go back and change it, but I can't,' Corin shrugged. 'We were twelve or thirteen, and I don't think any of us realised how much harm we were doing. We destroyed any relationship Zoë and Chris might have had. I think Zoë grew to resent us for it, in the end. I know she felt responsible when Chris tried to take her life, but she didn't know how to handle it, so she turned it around on on everybody else. That's why so many people thought she was a bitch.'

'You don't agree?'

'No. I think she hurt other people to stop them getting close enough to hurt her.'

'Well, you've certainly painted a very different picture of her from everybody else I've spoken to.'

'She was my girlfriend for two years,' Corin revealed. 'I saw what she went through when Chris took that overdose. I don't think anybody's seen the real Zoë since.'

When Carrina Mitchell opened the front door to Lawrence, it was clear she had been crying. Standing back from the door to allow him to enter, she asked whether he would like a drink. Lawrence declined, stopping in the hallway and waiting for Carrina to close the door.

'Somebody saw your husband leaving the house shortly after two on Thursday morning,' Lawrence informed her as she turned to face him. 'Would you like to tell me why you lied about that?'

'Oh –' Carrina raised a nervous hand to smooth her hair. 'Well – I – I – didn't know he'd gone anywhere – he was here when I went to sleep, and again when I awoke –' she swallowed. 'I expect the hospital called him in – they do quite often, and I'm a deep sleeper – I don't often hear his pager alarm, and he always dresses in his study so as not to disturb me –' she trailed off, evidently rattled.

'Is he in?'

'No.'

'When he left, did he give any indication of when he might be back?'

Carrina shook her head.

Lawrence sighed. 'Ok. Well, I'd like a few minutes of your time while I'm here. Is this a convenient time?'

'Oh – yes – please, come through.' She turned towards the living room. Lawrence followed, looking about himself and thinking back to previous visits to the house.

'You don't have any family photographs on display,' he observed, as Carrina perched anxiously on the sofa.

'No.'

'Is there any reason why not?'

Carrina frowned. 'That's a very strange question. How does it help you?'

Lawrence sat in an armchair. 'It may not help me at all, but I'd rather judge that for myself.'

'Oh,' Carrina nodded slightly, failing to provide him with an explanation.

'So?' Lawrence prompted, expectantly.

Carrina cast her eyes down. 'We did have some. Quite a few, actually. Christia smashed them up – some time ago now. Gavin wouldn't let me replace them.'

'Do you know why she smashed them?'

'She was rather upset at the time.'

'What about?'

'She felt that everybody compared her unfavourably with Zoë. As far as looks went, at least.'

'When was this?'

'Oh – about three years ago.'

'And your husband still won't allow you to replace the photographs?'

'No.'

'Why not?'

'I don't really know,' Carrina responded, after a brief pause. Lawrence wondered whether she was telling the truth, thinking that, if she was, it didn't say much for her marriage.

'Do you think perhaps Christia still feels insecure about her appearance?'

'I don't know,' Carrina shook her head. 'She never talks to me about anything.'

'Does she talk to your husband?'

'She may do, but I doubt she sees a lot of him at the moment. He's been working very hard recently – I've barely seen him myself.'

'From what she's said to us, she seems to be under the impression that you judge her on account of her weight.'

Carrina sighed. 'I'm a dietician. It worries me that she's put on so much weight – it really isn't healthy. Gavin knows that as well as I do, but he gets angry if I bring it up.'

116

Lawrence nodded, pausing for a moment before changing direction. 'This morning I interviewed some of the residents of Grosvenor Street, and one of them told me she saw somebody enter Zoë's flat at about three o'clock last Thursday morning. She's given me a description, which isn't all that detailed, but I was hoping that if I ran it past you you might be able to tell me whether it fits anybody we might not yet have come across.'

'How did this person get into the flat?'

'Through the front door. It would seem that whoever it was had a key.'

Carrina paled, but said nothing.

'Do you know of anybody who held a key other than Zoë, Pete and yourselves?'

'No. No, I don't.'

'Ok,' Lawrence flicked through his notes to find Antonia's description, and presented it to Carrina. She read through it, still terribly pale.

'I don't know,' she whispered, shaking her head. 'There isn't really enough to go on – I think half the men in Britain would fit this –' she looked up, tears in her eyes. 'I just don't know.' She pursed her lips, clearly struggling not to cry.

'I realise it was a long shot,' Lawrence reached to retrieve the notes. 'I'll run it past your husband later on, just in case.'

Carrina nodded, swallowing hard. Lawrence felt for her.

'I will do my utmost to find the person responsible for Zoë's death,' he promised, replacing his pen in the breast pocket of his jacket. He could only hope that, in so doing, he wouldn't add to her pain.

'Ray! Can you turn my mic down a bit?' Ian called to Astatine's sound technician five minutes into the sound check.

'It'll be a great relief to us all!' Ray responded, laughingly.

'Piss off,' Ian retorted, pleasantly. 'And give me some more bass – this chorus needs to be fucking huge!'

'Any more bass and nobody will be able to hear a word I'm singing,' Elliot objected.

'Your diction's so shite no one will notice the difference,' Ian came back, grinning to detach any real meaning from the comment.

Elliot made no reply, returning his attention to the task in hand. Launching into the chorus again, he stopped after less than fifteen seconds. 'Can't anybody here *work* a sound desk? Do I have to come and do it for you?' He moved to leave the stage.

'Cool it,' Ian warned, pulling him back.

'But I –'

'Give Ray a chance to do his job.'

Elliot sighed heavily, nodding. 'Can we try that again, please?' He shouted to Ray, who was standing towards the rear of the club. Ray gave him a thumbs up sign and the band began again. Moments into the song there was soft thud before the sound cut out completely.

'What the fuck is going on now?' Ian demanded, as Squidsy, one of the band's road crew, disappeared behind the stacks of equipment lined up across the back of the stage.

'Jeebies,' Elliot shook his head. 'It's going to be Christmas by the time we're finished at this rate.' He set his guitar down, turning towards the drum kit. 'Damian, d'you have a tab?'

'Don't you?'

'In my jacket.'

'Useless twat,' Damian grinned, pulling a packet of cigarettes from his shirt pocket and tossing them in Elliot's direction.

'Silk Cut?' Elliot remarked, on catching them, clearly unimpressed. 'Christ. I might as well suck a straw in a smoky room.'

'Nobody's forcing you to smoke them.'

Trying to suppress a smile, Elliot raised his eyes momentarily heavenwards before opening the box and taking one. Feeling in his pocket for a lighter, he returned the packet to Damian. 'Cheers mate.'

'We aim to please,' Damian quipped, standing and following Elliot in the direction of the open emergency exit doors at the side of the venue, taking a cigarette himself before replacing the box in his pocket.

'I thought that was just the ladies?' Ian observed, wryly.

'That's where he fails to meet the aim,' Elliot returned, lighting up as he arrived in the doorway.

'Cheeky fucker,' Damian responded, good-naturedly, holding out a hand for Elliot's lighter.

'Ah, he's just jealous,' Ian waved a hand in Elliot's direction. 'You and I can get laid every night of the tour, meanwhile Mr-almost-married here has to keep his nose clean so's –'

Damian exploded into laughter. 'What a choice of words!'

'Obviously I didn't mean that literally,' Ian replied, unnecessarily.

'No shit!' Elliot sniggered.

'May your nose bleed and your fingers burn,' Ian retorted. 'And might I just add that –'

'Ok, we're good to go!' Squidsy shouted, reappearing at the side of the stage.

'About bloody time,' Ian muttered, his words lost as Elliot simultaneously came out with a cheerful, 'Top banana!'

'Where the hell did that come from?'

'What?' Elliot frowned.

'Top banana.'

'It's an expression, stupid.'

'I know *that* – but why banana?'

'Well top carrot doesn't exactly have the same ring to it, does it?'

'Elliot, if you aren't careful I'll shove a carrot up your –'

'Can we get a move on now, please?' Jeff interrupted, impatiently, joining them in the doorway.

Elliot held up his cigarette, raising his eyebrows pointedly.

'I don't give a shit! We haven't all day, Elliot!'

'I do apologise,' Elliot returned, with heavy sarcasm. 'I momentarily forgot that while we have sit about all day waiting for you, we're then expected to jump to as soon as you snap your fingers. *Sorry.*'

'This is in your interests, not mine!'

'Yeah right! You're giving up your time for free, I suppose? Nothing to do with the fact you want to make a lot of money and a name for yourself in the music business!'

'I'm not even going to dignify that with a reply!'

'You mean because it's true! This business is full of parasites freeloading on other people's success and at the same time trying to prevent others from doing likewise! *You* are a parasite!'

'Will you grow up!' Jeff exploded. 'We don't have time for you to throw a tantrum! Now shut the fuck up, put the fag out and get on with what you're here for!'

'All right,' Elliot shrugged, abruptly reverting to calm and cordial for no apparent reason. Flicking the remains of his cigarette out into the street, he turned towards the stage. 'Let's go.'

His face flushed, Jeff struggled to keep a lid on his temper. Elliot had an infuriating knack of winding him up to breaking point only to defer at the last minute, leaving him fuming yet unable to vent his anger without afterwards looking unreasonable. Walking back towards the centre of the venue, he thought wistfully of the banal pop band he had worked with the previous year. Admittedly he had opted for the change – working with teenage wannabes singing manufactured pap was not something he had been proud of, even less interested in, but they had at least respected him. They wanted fame and adulation, and were willing to do whatever they were told along the way, in part because they knew there were thousands of others who would only too happily replace them.

Astatine, or, more to the point, Elliot, was an entirely different scenario. Elliot wasn't a mediocre singer with a pretty face who could be taught a few dance routines and ordered about. He was a talented musician and an exceptional songwriter, and Jeff suspected he knew it as well as everybody else. There was no way the record company was about to drop him, regardless of how difficult he might be to work with. Jeff could shout and bully him until the cows came home, but Elliot was as intelligent as he was argumentative, and, when it came down to it, he held most of the cards.

Lawrence walked purposefully into the hospital's cardiology department. He had learned long ago that if he looked as if he knew where he was going, people were unlikely to stop him, and it didn't take him long to find what he was looking for. Glancing quickly up and down the corridor, he stepped swiftly into the darkened room and flicked on the light.

Two things struck him immediately about Gavin Mitchell's office: firstly, that it was as neat and tidy as his own; secondly, that a framed photograph sat atop the desk. This came as something of a surprise considering the blanket ban Gavin had supposedly imposed on photographs in the home, and, even more curiously, this picture featured only Gavin and Christia. Looking around himself, Lawrence noticed that a poem undersigned *Christia Danielle Mitchell* had been affixed to the pin board above the desk, as had a photograph of Christia and Lucian. Lawrence could see nothing to even hint at Zoë's existence, and was on the point of moving to open one of the desk drawers when a voice stopped him.

'May I ask what you're doing in here?'

Lawrence turned. The man in the doorway was, he guessed, in his mid-fifties, and his smart attire and absence of a laboratory coat indicated that he worked in management. He was tall and very overweight, his ample stomach overflowing the waistband of too-tight trousers and his double chin partly disguised by a neatly trimmed beard. His greying hair had receded only slightly and, although he wasn't wearing glasses, the indentations on the bridge of his nose revealed that he did wear them a good proportion of the time. It was clear from his expression that he was more than a little displeased to find Lawrence in Gavin's office.

'I'm looking for Dr Mitchell. Is he in today?'

'No, he's not. And I really don't see that it was necessary to come in here to determine that.'

Lawrence introduced himself and furnished the man with a glimpse of his warrant card before asking, 'You are?'

'Brian Meyers. I'm the director of this department.'

'Do you have an office where we can talk?'

'Certainly,' Brian nodded. He waited for Lawrence to step out into the corridor, moving to close the door behind him before heading in the direction from which Lawrence had originally come. After some forty yards, he opened a door onto an office almost identical to Gavin's, although considerably less well-ordered. Brian sat at his desk, swivelling his chair around to face the room as he did so, and before he had a chance to ask questions, Lawrence posed his.

'I assume you can tell me which members of your staff were and weren't on call at a particular date and time?'

'Within reason. We don't keep those sort of records indefinitely.'

'How about Wednesday night and Thursday morning last week?'

'Certainly.'

'Was Dr Mitchell on call?'

'Gavin?' Brian turned towards his desk, then stopped, looking sharply back to Lawrence. 'Are you suggesting he might have had something to do with what happened to his daughter?'

'Please just answer my question.'

Clearly put out, Brian took a file from the shelf above his desk and flicked through the first few pages. Pausing, he scanned the page in front of him. 'Uh – no. No, Gavin wasn't on call on Wednesday night.'

'Would you have been informed if somebody swapped something like that with a colleague?'

Brian's tone was rather sarcastic as he replied, 'If the staff kept those kind of changes to themselves it would make it very difficult for us to know who to contact in an emergency, wouldn't it?'

'Can I take that to be a yes?'

Brian looked irritated. 'Yes.'

Lawrence nodded. 'Do you know Dr Mitchell well?'

'As well as I know most of my staff members, I suppose. We're colleagues, not drinking buddies.'

'Have you ever met any members of his family?'

'His wife's accompanied him to a few hospital dinners, and I understand his daughter drops in occasionally, but I've never bumped into her.'

'What's he like to work with?'

'He's a brilliant surgeon. I've no complaints about his work at all.'

'How long has he been working here?'

Brian paused to consider his answer. 'Just over two years, I think. He used to work at a specialist private hospital.'

'Do you know what made him opt for the NHS after that? Obviously not the money.'

'You must have visited his home – somehow I don't think money's something he's short of.'

Lawrence raised his eyebrows quizzically. 'You've been there, then?'

Brian flinched, evidently aware he had caught himself out. 'Yes,' he admitted, warily.

'Often?'

'Not that often.'

'So when you said you didn't know Gavin Mitchell well, that wasn't true,' Lawrence concluded.

Brian sighed. 'We play golf occasionally, that's all.'

'Then why tell me you know him as nothing more than a colleague?'

'I don't want to get involved. Gavin's private life is his business, not mine.'

Lawrence felt irritated. 'This is a murder investigation. Whether or not it's your business doesn't change the fact you'll be breaking the law if you withhold information from us. Do you understand that?'

'But I don't think I know anything that *could* be relevant. Gavin wasn't on call last Wednesday night, and I don't know where he was. What more can I tell you?'

'I don't know, but I get the impression you know more than you're letting on.'

'Well there's not a lot I can do about that,' Brian snapped, defensively. 'I've told you, I don't know anything about what happened to Zoë. I've barely seen Gavin since her death – as far as I know, he's only been in once, and that was to collect something from his office.'

Guessing Brian wasn't about to give in, and was unlikely to be caught out a second time, Lawrence decided to abandon the interview. 'I'll leave you to it, then,' he said, as pleasantly as he could. 'If you think of anything that might be of help, please let me know as soon as possible. You'll find the numbers on here.' He handed the man a business card.

'Certainly.' Brian took the card and moved to pin it to his notice board. Lawrence left the office, closing the door behind himself and making a mental note of its location in case he should need to return. To his mind it was not so much a case of *if* Brian was hiding something, but *what*.

'Lucian?' Christia spoke his name again, sounding frightened this time. 'Lucian, I know this must be more than you need to deal with right now, but I can't go through it alone!'

Lucian didn't reply. He couldn't look at her without betraying something of the truth, and reached automatically for his cigarettes, unconsciously giving himself an excuse not to meet her eyes.

'Lucian, *please.*'

There were tears in her voice. Lucian hadn't a clue what to say to her. He couldn't tell her. He *couldn't*. And his mind wouldn't focus on anything else. He wasn't even sure he had fully absorbed what she had just told him. His fingers unsteady, it took three matches to light the cigarette.

'I thought you loved me.'

Head bowed, Lucian squeezed his eyes shut. He couldn't bring himself to say the words that might reassure her. That he would be speaking the truth seemed almost irrelevant.

'What, was all this a game to you?' Christia asked, with a subdued sob. 'I suppose you thought I'd be up for anything! Fat, lonely and desperate – not much of a challenge, was it? And all along I was stupid enough to think we might have something special!'

'It wasn't a game,' Lucian managed, his words clipped in the desperate struggle to keep his tone even. 'It's not you –'

'Don't insult me with the *it's not you, it's me* speech!'

'That's not –' he gulped. 'Not – what I was going to say.'

'So what were you going to say?'

'It has nothing to do with you and me, but –' he broke off for a pull on the cigarette. 'I can't tell you any more. Please don't ask that of me.'

Christia's response, when it came, sounded hollow. 'What?'

Lucian couldn't speak. He merely shook his head, his throat aching with suppressed tears. Some moments passed before Christia spoke again, and in the interim Lucian dared not look up. Eventually, her voice trembling, she whispered, 'No, please *no* –'

Wishing he could have lied his way clear of the subject, Lucian ran his free hand across his forehead. It felt clammy.

'Lucian – please – tell me you don't mean what I think you're trying to say –'

Lucian opened his mouth to speak. How could he explain that this was hurting him every bit as much as it was her?

'Look at me!' She yelled, edging on hysteria.

Biting into his lower lip, Lucian slowly raised his eyes. Christia hadn't moved from the sofa, her cheeks flushed and wet. Her whole body shook as she sobbed.

'I don't want to believe it,' she whispered. 'I don't! Where were you that night? Were you with her?'

Lucian gazed wretchedly back at her. Stubbing out his cigarette, he felt for another.

'*Were* you?'

Lucian said nothing. Raising the cigarette to his lips, he reached for the matches.

'Answer me!' Christia demanded, leaning forwards and snatching the cigarette from him. Lucian stared at her, feeling out of control. He couldn't remember what the original question had been.

'*Say something!*'

'What do you want me to say?' He asked, hopelessly.

'The truth might be a good start!'

Lucian just shook his head. What her understanding of the truth was now, he simply had no idea. He wasn't even sure what *his* understanding of the whole situation was. He couldn't think straight, and he needed to get out. He stumbled to his feet, his legs threatening to buckle, limbs almost numb.

'You can't go *now*!' Christia shrieked. 'You can't! Don't leave me! Please don't leave me!'

Lucian felt faint. Entering the hallway, he raised a hand to steady himself, catching his finger on the edge of a clip frame that hung on the wall. The light filtering through the panel above the door seemed incredibly bright. Reaching the door, he clung to the handle as he opened it, feeling hot and dizzy. Outside, he sank down onto the balcony, leaning forwards so that the black bars supported his shoulders, his head slotted between them. He closed his eyes, feeling nauseous. He had sat in this position so many times. As a child he had watched people appear around the corner of the block, waited for a daydream to become a reality. For so many years he had wanted the truth. Now all he wanted was to forget.

'Lucian?' Christia's tone had changed. Her voice shook. He looked around. 'Please,' she whispered. 'Please tell me it isn't true.'

Lucian couldn't speak. He dropped his eyes to the concrete on which she stood. Nobody else knew the truth. Nobody needed to. Nothing had to change; he could keep quiet, and nothing would change. Nothing had to change. Nothing had to change. He repeated it silently, again and again, despite knowing that the effort was futile. Everything had already changed.

By the time Lawrence revisited the Mitchells on Sunday evening, Gavin had returned home, and was reading the paper in the living room. He stood as Carrina showed Lawrence in, glancing at his watch.

'Good evening,' he greeted, evenly.

Lawrence responded in kind before adding, 'I'm sorry to call so late.'

'What can I help you with?'

'I'm hoping you can explain why when we spoke on Friday you omitted to mention that you left the house at approximately two-fifteen on Thursday morning?'

'I was on call,' Gavin countered, his eyes flickering momentarily in his wife's direction.

Lawrence turned to Carrina. 'Would you mind leaving us for a minute, please?'

Carrina frowned. 'But –'

'It's standard procedure,' he responded, pleasantly.

'Oh – ok –' Carrina nodded, turning to go. Lawrence moved to close the door behind her before sitting on the sofa and regarding Gavin expectantly.

'Right. Now, I know you weren't on call, because I've checked with the hospital. So where were you?'

Gavin sighed heavily, sitting in an armchair. 'I went to visit somebody,' he answered, ambiguously.

'Somebody you clearly don't want your wife to know about,' Lawrence surmised.

Gavin nodded. 'Yes.'

'So who? A mistress?'

'Not exactly.'

'Not exactly?'

'She was. Once. A long time ago.'

'And you're still in contact?'

'Not really.'

'Could we stop playing guessing games, please?' Lawrence asked, impatiently.

'She tracked me down, I'm not sure how. She called on Wednesday evening asking to see me.'

'At that time of night?'

Gavin nodded. 'Yes.'

'Why did she want to see you?'

'To ask me a favour.'

'Which was?'

'I don't think that's any of your business,' Gavin snapped.

'Could you give me this woman's address?'

'No.'

'No?' Lawrence echoed, incredulously.

'I've no idea what it is. We didn't meet at her home.'

'So where did you meet?'

'That's hardly relevant.'

'I disagree.'

Gavin didn't reply.

'Do you have any means of contacting this woman in order to confirm that you were with her?'

'No.'

'Then how do you expect me to believe you were with somebody else at the time of your daughter's death?'

'I don't, but you're the one who has to prove otherwise.'

'Would you rather I wasted my time doing that than trying to find out what happened to Zoë?'

Gavin shrugged. 'The speed at which you do that isn't going to bring her back, is it?'

Lawrence stared at him, momentarily speechless. Some seconds passed before he asked, 'Dr Mitchell, do you actually *care* whether or not I get to the bottom of this?'

'What sort of question is that?' Gavin shot back.

'If you weren't being so obstructive I wouldn't have felt the need to ask.'

'I'm not being obstructive! What I was doing had absolutely nothing to do with Zoë!'

'If that's the case I don't understand why you can't tell me what it was. It's not as if I'm going to broadcast it.'

'Because it's none of your damn business!' Gavin returned, hotly.

Lawrence sighed. 'I'm afraid that given the circumstances, it *is* my business.'

'No, it isn't! I never asked you to get involved!'

Lawrence lifted his eyebrows. 'So you don't care whether or not Zoë's killer is brought to justice,' he concluded, aloud.

Gavin looked furious. 'I never said that!'

'I never said you did. I based my assumption on your behaviour,' Lawrence baited, calmly, hoping that, in his anger, Gavin would reveal more than he had originally intended. Gavin clenched his fists, and for a second Lawrence thought he might have succeeded in pushing him to the brink of losing his temper altogether. Moments later, however, he sank back into the chair, his expression changing.

'I'm sorry,' he sighed. 'I'm not accustomed to feeling so useless.'

'What do you mean?'

'All I can do is wait. I can't *do* anything, and it's really getting to me.' He rubbed his brow. 'I do care about what happened – of course I do – and I know you're trying to help, but I feel intensely frustrated that I can't do any of this *myself*.'

Lawrence wondered whether Gavin was speaking the truth. Until now he had been so self-possessed and showed so little obvious distress that Lawrence found his sudden frankness rather implausible. He suspected Gavin was clever enough to play him at his own game, and guessed the little speech was his way of side-stepping the original issue. Alternatively, Lawrence supposed, sceptically, it was possible that Gavin was losing control of his impassive facade as the reality of what had happened began to hit home. Either way, Lawrence thought it unlikely he would succeed in drawing any further answers from the man on the subject of Wednesday night, and turned his mind to whether there might be another way in which to substantiate Gavin's claim. Assuming, of course, that there was anything *to* substantiate.

'How was your afternoon?' Lawrence asked, arriving back at the office to find Rebecca sitting at his desk, leafing wearily through the *NME*.

'Boring,' Rebecca responded, without raising her eyes. 'Complete waste of time.'

'Complete?'

'Yep,' she closed and folded the *NME*, looking up. 'Yours?'

'More interesting than I anticipated, actually.'

Rebecca regarded him expectantly. As she apparently had no intention of vacating his chair, Lawrence reached for one that sat nearby and pulled it up to the desk so that he could sit opposite her.

'It would seem Gavin Mitchell wasn't home all night last Wednesday after all.'

'Where was he?'

'I don't know. He wasn't particularly forthcoming. He claims to have been visiting an old mistress, but refused to tell me who, how I might contact her or where they met.'

'How odd.'

'I spoke to the director of his department at the hospital to establish whether he was on call that night, and at first he denied knowing Gavin as anything more than a colleague, but then tripped himself up – it turns out they play golf together. I'm fairly certain he was hiding something.'

'Maybe he knows about Gavin's infidelities and doesn't want to be responsible for the details getting back to Carrina.'

'Could be,' Lawrence nodded. 'I also discovered that Christia attempted suicide shortly before she was due to take her GCSEs.'

'Why?'

'She was bullied at school. By Zoë and her friends.'

Rebecca frowned. 'Are you going somewhere with that?'

'I don't know,' Lawrence shook his head. 'I'm starting to see where Gavin might have had a motive in all this.'

'Yes?' Rebecca leaned forward impatiently.

'I visited his office today. He wasn't there, but looking around, you wouldn't know he had two daughters. He has a photograph of himself and Christia on the desk, and a couple of mementoes that she clearly gave him – but nothing at all relating to Zoë. No pictures, nothing.'

'A bit like his home, then.'

'I asked Carrina about that. She said Christia destroyed all the family photographs they had on view a few years ago. As far as I can tell, that was about the same time as her suicide attempt, and apparently Gavin won't allow Carrina to replace the pictures. I get the impression he and Christia are very close, and I wonder whether he knew something Christia didn't, and was trying to protect her.'

'Like what? That Zoë was involved with Lucian?'

'It's possible.'

Rebecca nodded thoughtfully. 'I know you're not convinced Lucian is with Christia for the right reasons, but supposing he is, how might he have reacted if she'd shared with him just how bad Zoë made her feel?'

'Also a plausible scenario,' Lawrence acknowledged.

'At least we should be able to rule Gavin in or out when we get the DNA results back. Leighton was hoping they'd come through tomorrow.'

'I've a couple of other questions for him. I suppose he's long since gone?'

'I think expecting him still to be here at half nine on a Sunday night is a bit beyond the call of duty.'

'Did he get back to you about those letters?'

'Um – no.'

Lawrence felt frustrated. 'That's all he's had to do *all day.*'

'He does have other people making demands on his time, too, you know,' Rebecca pointed out. 'But I've not long been back myself – maybe he's left something on my desk.' She stood and walked around Lawrence's desk and out of the doorway onto the main office.

'He'd better have done,' Lawrence remarked, relocating to his own chair while he had the chance.

Rebecca shuffled through some papers, then triumphantly held up a small blue Post-it note before starting to read.

'Very professional,' Lawrence muttered, sarcastically, as she padded back into his office. 'Could he not have used email like the rest of us? What does it say?'

'Envelopes not sealed with saliva. Further tests inconclusive.'

'Too much to hope for an easy answer, I suppose,' Lawrence sighed. 'Let's call it a day. I'm shattered.'

'Can't take the late nights any more?' Rebecca teased.

'Unlike your fiancé, I don't regard morning as something that happens *before* bedtime,' Lawrence smiled, rising slowly from his chair.

'I don't think *bedtime* is part of his tour vocabulary at all,' Rebecca replied. She sounded upset, and Lawrence looked around.

'What's up?'

Rebecca shrugged. 'I really miss him,' she admitted.

'I'm sure he misses you too.'

'I know. Usually, I'm fine with it all – but sometimes –' she paused. 'Sometimes I have to stop myself from getting the first train to wherever he is. Right now, there's nothing I'd like more than to have him there to go home to.'

'He'll be home soon,' Lawrence ventured, at a loss to know what else to say. Rebecca nodded, and he asked, 'Would you like a lift back?'

'Would you mind?'

'Not at all.'

Rebecca sighed. 'I'm sorry – I'm just tired. It's been a long day.' She turned towards the door, forcing a smile. 'In a couple of weeks' time Elliot will be dragging me out to see all his mates' bands play and I'll be desperate for a quiet night in, just me, a book and the bath tub.'

Ten

'Morning,' Lawrence greeted the receptionist as he passed her desk en route from the lifts to his office.

'Sir?' She stopped him. 'There's someone here to see you.'

'Oh?'

The receptionist nodded in the direction opposite to that in which he had been heading. Turning, Lawrence was intrigued to see Christia Mitchell sitting waiting, her head bowed and hands clasped tightly in her lap. As he approached, she looked up, her eyes red.

'Hello,' Lawrence greeted her.

'Hi.'

'What brings you in here?'

'Could I talk to you, please?'

'Of course. Come through to my office.' Lawrence waited for her to stand before beginning to walk. 'Looks like we're in for another hot day,' he commented, conversationally.

Christia nodded. 'Yes.'

'Since you've just finished college, I imagine you'll be seeing more of the Sun than I will,' he continued.

She nodded again.

'Your father mentioned that you're off to university at the end of the summer.'

'Yes.'

'What are you planning to study?'

'English with French.'

'Whereabouts?'

'Cambridge, hopefully. If I get the grades.'

'Nice place to be a student,' Lawrence remarked, opening the door to his office. 'Can I get you a drink?'

'No, thanks.'

'Have a seat,' he indicated a chair by his desk, moving to sit in his own. Christia did as bid. Lawrence sat down and rested his forearms on the desk as he said, 'So, can I help you, or have you come to help me?'

'I don't know,' Christia responded, shaking her head slightly. 'I don't know what to do. I don't know if I should be here at all. I might be wasting your time, but –' she stopped, biting down on her lower lip.

'But?' Lawrence encouraged.

'But I'm terrified I might not be!' Christia revealed, very quickly, her voice breaking as she finished the sentence. She bowed her head, twisting her fingers roughly around one another and locking them tightly. Lawrence offered her the box of tissues that sat on his desk, and waited for her to regain a degree of composure.

'Sorry,' she muttered, at length.

'You don't need to apologise. I understand that the last few days must have been very traumatic for you.'

Christia's bloodshot eyes came up sharply. 'I'm not upset about *her*,' she snapped.

'So what is it that's upset you?'

'I think –' she swallowed hard. 'Lucian – and –' she stopped with a shrug, casting her eyes back down.

'You think Lucian might have been involved with Zoë?'

'Yeah.'

'Has he said something to give you that impression?'

'It's what he *didn't* say.'

Lawrence nodded.

'What – what if –' Christia gulped. 'Maybe he only went with me to get to her!'

'Did he know Zoë before you started dating?'

'He didn't exactly know her – but – they met, yeah,' Christia paused, drawing a sharp breath. 'I guess the suggestion was always there – in the back of my mind –' she sniffed almost involuntarily before finishing with, 'I just didn't want to – to admit it – to – myself!'

'And do you suppose that if they were involved he might have been responsible for her death?'

Lips pursed tightly, Christia nodded.

'What makes you think that?'

'She would have told me. Sooner or later.'

'Do you really think that threat is motive for murder?'

'When I'm twenty-one, I'll inherit over a million pounds.'

'And do you think that's why Lucian has attached himself to you?'

'It's possible. I mean, look at me,' she held her hands out.

'Did Zoë not stand to inherit an equal sum?'

'Lucian was hardly going to see it through her! Zoë used people, and all she wanted from him was a good fuck and another one up on me!'

Lawrence raised his eyebrows but didn't reply. Privately, he wondered whom Zoë's share of the inheritance would benefit in light of her death.

'Mum's always telling me I won't keep a man like him looking like I do,' Christia continued, bitterly. 'Maybe she's right. I just didn't want to believe her.'

'And how does your father feel about the relationship?'

'I don't really know what he thinks,' Christia admitted. 'He seems to like Lucian, and he's been very supportive – with his illness and everything – but he's always discouraged me from getting involved.'

'Perhaps he's concerned. From what I've gathered, Lucian's behaviour is rather erratic.'

'Yeah, but it's not as if he's *dangerous*,' Christia countered.

'Are you and your Dad close?'

Christia nodded, saying sadly, 'Dad's the only member of my family who accepts me as I am. I used to wish it was just the two of us. Mum and Zoë were always so wrapped up in one another that I doubt they'd even have noticed if we'd disappeared.'

'It must be difficult for him watching another man taking his place in your life. Maybe he doesn't want to let you go.'

There was a long pause before Christia spoke again. 'Do you have kids?' She asked, hesitantly.

'Two. A boy and a girl.'

'Dad always wanted a son, but Mum couldn't have any more – after –' she stopped awkwardly. 'I don't know. There's so much they never seem to talk about. Sometimes I wonder why they're still together at all.'

'You're late,' Lawrence observed, irritably, as Rebecca approached his desk. 'You said you had something quick to take care of – you do realise it's now gone eleven, don't you?'

'Sorry, I lost track of time,' Rebecca apologised, before presenting him with a black and white photograph. 'Does this guy look familiar?'

Lawrence frowned. The young man in the picture was leaning against a brick wall, thumbs hooked into the pockets of his jeans, well-toned arms exposed by a white tank top. Dark, jauntily layered hair framed his finely contoured face, emphasising his cheekbones, and his dark eyes were accentuated by long, thick lashes. His head was tipped to one side, and he was gazing moodily at a point some way to the left of the camera.

'Should he?'

'That's Dayv Roberts.'

'Goodness,' Lawrence raised his eyebrows. 'Now I see how he made it into the modelling world.'

'I take it he looks rather different now?' Rebecca reached for a chair.

'Just a bit. Where did you find this?'

'I visited Electra – the modelling agency – it's just down the road from my flat. I also caught up with Dayv's doctor. If Pete's found guilty of GBH, he's looking at quite a lengthy sentence. He's not only caused lasting damage, but he's quite possibly ended Dayv's career.'

'How?'

'Apparently Dayv now suffers from epilepsy, dizziness and blackouts, and his eyesight has been permanently damaged. The doctor said that while there is likely to be some improvement, there's little chance he'll ever fully recover, and it's going to be a long time before he's well enough to work, if he ever is. As for the agency, they're putting on a good show of being sympathetic, but the woman I spoke to made it pretty clear that Dayv would be something of a liability to them if they were to keep him on their books.'

'That's rough.'

'And as you've just observed, he doesn't exactly look the part these days.'

'No,' Lawrence acknowledged. 'More evidence for the case against Pete, then. Zoë was a witness.'

'Exactly.'

Lawrence nodded. 'I had an interesting visit this morning myself.'

'Who?'

'Christia Mitchell. She seems to think Lucian might have been involved with Zoë after all. Apparently he didn't confirm being with her on Wednesday night, but refused to deny it, and couldn't even look her in the eye. I also had a phone call from Antonia Villar. She remembered something else about the man she saw enter Zoë's flat – he was smoking. Apparently he flung the cigarette butt into the flower bed outside Zoë's front door. I've

134

asked Leighton to chase up the DNA results from the postmortem and the cigarette butts that were picked up when the garden was combed last Thursday night – with any luck that might help us to establish whether the man Antonia saw was connected to what happened to Zoë. We may even get a further clue from the brand.'

'Which would count Pete out, wouldn't it?' Rebecca observed. 'Since he doesn't smoke.'

'Gavin Mitchell too,' Lawrence agreed. 'Although we have to bear in mind that some people are inclined to smoke the occasional cigarette without taking it up as a regular habit. My father occasionally does that – especially after a few drinks – but I wouldn't describe him as a smoker.'

'I wish that applied to Elliot. If he's anxious about something he can chain his way through twenty in a matter of hours.'

'That's another good point. How many people give up for a few weeks or months and then crack when they're under stress? Just because we've not seen Pete or Gavin smoke doesn't mean they never have.'

'True, but I'm guessing Lucian is still your number-one suspect.'

'Yes,' Lawrence leaned back in his chair. 'Although Dayv also smokes.'

'I think it's highly unlikely he had anything to do with it after what his doctor told me this morning.'

'Well, we don't know how much of that is true. It's very difficult to prove how much damage a person may or may not have sustained through a head injury. And on top of that, brain damage can cause behavioural changes – who knows what he may now be capable of.'

'We're forgetting the fact he's now in intensive care.'

Lawrence shook his head wearily. 'It feels as though we're going around in circles. We seem to have a case against half the men we've interviewed, and for all we know it may not be any one of them.'

Rebecca didn't immediately answer. 'I don't really understand why Lucian would have wanted Zoë dead,' she admitted, at length. 'If he cared enough for Christia to not want to lose her, why embark on an affair with her sister?'

'Christia stands to inherit a large sum of money in a couple of years' time. I think that's a pretty strong motive. I suppose she may inherit even more now Zoë's out of the picture.'

Rebecca sat forwards. 'Which could also represent a motive for Christia and Lucian acting together.'

'Indeed. We can look into that later on. I'd like to visit Lucian before we go any further, but after that –' Lawrence was interrupted by his desktop telephone, and reached to answer it. 'Hello? ... Really?' He looked surprised. 'Thanks very much for letting me know. We'll be right over.' Replacing the receiver, he looked to Rebecca. 'Ever been to St Albans?'

'No. Why?'

'That's where we're going next. The police there have arrested a young man trying to use a stolen credit card.'

'So?'

Lawrence moved to stand. 'The card belongs to one David Roberts.'

Rebecca and Lawrence were met at St Albans Police Station by a young Indian woman who introduced herself as Police Constable Nasim. Tall, with narrow shoulders and hips, she looked to be in her early twenties. Her slender face was surrounded by thick black hair cut in a neat bob, and the small indentation on the left side of her nose indicated that, outside work, she wore a nose stud.

'You're lucky we were able to contact you so quickly,' she said, showing them through to the interview rooms. 'One of our lads was down in London over the weekend, and saw the local news – he recognised the name on the credit card when he was called to the store.'

'How was the card identified as stolen in the first place?' Rebecca enquired. 'The owner can't have been in any state to report it missing.'

'Stupidity on the part of the thief,' PC Nasim replied. 'Combined with greed. If you're using a stolen credit card in a shop, don't use it in conjunction with your own store reward card.' She grinned. 'We've caught several that way.'

'What's he had to say about how he came to be in possession of the card?' Lawrence asked.

'Claims he found it.'

'Where?'

'St Catherine's Street. That's about ten minutes' walk from here.'

'Right, we'll see what we can get out of him – in the meantime, could you have someone see about getting us a search warrant for his home? At the moment the owner of that credit card is seriously ill in hospital, and even if he does pull through there may be a connection to our investigation.'

'Sure,' PC Nasim nodded. 'I'll get onto that right away. If you want to wait in here –' she opened a door to an interview room, 'I'll bring the lad in.'

'Thanks,' Lawrence smiled. As PC Nasim turned to go, he stopped her. 'Oh, one more thing. Does he smoke?'

'Yes. He was trying to buy cigarettes with the credit card as it happens – although I don't know whether they were intended solely for personal use.'

'What does he smoke?'

PC Nasim gave this a moment's thought before saying, 'Sorry, I don't know. I expect you'll find out soon enough, though.'

Sturdily built, with mild acne and unruly ginger hair, Lawrence put Toby Fielding in his late teens. There were two rings through his left eyebrow, and the rash around his mouth and nostrils suggested he either suffered from eczema or regularly inhaled solvents. He wore khaki combat trousers and a white t-shirt depicting a patch of cannabis plants accompanied by the slogan *don't walk on the grass, smoke it.* He looked mildly uncomfortable, and Lawrence guessed he was trying to conceal his anxiety at having been detained by the police.

'Toby Fielding?' He began.

'Yes,' Toby muttered, staring down at the table.

'I'm Detective Chief Inspector Forrester, this is Detective Sergeant Palmer. Could you tell us how you came to be in possession of a credit card in the name of David Roberts?'

'Found it,' Toby replied, without looking up.

'Where did you find it?'

'St Catherine Street. On the pavement.'

'Was it in a wallet?'

'No.'

'So it was just lying on the pavement by itself, was it?'

'Yes.'

Lawrence paused, more for effect than anything, before saying, 'Can you tell me where you were between eleven o'clock on Saturday night and two o'clock on Sunday morning?'

'At home.'

'Where's home?'

'Park Street.'

'Do you live alone?'

'With my Mum.'

'Can she confirm that you were home?'

'No,' Toby reached into his pocket, pulling out a packet of cigarettes. Lawrence made a mental note of the brand.

'Is that because she wasn't there, or because *you* weren't?'

'She works nights.'

'Is there anybody else who can confirm your whereabouts?'

'No.' Toby tapped a cigarette out of the packet.

'You can't smoke in here.'

He sighed.

'What were you doing at home?'

'Watching videos.'

Lawrence sat back in his chair. 'At present, the owner of that credit card is critically ill in hospital. Theft of a credit card is a minor offence compared with GBH, or, depending on how the situation progresses, possibly manslaughter or even murder. Do you understand that?'

'Yes,' Toby nodded, his gaze still fixed on the table.

'That being the case, if you have anything else to say about the origins of that credit card, you would be wise to say it now.'

'I *found* it,' Toby repeated, his voice strained.

'Where were you between midnight and four o'clock last Thursday morning?'

Toby raised his eyes, a puzzled expression on his face. 'What?'

Lawrence repeated the question.

'I was at home,' Toby responded, anxiously.

'Alone again?'

He swallowed. 'Yes.'

'Does the name Zoë Mitchell mean anything to you?'

'No.'

'We're currently in the process of obtaining a search warrant for your home,' Lawrence revealed. 'With that in mind, is there anything you'd like to add?'

Toby shifted uneasily in his seat, but made no reply.

'Yes or no?'

'I didn't just find the card,' he admitted, at length.

'So what did happen?'

'It –' he stopped. 'I found a wallet – the card was in there.'

'And why did you lie about that?'

'There was some cash. In the wallet, I mean.' Toby shrugged. 'I thought I might have to pay it back, or something.'

'Are you sure that's the whole truth? There's nothing else you've neglected to mention?'

'No. That's it.'

'All right, we'll leave it there for now. For your sake I hope it won't be necessary for me to have to speak to you again.' Lawrence rose to his feet. From his point of view, he hoped it *would* be necessary, given that he was unlikely to be questioning Toby again unless he could connect the boy to Zoë Mitchell. Disappointingly, however, he suspected such a connection was unlikely.

Mrs Fielding had been visibly shocked when Lawrence explained the reason for his and Rebecca's arrival on her doorstep, and put up no resistance when presented with a search warrant. She showed them upstairs to Toby's bedroom, and hovered anxiously on the landing before offering them a drink. Lawrence accepted, probably, Rebecca suspected, to get her out of the way, and opened the door onto Toby's room.

'Tasteful décor,' he remarked, drily, as they surveyed their surroundings. The bedroom was plastered floor to ceiling with posters and photographs of nude and near-naked girls. Aside from this, it wasn't noticeably different from that of the average adolescent – the bed unmade, various items of clothing strewn across the floor, dirty mugs lined up along the windowsill. It was sparsely furnished with a narrow wardrobe, a battered chest of drawers and a desk, the last of which acted principally as a stand for a wide-screen television. This looked to be brand new, as did the DVD recorder that crouched on the chair pushed beneath the desktop, and Rebecca wondered whether Toby had paid for them himself.

'Nice TV,' she remarked, pointedly.

'Wouldn't mind one like that myself,' Lawrence replied, moving to open the top drawer. 'Do you want to take the wardrobe?'

Rebecca nodded in agreement, and reached to open the single door. 'Ah,' she stood back. 'That's that job done, then.'

Lawrence looked up from his search of the desk drawers. 'Don't tell me it's empty?'

'No Sir, not exactly,' Rebecca stepped aside to give him a clear view. Inside the wardrobe sat a large plastic vat, and the strong smell of yeast that was fast filling the room left little doubt as to what it contained.

'Ah,' Lawrence acknowledged, lifting his eyebrows. 'I wonder if it's warm enough in here for that? We always kept ours in the airing cupboard.'

'We?'

'Student days,' he replied, with a smile. 'Well, that at least narrows down the search.'

Rebecca nodded, crouching down to check underneath the bed and simultaneously lifting the duvet, which spilled over the edge of the mattress and down onto the floor, concealing two drawers in the base of the bed. Feeling a momentary rush of excitement, she was disappointed to discover that the contents of the drawers were merely a continuation of the bedroom walls – top-shelf magazines, lingerie and swimwear catalogues, and a limited selection of photographs and posters. With a sigh, she moved to close them.

'What's up?' Lawrence enquired.

'Just a bunch of girlie mags.'

'We want those,' he replied, not looking around from what he was doing. 'Bag them up.'

Rebecca frowned. 'What for?'

'We don't yet know whether what happened to Dayv was in any way related to Zoë's death – and Zoë was a model. I want to see whether she appears in any of Toby's magazines.'

'Oh, right, yes,' Rebecca agreed. 'Do you want me to go through them this afternoon?'

'Yes please. Ordinarily I would ask Jamie or Danny to help you, but given the subject matter –' he gave her a knowing look. 'Somehow I suspect you'll conduct a quicker and rather more reliable search.'

'True,' Rebecca smiled, neatly stacking the magazines and depositing them by the door. Returning to the bed, she dragged it a few inches away from the wall and peered down into the dim crack between the two. Against the rather busy carpet, it was difficult to ascertain how many of the darkened shapes were actual belongings, so, hoping there were no large spiders lurking just out of sight, she reached in and drew out the first handful of items that her fingers came into contact with.

140

Spreading them across the bed, the first to catch her attention was a black leather wallet. Her initial disappointment on finding that the wallet hadn't belonged to Dayv lifted with the realisation that it didn't belong to Toby either, and she leaned to see what else might be hidden behind the bed. Amongst fluff, odd socks, chewing gum wrappers and other odds and ends, she retrieved several more wallets and a purse, and it came as little surprise that one of the former was embossed with the initials D.W.R. A club membership card and an uncollected prescription – all that remained of the contents – confirmed that it had indeed belonged to Dayv Roberts. A quick examination of the other wallets established little; that they were stolen Rebecca had no doubt, but the names of their original owners were disappointingly unfamiliar.

'Sir?'

Lawrence turned.

'I've found Dayv's wallet.'

'Good work,' he straightened up. 'Anything much left inside?'

'Not a lot. But I don't think Toby had anything to do with Zoë's death.'

'No?'

'He's amassed five wallets and a purse – I'm guessing he's little more than a petty thief.'

'One who's now going to be up on GBH charges,' Lawrence observed. 'I'd be interested to know whether he did that much damage every time. Could you look into that this afternoon?'

'Sure.'

'Great,' Lawrence turned back to the job in hand. 'Let's keep going. We're not leaving until we've taken this room apart.'

Rebecca jumped as a balled up piece of paper hit her on the forehead and fell into her lap. She raised her eyes from the magazine in her hands to see Jamie leaning against Lawrence's office doorframe, a mug in one hand and a bored expression on his face.

'Hi Jay.'

'What are you up to?' He asked, advancing towards her.

'I'm looking for our murdered model.'

Jamie cast his eyes over the piles of magazines and catalogues stacked on the floor around her feet. 'Sifting through porn counts as work now, does it?' He bent to reach for one of the magazines. Rebecca swatted his hand away.

'Oh come on!' Jamie protested.

'Jay, please, I'm not in the mood for this. Don't you have work to be getting on with?'

'Boring work, yeah. How come you get all the good jobs?'

'You may find it difficult to comprehend, but this really doesn't feature in my top ten.'

'I'll do it for you,' Jamie offered.

'Forrester asked me not to delegate this one.'

'You're having me on!'

'No Jay, I'm quite serious and very busy. Ok?' Rebecca snapped, impatiently.

'Well if you're so busy, how come Forrester won't let anyone help you?' Jamie persisted.

'Oh, I don't know,' Rebecca responded, sarcastically. 'Perhaps he's concerned about the pages of potential evidence getting stuck together?'

Jamie didn't look amused. 'Funny,' he retorted.

'What are you supposed to be doing?'

'Paperwork. Boring boring.'

'Where did you get to on Saturday night?' Rebecca asked, suddenly realising she hadn't seen Jamie since.

'I got a better offer, if you know what I mean,' Jamie replied, with a meaningful lift of his eyebrows.

'Did you now. You might have told me, Jay. I spent ages looking for you.'

'Ah, but *then* you'd have had to lie to Forrester for me, and you'd have liked that even less.'

That, Rebecca had to admit to herself, was true. 'What did you tell him?'

'Oh, just that I lost track of you, so in the end I went home. I don't suppose he believed me, but there's not much he can do about it.'

'Well, I think the least you can do is fill me in on the details.'

'I got her first name, if that counts as details,' Jamie responded, offhandedly. 'This, however, looks far more interesting.' He tried again to take one of the magazines.

'*Don't!*' Rebecca exclaimed, seizing hold of his wrist. 'If you want to touch any of this, get some gloves on first.'

Jamie rolled his eyes. 'Where's the fun in that?'

'This isn't a joke! If you're not going to treat it seriously, then go and be bored somewhere else!'

'Jesus, calm down!'

'Then stop pissing about!'

Jamie pulled a face just as Leighton wandered into the room.

'Sorry – am I interrupting?'

'She's all yours, mate,' Jamie responded, starting towards the door. 'Be warned,' he added, as he passed Leighton. 'PMT alert.'

Leighton's eyebrows rose.

'I could have him for saying that,' Rebecca snapped, when Jamie had gone.

'Yeah, you could, but he knows you're too soft. Are you busy?'

'I am, but if you're here about work, rather than just to annoy me because you're bored, you can stay.'

'Why thank you.' Leighton bowed slightly, doffing an imaginary hat.

Rebecca couldn't help smiling. 'Forrester's looking for you.'

'Yeah, I know,' Leighton grinned. 'I figured I'd best come and find you before he caught up with me – that way I might escape another ticking off.'

'Where've you been?'

'Playing pool with Jon,' he replied, perching on the edge of Lawrence's desk and shunting the resident pencil holder and Post-it block backwards as he did so. 'Trying to salvage some vestige of self respect.'

'Thrashed you again, did he?'

'Yeah.'

'Bad luck.'

'D'you fancy letting me beat you sometime? Help restore the battered male ego and all that?'

'I get beaten at pool quite enough by Elliot, thanks.'

'Is he any good?'

Rebecca nodded. 'Elliot's spent a disproportionate amount of the last ten years hanging around bars and clubs. Practise makes perfect, and he's had plenty of practise.'

'Sounds like Tom,' Leighton remarked. 'He once worked out how to override the payment system on the table at the local community centre so that we could play for free.'

Rebecca smiled. She had heard many tales of Leighton and his elder brother's exploits as teenagers, but little that had happened more recently. In fact, further than that he lived in Wakefield, she realised, she knew next to nothing about Tom. With this in mind, she asked, 'What's he doing now?'

'Time,' Leighton replied, shortly, extracting a rather crumpled piece of paper from his jeans pocket and flattening it out.

Rebecca started to laugh, then stopped short, realising from Leighton's expression that he wasn't joking. 'Seriously?'

He nodded.

'I'm sorry,' she offered, after a moment. 'That can't be easy.'

Leighton shrugged. 'I'm used to it. He's been in and out since I was fifteen.'

'Fifteen?' Rebecca exclaimed. 'Wow. That must've been tough.'

'I dunno. I think it probably did me a favour. If he hadn't gone down when he did I'd probably be in there with him. It wasn't as if I was sitting quietly at home doing my school work while he was out twocking cars and pillaging off licences. That I never got caught was more luck than judgement.'

Rebecca didn't know how to respond. There was a pause before Leighton added, 'It's not something I'm proud of. But I can't pretend it didn't happen.' He held up the piece of paper in his hand. 'Anyway, I came to say that we've a cigarette butt with salivary traces to match your killer.'

Rebecca sat forwards. 'Really? What brand?'

'Unfortunately I don't know. It's been smoked right down to the stub.'

'Oh.' Rebecca felt disappointed.

'All I can tell you is that the stub is white. I don't know if that helps at all.'

'I –' Rebecca stopped as Lawrence appeared in the doorway.

'Dr Campbell. I wondered where you'd got to.'

'Leighton's come bearing DNA results,' Rebecca offered, hoping to defuse her superior's irritation.

'At last,' Lawrence remarked, observing Leighton's position on the edge of his desk with visible disapproval. 'So. What've we got?'

'No hit on the database, I'm afraid, but I have succeeded in matching a cigarette butt to the killer. Although, as I was just saying to Becks, the only additional information I can give you is that the stub is white.'

Lawrence's eyebrows rose. 'Ah. Now, as I recall, Lucian smokes Berkeley menthols, which have a white tip.'

'So do duty free Marlboro lights,' Leighton observed. 'Or whatever they're called now they're not allowed to use *light* in case someone is deluded enough to think it makes them healthy.'

'So we could be looking for somebody who's been out of the country recently,' Lawrence surmised. 'Did you find any other white cigarette butts in the garden?'

'Nope.' Leighton pushed himself off from the desk. 'Quite a few Silk Cut – those were Zoë's – plus a couple of others. None of them matched.'

'Has anyone checked the garden again?' Lawrence asked.

Leighton looked put out. 'We did a damn good job the first time.'

'I'm not disputing that, but it's still possible you might have missed something – or that the killer has since returned to the scene.'

Leighton sounded irked as he said, 'Ok, ok, I'll have someone take another look.' He turned for the door. 'I'll give you a call if anything turns up. Otherwise I'll see you tomorrow.'

'Before you go, did you check whether Zoë's killer was related to her?'

'I did, and he wasn't,' Leighton replied, succinctly. 'But bear in mind the possibility of infidelity means I can only guarantee no relationship as far as the maternal line goes.'

Lawrence nodded. 'Understood. Thank you.'

Leighton disappeared through the doorway and Lawrence looked to Rebecca. 'Right. I think we need to have another chat with Lucian. Have you found anything of interest in these?' He indicated the stack of magazines.

'Not yet.'

'We'll worry about the rest of them tomorrow. Let's go.'

Gavin Mitchell didn't even try to disguise his displeasure at finding Lawrence and Rebecca on his doorstep, presumably because he expected further questions on the subject of his whereabouts at the time of his daughter's death.

'We're looking for Lucian,' Lawrence began. 'He isn't home – have you seen him at all?'

Gavin nodded, stepping back from the doorway to allow them to enter. 'He's here.'

'Here?' Lawrence exclaimed, surprised that he would be after all Christia had said that morning.

145

'I brought him home from the hospital a little while ago – his mother passed away earlier today. I don't know whether he's really up to answering questions at the moment.'

'I see.' Lawrence paused for a moment's thought. 'Do you think we might see him for just a few minutes?'

'I don't suppose I can stop you,' Gavin responded, wearily, turning towards the living room. Pushing the door open, he held it for Lawrence and Rebecca before closing it behind them.

Lucian was sitting on the sofa, his face white and expression rather vacant. He didn't react to their arrival, staring blankly at the coffee table directly ahead of him.

'Lucian?' Lawrence perched on a chair near where he sat.

'Yuh?' He didn't move.

'Do you think you're up to answering a few questions for us?'

Lucian shrugged.

'I'm sorry we have to put you through this now. If you don't feel you can cope –'

'Just get it over with.'

'All right.' Lawrence paused. 'Christia came to see me this morning. She seems to think you might have been involved with Zoë.'

'Oh,' came the empty response.

'Lucian, do you understand what I'm saying?'

'I didn't hurt her.'

'Who?'

'Zoë. I never hurt her.' Lucian shook his head, looking dazed.

'Perhaps you could answer the original question.'

'What?'

Lawrence sighed, feeling unreasonably impatient. 'How about you just tell us the truth?' He suggested. 'I doubt there's much we don't already know.'

Lucian paled further. '*What?*' He whispered, looking directly at Lawrence in something close to horror. He reached for the cigarettes on the table, his hands shaking violently. The first match he struck snapped, and he dropped the box to the floor. Bowing his head, he raised a hand to his forehead, closing his eyes.

Rebecca retrieved the matches and provided a flame for him. He gulped the smoke in relief.

At length, Lawrence tried again. 'Lucian?'

'I can't,' he whispered, his voice breaking. 'I *can't!*'

'Did you have a fling with Zoë?'

146

Lucian shook his head. 'No. I love Chris. She's all I have left and –' he took another pull on the cigarette, tears starting to run down his cheeks. 'And I'm going to lose her!' He coughed.

'Why? Because of what happened to Zoë?'

Lucian closed his eyes, shaking his head again.

'Where were you on Wednesday night?'

'I didn't! I wasn't!'

'Didn't what?'

'I didn't see Zoë! I didn't – even if – if I had – I –' Lucian shuddered, then gasped, and for a moment Lawrence thought he was about to vomit. 'I –' he stopped, roughly drying his tears with the back of his hand. 'I – I was – I –'

'Calm down,' Rebecca said, gently. 'Just tell us what you were doing.'

'Nothing,' he sniffed. 'I was at home. Alone.'

'Are you sure?'

'I couldn't have raped Zoë! I *couldn't*! Now even – with Chris – I can't – I can't –' he broke off, shaking his head.

'Why not?' Lawrence persisted.

Lucian closed his eyes, bowing his head. His words, when they came, were barely audible. 'She's –' he paused. 'She's my *sister*.' Then, more mouthed than spoken, 'And she's pregnant.'

Eleven

Some moments passed before Lucian found the courage to look up. When he did, his eyes were wet. He was shaking violently.

'How long have you known?' Lawrence asked.

'Since Wednesday.'

'How did you find out?'

'I –' Lucian took a desperate gulp on the cigarette. 'I asked – Mum – about –' he swallowed hard, bowing his head again. 'I wanted to know. About my father.'

'Gavin Mitchell,' Lawrence offered, as much to clarify the situation for himself as anything else.

Lucian nodded.

'Does he know?'

'I don't know. He's never said.'

'Did your mother not know about your relationship with Christia?'

'Not really. She knew I had a girlfriend, but –' he shrugged weakly.

'Given that you're about the same age as Christia and Zoë, I'm guessing she and Gavin had an affair?'

'Yuh.'

'Do you have any idea whether they remained in contact?'

Lucian shrugged again. 'Mum never said.'

'Did you tell her that you already knew Gavin?'

'No.' Lucian drew a deep, unsteady breath.

Lawrence gave him a few moments to gather his thoughts before saying, 'Is that why you didn't want to see Christia on Wednesday night?'

'Yuh,' Lucian whispered. 'I just couldn't face her. I didn't know what to do.'

'Did you know about her pregnancy at that point?'

Lucian blinked, and tears ran from his eyes. 'No,' he managed, pursing his lips.

'When did you find out about that?'

'Yesterday.' He shuddered, reaching to stub out his cigarette. 'I –' he swallowed. 'I didn't know what to say. It was so confusing.

Chris jumped to all sorts of conclusions – I don't even know what she thinks now. She hasn't spoken to me since.'

'You haven't told her, then?'

Lucian shook his head, closing his eyes. 'How could I?' He asked, brokenly. 'I just – had – to sit there – watching her cry – and – I – I –' he coughed. 'I want-ed to – to –' he stopped, his breathing growing rather convulsive. As he began gasping and raised a hand to his chest, Lawrence looked to Rebecca in some concern. 'I think it might be a good idea for you to call Gavin.'

Rebecca nodded, making for the door.

Gavin was hovering in the kitchen, clearly very uneasy. He looked up as Rebecca approached the doorway.

'Lucian's quite upset – we're a bit worried about him –'

Gavin was halfway across the hallway before Rebecca had time to finish, and she followed him back to the living room. He went straight to Lucian, joining him on the sofa.

'Ok,' he rested a hand on the boy's shoulder. 'It's all right, Luke, calm down.'

Lucian tried to speak but didn't manage to get the words out.

'Come on, try to breathe slowly.' Gavin turned to Lawrence. 'Could you wait outside, please?'

'Of course.' Lawrence stood, and he and Rebecca retreated to the hallway. Rebecca perched at the foot of the staircase, looking up at her superior with her eyebrows raised.

'What a mess,' Lawrence remarked.

'Poor kid. What a time to find out,' Rebecca replied, her voice lowered.

'It never rains, does it?'

'If Gavin knows, it might explain why he's been so unhelpful,' Rebecca suggested.

'He knows,' Lawrence responded, decidedly. 'And as far as Zoë goes, I think we're more or less back at square one. I'm fairly sure I know exactly where Gavin was on Thursday morning.'

Several minutes elapsed before the living room door opened and Gavin reappeared. Closing the door behind himself, he turned to Lawrence and Rebecca.

'I can't let you ask him anything else tonight – he's really not up to it. You might be able to finish up in the morning, but I doubt he'll be well enough.'

Lawrence nodded. 'I understand that.'

'Great. Well, if you don't mind, I'd like to find him a sedative before he works himself into any more of a state, so if you –'

'We'd like a word with you before we go, actually.'

Gavin frowned. 'It'll have to be quick – I don't want to leave him for long.'

'It won't take a minute,' Lawrence assured him. 'Is there somewhere we can talk?'

'Um – ok – come through to the dining room.' Gavin turned and walked to a door at the far end of the hallway. Opening it, he flicked on the light, holding the door for Rebecca and Lawrence before closing it behind them.

'Will Lucian be staying here tonight?' Lawrence enquired.

'He's in no state to be going home alone, is he?'

'No,' Lawrence agreed. 'Besides, I imagine you feel some responsibility towards him.'

Gavin frowned. 'What's that supposed to mean?'

'You weren't lying when you told me your whereabouts at the time of Zoë's death, were you? You *did* visit an old mistress. Lucian's mother, to be precise.'

Gavin closed his eyes momentarily. 'Yes,' he admitted, at length. 'She asked if I'd contact him after her death – she was afraid he wouldn't be able to cope alone.' He paused before finishing, 'She was probably right.'

'What was your response to that?'

'How many responses are there that you can give to someone with a terminal illness?'

'I take it you didn't tell her that you already knew your son.'

'Of course not.'

'Did she mention that she'd given your name to Lucian?'

Gavin stared at Lawrence. 'She *what*?' He managed, at length, sinking down onto a chair. 'Oh good grief.'

'Does your wife know?'

'She knows I have a son, but that's all.'

'Have you known all along?'

Gavin sighed heavily. 'Yes,' he nodded. 'I even have a photograph – Maria sent it to me shortly after he was born –' he cast his eyes down. 'If he and Chris hadn't become so involved, it wouldn't have been a problem. I always wanted contact with him, but Carrina threatened to leave me if she found out that I'd seen anything more of Maria, and at the time –' he shrugged. 'Zoë and Chris had just come along – I wasn't going to risk losing them.' He paused. 'And now I have a horrible feeling I'm going to lose everything.'

The progress of the red 23° marker up the shaft of the Galileo thermometer was so gradual as to be imperceptible, but Daniel Freeman was convinced it had moved during the previous twenty-five minutes. He had spent that time watching it intently, a welcome alternative to the report on which he couldn't concentrate and a distraction from the emotional tumult behind his inability to focus.

It was five to eight, the report wasn't due for ten days, and, since he had nothing more pressing to do, Daniel would ordinarily have been home by now. As it was, he was still seated at his desk, absently gnawing the lid of a new biro and trying to remember why it was that the markers rose as the temperature fell. His elder brother, a lecturer in thermodynamics at Southampton University, had explained the theory behind it when he gave Daniel the thermometer the previous Christmas, but at the time Daniel had been closer to drunk than sober, and had taken little on board. Jessica had hated it, which was why it had come to be on his desk at work, where, until recently, it had been little more than a novelty. Now it was one of the many excuses Daniel had found, consciously or subconsciously, to put off going home – and to put off facing Jessica.

He sighed, tossing the pen onto the desk and leaning back in his chair, eyes still fixed on the glass ball that hovered two-thirds of the way up the tube. He had devoted most of the afternoon to analysing his crumbling relationship with Jessica, with whom he had been cohabiting for over four years, and had spent the majority of that time trying to convince himself that he wasn't primarily responsible for the relationship's demise.

He had never wanted children. Jessica had always known that, which was why she hadn't told him when she came off the pill. Within six months, she had fallen pregnant. Initially, he had been stunned and the whole situation had seemed unreal. When he had learned of her deception, his disbelief had turned first to shock, then to anger, and the subsequent weeks of rows, threats, silences and bitter words had culminated in Jessica's terminating the pregnancy. The news had been an incredible relief to Daniel at first, and he had given little thought to what the long-term implications might be for Jessica and their relationship. Looking back, he wondered how he could have been so naive, but at the time he had felt hopelessly trapped, and hadn't approached the situation with much objectivity. Now he was beginning to face up to reality, and trying to acknowledge that that reality was a future without Jessica.

'Dan?'

The voice made him jump, and he looked around from the thermometer. Rebecca Palmer, a colleague who had become a friend in his fifteen months at Scotland Yard, was standing in front of the desk that backed onto his own.

'Hi. You're here late,' he greeted, unimaginatively.

'So are you, given that you don't appear to be doing anything,' Rebecca replied, walking around his desk and sitting in the chair at her own before swivelling it through ninety degrees to face him.

'Yeah,' Daniel shrugged, unable to think of a realistic lie to cover his reluctance to go home.

To his relief, Rebecca didn't question him. Instead, she offered him a new diversion. 'Fancy a pint?'

'Don't you have to get back?'

'Elliot's away.'

Daniel nodded. He had known that, he realised; he'd seen the tour dates in the crumpled copy of the *NME* that had been knocking around her desk.

'Come on,' Rebecca smiled. 'My treat.'

On their arrival, the pub had appeared almost deserted, and the heat at the bar had been approaching unbearable. Rebecca and Daniel had headed straight for the beer garden and found a quiet table away from the cluster of patrons standing in and around the back door. Rebecca took a long drink, suddenly realising how tired she felt.

'Are you happy?' Daniel asked at length. 'You and Elliot, I mean.'

'Mostly.'

'So not entirely.'

Rebecca considered her response carefully. 'I do love him. It's just –' she paused. 'It's difficult trying to balance two very different lifestyles, and –' she sighed. 'Recently, I've barely seen him.'

'You must miss him.'

'I do miss him when he's away – I'd be worried if I didn't – but I don't think the problem lies with his absence. I think it's more that we don't have enough time together in between.'

Daniel frowned. 'Meaning what?'

'He'll be away three or four weeks, and I'll then only see him for a couple of days before he's off again. With such finite periods of time together, we tend to try too hard to make everything perfect. It doesn't feel so –' Rebecca frowned. 'What's the word I'm looking for?'

'Natural?'

Rebecca shook her head. 'Spontaneous,' she said, suddenly, her frown lifting. 'Even if we've not planned anything – supposedly impromptu acts still wind up seeming contrived. Does that make sense?'

'I think so.'

Rebecca didn't respond, reaching for her beer.

'Can I ask you something?' Daniel enquired, as she took a mouthful.

'You can ask.'

'How on earth did you and he get together in the first place?' When Rebecca didn't immediately respond, Daniel added, 'I'm just curious. I can't help wondering what you have in common.'

Rebecca shrugged. 'Our lives weren't quite so different when we met. The band wasn't much more than a pipe dream in those days. Or at least that's what it seemed like to me. Back then Elliot was working six days a week and playing the odd gig in his spare time. He's put a phenomenal amount of work into getting the band to where it is now.'

'What was he doing before?'

'Sound engineering. He had a job at a studio in Docklands.'

Daniel looked surprised.

'I met him at an aftershow party, which isn't as glamorous as it sounds. It was for Vicious Circle, but nobody had heard of them then, either, and it was in the back room of a pub. My mate had a crush on the drummer and wouldn't go by herself, so she dragged me along. Elliot had been working the sound desk during the gig – as a favour, I later found out – and I just assumed he was a member of the band's crew. He was charming and entertaining, so when he asked for my number I gave it to him. I didn't think he was actually going to call.' She smiled. 'In fact, he didn't – he turned up outside the office four days later because he'd lost the number.'

'He must have been pretty taken with you to stand around outside just waiting for you to show up.'

'I didn't know quite what to make of it. On the one hand, I felt flattered – but on the other I wondered whether he was going to turn out to be some weird stalker type.'

Daniel smiled. After a moment, he said, 'Do you not find it difficult fitting into his world?'

'Yes,' Rebecca admitted. 'I know it's not ideal. A lot of his friends have issues with what I do, and I often wish our lives weren't so different, but there's not a lot I can do about it. You don't choose who you fall in love with.'

'I guess not.'

'Why do you ask, anyway? Are you and Jess not happy?'

Daniel dropped his eyes to the tabletop. 'It's all going wrong, and I don't know how to stop it,' he said, with a heavy sigh.

'What do you mean?'

'These days we don't even seem to need a *reason* to have a row. I don't know. It isn't working, and I came to the conclusion this afternoon that we're both just waiting for the other to find the guts to end it.'

'I'm sorry.'

Daniel shrugged. 'I sometimes think the only reason we're still together at all is because we live in the same house. It was never going to work long term. Jess loves kids, and I hate them. There's no way I could even contemplate having children.'

'Is that what she wants?'

'Yeah.'

'Is that the only problem?'

Daniel shook his head. 'I don't know. Sometimes you reach a point where you can't see the relationship going any further, and you either accept it and move on or you just watch it slowly falling apart. I think I've been trying to ignore that for months now. We've been together five years, and I've never seriously considered asking her to marry me.' He reached for his drink. 'How long had you been with Elliot before he proposed?'

'Six weeks.'

'Six *weeks*?'

'I didn't say yes!'

'Was he serious?'

154

Rebecca nodded. 'According to Ian, Elliot announced that he wanted to marry me within a week of meeting me.'

'Wow.'

'He can be rather impulsive.'

'He was right, though, wasn't he?' Daniel rested his elbows on the table before adding, rather sadly, 'We weren't.'

'What do you mean?'

'We'd not been together long, the lease was up on Jess's flat and my brother was fed up with putting me up in his spare room, so we decided to move in together. In retrospect, that was huge mistake. Now I have no idea what to do.'

'It sounds to me like you've already made your decision, Dan,' Rebecca responded, gently. 'Now you're just delaying the inevitable.'

'Where's my welcome committee?' Lawrence called, closing the front door behind himself and hanging his jacket over the baluster at the foot of the staircase.

'Daddy!' Elise came tumbling down the stairs. 'Daddy, Mummy said you'd help me with my castle! Can you come?'

'What castle?'

'The one Uncle Jethro gave me for my birthday,' Elise replied, impatiently, as if he ought not to have needed to ask.

'Ah. Yes.' Lawrence nodded, wondering how he might postpone the task. The model castle was to be assembled entirely from match sticks, minus their inflammable heads, and served, in Lawrence's opinion, to highlight the fact that his brother-in-law did not have children.

'*Now* Daddy!' Elise dictated, taking his hand and pulling him up the stairs.

Reluctantly, Lawrence followed.

Arriving in Elise's bedroom doorway, he regarded the sticky mess of newspaper, match sticks and glue from a distance. 'I hope that isn't today's paper.'

'No,' Elise frowned, looking indignant.

'Small mercies,' Lawrence muttered, unbuttoning his cuffs and rolling his shirt sleeves up to his elbows. 'All right, what's the problem?'

'I can't get this bit to attach *here*,' Elise indicated two pieces of card, both neatly covered with a layer of match sticks. The pieces had small tabs down each side, labelled with various letters indicating to which other sections they ought to be joined.

'Ok,' Lawrence took the two pieces and lifted them to eye level. As he did so, the top sheets of paper rose from the table and swung precariously close to his tie. Catching the errant pages, Lawrence carefully separated them from the section of the model they'd attached themselves to, then folded them to contain the glue before balling the paper up and aiming it at Elise's rubbish bin. This done, he returned his attention to the model.

'Sweetheart, I don't think these two pieces go together at all.' He set them down on the clean paper now blanketing the table. 'You've got this one upside down. This is an M, not a W.'

Elise leaned in to look, her expression perplexed. 'Oh,' she acknowledged, after a moment.

'I think you might –' Lawrence stopped short as a newspaper headline caught his eye. *Dancer's mutilated body 'like something from a horror film'.* The paper was dated almost a year previously, although Lawrence remembered something of the case since the woman in question had been the wife of Derek Winterton, a Premier-league football player. Scanning the article, the similarities between the late Mrs Winterton's death and that of Zoë Mitchell struck him immediately, and he suspected that might be no coincidence. Taking the page and replacing Elise's model on the one that followed, he folded the article carefully and slipped it into his shirt pocket. He wondered whether the case had ever been solved. If not, an examination of the basic facts might prove very interesting.

It was nearly eleven by the time Rebecca arrived back in Highgate to find that the almost unbearable humidity had finally culminated in another storm. Cursing the loss of her umbrella, she hurried home from the tube station, keeping well away from the edge of the pavement lest a passing car should plough through the already flooded gutter. Turning into the street she and Elliot called home, she searched her handbag for the front door keys. For a moment she thought she might have lost them, but then located them in a side pocket, wedged beneath a compact and a pair of nail clippers. Elliot had lost his keys some weeks earlier, and the inconvenience of changing the locks – despite Elliot having done the job himself – was something she could do without a second time. Stepping carefully up to the front door of the ground floor flat, she let herself in, closing the door behind herself in relief.

'Hell,' she muttered, inspecting her drenched silk blouse and wondering whether it would ever be wearable again. Supposing that the best thing for it was probably to hang it up, she headed straight for the bedroom to change. She reached for the door handle, but as her fingers made contact it moved away from her, as if of its own accord, and the door swung open. Rebecca screamed.

Twelve

'Elliot!' Rebecca exclaimed, raising a hand to her chest. 'You scared the life out of me!'

'Sorry,' Elliot replied, sheepishly, leaning to kiss her.

'God, you gave me such a fright!' Rebecca embraced him.

'Yeah, well, you made me jump and all with that scream.'

'What are you doing here?' She asked, as she released him.

'We quit the tour,' Elliot shrugged, rather despondently.

'Why? What happened? You didn't have a fight with Jeff, did you?'

Elliot didn't reply, he simply shrugged again and directed his gaze at the floor.

'Oh Elliot –'

'I told him he was sacked.' Elliot coughed, rubbing his eyes. Rebecca guessed he had been asleep prior to her arrival home.

'Can you *do* that?'

'I dunno.'

'Surely that's a matter for the record company.'

Elliot shrugged a third time.

'Have you spoken to anybody there since?'

'No.'

'Do you not think you ought to?'

'They can call me,' Elliot responded, sullenly.

'It might be better if you made the first move, Elliot.'

'Jeff's an arsehole.'

'That's as may be, but I think it's a little early to start playing the temperamental artist part, don't you? Your career is just getting started, and you're risking throwing it all away just to make a point!'

Elliot glared at her. 'I do apologise,' he snapped. 'Obviously I'm just supposed to stand around and tolerate gross insensitivity and put my career ahead of my mate's feelings!'

'What?'

'Ian's dad had a massive heart attack – last night – they still don't know if he's going to make it, and Jeff told him that wasn't a good enough reason to abandon the tour –' Elliot pulled his

Marlboros from his pocket. 'That was about the point that I lost it with him,' he sighed. 'Do you think that was so unreasonable?'

'No.' Rebecca reached for his free hand. 'I think a lot of people would have done the same.'

'I did call and leave a voicemail, but I guess you didn't get it.'

'It keeps dying on me – I think it needs a new battery.'

'You might as well just get a new phone,' Elliot observed, turning towards the living room and making for the sofa.

'Probably.'

Elliot dropped onto the sofa, tossing his cigarettes onto the coffee table without taking one.

'How's Ian?' Rebecca asked, sitting beside him.

'Not so great,' Elliot coughed, relaxing back against the cushions.

'And how are you?'

Elliot frowned. 'Meaning what?'

'Just that. How are you?'

'Fine,' Elliot replied guardedly, still frowning. 'Shouldn't I be?'

'There's no need to be so defensive. It wasn't a loaded question.'

'I'm not being defensive,' Elliot snapped, reaching for his cigarettes and fishing one out of the packet. Lighting up, he began coughing.

'You sound like you have a cold.'

'It's nothing,' Elliot muttered. After a moment he continued, Rebecca guessed to change the subject, with, 'How's work?'

'Until this afternoon we thought we were getting somewhere, but it looks like we've been heading in completely the wrong direction. I'm not sure where we're going to go from here.'

'I know the feeling,' Elliot remarked, returning the cigarette to his lips, which immediately set him off coughing again. He raised a hand to rub his chest and, seeing the look on Rebecca's face said, 'Please don't.'

'I'm worried about you. You spent half of last winter on antibiotics, and between the smoking and the touring I'm afraid you're going to wind up seriously ill.'

'What the hell is that supposed to mean? You think I'm taking drugs as well?'

'No, that's not what I meant at all.'

'Right,' Elliot snapped, turning away.

'Elliot, look at yourself! You're ill, you've lost weight, you look exhausted – and you've barely been away three weeks! What –'

'Oh, well, obviously I must be on something then! Why do you have to think the worst of me just because I come home with a cold?'

'I'm not accusing you of anything! If you hadn't been so defensive, I wouldn't have given the matter much thought! As it is, I find myself wondering why you're getting so hot and bothered when all I said was that I was worried about you smoking!'

'That wasn't all you said!' Elliot returned. 'You –' he broke off, coughing. It was some time before he managed to stop, and he leaned back against the sofa, closing his eyes. When he spoke again, it was in a very different tone. 'I'm sorry.' He drew a careful deep breath. 'I've had a really lousy day. I know I shouldn't take it out on you.'

'I'm not trying to give you a hard time.'

'I know. I just – I just feel like –' he stopped, shaking his head.

'Go on,' Rebecca encouraged.

'I feel like everything I do is under scrutiny. Because of your career. I'm terrified of losing you, but I can't help thinking that one day it's going to happen.'

'Why?'

Elliot looked down. 'I don't know,' he answered, miserably. 'It just seems inevitable.'

'If you think like that you're never going to be happy,' Rebecca wrapped her arms around him. 'I don't want you to feel under pressure all the time, and I'm sorry if I've made you feel like that. I'm just concerned for you. I don't want to see you making yourself ill simply because you don't take good care of yourself on tour. And because you smoke so much.'

'I can't.'

'You can't what?'

'I can't quit smoking. Please don't ask that of me.'

'But if you keep on like this –'

'Yes, I know, I will have chronic bronchitis before I am thirty-five, thanks very much for the reminder!'

Rebecca frowned. 'What on earth makes you say that?'

Elliot closed his eyes momentarily. 'That's what the doctor told me last year.'

'Oh Elliot,' Rebecca sighed.

'I'm sorry,' he repeated with a cough. 'I'm paranoid and I misinterpret how much meaning there is in some of what you say. The stupid thing is, half the time I know I'm doing it. I don't know what's wrong with me.'

Rebecca reached to take his hand. 'You're just tired.'

Elliot nodded.

'Can I get you anything?'

'No. I'm ok.' Several seconds passed before he added, quietly, 'Thanks. For caring, I mean.'

'Of course I care. I love you.'

His expression told her just how much that meant to him. Rebecca squeezed his fingers, wondering what it must feel like when there was only one person in your world from whom to hear those words. Certainly Elliot had numerous friends, some of them very close to him, but when it came down to it, she was the nearest he had in terms of a family. The reasons why he no longer communicated with his parents he had never explained; probably, Rebecca suspected, because he found it too painful to talk about. What she did know was that she couldn't even begin to imagine life without her mother and father, her twin sister or cheeky younger brother, and, from that point of view, could understand why at times Elliot seemed so terribly insecure. She just hoped that one day he might be able to bring himself to tell her what had happened.

'Morning,' Rebecca greeted, with a smile, as she walked in through Lawrence's open office door at five to nine on Tuesday.

'You look very cheerful,' he observed. 'I'm sure I remember you saying that Tuesday was the worst day of the week.'

'Not when it starts with pancakes in bed.'

'Pancakes?'

'Elliot came home early.'

'Ah,' Lawrence nodded, with a lift of his eyebrows. 'That must have been a nice surprise.'

'He scared the life out of me, actually. He'd been asleep before I arrived home, and he heard me come in – when the bedroom door opened I nearly had a heart attack.'

'Why's he home early?'

'Ian's dad's seriously ill.' Rebecca sat beside the desk, adding, 'You look tired.'

'I couldn't sleep – too much going on up here,' he indicated his head. 'Have a read of that,' he handed her the sheet of newspaper he had come across the previous evening. 'If we can't find a link between this girl and Zoë, I think we may not be looking for somebody with motive at all. I think we're looking at a serial killer. Or someone with the potential to become one.'

'Crumbs,' Rebecca raised her eyebrows. She scanned the article quickly before asking, 'Where did you find this?'

'My garage,' Lawrence admitted, sheepishly.

'Your garage? Have you seen the date on here?'

'Yes, yes, I know – I need to clear it out. But that aside, I made some enquires, and this girl looks to have died in almost identical circumstances to Zoë.' Lawrence handed Rebecca a page of handwritten notes. 'I spoke to Leighton last night, and he managed to get hold of the relevant crime scene and postmortem reports. Unfortunately there isn't a DNA match, but on balance he agrees we're most likely dealing with the same perpetrator. I've contacted Derek Winterton, and we're going to head up to Liverpool to visit him this morning.'

'Liverpool?'

'That's who he plays for these days.'

'Is he a suspect?'

'No,' Lawrence reached for a pen. 'He was out of the country at the time of his wife's death, playing football in Germany. He found the body on his return.'

Rebecca made no further comment, looking back to Lawrence's notes.

'Suppose –' she stopped short.

'Suppose what?'

'I was just thinking. If the killer mutilated the bodies prior to death, is it not possible that on another occasion he might have launched a similar attack without, for some reason, managing to complete the job? Either because he was disturbed, or didn't realise his victim was still alive?'

'You thought of that too.'

'Did you sift through any files other than homicide last night?'

'I didn't have time – it was almost nine when I first found the article. Katie just about killed *me* when I turned around to come back here after barely five minutes at home. I had to promise not to be long.'

'So under the thumb,' Rebecca teased, shaking her head slightly.

'We'll have a hunt through the system this afternoon – see what else we can come up with,' Lawrence pushed his chair back from the desk and stood up. 'But first stop, Liverpool.'

* * * * *

Derek Winterton's build was much as Rebecca had expected of a professional footballer. Tall, athletic and broad-shouldered, he would have been indistinguishable from many of his peers had his thick black hair not fallen almost halfway to his waist. He was undeniably handsome, with a firm jaw and olive skin, which, combined with his dark eyes and hair, indicated that he was of Mediterranean or Hispanic descent. Rebecca guessed he was probably a favourite with the female fans, and wondered whether she might have recognised him had he been wearing his football strip rather than a t-shirt and jeans, quickly concluding that it was unlikely. Elliot was far more considerate of her dislike of football than some of her previous boyfriends had been, and rarely insisted on watching it when she was around. As a result, Rebecca suspected the only Premier-League players she would stand a chance of picking out of a line-up were those whose wives featured regularly in women's magazines.

Derek showed them straight through to the kitchen of his sizeable detached house before asking whether he could get either of them a drink.

Rebecca accepted gratefully, thirsty after the long drive.

'Coffee, tea, juice?'

'Coffee, thanks,' Rebecca replied, turning to look out of the window at the extensive garden to the rear of the house.

'Same for me, please,' Lawrence nodded as Derek moved to fill the kettle.

'Have a seat,' he gestured towards the kitchen table. Rebecca and Lawrence sat, and Rebecca opened her notebook to a clean page. Derek flicked the switch on the kettle, turning to face them. 'You wanted to ask me about Letty.'

'Yes,' Lawrence confirmed. 'I'm sorry to put you through talking about it all over again, but we're investigating the death of a young woman in London, and it's possible the two cases are connected.'

Derek nodded, but didn't immediately respond. At length, he said, 'What do you want to know?'

'I understand that when you found your wife's body, there was no sign of forced entry to the flat,' Lawrence rested his forearms on the table, linking his fingers together. 'Do you think she might have granted her killer access?'

'No.'

'You sound very sure about that.'

'Letty never let anybody she didn't know into the flat. If we needed work done on the place and she hadn't met the workman before, I had to stay home.'

Lawrence raised his eyebrows. 'Why?'

'Before she left home she was being harassed by her ex – she moved down to London to get away from him, but after we met she was concerned my public profile might make it possible for him to track her down again.'

'If she wouldn't have let someone she didn't know in, there's a good chance she knew her killer,' Lawrence observed.

'You *mean* there's a chance she was having an affair,' Derek assumed, sounding nettled.

'Do you think she was?'

'No, I don't, and I resent the way people always imply she was!'

Lawrence didn't comment, opting instead to change direction. 'Can you think of any way an intruder might have entered the flat without her knowledge?'

'He came in the front door,' Derek turned as the kettle came to the boil, reaching to take two mugs from the mug tree on the windowsill.

'How can you be so sure?'

'The week after she was –' Derek stopped. 'After she died. Somebody posted the keys back.'

'The *keys?*' Lawrence exclaimed.

'I thought you'd have known that already.'

'No, I'm afraid that information wasn't on file. Presumably you notified the police?'

'Yes. They thought Letty must have given whoever it was a set, which only fuelled their conviction that she was cheating on me.'

'Were you missing any sets of keys after her death?'

Derek shook his head. 'I honestly don't know,' he admitted. 'Letty had loads of copies made – her parents and brother had keys, as did the cleaning lady – and we had several sets in the flat. I don't even know how many we had in the first place.'

Lawrence nodded. 'How long had you been living in the flat when she died?'

'A couple of months. We hadn't even finished decorating.'

'Did you have the locks changed after you moved in?'

'Yes. It was practically the first thing Letty did.'

'And do you have any idea how somebody might have come by a set of keys other than directly from Letty or one of the other key holders?'

'I think somebody probably took her keys from her bag at work, had copies made and then returned them before she had a chance to notice they were missing.'

'Where did she work?'

'Several places. She was a dancer – she worked at two or three different clubs around the West End.' Derek paused, then added, in case there was any doubt, 'She didn't do anything else. She just danced.'

'Do you know whether the police examined the keys or the envelope used to return them?'

'They said there were no prints on the keys and that the envelope had been sealed using a sponge – but after it had been through the post and I'd opened it they couldn't ascertain much else.' Derek bowed his head. 'I just wish I'd taken Letty with me to Germany. Then maybe she'd still be here.'

'It would make life so much easier if people did their jobs properly,' Lawrence grumbled as he pulled his car away from the kerb. 'There was nothing on file about the keys being returned *or* the ex-boyfriend. Who knows whether either was even followed up!'

'I'll call Jamie to see whether he can look into that for us,' Rebecca offered. 'But as far as the keys go, Lars' letters to Zoë were also sealed using – well, maybe not a sponge, but something along those lines.'

'Yes. And, by all accounts, Lars spends a considerable amount of his time hanging around in clubs all over the West End. It might well be worth paying him another visit.'

'How about Zoë's flat?'

'What about it?'

'Is it worth going back to see if there's been any post?'

'Yes, it probably is. Can you take care of that this afternoon?'

'Sure,' Rebecca agreed. 'Are we going straight back to London, then?'

'Where else would we be going?'

'I thought we might be taking in Leicester on the way back.'

'Why Leicester?'

'That's where Letty's parents are. They might be able to give us some information about her ex. Even if they never met him I'm sure Letty would have had a few photos of him.'

'How do you know her parents live in Leicester?'

'It says so in your newspaper article.'

'Does it?'

'Yes.'

Lawrence raised his eyebrows. 'I'm glad one of us is awake. Well done, Becky. Next stop, Leicester.'

Disappointingly, Rebecca and Lawrence turned up little in Leicester, and there had been no mail of any interest delivered to Zoë's flat, either. It was late afternoon by the time they arrived back at Scotland Yard, and many of their colleagues were on the point of leaving for the day. Rebecca and Lawrence, meanwhile, sat down to repeat and extend the search that Lawrence had begun the night before, and, after three hours trawling the database, Rebecca had nothing to show for her evening but a headache from staring at the computer screen. With a sigh, she leaned back in her chair. Then, after a brief stretch of mental debate, she yielded to the temptation she'd been trying to resist for more than twenty-four hours. Her fingers slightly unsteady on the keys, she typed in a name and hit return.

Reading the words that scrolled down the screen, she caught her breath. Some of the offences – theft, aggravated vehicle taking, dangerous driving – she had anticipated, and others, such as affray and failing to stop after an accident, didn't come as much of a surprise. A few, including wounding with intent and assaulting a police officer, made for more uncomfortable viewing. But it was the most recent conviction that left her feeling shaken. Tom Campbell was currently serving twelve years for attempted murder. Of his *wife*.

'Are you all right?'

Rebecca looked up sharply, her rapid pulse sounding in her ears, to see Lawrence standing in his office doorway. 'What?'

'You look like you've seen a ghost.'

'No, I'm ok,' she closed the window with a click of her mouse. 'Tired.'

Her superior nodded. 'Found anything?'

'A big fat bagel.'

'What?'

'Nothing,' Rebecca expanded. 'A circle with a hole in the middle.'

Lawrence looked momentarily puzzled before getting the joke and smiling. 'Who came up with that one? Leighton?'

'I should think his preference would be for a ring doughnut,' Rebecca replied, returning her superior's smile. 'The bagel was Danny's choice. He calls pay-review time bagel day.'

'I'll use that next time Jimmy comes asking for pocket money twenty minutes after cycling through my flower beds,' Lawrence remarked, laying a computer printout on Rebecca's desk. 'All I've come across so far is a girl who was attacked in her home last April.'

'Oh?'

'There isn't a lot here, but it seems she was raped and her breasts mutilated in a similar fashion to both Zoë's and Letty's. She was then strangled. Unsuccessfully.'

'You mean she's still alive?'

Lawrence nodded.

'Wow,' Rebecca lifted her eyebrows. 'Do you think that was intentional?'

'What do you mean?'

'Leighton said Zoë was strangled twice. Originally she was rendered unconscious – presumably so that her attacker could mutilate her without much resistance – then the second time around it finished her off.'

'That's true, but we don't know whether her killer intended for her to still be alive at that point in time.'

'Well, what happened to Letty? Do we know?'

'Good question,' Lawrence turned back towards his office, returning moments later with the relevant paperwork. Skimming it briefly he shook his head. 'It doesn't say here – Leighton's the one with the pathologist's report – he should be able to answer that for us. But even if she was alive when her breasts were mutilated, I don't really see why Josephine – that's the other girl – should have been intentionally spared.'

Rebecca shrugged. 'I don't know – some serial killers start off with a trial run, don't they?'

'Do they?' Lawrence replied. 'I don't know. To be honest, I don't know an awful lot about serial killers – I've never had much involvement with one. Thankfully they don't crop up every five minutes.'

'Who knows. Maybe I just saw that on TV.'

'In that case, it must be true,' Lawrence smiled. 'We probably ought to have a chat with somebody who does know something about serial killers, though. I'll ask around tomorrow and see whether anybody can help us out with that.'

'Are we going to interview this Josephine tomorrow? Or do you want to do that now?'

'I don't think so – I've still got to find an up-to-date address for her, and it's gone eight o'clock already. I think we'll make that our first job in the morning. If I can track her down tonight, I'll give you a call first thing – I can pick you up and we'll go straight there.'

'All right,' Rebecca nodded. 'So what now?'

'You can get off home unless there's anything else that urgently requires your attention.'

'Are you sure?'

'Yes. You've not seen Elliot in weeks. I'm sorry you're so caught up with this – you must want to drop everything at the moment.'

'Pretty much,' Rebecca admitted.

'There's not much more to do here. I want to sift through the newspapers on the microfiche, but that's more to satisfy my own curiosity at this point – there's no need for you to stay.'

'Ok,' Rebecca smiled. 'Thanks.'

'Thank *you*. I know this job has a habit of infringing on other areas of our lives – not everybody's prepared to go that extra mile, and the fact that you are doesn't go unnoticed.'

Rebecca felt herself blush. 'I like my job.'

'So do I, but I'd still prefer a good game of golf.'

Rebecca laughed, closing her laptop and reaching for her handbag.

Lawrence turned back towards his office. 'I'll see you tomorrow. Have a good evening.'

'You too. Goodnight.' Rebecca stood to go, feeling suddenly less frustrated with her lack of success that day. Praise meant much more when it came from somebody who didn't hand it out every five minutes, especially somebody you liked and respected, and pushing her discovery about Leighton's brother to the back of her mind, she turned her thoughts to what was left of her evening. Tomorrow, she assured herself, would be a better day.

Thirteen

Rebecca arrived home to find Elliot lying asleep on the sofa, a cushion tucked beneath his head and one arm draped onto the floor, fingers spread across a battered copy of Albert Camus' *The Stranger*. His hair looked in need of a wash, and his choice of attire – an old pair of jeans and a tight, long-sleeved grey top – emphasised how thin he was, undeservedly and rather unfairly, Rebecca thought, considering the quantities he ate and drank. From the contents of the ashtray and the collection of beer tins on the coffee table, she guessed he had been there some time, and wondered whether he had ventured out at all that day.

'Hey,' she greeted, ruffling his hair as she sat in an armchair adjacent to the sofa.

'Uh?' Elliot started, opening his eyes. 'Oh – Becca – hi. What time is it?' He turned onto his back.

'Five to nine. Sorry I'm so late.'

'Not your fault,' Elliot replied mildly, pushing himself slowly up into a sitting position and coughing as he did so. 'Have you eaten?'

'Not yet. I'm absolutely starving. I'm too tired to cook – I thought I'd order in. Is there anything you fancy?'

'Well –' Elliot looked thoughtful. 'We could do that, but if you give me five minutes I'll throw something together for you.'

With a smile, Rebecca nodded, relaxing back in the chair. 'Thanks.'

'Would you like a drink?' Elliot moved to stand. 'There's some wine in the kitchen.'

'That sounds great. Yes please.'

'You just sit there.'

Rebecca willingly did so, closing her eyes as Elliot headed towards the kitchen. While she wanted to make the most of the unexpected time with him, that meant fighting the natural desire to catch up on sleep. With a sigh, she reopened her eyes, reaching for the newspaper. Maybe she would feel more awake when she'd eaten.

'Caught your killer yet?' Elliot asked as he returned, a glass of white wine in hand.

'I'm afraid not,' Rebecca raised her eyes from the paper, reaching to take the glass. 'It looks as if we might be dealing with a serial killer as opposed to somebody with motive, which makes things a whole lot more complicated.'

'Yikes.'

'I spent half my day trawling through records in search of related incidents.'

'Find many?'

'Not one. Forrester came up with one possibility, which we still have to look into.' Rebecca sipped her wine. Aware she shouldn't be discussing her work with Elliot, she changed the subject. 'Did you see Ian today?'

Elliot nodded, perching on the sofa's armrest.

'Any news on his dad?'

'It's not looking good.'

'How's Ian coping?'

Elliot shrugged. 'I dunno. It's hard to tell when he's acting tough for his mum and his little sister.'

'How old is she?'

'Fifteen.'

'Poor kid.'

'I don't think the reality of the situation has hit her yet, to be honest. When I was at the hospital earlier she seemed totally dazed.' Elliot pushed himself up off the chair. 'Usually with this sort of thing they say the first twenty-four hours are crucial, but apparently there've been some complications.'

Rebecca nodded. 'Did you talk to anyone at the record company?'

'I hung up on Scott a couple of times.'

'Elliot –'

'I spoke to Benny. He's a bit less of a twat.' Elliot made for the door.

Rebecca returned her attention to the paper, skimming over the political articles and settling on an unsolved homicide in Edinburgh. Part way through, she abandoned it, tossing the paper to the floor and sliding down the chair, resting her head on the armrest. She had just made herself comfortable when Elliot looked back in. 'Dinner's ready.'

'Mmm.'

'Come on.'

'What?'

'I thought we'd eat at the table.'

'Can't we just have it in here?'

'Nope,' Elliot replied, leaning against the door frame and raising his eyebrows expectantly.

Rebecca reluctantly struggled to sit up. Elliot grinned, turning back the way he had come. Rebecca stood to follow, feeling peeved. All she really wanted to do was curl up with her dinner in front of the television. Entering the kitchen, she stopped short. The table had been polished and neatly laid out, with candles burning at each end. A starter of smoked salmon sat at the two place settings, neatly garnished with cherry tomatoes and slices of iceberg lettuce. At her place, the dessert cutlery was accompanied by a small parcel, wrapped in silver paper and red ribbon. Smiling involuntarily, she looked to her fiancé. 'Elliot –' she reached to take his hand, trying to think of something to say. Suddenly at a loss for words she settled on, 'Thank you.'

Elliot moved to kiss her. 'I braved the rain and my adoring public to go shopping.'

'You're a star.'

'I know,' Elliot grinned. 'Do you think you could tell the rest of the world?' He kissed her again, holding her close. Rebecca giggled, linking her fingers behind his neck. 'I'll think about it.'

Elliot muttered something inaudible, kissing the side of her neck and simultaneously manoeuvring his fingers from around her waist up under her top, reaching to unfasten her bra.

'Shouldn't we eat before it gets cold?' Rebecca murmured, as Elliot kissed her again. Only when Elliot began laughing did she realise what she had said, and raised a hand to cover her eyes, shaking her head.

'You'll be waiting for it to swim upriver next,' Elliot managed, coughing and trying to stop laughing. Releasing her, he pulled a chair out from the table. 'Come on, sit down and eat before you lose the plot completely.' He coughed again, moving around the table. Glancing up with a mock serious expression as he sat down, he added, 'Just don't burn your tongue!'

'Becca!' Elliot's urgent voice jolted her awake. 'Becca, wake up!'

'Huh?'

Elliot flicked on the light and Rebecca squinted against the brightness. Elliot was sitting on the bed beside her, hyperventilating. His face was white, and he looked panicked.

'What?' She asked, pushing herself up onto one elbow. 'What's wrong?'

'There's someone here!'

'Where? What?'

'In the flat. There's someone here!'

Awake enough to understand what he was saying, Rebecca sat up. 'What? Are you sure?'

'Of course I'm bloody sure!' Elliot replied, sounding slightly hysterical.

'Calm down. What happened?'

'I went to – I –' Elliot swallowed hard. 'I heard something – in the hall – I –'

'Did you see anyone?'

Elliot shook his head. 'I wanted to check you were ok.'

'Are you sure it wasn't just the guys upstairs?'

'There are *footprints* in the hall!'

Immediately understanding why he looked so panicked, Rebecca moved to climb out of bed.

'*No!*' Elliot exclaimed, pulling her back. 'Don't go out there – what if something happens?'

'Ok,' Rebecca nodded, turning towards her bedside table for her mobile. She quickly dialled 999 while Elliot watched her anxiously, looking very shaken. As Rebecca terminated the brief telephone call, he reached for his cigarettes.

'What now?' He asked, his voice wavering.

'Someone will be here in a minute or two.' Rebecca reached to take his free hand. 'It's all right,' she reassured him, trying to appear calm, despite the fact her heart was racing. Part of her still couldn't believe this was real, and had Elliot not been quite so shaken she would have insisted on taking a look herself before doing anything else. *Elliot.* Her heart jumped as realisation hit home. Elliot was supposed to be in Scotland that night, and, by rights, she ought to have been alone in the flat. She felt cold, and gripped Elliot's hand more tightly, glancing at her watch. It was a little after two, and Rebecca wondered how long it would be before the police arrived. She just hoped Elliot might have been wrong.

He hadn't been. Had the carpet not been so pale, the footprints might not have been visible. As it was, they were little more than damp smudges, which, Rebecca guessed, would disappear as soon as they dried. It was difficult to ascertain from where, or in which direction, they were going, and Rebecca was still examining them when the young police constable who had arrived at the door minutes earlier rejoined her in the hallway.

'There's nobody here now,' he said, smoothing his goatee with the fingers of his left hand.

'Well there's been someone here at some point,' Rebecca observed, her eyes still on the carpet.

'I'm not disputing that, but there's nobody but us here now. I expect your –' he stopped awkwardly, perhaps struggling to decide how best to connect her to Elliot. 'I expect your friend frightened him off,' he finished, eventually.

'Well, thank you for your help.'

'No problem. Give us another call if anything else happens.'

'I will. Thanks.' Rebecca held the door for him, then closed it and returned to the bedroom. 'There's no one here.'

Elliot looked up, anxiously. 'But the footprints –'

'I know, I've seen them. But there's no one here now.'

'But –'

'Elliot, the police have checked in here and outside, and they've found nobody. Whoever it was is long gone.'

'But what if he *is* still here?' Elliot demanded. 'What if they missed something? I mean – how did anyone get in here in the first place?'

'I don't know.' Rebecca sat beside him. 'I'm going to have a look around to see if anything's missing. Why don't you get some rest?'

'Rest?' Elliot echoed, incredulously. 'You think I'll be able to *sleep* now?'

'Try to calm down. Nothing's happened.'

'How the hell can you take this so fucking calmly?' He exclaimed, hotly. 'Somebody breaks into our home in the middle of the bloody night and you seem about as concerned as if it were just the postman coming early!'

'Elliot, my job involves staying calm in this sort of situation. I know you've had a shock, and I know you're anxious, but getting worked up isn't going to help.'

'What if he comes back?'

'That's pretty unlikely.'

Elliot didn't look reassured, and Rebecca sighed. 'Ok, how about I give Forrester a call, see whether he has any advice?'

'Can you do that?'

'Sure,' Rebecca gave him a small smile. 'Give me two minutes.'

Elliot nodded, reaching for his cigarettes.

'I won't be long,' Rebecca promised, turning back towards the hallway, where she made a quick telephone call to her superior.

'Forrester will be over in about an hour,' she informed Elliot, looking back into the bedroom. He was leaning against the headboard, horribly pale, a cigarette clamped between shaking fingers. Rebecca perched on the edge of the bed beside him, reaching to take his hand. 'Are you all right?'

'I feel sick.'

'You've had a bad shock, love. It's all right.'

'What if I hadn't been here?' He looked tortured. 'What if I'd been in Glasgow – if – if you'd been alone –'

'Hey, you aren't in Glasgow, I'm not alone, and we're both still ok. Come here.' Rebecca moved to embrace him. Elliot held her tightly, which was when she realised he wasn't the only one shaking. She took a deep breath, wondering how she was going to feel the next time Elliot was away. She suspected it would come around all too soon.

By the time Lawrence arrived, Rebecca felt exhausted. Elliot had finally calmed down, and Rebecca left him to rest, sitting down with Lawrence in the living room to explain exactly what had happened.

'How's Elliot?' Lawrence enquired, once she had finished.

'I don't know,' Rebecca admitted. 'Very shaken. He isn't feeling too well. I expect he'll be all right later on, I think it's just the shock.'

'You must be fairly shaken yourself.'

Rebecca nodded, raising a hand to twirl a lock of hair around her finger. 'What most scares me is the fact I would have been alone if Ian's dad hadn't been taken ill.'

'Yes,' Lawrence agreed. 'Do you have any idea how anybody might have managed to get in?'

'No. I've checked all the windows – the only one we left open was in the bathroom, but it's pretty small, and anyway, it's en suite – I don't think it's likely anybody could have climbed in without one of us hearing something.'

'Did you have many windows open earlier in the evening?'

'Quite a few. It's been so hot.' Rebecca hesitated. 'Do you think somebody was here all that time?'

'It's possible. Is there anywhere they could have hidden?'

'I suppose the spare bedroom – although we didn't have windows open in there, so –' Rebecca stopped. 'But that still wouldn't explain the footprints on the hall carpet.'

'Who's to say whoever it was didn't come and go – have you noticed anything missing?'

No, nothing. I've not had a really good look around, but nothing obvious has disappeared.'

'How strange,' Lawrence frowned. 'I suppose it's possible Elliot disturbed whoever it was before they had a chance to take anything.'

'I don't understand why somebody would have waited so long. We were in bed by eleven-thirty.'

'Did you go straight to sleep?'

Rebecca felt her cheeks flush. 'No. But we can't have been awake *that* long.'

'So you don't know exactly what time you fell asleep?'

'No.'

There was a pause before Lawrence asked, 'Does Elliot ever sleepwalk?'

'Not as far as I know.'

'I just wondered whether he might have somehow wandered out of the door and back in again.'

'The prints on the carpet looked as if they'd been made by a shoe – I could pick out several tread marks –' Rebecca reached for her mobile to call up the photographs she had taken at the time. 'I doubt he'd have managed to put shoes on and then take them off again in his sleep. Besides, I don't think he sleeps deeply enough – you only have to cough and it wakes him up.'

'Ok,' Lawrence sighed. 'Well, I'll have a look around the place, see whether I can see anything unusual – you should try to get some sleep, you look shattered.'

'I'm sorry for calling you in the middle of the night – Elliot was in such a state, and –'

'Don't worry about it, I don't mind.'

'You're welcome to stay in the spare room – save you going all the way home again.'

'That sounds great.' Lawrence nodded.

'Then we can get straight down to work in the morning,' Rebecca suggested, with a weak smile.

'Let's see how you feel tomorrow before we worry about that,' Lawrence replied, standing and turning towards the windows.

'Now. How about you tell me where you and Elliot spent your evening so that we can try to get to the bottom of this case tonight?'

Lawrence and Rebecca had drawn no definite conclusions by the time they retired to bed, and next morning had a quick breakfast before setting off for an address in Richmond that Lawrence had obtained the previous evening. It turned out to be a large Victorian townhouse that must have looked majestic at some stage, but was now in dire need of a lick of paint and the ministrations of a gardener.

Lawrence knocked on the front door, and shortly it was opened by a stooped, weary-looking man who must have been at least sixty.

'Hello?'

'Good morning. I'm DCI Forrester –' Lawrence proffered his identification, 'And this is DS Palmer. We're looking for Josephine Islington.'

'Oh –' the man hesitated.

'Is there a problem?'

'It's just – I – do you really need to speak to Jo? What's all this about?'

'We'd like to ask her a few questions about the attack last spring. It's possible it may be connected to our current investigation.'

'I see,' the man conceded, rather reluctantly, stepping back from the door. 'You'd best come in, then. I'll call Jo for you. You will be gentle with her, won't you?'

'Of course.'

'Take a seat through there –' he waved a hand in the direction of the living room before beginning a slow ascent of the stairs. Rebecca and Lawrence made themselves comfortable, taking in their surroundings. Although large, the room was sparsely furnished, looking almost as if it had only just been occupied and was awaiting a further load from the removal company. What furniture there was looked to be of good quality, however – a solid oak sideboard, a plush three piece suite, a sturdy coffee table and, ticking loudly in one corner, an antique grandfather clock.

Several minutes passed before they were joined by a young woman who looked no older than her late teens. She was petite and appeared too thin even for her small frame. Untidy dark hair fell over her pale face, and both her expression and demeanour were anxious. She hesitated in the doorway for some moments, clinging to the cuffs of her shirt, until the man who had answered the door appeared at her side.

'Sit down, Jo dear.' He nudged her towards an armchair. Josephine did as bid, wrapping her arms around herself protectively, never raising her eyes from the floor.

'I'm sorry to ask you to relive it, but we've a few questions about the night of April the eighteenth last year,' Lawrence began.

Josephine nodded wordlessly, eyes still cast down.

'Do you think you could tell us, in your own words, what happened that night?'

'Uh –' Josephine gulped. 'I – um – came home – my flatmate was working nights, so I was alone. I watched a film and went to bed. I – I heard him – enter the flat – because –' she drew a sharp breath. 'He came through the front door. I heard the key turn –' she broke off, raising a hand to her mouth.

'Can you be sure about that?'

Josephine nodded. 'I heard the key, but I was half asleep, and I didn't know what time it was. I just assumed it was Maud getting home. She used to get in at about five, when it was still dark.'

'What happened next?'

'I don't remember exactly – I wasn't really awake – he – he was –' she swallowed. 'He pinned me down and had tape over my mouth before I even knew what was happening.' She bit into her lip. 'He – um –' she lowered her voice almost to a whisper, 'He pulled off my underwear and – and –' she shook her head rather than complete the sentence. 'After –' she hesitated before settling on, '*That* – his hands were around my neck. I can't remember much after that – just coming to – and the blood –' she trailed off.

'How long had you been living at the flat?'

'About ten days.'

'Did you have the locks changed when you moved in?'

Josephine shook her head. 'No. We should have done. They tried to trace the guy who was living there before, but –' she shook her head slightly. 'He hadn't left a forwarding address – and the man whose name was on the lease had moved out early without telling the landlord – so nobody knew who he was.'

Lawrence nodded, guessing that his and Rebecca's next job would be to trace the landlord. 'I know this must be very difficult for you, and I'm sorry to have to ask you anything further, but can you remember anything at all of what the man who attacked you looked like?'

'It was dark –' Josephine shrugged. 'I couldn't see much – and I was so scared –'

'How about the colour of his skin?'

'He wasn't black, but further than that –' she shook her head.

'And his build?'

'I've no idea how tall he was, but he was slender.'

'Could you describe any of his facial features?'

'No,' Josephine pursed her lips, looking on the verge of tears. 'I'm sorry – I can't remember anything, and I don't know why! His face haunts me every night, and I've tried – I've tried *so* hard to remember – but – when I wake up –' she paused, swallowing hard. 'When I wake up, it's gone.'

Rebecca approached Lawrence's desk, a mug of coffee in each hand, to find him compiling a table. There were four columns, containing assorted ticks and crosses, presumably, she surmised, relevant to the notes jotted down the margin.

'Meeting with your accountant again?' She joked, setting his mug down on the pottery drink mat fashioned into a fish shape by Elise in art class.

Lawrence didn't immediately look up, and when he did his expression was uneasy. 'I don't think these attacks are as random as they first appeared.'

'Oh?' Rebecca sat on a chair by the desk and slid down it so that her bottom rested close to the edge of the seat.

'All three made the papers. Not the headlines, but most of the national papers none the less.'

'How?'

'Zoë was a model. Not a supermodel, but her face has been seen enough to make her death newsworthy. Letty was married to a famous football player. She might not have been news, but he certainly was, and she made a footnote on the front page of my *Times*.'

'And Josephine?'

'Does the name Catherine Dixon mean anything to you?'

'Yes, but I can't place it.'

'She's a writer.'

'Oh – yes – is it horror?'

'That's right.'

'Elliot reads them. What's the connection?'

'She's Josephine's mother.'

'Mother?'

'Yes,' Lawrence reached for his coffee. 'It's almost as if our killer wants nationwide recognition without making too big a splash. He doesn't want to take it too far, because then he'll risk mass media attention. Quite whether that would have been his original intention, or whether he found it a pleasing side effect of the attack on Josephine and decided to keep it up, I'm not sure.'

'Good point.'

There was a long pause before Lawrence replied. 'I think we might have another piece of this jigsaw right in front of us.'

'Uh-huh?'

'Becky, who are you engaged to?'

As realisation of what her superior meant sunk in, Rebecca felt sick. 'No – *no* –'

'I would think enough radio listeners would know the name Astatine, if nothing else. You're a pretty young woman with a link to publicity, and anybody reading the *NME* knew exactly where Elliot was supposed to be last night. Four hundred miles away.'

Rebecca swallowed hard.

'Letty and Derek lived less than fifteen minutes' walk from your flat, and as you said, Zoë's agency is just down the road. I'm guessing that's no coincidence.'

'But I don't understand how anybody could have come by a set of our keys,' Rebecca countered. 'That just doesn't make sense!'

'Have either you or Elliot lost your keys recently?'

'Elliot lost his a month or two ago – but he changed the locks the following day.'

'Did he do that himself?'

Rebecca nodded.

'And did he subsequently have any extra sets made?'

Rebecca thought back. 'I'm not sure,' she admitted, after a moment.

'Well my guess is that we're dealing with somebody who has a means of *cutting* keys. Zoë had keys cut for Pete a few months before her death, and it sounds as if Letty had a score of extra keys made when she and Derek moved into their flat.'

Rebecca stared at Lawrence in horror. 'You mean a *locksmith*?'

Lawrence didn't respond verbally, but his expression told Rebecca that was exactly what he was thinking.

'What about Josephine? She'd only been in the flat a week – and she –' Rebecca stopped as she added two and two. 'She didn't have the locks changed when she moved in.'

'No.' Lawrence lifted his eyebrows. 'I've managed to get hold of the name and address of Josephine's landlord, although that's all the information that's available thus far. We need to track him down, but first –' Lawrence moved to stand. 'First, I want a word with Elliot.'

Elliot was sitting in the living room with his laptop open on his knees, a bottle of vodka and a glass on the table in front of him. Rebecca noticed that a good third of the bottle had gone, and wondered how coherent Elliot was going to be. He was typing something as they entered, and Rebecca guessed he was posting on the band's website or one of its associated social media pages.

'Back already?' He greeted her, eyebrows raised.

Rebecca translated the meaning behind his comment. Had he known she was on her way home, he would have put the vodka away. As it was, he reached for the glass on the table top and drained the contents.

'I need to ask you a few questions about last night,' Lawrence began. 'Do you feel up to answering them?'

Elliot frowned. 'Why wouldn't I?'

'Elliot, you had a bad shock, and when I saw you this morning you weren't in much of a state to talk to anyone.'

'I'm fine,' Elliot replied, curtly, snapping the laptop shut and setting it down beside himself on the sofa. 'So. What do you want to know?'

Lawrence turned to Rebecca. 'I think it would be best if I went over this with Elliot. Do you mind leaving us to it for a few minutes?'

Rebecca would have liked to stay, if only to control Elliot's alcohol consumption, but appreciated that when it came to questioning Elliot she was too involved to approach the situation objectively. Nodding, she turned back towards the hallway. 'Can I get either of you anything?' She asked, from the doorway.

Elliot shook his head, reaching for the bottle on the table and starting to unscrew the lid.

'I wouldn't say no to a coffee,' Lawrence answered, slipping his notebook out of his pocket and flicking it open.

Rebecca pulled the door shut. She had never before found her job and her home life so entangled, and felt suddenly very vulnerable. This wasn't simply another case.

Elliot said nothing until he had poured a large measure of vodka into his glass. Having done so, he looked up at Lawrence, who had made himself comfortable in a nearby armchair. 'So. What now?'

'Could you describe exactly what happened last night? As you remember it.'

'Um – I woke up – just before two. All I did was go to the kitchen to fetch a glass of water. I didn't bother turning the light on, because I know the layout of the flat well enough by now. I was in the kitchen and I heard a noise in the hallway, so I flicked the light on. Originally I thought it might be our neighbour's cat, because he sometimes climbs in through the bathroom window, and if it was I wanted to put him out before he sprayed all over the sofa or something. Once I saw those footprints I just freaked. The only thing I could think of was whether Becca was all right. It all goes a bit blurry after that.'

'What sort of noise did you hear?'

Elliot appeared to give this a moment's consideration before saying, 'Kind of – scraping – and then a click.'

'What sort of scraping?'

'Um – well, you know the sound you get when you rub up against a plastic Mac, or something like that? Or if you're wearing one and –' Elliot stopped, his expression changing. 'If you're wearing one and you brush past something –'

'Do you think the click could have been the front door closing?'

Elliot didn't answer immediately, reaching for his cigarettes. When he spoke, his voice was unsteady. 'Yeah.' He paused 'I heard him leave, didn't I? Slip out through the door and pull it shut.'

'I suspect so.'

'God,' he fished a cigarette out of the packet and lit it, his hands trembling.

'Where did you get the keys for your front door cut?'

Looking surprised by the change in direction, Elliot went to answer, then paled, his eyes widening. 'You mean – that – no – no –' he shook his head. 'Last night –' he swallowed hard. 'Someone else has a *key*?'

181

Lawrence hadn't expected Elliot to reach that conclusion quite so quickly, and wasn't prepared for the question. 'Where did you get the keys cut?' He repeated.

'Sibson and Son. Just down the road. Becca takes her dry cleaning there.' He took a long pull on his cigarette.

'Can you remember anything about the person who served you?'

'Uh –' Elliot hesitated. 'He was youngish – thirty-something – his name was Brett.'

'Are you absolutely certain of that?'

'Yes,' Elliot drew deeply on his cigarette, reaching for the glass of vodka, which he drained.

'How?'

'He had a name tag.'

'How long ago was this?'

'May seventh.'

'Are you sure?' Lawrence asked, surprised Elliot remembered the date, given that it was now mid-June.

'They had one of those day-to-day displays in the shop. You know, time, date, that sort of thing. I'm going on that being right – if it isn't – wasn't –' he shrugged, bowing his head and raising a hand to his forehead.

'Elliot, are you all right to continue with this?'

'Yuh,' he nodded, his voice wavering. He didn't sound very sure.

'Did he cut the keys while you were there?'

Elliot shook his head. 'He said – something about the gadget not working right – but that if I left them there he'd do them for me to collect on my way back – I was on my way to the supermarket –' Elliot paused, looking up as Rebecca reappeared with a mug of coffee. 'How could I be so fucking stupid?'

'Did you tell him where you live at any stage?' Lawrence asked, as Rebecca joined Elliot on the sofa, slipping an arm around him.

'God. Yeah, I did. He said he'd seen me around, and did I live around here – I never even thought about it – I just said yes – I told him the street, and everything!' He ran a shaking hand through his hair. 'The last couple of months I've grown kind of accustomed to being asked questions like that – to being recognised in pubs –' he paused, blinking hard. 'I even talked about Becca – I told him I was in trouble for losing my door keys. He said he'd seen me with her – that I was lucky to have such a

182

gorgeous girlfriend, and –' Elliot stopped, bowing his head. 'And because I have a fucking big ego she could have died!'

'Elliot, none of this is your fault,' Rebecca replied gently, leaning to kiss his forehead.

'Of course it's my fucking fault!' Elliot yelled, wrenching himself away from her embrace and jumping up from the sofa. 'If I hadn't been so busy enjoying thinking I was a celebrity and lapping up all the attention, I might have thought about what I was doing! As it was, I nearly killed you!' He turned and left the room, slamming the door shut behind himself.

'I'd better go and see he's all right,' Rebecca said, standing and moving towards the door. 'I won't be long.'

'No rush,' Lawrence replied tactfully, reaching for Rebecca's notebook and flipping the cover back. He had only had the chance to peruse the first few pages before Rebecca returned, sooner than he had expected.

'How's Elliot?'

'I don't know. He's locked himself in the bathroom – I'll give him a few minutes to calm down.'

'I'd like to make a trip to this locksmith's as soon as possible, so –'

'I can't leave Elliot now.' Rebecca raised an anxious hand to the pendant around her neck and pulled unconsciously on the chain. 'I'm sorry, but –'

'Becky, I'm not expecting you to. Besides, all things considered I don't think it would be a particularly good idea for you to come with me. Now, Elliot seems to think he was served by a young man named Brett, so assuming there is somebody of that name working there I'll –'

'Why wouldn't there be?' Rebecca asked, with a frown.

'Do you think Elliot would remember something like that? From over a month ago?'

'Probably. He has a photographic memory.'

'Does he?'

'Yes he does!' Rebecca snapped, defensively. 'He isn't stupid, you know – he does understand how important this is!'

'I never said he was stupid,' Lawrence replied, calmly.

Rebecca sighed. 'I'm sorry. I didn't mean that to sound so pointed. I'm just fed up with everyone I know thinking that because he plays in a band he doesn't have a brain. Elliot's very bright, he just doesn't have a lot of common sense.'

'How about you tell me where the locksmith's is, and I'll pop down there now? Give you some time with Elliot.'

'Yes, ok. Thanks.' Rebecca forced a small smile. 'I'll draw you a map.'

Once Lawrence had departed, Rebecca returned to the bedroom. The door to the en suite bathroom was still locked, and she knocked softly. 'Elliot?' She paused. 'Elliot, please let me in. I'm worried about you.'

There was no response, and after a moment Rebecca tried again. 'Elliot, come on, sweetheart, I don't like you being alone in there. Please.'

Again there was no answer, and Rebecca knocked harder. 'Elliot, please at least say something – you're scaring me!'

Beginning to feel panicked when there was still no sound from within, she spoke more sharply. 'If you don't let me in, I'll break the lock! Now open the door!'

There was a short pause before Rebecca heard the key turn and Elliot partially opened the door. He had clearly been crying, but said, rather impatiently, 'I'm ok. See?'

'You're not ok.'

'I'm alive. Isn't that what you wanted to check?' He snapped. 'Now do you think you could leave me in peace for five minutes? Would that be too much to ask?'

'Elliot –'

'Leave me alone!' He tried to close the door.

Rebecca stopped him. 'Please don't shut me out.'

'*Leave me alone!*' He enunciated, giving the door another shove. Rebecca instinctively pushed back, catching him off guard. The door flew open, almost knocking him backwards into the bath. As he steadied himself, Rebecca realised why he had wanted to be alone. His left forearm was red with blood.

'Jesus Elliot – what have you done –' Rebecca stood staring at him in shock, immediately assuming the worst. Exposed, he didn't seem to know how to react, and looked rather panicked. 'Oh God –' Rebecca moved towards him, taking his shoulders firmly in her hands. 'Sit down.' She manoeuvred him backwards towards the toilet, feeling sick. 'Sit.'

Elliot obeyed, wrapping his arms around himself.

'Let me see.'

Elliot didn't move.

184

'Let me see your arm.' The control with which she managed to speak was borne more of urgency than strength. 'Then I'll call an ambulance.'

'No!' Elliot exclaimed, looking up. 'No, I don't need an ambulance!'

'I'll be the judge of that. Now let me see.'

Elliot shook his head.

'Either you let me see or I'll call for an ambulance.'

Seconds ticked by.

'*Elliot!*'

He closed his eyes, biting his lip. Slowly he loosened his left arm and held it out, turning his forearm so that the palm of his hand faced upwards. Blood dripped onto the tiled floor.

'I'm sorry,' he whispered. 'I'm sorry, Becca.'

Fourteen

A bell rang to announce Lawrence's arrival at Sibson and Son, prompting the single occupant of the shop to glance up. A portly man in his mid-fifties with thick grey hair and a carefully sculpted moustache, his name tag revealed him to be Cliff Sibson, and Lawrence wondered whether this was the original Mr Sibson or his son. He was standing behind the shop's small counter, polishing a trophy of some sort, and smiled as Lawrence approached.

'Good afternoon.'

'Afternoon,' Lawrence proffered his warrant card. 'I'm DCI Forrester – I believe you have a young man named Brett working here. I'd like a word with him.'

'He doesn't work here any more.'

'Oh? Why not?'

'I fired him.'

'Would you mind telling me why?'

'He was cutting keys on the sly at a discounted rate.'

'How did you find out?'

'I caught him slipping a handful of keys into his bag. When I confronted him, he admitted to it.'

'I see,' Lawrence nodded. 'When was this?'

Cliff's eyebrows contracted in thought. 'Last Tuesday, I think,' he said, at length. 'Monday or Tuesday, at any rate.'

'Do you have a home address for him?'

'Yes.'

'Could I have it, please?'

'Certainly,' Cliff turned to a chest of drawers behind the counter.

'How long had he been working here?'

'Oh –' Cliff paused for thought. 'Just over a year. He started in May last year.'

'I understand you also provide a dry cleaning service.'

'Yes.'

'Do you have a fairly established clientele?'

'We do see a number of people on a regular basis, if that's what you're asking.' Cliff took a envelope wallet from the drawer he had been searching through and drew out a sheaf of papers. 'What's all this about?'

'I'm afraid I can't go into that.'

Cliff nodded, apparently not overly surprised by this response, and passed Lawrence a sheet of paper. 'That's the address I have for him – although he filled this in when he began working here, so if he's moved in the meantime I'm afraid I can't help you.'

'Thank you.' Lawrence cast his eyes over the details before folding it and slipping it into his pocket. 'How did Brett get on with your customers?'

'Fine, I think. He seemed a very personable young man – I was shocked when I learned what he'd been up to, because I'd always felt I could trust him.'

'Did you ever leave him alone in the shop?'

'Frequently. As I said, I was under the misapprehension he was trustworthy.'

'Can you tell me much about him?'

'Further than that he worked hard and was always punctual, no, not really. He was quite chatty, but he didn't talk a lot about himself. He struck me as rather a private person in that respect.'

'So you don't know what he did with his spare time?'

'No.'

Lawrence nodded. 'Did you ask for any references when he first applied for the job?'

'I did, but he'd been working abroad for some time, so it was quite difficult to verify them. He came to work on a month's trial – he was good at the job and everybody seemed to like him, so I kept him on.'

'And did he know how to cut keys when he first arrived?'

'No, but he picked it up quickly. I was quite impressed.'

'Could you give me a physical description?'

'Certainly. He's quite tall – about six foot – fairly athletic – wiry would probably be the best way of putting it. His hair's blonde and he keeps it quite short, but not spiky – and he has very blue eyes. Almost unnaturally so. Oh, and he has a small scar here –' Cliff indicated his upper lip.

Lawrence nodded. 'All right, thank you very much for your help. If anything else comes to mind, or if you see Brett again, please give me a call on this number.' He handed Cliff his card.

'Righty-ho.'

'Thanks,' Lawrence smiled, feeling both excited and apprehensive as he turned to leave. He was either almost there or back at square one, and, until he arrived in Nether Street, he had no way of knowing which.

'Are you feeling any better now?' Rebecca asked, joining Elliot on the sofa. He was smoking his third cigarette in ten minutes, his arm now neatly bandaged, his bloodstained t-shirt a vivid reminder of recent events. Rebecca still felt very shaken. That Elliot had at one time indulged in self-harm had been evident from the faded scars on his forearm, but they had been there for as long as Rebecca had known him, allowing her to distance herself from the reality surrounding them. The additional scars that ran down his wrists, now white and smooth with age, indicated of what else he was capable, although he had refused to discuss either issue throughout their two-year relationship. Whenever questioned, he had said only, 'That was a long time ago. I've sorted myself out since then. Subject closed.' And while his temperament tended towards erratic, Rebecca had had little reason to doubt him. Until now, that was.

'Sorry,' Elliot muttered, for what seemed like the hundredth time in half an hour.

Rebecca felt irritated. 'Stop apologising.'

'I don't know what else to say.'

'An explanation wouldn't go amiss.'

Elliot shrugged.

'I understand that the past twelve hours have been very distressing for you, but –' she paused. 'This really isn't a normal reaction, Elliot.'

'Whoever said *I* was normal?' Elliot returned, defensively.

'What is all this about? Did you really need to go to such lengths to get my attention?'

'That has nothing to do with it! You're the one who made me open the fucking door!'

'Oh for God's sake, did you honestly think I wouldn't notice? Were you planning to wear a longsleeved t-shirt to bed for the foreseeable or what?'

'Stop shouting at me!'

'I'm worried about you! What if that happens again? What if you do more damage and I'm not here with you?'

Elliot met her eyes with a cold glare. 'If I wanted to kill myself I would. It's not something I'd do accidentally.'

'I'm sorry, Elliot, but I don't see where the boundary lies! To me the distinction between self-harm and suicide is all rather hazy!'

'That's because you're judging something you don't understand,' Elliot replied, acidly.

Rebecca felt exasperated. 'Well, could you please explain to me so that I *might* be able to understand what possible reason you could have for doing something so *stupid*?'

'It makes me feel better, all right?' Elliot crushed his cigarette viciously into the ashtray. 'It *prevents* me from reaching a point where I might take things further!'

'But you have done before.'

'That was an entirely different situation!'

'How?'

'I don't want to talk about it!'

'But –'

'No! That was ten years ago, I was having a very bad time, and I couldn't cope! It was a whole other lifetime, and I don't want to have to think about it now!'

'All right, we won't talk about that,' Rebecca replied, trying to keep her tone reasonably even. 'But I think you ought to see someone about what happened today.'

'I don't need to see anyone.'

'I think you do! Hurting yourself like that isn't –'

'Isn't normal, yes, so you've already said! So how about you tell me what you think a normal reaction *is* to discovering the person you love most in the world could have died thanks to your stupidity? Because obviously the rest of the population have some great answer to that sort of shock!'

'Elliot –'

'You're all I have, and I could have killed you! How do you think that makes me feel?'

'How do you think *I* felt opening that door and seeing you covered in blood?'

'Stop shouting at me!' Elliot managed, his voice unsteady, bowing his head to hide his face from hers. Rebecca sensed that he was in tears, and sighed, in two minds about how to respond. What she wanted to do was walk out and slam the door, but at the same time she felt uneasy about leaving Elliot on his own. He had refused to let her take him to A and E, despite the fact that several of the cuts on his arm looked as if they needed stitching, and she suspected that were she to suggest calling the doctor it would be equally ill-received. She had never seen him so upset, and guessed the quantity of vodka he had consumed that morning was at least partly to blame. Had circumstances been different she would have contacted Ian. He and Elliot had been friends for almost a decade, and Rebecca felt sure he would have more idea than she did of how to deal with this situation.

Elliot raised his hands to cover his face, his respirations uneven. Reluctantly, Rebecca moved closer to him, reaching to hold him. He was shaking.

'Calm down.'

'I'm sorry,' he whispered. 'I'm sorry, Becca, please don't leave me!'

'I'm not going to leave you. There's no need to get so upset.'

'I didn't ask to feel like this!'

Rebecca took a deep breath. 'Why don't you go back to bed?' She suggested, eventually. 'Maybe you'll feel better when you've had some sleep. I'll call somebody about getting the locks changed on the front door.'

'Call someone?' Elliot jerked away from her embrace. 'You're going to trust someone *else* with our locks after what just happened?'

'Well what do you suggest?'

'I'll do it myself!'

'Elliot, you're in no fit state to do anything of the sort!'

'I'll do it my fucking self, all right?'

'Fine,' Rebecca snapped. 'You do whatever you want! I'm going out!' She stood and left the room, not looking back. After all that had happened, she needed some time to herself, time she suspected she wouldn't get if Elliot knew where she was. Despite her frustration, she felt bad leaving him alone, but decided it was probably for the best. Were she to stay, it would only be a matter of time before she said something she'd later regret.

Lawrence was waiting for Google Maps to load on his mobile and provide him with directions to Nether Street when the phone rang. Expecting the call to be from Rebecca, he was more than a little surprised to see Leighton's name and number flash up on screen.

'Have you seen the news?' Leighton opened, rather urgently, without even saying hello.

'No. Why?'

'A body's been found in an alley near Tufnell Park station – I've not been able to get hold of much information yet, but it sounds like the same killer.'

'Where are you now?'

'On my way there. I put in a call to the Kentish Town constabulary as soon as I heard about it – asked them to hold everything until I get there.'

'How did you hear about it?'

'Early lunch in the pub,' Leighton admitted, continuing, before Lawrence could comment, with, 'Can you meet me there? I shouldn't be more than twenty minutes.'

'I've an important visit to make – do you need me there?'

'No, not if you're busy. How about Becks, is she with you?'

'Becky isn't working this afternoon.'

'Oh. Ok, well don't worry about it, I'll let you know if anything comes up. Give me a call when you're done.'

'I'll do that. Thank you for letting me know.' Lawrence terminated the call. Starting the car's ignition, he glanced over his shoulder before pulling out into the road, his excitement now tinged with sadness. If he'd thought of the possibility of a locksmith's involvement just twenty-four hours earlier, perhaps one life might have been saved.

Nether Street was located in a leafy suburb of North London, and the semi-detached red brick house whose address Lawrence held was much like many of its neighbours. The small front garden was beautifully manicured, and a climbing rose in full bloom clung to the trellis around the front door. Pretty net curtains hung in the downstairs windows, and a black and white cat on the near side of the netting gazed out impassively. Stepping up to the front door, Lawrence discovered that there were two door bells, labelled with no more information than 'ground floor flat' and 'top floor flat'. He recalled no mention of either of these, and a quick consultation of the information provided by Cliff Sibson left him none the wiser. After a moment's thought, he pressed both bells, hoping that an occupant of at least one of the flats would be at home. When, after a time, there had been no response, he stepped back from the door to take another look at his surroundings.

From where he stood, he could see a narrow corridor running down the side of the house, only partly obscured by a rhododendron bush that rendered it invisible from the street. Moving carefully between the flower beds, Lawrence peered around the corner of the house, finding, to his surprise, that the gate leading to the back garden had been left open. Making sure he had his warrant card to hand, he made his way along the side of the house and into the back garden, which was as carefully tended as its partner at the front, and more than twice the size.

June was perhaps an ideal time to visit; the herbaceous border was alive with colour, the grass had not yet been burned by the summer sun, and a laburnum tree in the far corner had been almost engulfed by chains of its small yellow flowers. Central to the garden was an oval pond, crowded with irises, water lilies and plump red goldfish; these apparently of little interest to the tortoiseshell cat who lay sunning herself just inches from the pondside. A garden shed had been partially disguised by a yew hedge, and, no sooner had Lawrence noticed its presence, the door opened and a petite woman he guessed was in her sixties appeared. Clad in threadbare cotton trousers and a dirty blue shirt, she carried a tray of seedlings in one hand and a trowel in the other. Several seconds passed before she noticed Lawrence, and, when she did, she stopped dead, clearly startled.

'Police,' Lawrence announced, holding up his identification to allay any fears she might have as early as possible.

'Oh –' the woman swallowed. 'Oh, I see.' She set the seedlings down on the lawn and moved towards him. Her hair was mostly grey, although from the colour that remained it was apparent that she had, in her younger days, been brunette. Her posture was good, though the lines surrounding her blue eyes and her slightly drooping jowls gave away her age, and Lawrence wondered whether she might, in fact, be some years older than he had first thought.

'I'm DCI Forrester – I've been given this address for a young man called Brett Lindquist. Do you know him?'

'Yes. He lives in the upstairs flat.'

'There's no answer at present – I don't suppose you know who he rents the flat from, do you?'

'Yes. I'm his landlady.'

'Ah,' Lawrence raised his eyebrows. 'Could I take your name, please?'

'Cara Townsend. Mrs.'

'Do you have a key to the upstairs flat?'

'Yes,' Cara frowned. 'Why? What's happened?'

'I need to speak to Brett in connection with a serious crime. Would you mind letting me into his flat?'

'Don't you need a warrant?'

'I don't want to search the flat, I just want to know whether he's there.'

'Oh,' Cara nodded. 'Oh, well, I suppose that would be all right.' She glanced towards the house. 'Would you mind going back round to the front door? I'd rather not have outdoor shoes on my carpets.'

'Not at all,' Lawrence agreed, turning back the way he had come, keen to minimise the wait for access to Brett's flat.

The first surprise – which shouldn't have come as a surprise at all – was that the lock on the front door had been changed. Cara tried the key several times, looking puzzled, before turning to Lawrence.

'I'm sure this is the right one.'

'I imagine the lock's been changed,' Lawrence sighed. Knocking on the door, he added, 'If there's still no answer I'm going to have to force my way in.'

This suggestion clearly came as a shock to Cara. 'Surely there must be some other way?' She asked, apprehensively. 'Is it really necessary? What's so important that you can't wait –'

'I'm afraid all I can say at the moment is that it's imperative I speak to Brett as soon as possible,' Lawrence responded, putting his shoulder to the door.

Cara's concerned expression didn't diminish, but she said nothing further.

The door creaked and shuddered at Lawrence's first attempt to force it, and he tried again. This time, the door flew open and Lawrence fell into the room, only just managing to keep his balance. Straightening up, he found himself in a narrow hallway with a doorway on either side and one up ahead. On his right was a bedroom, and the first thing to catch his attention was that the bed was nothing more than a naked mattress on a frame. The room also contained a pine wardrobe and chest of drawers, and given that the top of the chest was completely bare, Lawrence suspected he had arrived too late. This was confirmed by the fact the drawers and wardrobe were also empty, and with a sigh he returned to the hallway. He checked the kitchen and bathroom more as a matter of protocol than through any real hope of finding something useful, before returning to Cara, who was inspecting the damage to her door.

'He's gone,' he informed her. 'When did you last see him?'

'Yesterday evening. He came in while I was working in the front garden. I heard him leave a few hours later. Around ten.'

'Do you know whether he came back after that?'

'No. That is, I don't. He might have.'

'All right,' Lawrence continued. 'I'm going to arrange for a police officer to keep an eye on this flat – I'll be sending a forensic scientist around later to take a look at the place, and I don't want it disturbed in the meantime. Once I've sorted that out, I'd like to have a chat with you about Brett.'

Cara nodded. 'I'll tell you what I can, but I'm not sure I'll be a lot of help. He seemed a nice enough lad – he was very polite – but he kept himself to himself.'

That sounded familiar, Lawrence thought, remembering his earlier conversation with Cliff Sibson. Feeling intensely disappointed, he slid his hand into his pocket for his mobile, wondering how Rebecca would take the news. Their chances of finding Brett now seemed remote.

Gavin Mitchell appeared rather less composed than on previous occasions when he opened the front door to Lawrence late on Wednesday afternoon. He was pale and visibly tired, and Lawrence guessed he hadn't had much sleep in the past couple of days.

'Good afternoon – um – come in – please –' he stepped back from the door.

Lawrence thanked him, entering the hallway and asking, conversationally, 'How's Lucian?'

Concern clouded Gavin's face. 'You're not here to speak to him again, are you? I really don't think he's up to it.'

'No, no, it's you and your wife I'm here to see. I just wondered how he was.'

'Oh, I see,' Gavin nodded. 'He's in quite a bad way, which isn't entirely surprising, given everything that's happened. It's not as if he was well before all of this.'

'Will he be staying here long?'

'I don't know. That's up to him, really.' Gavin turned towards the drawing room and Lawrence followed. 'Carrina's not here at the moment – she's gone to stay with her brother for a few days.'

Lawrence didn't feel particularly surprised, and wondered whether she had any intention of returning. Quite how he might have reacted in her position, he had no idea. Gavin took a seat on the sofa, looking up expectantly. 'So. What is it you need to know now?'

'I actually came to update you on our progress.' Lawrence sat opposite him. 'I wanted to let you know where we're at before it gets splashed across the papers.'

Gavin's eyebrows rose. 'Have you made an arrest?'

'No, and although we aren't one hundred per cent certain who was responsible for Zoë's death, we do have a pretty good idea. Unfortunately the man we're looking for has made himself scarce.'

'Who is he?'

'I'm afraid I can't give you a name at this point, but it's unlikely it would mean anything to you. It looks as though Zoë was the victim of a serial killer.'

Gavin stared at Lawrence. 'A serial killer?' He echoed, at length.

'Yes.'

'Well what exactly does that mean?' He demanded. 'I mean, obviously I know what a serial killer is, but what does it mean in this case? Do you have any idea who you're looking for, or have you just linked it to a few similar cases and given the perpetrator some graphic nickname that's going to be bandied around by journalists for however many months or years it takes to track him down?'

'I think you'll find it's the journalists who are responsible for the nicknames.'

'I couldn't give a damn who thinks up the nicknames! What I want to know is whether you've any real chance of tracking down my daughter's killer!'

'I'm afraid I can't give you a satisfactory answer to that question at this juncture. We do have a name, but he's no longer at his most recent address and we don't yet know where he went from there. We will be following up every avenue, and I can assure you we will do our utmost to find him and bring him to justice.'

'That means no, doesn't it?' Gavin snapped. 'Perhaps if you'd wasted less time prying into my family's private affairs you might have succeeded in tracking the guy down *before* he disappeared!'

'Dr Mitchell –'

'No! What is it with you people? Why do you automatically assume that when a murder is committed it must have something to do with the victim's friends and family? Is it too much trouble for you to check your records *first*?'

'That really wouldn't have taken us any further forwards. The only reason we have succeeded in identifying a suspect is because of his activities since Zoë's death. Naturally we're as keen as you are to see him brought to justice, but –'

'I bet you are! It doesn't reflect well on you when somebody's running about killing people left, right and centre, does it?'

'Dr Mitchell, *please*. I understand you're upset, but we really are doing everything we can.'

Gavin didn't respond.

'I'm sorry if this is taking longer than you had hoped, but in cases such as this the absence of any links between a killer and his victims can make it very difficult to even identify the perpetrator. We do have a name and a description for our suspect, and I'm hopeful we will track him down.'

Gavin grunted in reply, still saying nothing.

'Now, if you'd rather I broke the news to your wife you can give me her current address and I'll –'

'She's in Leeds,' Gavin interrupted. 'You're hardly going to go all the way up there now, are you?'

'I can drive up there this evening, that's not a problem.'

'What, and waste even more time than you have already?'

Lawrence tried to keep his tone reasonable as he said, 'If you'd prefer to tell her yourself –'

'I would.'

'Are you sure?'

Gavin nodded. 'I'll tell her.' He looked down with a heavy sigh. 'After everything else, I think she deserves that much.'

On his way back to Scotland Yard, Lawrence looked into the mortuary, where Leighton and two technicians were in the midst of a postmortem. With its stainless steel surfaces, unnaturally bright lights and the scent of chemicals heavy in the air, the room was unwelcomely sterile, and Lawrence wondered, not for the first time, exactly what it was that drew anyone to a career in the rather grisly field of forensic pathology.

Hearing the door open, Leighton glanced up, and, seeing Lawrence, left what he was doing and walked towards him.

'How's it going?' Lawrence enquired, as his colleague snapped off his gloves and removed his face mask.

'Slowly.'

'Anything you can tell me at this stage?'

'It'll be a couple of days before I have any DNA results, but I think that's just going to be a formality.'

'So you think we're looking at the same man?'

Leighton nodded. 'Strangulation, rape, mutilation of the breasts –' he raised his eyebrows expressively. 'The mutilation's rougher than on previous occasions, but that's not altogether surprising given that this attack took place out in the open. I expect the perpetrator was in something of a hurry.'

'Why do you think this one did occur outdoors?'

Leighton shrugged. 'I'm not a psychologist.'

'Fair point,' Lawrence conceded. 'Any idea about time of death?'

'Early hours of this morning. If you want to narrow it down further, CCTV is probably your best bet.'

'I was really looking to find out what sort of window we should concentrate on when we check the CCTV,' Lawrence replied. 'How much longer do you think you're likely to be?'

'A while.'

'When you're done, there's a flat in North London I'd like you to take a look at.'

Lawrence had expected Leighton to protest at the prospect of another job that would doubtless take him late into the night, and was pleasantly surprised when he nodded and said, 'No problem, but you might want to have someone keep an eye on the place, make sure nobody disturbs it in the meantime. I don't know how long I'm going to be here.'

'Already done.'

'Great. Can you send the address and any other details through to my phone?'

'Sure. And on another note, I need to know whether or not Letty Winterton's breasts were mutilated prior to death or after the event.'

'What do you need to know that for?'

'I've arranged a meeting for tomorrow morning with a criminal psychologist who's done a lot of work with serial killers, and I'd like to make sure I have all the available information.'

'Sounds interesting. Any chance I could tag along?'

'If you've time.'

'I'll see how it goes.'

'And how about Letty?'

'Oh – um – I think the attack was a virtual carbon copy of that on Zoë, but I'll check that for you. Do you want me to do that now?'

'No, don't let me interrupt – just give me a call when you can.'

'Will do. This one here's been mutilated prior to death, if that's of any interest.'

'Out in the *street*?'

'Hardly the street.' Leighton leaned against the bench behind him. 'Shoot-up alley, I think they called it – I don't imagine it would have been a busy thoroughfare in the wee small hours.'

'Even so, it's a big risk – all it would take would be for the girl to scream at the wrong moment.'

'She wouldn't have been able to even if she had been conscious. The killer taped her mouth shut – you can see the damage to the tissue where it's been ripped off.'

Lawrence immediately thought of what Josephine had told him that morning. 'Did you notice any similar marks when you examined Zoë's body?'

Leighton shook his head. 'No, but I guess it might have been removed more carefully on that occasion – I noticed it this time because there's a tear to the girl's lip.'

'And Letty?'

'I don't recall any mention of tape. I'll go and check the report for you now. Would it make life easier if I just made you a copy?'

'If you tell me where the report is, I can copy it myself.'

Leighton effected an exaggerated wince. 'You might have trouble finding it. My desk is mess.'

Lawrence sighed. 'All right, well when you do manage to find it, please let me know. And if you could let me have some sort of report on this one by the morning, that would be very much appreciated.'

'I'll do my best. Don't forget to send me that address.'

'I'll email it through.' Lawrence turned to go. 'Give me a call if anything comes up. Otherwise I'll be here tomorrow. First thing.'

'Marvellous,' Lawrence muttered, sarcastically, arriving home on Wednesday evening to find a copy of *The Evening Standard* lying on the kitchen table, complete with the front-page headline *London Slasher Strikes Again*. Picking it up, he scanned the first paragraph, and wasn't particularly surprised to learn that the journalist had managed to link the most recent killing to not only the death of Zoë Mitchell, but also that of Letty Winterton. The article was accompanied by a photograph of the alley in which the previous night's victim had been found, complete with police tape and a hastily erected tarpaulin tent. Several uniformed police officers were clustered in the foreground, and behind them and the tape Lawrence could just make out Leighton gesturing to another uniformed officer.

'I was starting to think you might have forgotten where we live,' Katie's voice remarked, coolly, from behind him.

'Sorry,' Lawrence replied, looking up as she entered the kitchen. 'It's been rather a hectic day.'

'Just for a change,' Katie returned. 'What kept you this time?'

'Have a read,' Lawrence replied, handing her the paper and moving to loosen his tie.

Katie glanced down at it, then looked sharply back up. 'This is *your* case?' She exclaimed, as Jimmy came wandering into the kitchen.

'It is.'

'Goodness.'

Jimmy's reaction was quite different. 'Wow!' He responded, excitedly. 'Cool!'

'Jimmy –'

'Was there, like, loads of blood?'

'Was there loads of blood,' Lawrence corrected.

'Whatever,' Jimmy responded, impatiently, and, when Lawrence didn't immediately reply, 'Well, *was* there?'

Lawrence sat at the kitchen table. 'I'm not going into the gory details.'

'But –'

'Give your dad five minutes to unwind, Jim. He's had a long day.' Katie handed Lawrence a glass of water.

'But this is *cool!*' Jimmy enthused. 'Wait till I tell the kids at school! Are you gonna get to go on TV, Dad?'

'Sit down a minute,' Lawrence pulled a chair out from the table. Jimmy obliged, looking expectant, and Lawrence took a sip of his drink before continuing, 'Now I know this must all look very exciting, and when I was your age I probably would have reacted in much the same way, but murder really isn't cool, Jim. We're not talking about a film here; this girl suffered a terrifying and violent death. She most probably has a family somewhere, and friends – just try to imagine how they're going to feel when they find out what's happened to her.'

Jimmy cast his eyes down, chastened. There was a pause before he asked, 'Does that mean I can't tell everyone at school?'

Lawrence sighed. 'I can't stop you, can I?'

Jimmy shrugged.

'There's some leftover dinner if you're hungry, Larry,' Katie put in, resting a hand on his shoulder.

'Thanks, but I grabbed something at work in the end – I'm sorry, I should have called, I know.'

Katie absolved him with a small smile and a shake of her head.

'Can we go to Alton Towers in the holidays Dad?' Jimmy asked, perking up again. 'Ricky went on Saturday, and he said it was ace!'

'I should think that could be arranged,' Lawrence replied. 'Just so long as you don't expect me to accompany you on anything that goes upside down.'

'But it'll be *boring* going by myself!'

'Well perhaps you could bring a friend along.'

Jimmy's face lit up. 'Can I? Can I ask Mal?'

'Sure, why not.'

'Excellent!' Jimmy jumped up from the table. 'Mum, can I go and call him now?'

'It's nearly ten o'clock, Jim – Malcolm's probably in bed by now. You can ask him tomorrow at school. You should be getting ready for bed yourself. Go and clean your teeth and I'll be up to say goodnight in five minutes.'

'But –'

'Bedtime,' Katie interrupted, firmly. 'Go on, before your dad changes his mind.'

This was enough for Jimmy, who turned and scurried from the kitchen without another word. Katie joined Lawrence at the table. 'You've just made his week. He's been talking about nothing else since he arrived home from school.'

'Anything for peace and quiet,' Lawrence joked. 'How's Elise?'

'Sulking. I wouldn't let her have a little top she wanted from that shop up near the station, so now I'm public enemy number one.'

'How much was it?'

'Oh, it wasn't the price tag that was the problem – although she tried to persuade me to let her have it if she paid for it out of her pocket money – but there's no way she's walking around in a t-shirt with *sex kitten* printed across it.'

Lawrence raised his eyebrows.

'Obviously that makes me a *terrible* mother, because *all* her friends' mothers would have let *their* daughters have it.'

'Of course.'

Katie smiled. 'And apparently Daddy would have let her have it too, so you can expect the matter to come up over breakfast.'

'That's going to be a very short conversation,' Lawrence replied, shaking his head. 'I don't know. There's something very wrong with a world in which nine-year-old girls want mobile phones and sexually suggestive clothing – my sister was still wearing Snoopy pyjamas and climbing trees at the age of thirteen.' He sighed. 'Sometimes I wonder what happened to childhood. These days it seems as if girls learn to apply make-up before they even learn to write.'

Fifteen

Unless he was on call, Leighton rarely made it in to the pathology unit much before half-past nine, so Lawrence had been under no illusion that he might get an update in person when he arrived at seven-thirty on Thursday morning. Having received nothing from the pathologist by email overnight, he was expecting to find a summary of the previous day's postmortem waiting for him at the front desk, and was more than a little surprised when the security guard on duty told him that no, Dr Campbell hadn't left anything out for collection, but was around somewhere if he wanted to go through. Even more surprisingly, Leighton wasn't lounging at his desk with a coffee, but already at work in the lab.

'I thought *I* was in early,' Lawrence remarked, approaching the bench where his colleague was sitting, peering down a microscope.

'I'm working late as it happens,' Leighton responded as he raised his gaze, his blue eyes faintly bloodshot.

'Have you been here all night?'

'Yep – well, since I finished up at that flat, which was some time around three.'

'Have you much more to do?'

'I hope not – I'll need Red Bull on an IV drip if I have to stay here much longer,' he replied, with a weary smile, raising a hand to rub his eyes.

'Where are you at?'

'Report on the dead girl is on your desk, as requested. On the subject of that flat, you're either after one clever killer or he's been paying close attention while watching *Gattaca*.'

Lawrence frowned. 'Meaning what?'

'I think he went over the place with a mega-powerful vacuum cleaner before leaving. He's certainly done his best to remove all traces of himself – and added a few foreign samples to confuse me.'

'Did you find anything?'

Leighton lifted one eyebrow. 'Well, you clearly *didn't* pay attention to the *X-Files*. *Nothing* disappears without a trace.'

'Do you think we could just get to the point?'

'I can't tell you anything for certain until the lab gets back to me with the DNA results, but I'd put money on getting a positive match from a couple of hairs I found caught in the u-bend under the sink. They'd been bleached, and they're exactly the same colour and have an identical degree of root growth to one I found at yesterday's crime scene.'

'How about fingerprints?'

'I managed to find a few, although it took forever. I've run them through the computer, but so far I've come up with nothing. Not that there's any guarantee they're his.' Leighton rearranged himself on his stool, looking suddenly animated. 'Has anybody you've spoken to commented on his eyes?'

'A couple of people mentioned that they were very blue. Azure was one description, I think.'

'Tinted contact lenses,' Leighton revealed, looking pleased with himself. 'I found one on the ground beneath the body, I suspect it fell out while he was struggling with the girl.'

'So he may have altered his hair and eye colour as part of a disguise,' Lawrence concluded.

'Makes sense to me. If you're running the risk of your description being widely circulated, and perhaps even given out on television, the last thing you want is for your friends and family to identify you. People are more likely to dismiss a different hair colour, because most of us have dabbled with colourants at some stage – but tinted contact lenses are still something of a rarity.'

Lawrence nodded. 'Is there any way of finding out what colour his eyes actually are?'

'I'm not a magician,' Leighton shrugged. 'What I am going to do, though, is ask an optician to look at the lens for me. In the unlikely event that it's a prescription one, we might be able to trace where it came from. There can't be many people out there buying them for anything more than novelty value.'

'How will that help?'

'There's a chance an optician might have a record of past addresses, email, mobile number – that kind of thing.'

'Good point.'

'I think that's about all I can give you at the moment.' Leighton rested an elbow on the surface of the laboratory bench, propping his head up with his hand. 'I'll be about for another hour or two, and then I'm going to head off. My mobile's playing up, so I'll leave you my home number – if anything comes up, give me a call.'

'Thanks. I'll try not to disturb you unless it's urgent.'

'Isn't it always?'

'Usually,' Lawrence admitted. 'But I don't get impatient out of some exaggerated sense of self-importance. Homicide cases have a habit of becoming a race against the clock.'

'Yeah, I know,' Leighton replied, amicably. 'I don't take it personally.'

Lawrence didn't say that perhaps he ought to. The pathologist's relaxed attitude to working hours and time management was frustrating for more reasons than one, but it seemed churlish to say as much when he'd been working all night. Lawrence might have been thinking aloud, however, because his colleague added, as if in defence, 'We do tend to have a lot of balls in the air in these parts, though.' He tweaked one of the dials on the side of the microscope before looking back up. 'The fact I'm not doing something for you doesn't necessarily mean I'm doing nothing.'

Academics had apparently smartened themselves up since Lawrence's time at university, and in his neat grey suit, white shirt and nondescript tie, George Cooke would have blended in easily at a city bank or law firm. He looked to be in his forties, his hair still relatively dark, although thinning, his eyes a dark caramel colour. He took his time reading the notes Lawrence had compiled on the circumstances and details of the four crimes involved in the investigation, and examined a number of the crime scene photographs before raising his eyes to meet Lawrence's and leaning back in his chair.

'Organised nonsocial lust murderer,' he concluded, shortly.

'What does that mean?'

'Lust murderers tend to mutilate or displace the breasts or genitals of their victims. As a rule they like to use their hands during the killing – strangulation is fairly common.' George sat forwards, reaching for the pages of notes, which he had placed on Lawrence's desk a few minutes earlier. 'There are two basic types of lust killer, and from a number of the details in here, there's little doubt you're looking at an organised nonsocial killer as opposed to the disorganised asocial type.'

'What's the difference?'

'Well, for starters, with the exception of yesterday's victim – who I'll come to later – these crimes have been very carefully planned. Your typical disorganised killer is more of an opportunist.' George glanced down at the printout in his hand before continuing. 'He's obviously very aware of the effect these murders are going to have on society – he *wants* the publicity that will stem from his crimes. That much is evident from his careful choice of victims.'

'What were you going to say about yesterday's victim?'

'Oh, yes – obviously not planned like the others, however, as you've stated in this report it's likely his original plan fell through. I suspect he found the first available replacement. The serial killer's compulsion to kill will often overtake everything else, and the ritual is of the utmost importance to him. It's likely that by the time he discovered his intended victim was unavailable, the first and foremost thought in his mind was to kill. He then had to find another woman to satisfy that urge.'

Lawrence nodded.

'The fact that he's mutilated the bodies prior to death, and that he's made no effort whatsoever to conceal them also indicate the type of killer you're looking for.'

'I assume the mutilation is part of the ritual you mentioned earlier?'

'Yes.'

'I suppose that might explain why he took the risk of carrying it out in the street yesterday morning.'

'Oh, absolutely. That risk would be overridden by the need to complete the ritual.'

'Do you have any idea what sort of person we might be looking for in a more day-to-day sense?'

'Unfortunately he probably seems like a perfectly normal member of society. Your typical organised nonsocial killer is very cunning and comes across as friendly and personable. Although they generally dislike people, this type of killer is very adept at hiding that.'

'Do you think he's likely to continue killing until he's caught?'

'Almost certainly. Serial killers rarely stop killing of their own accord. On occasion they take their own lives, but I seriously doubt your killer is going to do that.'

'And God knows how many other door keys he's managed to amass in the last eighteen months,' Lawrence remarked.

'There must be a limited number of newsworthy customers using one particular locksmith's. Especially considering that all the victims so far have not only had a link to the public eye but have also been slim, young, attractive women with long or mid-length brown hair.'

'But the locksmith fired him after he caught the man – Brett – stealing a handful of keys.'

'Did he ask what they were for?'

'The story Brett gave him was that he was cutting keys at a discount and pocketing the cash.'

'That's quite possible,' George replied. 'Serial killers often commit crimes other than homicide. Sometimes you'll see a gap in a series of murders, which turns out to correspond to a time when the killer was imprisoned for a completely different offence. I assume you've already run a check for fingerprints?'

'Yes.'

'Well, I don't think there's much else I can tell you at this point. Give me a call if you've any questions, or if anything else comes to light.'

'I will, thank you.'

George stood to leave. 'Good luck.'

Lawrence nodded. He suspected he was going to need it.

'Sorry I'm late,' Rebecca apologised as she hurried into Lawrence's office at twenty-five to ten. 'I didn't have a very good night, and I overslept.'

'Don't worry about it. I've only just managed to round these two up anyway.' Lawrence indicated Daniel and Jamie, who were sitting around his desk. 'Come and join us.'

Rebecca sat beside Daniel, who took a mug of coffee from Lawrence's desk and handed it to her.

'Thanks.'

'Ok,' Lawrence sat back in his chair. 'It seems likely we're looking for a serial killer, and one whose whereabouts are now completely unknown. We do know that he was at a rented flat in North Finchley until Tuesday evening, and that he was in Tufnell Park during the early hours of Wednesday morning. From then on is a total blank. He's cleared the flat, so we've very little to go on. I'm going to arrange for someone to draw up a photofit with the assistance of his landlady and his employer, and I'll have that circulated as widely as possible. The flat's being kept under surveillance on the off-chance he might return. I'd like to try to trace his movements from Tuesday evening onwards via CCTV –

perhaps you two could look into that?' Lawrence looked to Daniel and Rebecca.

Daniel raised his eyebrows. 'I don't mean to be unhelpful, Sir, but I doubt there's much CCTV to find. The flat's slap bang in the middle of a residential area.'

'I know it's a long shot, but let's not write it off before we've even begun. Start with local cab companies, and if you draw a blank with them try TfL – nearest tube stations, and local buses if need be. You'll need somebody who recognises him to help you out with that initially – I'll ask his landlady if she'd mind, because she's retired – somehow I don't think the locksmith's going to be keen to give up too much his time.'

'It might be worth checking with the local station ticket offices before we do that,' Rebecca suggested. 'See whether we can track him through Oyster. Although I'm guessing he'll have thought of that.'

'Good idea.'

'What do you want me to do?' Jamie asked.

'See what you can trace in terms of bank accounts and credit cards in the name of Brett Lindquist. Even if he's no longer using them we might get some clues to his identity from previous or alternative addresses. Hopefully the locksmith has a record of his National Insurance number; if so you should be able to track down the details of his previous employers. An old colleague may still be in touch with him, or know his family – even tracing them would be a start. And see what you can get from the phone companies.'

'Do we have a mobile number?'

'Unfortunately not, but there was an active landline at the flat, although the landlady wasn't sure about Internet connectivity.'

Jamie nodded. 'Do we know how his salary or rent was paid?'

'No, I'll look into that as soon as we're done here and let you know. After that I'm going to make a start on tracing the previous tenant of Josephine's flat, and I'll see what help we can get on house-to-house enquires around Tufnell Park and Highgate – if any of you comes up against a dead end, you can lend a hand there.'

'I assume you're going to have posters put up in the area?' Daniel remarked.

'If the Kentish Town police haven't already seen to that, yes,' Lawrence reached for a pen. 'And before I forget, the current description we have of Brett may no longer be accurate. I spoke to Leighton earlier, and he seems to think Brett not only bleached his hair but also wore coloured contact lenses. I'll see whether we can get some photofits with different eye and hair colours for reference.'

'The words *needle* and *haystack* spring to mind,' Daniel remarked, gloomily.

'Nah, finding a needle in a haystack would be easy,' Jamie responded. 'You could just crack out a metal detector.' He paused, then added, 'What we're looking for is a chameleon in the jungle.'

According to the original police report detailing the violent attack on Josephine Islington, the previous tenant named on the lease of the rental flat was one Alan Newman. He had been cleared of any involvement in the crime, as he had been working abroad on the night in question, and claimed to have sublet the flat for the final five months of his contract. Unfortunately, however, he had been able to provide the police with little more than a Christian name for the man who had taken his place in the property.

Lawrence had had little difficulty locating Alan, who was still living at the same address he had given the police some thirteen months earlier, but had been unable to interview him before Saturday lunch time, as Alan had once again been out of the country. A hefty man in his thirties with wide-set eyes and dark hair that was little more than stubble, he had several rings in each ear, and one through his left eyebrow. There was more hair on his chin than on his head, although this did little to disguise the fact that the feature was almost non-existent. Clad in black jeans and a white vest that exposed arms tattooed from his shoulders to his wrists, he was watching the cricket when his girlfriend showed Lawrence into the living room, and looked none too pleased at the interruption.

'Good afternoon,' Lawrence began, presenting Alan with his warrant card. 'I'm DCI Forrester. I'm sorry to disturb you on a Saturday, but it is rather urgent.'

'Lindy said you'd been round.'

'Yes. I understand you've been away.'

'San Francisco. What d'you want from me?'

'I'd like to ask you a few questions about the flat you rented in Black Horse Road the year before last.'

Alan frowned. 'Why? I've already told the police everything I know about that.'

'It's possible that the attack that occurred there is related to several other serious crimes, so I'm keen to gather all the information I can.'

'Well I don't really see how I'm going to be of much help.'

Lawrence felt irritated. 'Perhaps you could reserve judgement until you've heard what I'm going to ask.'

Alan shrugged wordlessly.

'As I understand it, you sublet the flat for the final five months of the lease without notifying the landlord. Why was that?'

'The lease stated that I wasn't allowed to sublet – I was hardly gonna tell the landlord, was I?'

'My question is why you sublet the flat at all.'

'Oh,' Alan nodded. 'I moved in here with Lindy. She lost her job and was afraid she'd lose the house, so I offered to cover the mortgage payments. I couldn't keep up the rent on the flat as well, and the landlord refused to release me from the contract, so subletting seemed the best option.'

'And how did you go about finding a tenant?'

'Is this information not on file somewhere?'

'Not in detail, no. Please just answer the question.'

Looking vexed, Alan said, 'I put an add on Gumtree.'

'What happened after that?'

'Several people enquired about it – I met Rhys in my local – he seemed all right, and he paid me two month's rent in advance, so I agreed he could take the flat.'

'Can you remember his surname?'

'I don't know that he even told me what it was.'

'How did he pay the rent?'

'In cash. Once a month.'

'And the bills on the property?'

'Cash. I included them in the rent and left the accounts in my name.'

Lawrence nodded. 'Could you give me a description of Rhys, please?'

'Christ, I haven't seen the man in well over a year! And I only ever met up with him half a dozen times!'

'Would you recognise him if you saw him?'

'Probably, but that doesn't mean I'd be able to give you much of a description.'

Lawrence presented Alan with a black and white photofit diagram. 'Does this look anything like him?'

Alan scrutinised the picture before nodding slowly. 'Yeah, kind of. I remember that scar on his upper lip.'

'Can you tell me what colour his hair was at the time?'

'Brown.'

'How about his eyes?'

'I've no idea.'

'Do you know what line of work he was in?'

'*No.*' Alan sat forwards in his chair. 'Look, I didn't know the guy! We met up for five minutes once a month for me to collect the money, that was as far as it went! If I'd known subletting the flat was going to cause me this much grief I'd've asked for references!'

Lawrence sighed. 'All right, I'll get out of your way. If you think of anything else – however small – please let me know.' Leaving his card on the coffee table, he stood up. 'Thank you for your time.'

Alan nodded in response, returning his attention to the cricket, and Lawrence headed towards the door. Although he had learned little from the interview, he felt heartened that the visit had not been entirely in vain: it had at least provided reasonable confirmation that, whatever his name, the previous tenant of Josephine's flat and the man who had worked at Sibson and Son were one and the same. Until Lawrence had a full name with which to attempt to trace him, however, that knowledge was of little use.

By the time Rebecca arrived home on Saturday evening, she was exhausted. She and Daniel had spent the previous two and a half days trying to trace Brett's movements after his departure from the flat in Nether Street on Tuesday night. Relying mainly on CCTV, they had succeeded in tracking him to Euston Station, via the Northern Line. There, he had placed the holdall he carried in left luggage before heading off above ground. Having returned early the following morning to collect the bag, he once again departed the station, and it had taken Rebecca and Daniel the best part of Friday to establish that he had chosen to walk the short distance from Euston to St Pancras, rather than take the tube.

There, he boarded a train bound for Bedford, and disembarked at the small Hertfordshire town of Harpenden. Rebecca and Daniel had lost track of him shortly thereafter, and, having spent the afternoon in the town, Rebecca suspected they were unlikely to pick the trail up again. Despite this, she and Daniel were to head back out to Harpenden the following morning, when all Rebecca wanted to do was have a long lie in followed by a lazy afternoon on Hampstead Heath.

The phone was ringing as she unlocked the door, and she hurried to answer it. 'Hello?'

'Hiya Becks. Is Elliot there?'

'I'm not sure – I just walked in the door. Hold on.' Rebecca set the receiver down and turned towards the bedroom, guessing that was where she was most likely to find him. He had barely been out of bed since Wednesday evening, and Rebecca was beginning to feel seriously concerned. She eased open the door to find the curtains closed and the room in semi-darkness. Elliot was curled up on his side, one arm tucked beneath his head. He had his back to the door, and was staring rather vacantly at the wall.

'Elliot, Damian's on the phone for you.'

'I don't want to talk to him.'

'But –'

'I don't want to talk to him!' Elliot repeated, more forcefully.

'All right,' Rebecca acknowledged, leaving the room and returning to the telephone. 'Damian, this isn't a very good time – can I give him a message for you?'

'No, not really,' Damian responded, sounding peeved. 'Scott's been on my back because Elliot's gone AWOL – he's not answering his mobile and he hasn't been online since Wednesday. I wondered whether everything was all right.'

'I don't really know, to be honest – he's not been very communicative.'

'Well Scott's pretty pissed off, so he might want to communicate with him. I can look after the website, but do you think you could tell Elliot to get his act together in time for next weekend?'

'Next weekend?'

'Glastonbury.'

'Oh – yes – of course.'

'Ok, I'll let you go. See you soon.'

'Sure. Goodbye.'

Replacing the receiver, Rebecca turned back towards the bedroom. Elliot was as she had left him, and, moving closer, she noticed that his eyes were bloodshot.

'Damian said Scott's been trying to get hold of you.'

Elliot didn't respond. Rebecca sighed, perching on the bed beside him and reaching to stroke his hair out of his eyes. It needed washing. 'What's up, sweetheart?'

'I don't know,' Elliot responded, weakly.

'Would you like me to call the doctor?'

'No.'

'How about you get up and take a shower and I'll cook you some dinner? Maybe you'll feel better when you've eaten.'

'I'm too tired.'

'Would you like something to eat in here?'

'Not hungry.'

'Elliot, if you don't eat you're going to make yourself ill.'

'I'm not fucking hungry! All right?'

'I'm only trying to help!'

'Just leave me alone.'

'Elliot –'

'Please just *go*.'

'Go? Where? Next door? The other side of town? What do you want me to do? Go to another room, or pack a suitcase and leave?'

Elliot met her eyes for the first time, his expression panicked. 'You can't *leave*! You *can't*!'

'So what am I supposed to do? Sit around waiting for you to pull yourself together? Don't you think I've enough on at the moment without having this to come home to?'

'Pull myself together?' Elliot repeated, his tone one of total disbelief. 'Do you really think it's that fucking easy? You have no fucking *idea* how I feel!'

'No, I don't! And if you won't tell me, how the hell am I supposed to know? I'm not a mind reader!'

'Don't leave me!' Elliot implored, rather desperately. 'Please don't go, I don't think I could cope without you!'

'You call this coping?'

'Please don't leave me!'

'You're the one that told me to go!'

'I didn't mean for you to *leave*!' He reached for her hand. Rebecca snatched it away, and Elliot pursed his lips tightly, his eyes filling with tears.

'Will you grow up!' Rebecca exclaimed, jumping to her feet. 'Every time I try to help you, you treat me like crap, and then start crying when I lose my temper! I never said I was going to leave, but I'm beginning to think it might be a good idea!'

'I'm sorry!' Elliot managed, struggling to sit up. 'Please don't leave! *Please!*'

'Give me one good reason why I should stay?'

Elliot shrugged. 'Because I love you,' he offered, weakly, after a moment.

'Shutting me out. That's love, is it?'

'*Please!* Please don't go, it'll kill me!'

Rebecca shook her head. 'Ultimatums aren't going to keep me here, Elliot.'

'I'm *sorry!*'

'Stop apologising all the bloody time! Saying sorry doesn't make everything all right when you continue to behave like a stroppy teenager!'

Elliot bowed his head, raising a hand to cover his eyes. He was shaking, and Rebecca noticed that there were fresh cuts to his arm. She remained where she was for a moment before turning to leave the room. In the kitchen she sank down into a chair at the table, starting to cry herself. The past week had been incredibly draining, both mentally and emotionally, and having to deal with Elliot on top of everything else was just too much. For months she had relied on him for a hug and some reassurance at the end of a tough day, and recently she had rather forgotten what life had been like before they met. Wishing her mother didn't live so far away, Rebecca reached for the telephone and started to dial her sister's number. Assuming that Angela was in on a Saturday night, Rebecca hoped her reaction wouldn't be a blunt *I told you so.*

Katie looked up as Lawrence appeared in the living room doorway at quarter to ten. 'They ought to be paying you overtime,' she remarked, lightly.

'Sorry.'

'How was your day?'

'Long and frustrating. Once again.' Lawrence sighed, sitting in his favourite armchair. 'I've been knocking on doors since one o'clock this afternoon.'

'Have you eaten?'

'Not since lunch time. I'll make a sandwich in a minute.'

'There's soup in the fridge if you'd like some.'

'What sort of soup?' Lawrence asked, before a loud thud from upstairs made him jump. 'What the hell was that?' He exclaimed, moving to stand.

'Malcolm's staying over – he and Jimmy are constructing some sort of fort. They wanted to camp out in the garden, but I said no, so I think they're planning on camping out indoors instead.'

Lawrence glanced at his watch with a frown. 'They ought to be in bed by now.'

'I said they could stay up for an extra hour.'

Lawrence nodded. 'I suppose I'd better go and water the garden while it's still light enough for me to see what I'm doing.' He stood up reluctantly. 'I won't be long.'

Moving the sprinkler towards the end of the garden, Lawrence stopped, trying to put his finger on what it was about the flower bed that wasn't right. Some moments passed before he realised that the red-hot poker that had towered proudly amidst the snapdragons and dahlias was missing. Close up, all that remained was the leaves; the flowers and stalk were nowhere to be found. Returning to the house, he looked back into the living room.

'Have Jimmy and Malcolm been playing in the garden?'

Katie glanced up from her book. 'Pardon?'

'Have the boys been playing in the garden?'

'They were out there for a while this afternoon. Why?'

Lawrence shook his head angrily, turning to call up the stairs. 'Jimmy? Down here now, please!'

'What's happened?' Katie asked, joining him in the hallway as Jimmy and Malcolm careered noisily down the stairs.

'Can either of you explain the absence of the red-hot poker that was in the garden when I left the house this morning?' Lawrence asked, sharply, as they skidded to a halt in front of him.

Jimmy fixed his eyes on the floor, thrusting his hands into his pockets, and Malcolm shuffled his feet, clearly uncomfortable.

'I'm waiting.'

'Sorry Dad,' Jimmy muttered, without lifting his gaze.

Lawrence sighed. 'What happened?'

'Hit it with a football.'

'What have I said about playing football?'

Jimmy shrugged, eyes still on the floor. 'Not in the garden.'

Lawrence felt vexed. 'How many times do we have to go over this? The flower beds are *not* a playground! It's not as if there's nowhere else for you to go, is it? There's a park just down the road! *Why* do you find it necessary to persistently disobey me?'

Jimmy shrugged again. 'Sorry.'

'You're old enough to know better! I don't *want* to have to confiscate your football, but if this happens again, I'm going to have no other option! Is that understood?'

'Yes Dad. Sorry.'

'Go on, upstairs. It's past your bedtime.'

The two boys turned to go. Lawrence remained where he was, and heard Jimmy say as he and Malcolm reached the top of the stairs, 'I *told* you Dad'd notice. I think he knows where every plant in the garden is. He must *count* them, or something.'

Looking to his wife, Lawrence guessed from the suppressed half smile on her face that he hadn't been the only one to overhear.

'You wouldn't be laughing if it was your geraniums.'

'Ah, but I don't count my geraniums,' Katie teased, before her expression grew more serious. 'I'm sorry Larry – I should have kept a closer eye on them.'

'It's not your fault. Jimmy's quite old enough to take responsibility for his actions. Sometimes I –' he stopped suddenly as a thought hit him. Glancing at his watch, he started up the stairs. 'He's given me an idea. I'm going to make some calls. I'll be in the study.'

'But –' Katie began.

'I'll try not to be long,' Lawrence promised, guessing that his chances of getting the information he wanted on a Saturday night were minimal. Jimmy's words went round and round in his head, and, reaching his study, he took the calendar from the desk and flicked straight to the back to check the dates of previous years. Counting back the months, he tried to suppress his excitement. This was a long shot, and he suspected it would leave him disappointed. Even so, it had to be worth a try.

Sixteen

'Morning,' Lawrence opened, as Daniel entered the office a few minutes after eight on Monday morning.

'Yeah, don't rub it in,' Daniel responded, wearily, dropping into a chair to the left of Lawrence's desk. 'I hope there's a good reason for dragging us out of bed so early when we've been working all weekend.'

'I'm meeting somebody over in East London at nine, and I wanted all of us to sit down for a few minutes before the week gets underway.'

Daniel's dark eyebrows rose. '*All* of us?'

'Assuming Becky and Jamie intend to join us.'

'Nobody told me it was optional.'

'It isn't,' Lawrence responded, shortly, turning towards the shelves behind his desk and reaching for a folder.

Daniel sighed loudly, reaching to his pocket for his phone. 'Well, while we wait I might as well –'

He was interrupted by Rebecca's arrival. She looked flustered, and was out of breath. 'Sorry, Northern Line's shafted again.'

'Let me guess,' Lawrence replied, drily. 'Aliens from planet Zog abducted the driver?'

'How did you know?' Rebecca reached for a chair. 'No, this time they closed the Charing Cross branch because somebody *stole* a train.' She held out her hands in disbelief as she sat down. 'Can you actually believe that? Where the hell did they think they could take it?'

'Great train robbers strike at Mornington Crescent,' Daniel remarked, sarcastically. 'Perhaps they kidnapped Jamie as well.'

Lawrence glanced at his watch. 'We'll make a start without him – I haven't time to sit around waiting for any more excuses. Have you two made any progress since we spoke on Saturday?'

Rebecca shook her head. 'We spent most of the weekend in Harpenden, but nobody recognised the photofits, and we drew a blank on what CCTV there was.'

Lawrence sighed. 'I think we're looking for the invisible man. Most of the people living in Nether Street didn't even recognise him.'

'Perhaps he goes around in a hat and dark glasses,' Daniel suggested, unhelpfully.

Rebecca rolled her eyes. 'Yeah, Dan, great idea. That wouldn't attract any attention whatsoever.'

'This isn't a joke,' Lawrence snapped. 'Now, do you think it would be worthwhile spending any more time in Harpenden?'

'No,' Rebecca replied, definitively. 'We've no further leads, and given that the last time we know he was actually there was on Thursday morning, I doubt we're going to come up with anything else.'

'All right, I'll arrange to have some flyers distributed in the area, and you two can join in with making enquires around the locksmith's. I'd like to –'

'Sorry,' Jamie apologised, as he hurried in. 'I was –'

Lawrence held up a hand. 'I don't want to hear it. Grab a seat and give us all some idea of where you're at.'

Jamie sat down, asking, as he did so, 'Where do you want me to start?'

'How about the banks and credit card companies?'

'Nothing. Well, not for the guy we're after.'

Lawrence frowned. 'What does that mean?'

'The account his salary was paid into was cleared out several days before he disappeared and there's been no activity since. I did find a couple of other accounts in the name of Brett Lindquist, but that Brett is a fourteen-year-old schoolboy living in Aberdeen.'

'I assume you contacted the family to check they have no other relations of that name?'

Jamie shifted uncomfortably in his chair. 'Not yet.'

Lawrence felt irritated. 'You mean you didn't think of that. This morning, please,' he said, pointedly. 'How about the National Insurance search?'

'Somebody's supposed to be getting back to me today.'

'I'll leave that with you, then.' Lawrence checked his notes. 'Oh, and how did you get on with the phone line?'

'There is a line to the flat, but he doesn't seem to have used it.'

'Damn. I was hoping we might find something there.' Lawrence reached for a pen. 'How about Internet?'

'Nothing. At a guess – if he had a computer – he used one of those pay-as-you-go dongles. Or a smartphone hotspot.'

'Ok.' Lawrence nodded. 'Now I don't know whether my meeting this morning is going to yield anything at all, but if it does

I may be tied up for the next day or two. If you need me for any reason, don't hesitate to call.' He pushed his chair back from the desk and stood up.

'Who are you meeting this morning?' Rebecca enquired.

'A librarian.'

'A *librarian*? How come?'

'Probably just to waste a couple of hours of my morning,' Lawrence replied, pulling on his jacket. 'But if I strike lucky, all will be revealed.'

Daniel knocked on the front door of the final house in the terrace, glancing at his watch as he did so. 'Shall we make this the last one?'

Rebecca nodded. They had spent most of Wednesday afternoon and half the evening continuing the extended house-to-house enquires Lawrence had requested around Brett's North London flat, and so far not one person they had spoken to had even recognised the photofit picture they carried, much less known anything about him. Rebecca had been convinced the task was a waste of time before they had even begun, and was growing increasingly frustrated with knocking on one door after another.

'Do you have any plans for what's left of the evening?' She asked, as Daniel stepped back from the door.

'Packing.'

'Oh?'

'I'm moving out.'

'You decided to make the break, then.'

'Yeah,' Daniel confirmed. 'It's a relief, to be honest.'

'How's Jess taking it?'

'I dunno. She's hardly going to tell me.'

'Where are you moving to?'

'Acton. It's not my first choice of location, but the rent where I am now is going to take too big a bite out of one salary, and I can't be doing with sharing with random strangers.'

'When are you moving?'

'Saturday. It's a nightmare working out what's mine to take – there are so many things we bought together.' Daniel knocked on the door again.

'Is that causing problems?' Rebecca asked, thinking of the numerous shared possessions she and Elliot had amassed in just a few months.

'World war three.'

'Will Jess be staying on at the flat?'

'I doubt it – unless she turns the living room into a second bedroom and rents it out.' He paused. 'Mind you, she's effectively done that already – I've been sleeping in there for weeks.'

'Next time you move in with a girl, make sure you get a spare room.'

'Do you have one?'

'Oh yes.'

Daniel raised his eyebrows. 'Like that, is it?'

'Not yet. Elliot keeps all his guitars and other equipment in there. I think he likes to have somewhere to retreat into his music. Quite often he disappears for hours at a time.'

'Is *that* what he tells you he's doing?' Daniel grinned.

Rebecca ignored the comment, looking up at the house in front of them. 'At a guess, I'd say there's nobody home. Let's make a move.' She turned back down the path.

'What are you doing tonight?'

'As little as possible. I'm knackered.'

'Will Elliot be home?'

'Probably.'

There was a pause before Daniel asked, rather awkwardly, 'Do you not feel anxious being alone at night – after – what happened?'

'I don't know. I might do, if I were alone – but as yet I haven't been.'

'Elliot staying home to look after you, is he?'

Rebecca grunted noncommittally to avoid answering the question. She wasn't about to go into the details of the nightmare that her personal life had become over the course of the past week.

'It must be difficult for you working on this investigation, given the circumstances.'

Rebecca shrugged.

'Did Forrester not view it as a conflict of interest?'

'He suggested I take some time off, but I didn't want to. Sitting around at home isn't going to make me feel any better about things.'

Daniel hesitated before asking, 'How are you going to feel if we don't find Brett?'

'If I have anything to do with it, we *will*.'

'Do you really believe that?'

Rebecca chose to sidestep the question, saying instead, 'The more I think about what could have happened, the more terrifying it all seems. I've tried thinking about it rationally – I mean, nothing *did* happen – but somehow that doesn't make me feel any better. And at the same time, I feel guilty, because I'm so glad Elliot was there, and he wouldn't have been if Ian's dad hadn't been so ill.'

'Why does that make you feel guilty?'

'He's dead,' Rebecca revealed, wishing her voice didn't sound so unsteady. 'Ian's dad. He died over the weekend. If he was still here, maybe I wouldn't be.'

'That's hardly your fault.'

'I know that, but it doesn't make me feel any better about it! All right?'

Daniel didn't answer.

'I'm sorry,' Rebecca offered, at length. 'I didn't mean to have a go at you. I know you're only trying to help. I just don't know how I feel about everything at the moment. I'm used to my job being about other people.'

'Do you want to go for a drink?'

Rebecca shook her head. 'Not tonight. Maybe some other time, but right now I just want to go home.' She forced a smile. 'Thanks anyway.'

'I'm sorry if I'm sticking my nose in. You helped me make a decision about Jess, and I suppose I want to return the favour – but I guess you'd rather talk to Elliot.'

Rebecca didn't respond. She suspected *her* feelings were the last thing she and Elliot would be discussing that evening.

Lawrence replaced the telephone handset and looked back to the list he had been reviewing minutes earlier. He had already scored out most of the points, and suspected it was only a matter of time before he came up against another dead end. Glancing at his watch, he was considering calling it a day when Leighton tapped on his open office door.

'Is this a good time?'

'If you're here with information, any time's a good time,' Lawrence replied, leaning his elbows on his desk.

'I've fingerprints for you.' Leighton settled himself in a chair the other side of the desk. 'Or at least, *a* fingerprint.'

'I thought you couldn't match any of them?'

Leighton shook his head, waving a hand in emphasis. 'Not the ones from the flat. I came up with another idea while I was writing a Post-it note for Jon this afternoon.'

'What idea?'

'Well, it occurred to me that if our final victim – does she have a name yet, by the way?'

'Monica Hudson.'

'Ok. Anyway, I figured that if she had tape stuck over her mouth when she was attacked, but not when she was found, the killer had most probably pulled it off before leaving. Now, if you get hold of the end of a piece of tape –' Leighton reached for the Sellotape dispenser on Lawrence's desk and took hold of the end to demonstrate. 'You more often than not have your thumb held firmly on top.' He replaced the dispenser. 'So I had another look through everything we collected at the crime scene, and found a fragment of duct tape. I can't say one hundred per cent that the print on it is the killer's, but I ran it through the computer anyway, and I have a name for you. It's not the one you're looking for, but the man in question has previously served time in connection with a serious sexual assault.'

'What is the name?' Lawrence chivvied, impatiently.

'Rhys Williams.'

'Rhys Williams?' He exclaimed. 'But I ran that name through the computer on Monday! I didn't find anything!'

'Well, you know what they say. If you want a job done badly, do it yourself, if you want a spectacular cock-up, use a computer.'

'I must have done something wrong,' Lawrence sighed.

'Or there was a problem with the system,' Leighton ventured.

'When did the assault take place?'

'Some years ago now. It's all in here.' Leighton tossed a computer printout onto Lawrence's desk. 'There's also a photo, although it'll be rather out of date.'

'Thank you,' Lawrence reached for it before stopping with a frown. 'If he was convicted of sexual assault, surely there ought to be a DNA profile on file?'

'Yeah, there ought to be, but there isn't.'

'Is there any way we can chase that up manually?'

'Already tried. I got the email equivalent of a shrug.'

'Fantastic,' Lawrence muttered, sarcastically.

'Not that it makes a lot of difference, at this stage.'

'It does if it prevents it happening again. If the information had been on file, it might have saved lives.'

Leighton conceded the point with a change in expression.

'I'll follow it up with the relevant force,' Lawrence concluded.

'Am I interrupting?'

Lawrence glanced up to see Jamie hovering in the doorway. 'Um – no, I don't think so –' he looked back to Leighton. 'Unless you've anything else?'

'I'm not a genie.' Leighton peeled himself reluctantly from his chair. 'I'm off home now – call me if you need me, but please try not to need me.' He grinned, making for the door.

Lawrence returned his attention to Jamie. 'Go ahead.'

'There's a nineteen-month gap in National Insurance payments prior to Brett's taking the job at the locksmith's.' Jamie laid a computer printout on top of the one Leighton had left moments earlier, indicating the dates.

'And?' Lawrence responded, guessing Jamie had something more to add.

'I finally managed to track his family down. Brett Lindquist's dead. He died in a fire three years ago. That isn't something that National Insurance records always take into account, hence the enormous degree of benefit fraud that goes on in this country.'

Lawrence sighed. 'Why am I not surprised?'

Jamie frowned. 'What?'

'I'm fairly sure that prior to moving to Nether Street, he was living in a flat on Black Horse Road, and it occurred to me that if that were the case, he was living there at the time of the last census. I visited the local library on Monday, but there was nobody called Brett living at that address at the time.'

'And?'

'According to the census, there was a man by the name of Rhys Williams living there. He had an American Express card, which he cancelled just last week.' Lawrence leaned back in his chair. 'American Express were good enough to provide me with a sample of his handwriting, and I asked a graphologist to compare that with a form that Brett filled in for the locksmith when he first started work for him. She's just called to say that she's almost certain that the two were written by the same person, and Leighton has managed to link his fingerprint to the scene of Monica Hudson's death.'

'So what next? Start the search over again?'

'We'll try, but I'm not sure how far we'll get. I made a start on trying to trace him on Monday, and he's not only cancelled his Amex card, but also emptied two bank accounts, and he hasn't made any National Insurance contributions in over a year. I suspect he's either already created another alter ego or is in the process of doing so.'

'Would you like me to have a go at tracking down a family for Rhys Williams?'

'Certainly. We'll keep going until we run out of options, but I'm not hugely optimistic.'

'Becky's not going to like that,' Jamie observed.

'I know.' Lawrence reached for a pen. 'I'd appreciate it if you could keep this to yourself for now. I'll speak to her tomorrow.'

Rebecca arrived home to find Elliot half-sitting, half-lying on the sofa, staring blankly at MTV, a bottle of Jack Daniels on the floor beside him. He looked desperately tired, and there were dark shadows beneath his eyes, which were bloodshot. He had lost weight, and his pale cheeks looked hollow. His bleached hair hadn't been washed in days, and although it was gone nine, he was still in his dressing gown. Rebecca wondered how long he had been out of bed.

'Elliot, you *have* to see a doctor!'

'I don't want a doctor,' he returned, tersely.

'Well you can't go on like this! The only occasions I've seen you out of bed in the last week it's been to either hurt yourself or visit the drinks cupboard!'

'Get off my back.'

Rebecca bit her tongue, struggling not to snap at him. She was running out of both patience and sympathy, and she didn't think she could take a lot more. 'Then please talk to me. Tell me what's wrong.'

Elliot made no reply.

Rebecca moved to sit beside him, resting a hand on his arm. He flinched on contact, and she felt the bandages through the sleeve of his gown.

'How about you give me custody of your razors?' She suggested, trying to keep her tone gentle.

'Like that'll help.'

'It might stop you hurting yourself.'

'You really don't get it, do you?' Elliot demanded, meeting her eyes for the first time. 'I don't have to use razors, you know! Take those away and I'll find something else!'

'Would you not at least think about what you were doing if they weren't so readily available?'

'Thinking barely even comes into it.'

'Have you tried?'

'Tried what?'

'Thinking about it.'

'Of course I've thought about it! I used to cut myself all the time! I made myself stop, but it doesn't matter how long you give it up for, it doesn't get any easier! It's almost like a drug, because you know that you'll instantly feel so much better –' he shook his head. 'You have no idea how often I've had a bad day in the past and had to almost force myself not to – to –' he stopped.

'Do you not think you might be able to stop again if you didn't have the razors?'

'No.'

'Why not?'

'Because sometimes I –' Elliot bit his lip, drawing a deep breath. 'I get to a point where I barely even think about what I'm doing – it's like – like – a total frenzy. When I lived with Alec he once took my razors off me and I smashed up a plastic one with a fork just to get the blade out!'

Rebecca didn't immediately respond, wrestling with how to word what she wanted to say. 'Ok, I hear what you're saying, but I still don't understand exactly how you feel. You've explained that doing this to yourself makes you feel better, but you haven't said how.'

Elliot cast his eyes down. 'You know –' he broke off. 'You know when you get really upset how your chest feels tight – and it's hard to breathe – and you're trying not to think about what it is that's upset you because that's only going to make it worse, but at the same time you can't think about anything else – and – and you're trying to breathe slowly and stay calm but –' he swallowed. 'But that feeling won't go away. Not until you scream, or throw something, or – or –' Elliot stopped again. 'The moment I cut myself it's almost like all that gets released. Somehow it's easier when it's your arm that's hurting than when the pain's inside.'

Rebecca took a moment to absorb this before responding. 'So what is it that's upset you today?'

'I don't know,' Elliot whispered, brokenly, tears filling his eyes. 'I just feel so bad that all I can do is curl up and wrap my arms around myself as if that might somehow stop me from falling apart!' He sat forwards, raising his hands to cover his face.

Feeling less impatient now that he had at least made an effort to explain how he felt, Rebecca slipped an arm around him. In recent days she had been increasingly concerned by his behaviour, but after what he had just told her she felt seriously alarmed.

'Elliot, please let me call a doctor. You have to sort this out.'

'I don't want to take antidepressants!'

'Have you been on them before?'

Rebecca wasn't altogether surprised when Elliot nodded. He dropped his hands into his lap and twisted his fingers together until his knuckles turned white.

'Nobody can force you to do anything, but please at least talk to somebody. I can't bear seeing you like this.'

'I don't want to talk to anyone.'

'Please.'

Elliot closed his eyes but didn't reply.

'*Please*,' Rebecca repeated. 'Let me call a doctor. You don't have to do anything you don't want to do, but at least see someone.'

'I don't want to.'

'I know you don't, but you can't continue living like this! You're not eating, you're barely sleeping – despite the amount of time you're spending in bed –' Rebecca reached to take his hand, keeping an arm around him. 'You're clearly desperately unhappy. Please let someone help you.'

There was a long silence before Elliot mumbled something indistinguishable.

'What was that?'

'All right,' he whispered.

'All right? You mean you'll let me call a doctor?'

Eyes on the floor, Elliot nodded.

Rebecca felt enormously relieved. 'Thank you.' She squeezed his fingers.

'I'll see a doctor, but I'm not going to any hospital.' He raised his eyes to meet hers. 'And if you sign anything letting them take me, I'll never forgive you.'

'Becky,' Lawrence sat back in his chair as she entered the office. 'Could you close the door, please?'

Rebecca frowned. 'What about Danny and Jamie?'

'I want a word with you. Sit down.'

Rebecca obediently closed the door and perched anxiously on the edge of a chair. 'Have I done something wrong?'

'No, no, nothing like that.'

'So?'

'Jamie's managed to dig up some information on Brett Lindquist,' Lawrence revealed, rather reluctantly.

Rebecca's expression turned to one of relief, and she opened her mouth to speak. Lawrence held up a hand to silence her. 'He's been dead three years.'

'*What?*'

'We're not looking for Brett Lindquist at all. The guy we're after simply took on that name and identity. We're actually looking for a man named Rhys Williams, and he, like Brett, seems to have disappeared. If he can transform himself once, he can do it again – effectively we could be looking for anybody. I'm afraid our chances of finding him may be remote.'

'But – we've a description – surely –'

'I will do everything in my power to make sure this investigation gets all the time and resources available, but the fact remains that our options are finite, and we need to be realistic about the likely outcome. I suspect we may reach a point where we have no choice but to leave the case open.'

Rebecca shook her head. 'We can't!'

'Becky, the decision won't be down to me.'

'But there's still time, I mean, we've barely started –'

'I know,' Lawrence stopped her. 'I just want to make sure you understand the situation. I don't want you getting your hopes up.'

Rebecca pursed her lips and said nothing further, clearly struggling not to cry.

'Would you like me to drop you back home?' Lawrence offered, at length.

Rebecca nodded, swallowing hard.

'I think it might be a good idea for you to take some time off. Go to Glastonbury at the weekend as planned, and if you don't think you can cope with coming back in next week, just give me a call.'

'We're not going,' Rebecca managed, her voice wavering.

'What?'

'At the weekend.'

'I think it would do you good.'

Rebecca shook her head. 'Ian's dad died on Sunday, so the band aren't playing – but Elliot wouldn't be up to it anyway.'

Lawrence frowned. 'Why not?'

'He hasn't left the house in over a week. He's so depressed he isn't even eating!' Raising a hand to her mouth she bit into her forefinger in an fruitless attempt to check her tears. 'I don't know what to do! I'm so worried about him!' Bowing her head, she covered her eyes with her fingers.

Lawrence sighed, standing and moving to sit beside her. 'Becky, why didn't you mention this before? You could have taken some time off.'

'How would that have helped?' She gulped. 'He barely even wants to talk to me!'

'Has he seen a doctor?'

'Yuh. Last night. He said Elliot ought to be on Prozac, but he's refusing to take it.'

'Why?'

'I don't know.' Rebecca reached to take a tissue from the box on Lawrence's desk.

'Have you explained how you feel?'

'I might as well talk to myself. The state he's in at the moment, I don't think he's capable of registering that I *have* feelings.'

Lawrence suspected that was as much a part of the problem as was her anxiety for Elliot. Although she had refused to admit it, he knew she had been struggling to cope with being so involved with the investigation, and, in hindsight, wished he had insisted on taking her off the case.

Rebecca blew her nose. 'I'm sorry,' she muttered, looking at the floor.

'No, I'm sorry – I shouldn't have let you continue working on this.'

'I never thought I'd feel so isolated,' Rebecca said, after a long pause. 'I used to wonder how anybody could be so short-sighted as to neglect their friendships in favour of a relationship – but that's exactly what I've done! I go to work, I go home, I see Elliot, I see his friends – I've made no real effort to keep in touch with any of my friends over the last year or two, and until recently I never even realised that was what I'd done! It's only over the last few months that it's occurred to me – with Elliot being away so much of the time –' she trailed off with a shrug.

'That's not necessarily irreversible.'

Rebecca didn't respond.

'Can you not talk to your sister?'

'I already tried. All she was interested in was telling me that my relationship with Elliot was never going to work.'

'There are people here you can talk to, if you feel that it would help.'

Rebecca shook her head. 'I'll be ok.'

'Are you sure?'

'Yes.'

'At least think about it.'

'I will. Thanks.'

'Why don't we go for a coffee before I drop you home? I'm sure Jamie and Danny can manage without me for an hour or two.'

'That'd be good,' Rebecca nodded, forcing a smile. 'You can tell me what you know about this Rhys –' she frowned. 'What was his name again?'

'Rhys Williams,' Lawrence replied, with a sigh. He had hoped to take her mind off the investigation, although he knew that if the circumstances had been reversed he would have been just as keen to know the details. He was more concerned about how she would react if – or, he suspected, *when* – the case was left open and they were assigned another job. Much as he had made her aware of the likelihood of that eventuality, he was only too aware that until they had a definitive answer one way or the other she would cling to the hope that they might still succeed. Quite how she would deal with the situation were Rhys Williams to escape justice, he had no idea.

Epilogue

Glancing across the street as he turned the sign on the door from *open* to *closed*, Charles Bowman noticed that members of staff in the shop opposite were plastering *SALE* notices across the windows, and thought, not for the first time, how fortunate he was. Whatever downturns or recessions might blight the economy, people would always need keys, and in a slump were probably more likely to have their shoes re-healed than usual, thus saving on the cost of a new pair. In recent months his income had been stretched to the limit as it was, given that he was now supporting not only himself, but also his daughter and grandchildren. The children's father had thus far refused to pay maintenance, and the cost of childcare had made it impossible for his daughter to work. For some time she had fought to retain her independence, but had, in the end, reluctantly accepted Charles' help rather than see her son and daughter go without. Charles himself would have liked nothing more than to give her now ex-boyfriend a piece of his mind, but had respected his daughter's wishes, and kept out of the dispute.

Turning back towards the shop counter, his musings on the matter were interrupted by a sharp knock at the door.

'We're closed,' he responded, barely glancing around.

'It's about the job,' came the reply, muted by the glass.

'The job?' Charles hurried to open the door. The card in the shop window advertising for an assistant had for so long gone unnoticed that he had all but forgotten it himself.

'Ewan Anderson,' the thirty-something man outside introduced himself, shaking his umbrella before entering the shop. He was tall and slender, his short dark hair carefully teased with wax and grey eyes mildly distorted by rain-splashed spectacles. He wore blue jeans, Chelsea boots and a leather jacket, from the pocket of which he pulled a handkerchief before setting about drying his glasses. 'I've just moved up here – I'm looking for work – I was just passing, and –' he trailed off, indicating the card in the window with a flick of his wrist.

'Have you done this sort of work before?'

'Some time ago. My father was a locksmith, and I used to help out on weekends when I was at school. Since he died, I've been travelling around Europe, but I think it's time I settled down and stopped living like a nomad.' Ewan replaced his glasses and returned the handkerchief to his pocket. 'I might need a little retraining, but I pick things up pretty quickly.'

'How about shoe repairs?'

'That I haven't done before. But I'll give it a shot.'

'What draws you back to the job? It must be a fair few years since you finished school.'

'I miss the people, really. I've worked in a couple of offices, but technology seems to be replacing the need to communicate,' he smiled ruefully. 'Why speak to anybody when you can send them an email?'

'This is hardly a small village community – in a city like this you're unlikely to see many customers more than once or twice.'

'I'd just be happy working face-to-face with people rather than computer screens.'

'How would you feel about looking after the shop some of the time?'

'By myself, you mean?'

Charles nodded. 'Yes. I'm hoping to spend a few afternoons a week with my grandchildren.'

'No problem. How old are they?'

'Five and two,' Charles smiled fondly. 'My daughter moved up here earlier in the year, and even though they're so close by I feel as if I hardly see them. Kids grow up so fast, and I –' he stopped. 'Sorry – I'm waffling – you probably want to be getting on. Would you be able to come in tomorrow so that I can see you in action?'

'Sounds good.'

'After that I might be able to offer you a trial period – although I'll obviously require some references as well.'

'I don't know how easy they'll be to get hold of – most of the places I've worked are on the Continent, and I didn't stay in one place for more than four or five months at a time – but I'll let you have what information I have.'

'Do you have any identification with you?'

'I've a passport.' Ewan reached inside his jacket and drew out an immaculate British passport.

'That's travelled well,' Charles remarked, surprised.

'Oh – no – this is a new one. I'm not planning on going far, but it's easier to renew the old one than have to start again from scratch.' Ewan handed it over. 'Oh, and I've my National Insurance card somewhere, too –' he pulled a wallet out of his jeans pocket as Charles opened the passport, moments later presenting the plastic card, slightly bent. Both looked to be in order, and Charles returned them to their owner.

'All right, I'll see you tomorrow morning, then.'

'What time?'

'Eight forty-five?'

'Great,' Ewan smiled warmly, holding out a hand. 'Thanks very much.'

'Thank you for dropping by.' Charles shook his hand.

'See you tomorrow.' Ewan turned for the door. Opening it, he paused in the doorway. 'Good night.'

Nobody paid any attention to the man leaving the locksmith's at five-fifteen on a cold November evening. Closing the shop door behind himself, he opened his umbrella before setting off down the high street. Pausing at a pelican crossing, he lit a cigarette and watched a pretty young shop assistant dart out of Next and run for a waiting bus. Reaching into his back pocket, he extracted a yellowing scrap of newspaper, worn almost in two through repeated folding and unfolding. He read it one final time before casting it into the wind and stepping out onto the crossing. The discarded cutting fluttered unseen onto the wet tarmac of the road, the minuscule print still legible.

DEATHS

ANDERSON.—On April 17, as the result of a tragic accident, EWAN PATRICK, aged 38. Much loved son of Margaret and Thomas. Funeral service at Worthing Crematorium on Wednesday, May 26 at 12.30pm. Family flowers only please, but donations, if desired, to the National Trust.

The lights changed, tyres slithered in the rain, and it was gone.

A note from Sadie

Thank you for choosing to read my first book. If you have enjoyed *Front Page News*, I would be very grateful if you would consider rating it, or even writing a review – just a few words can make a difference in helping to persuade others to give my books a try.

PENGUIN BOOKS

The Malice of Waves

Mark Douglas-Home is a journalist turned author. Before writing books, Mark was the editor of a daily newspaper in Scotland. As Scottish correspondent for the *Independent*, he reported on both the Lockerbie and Piper Alpha disasters.

His career in journalism began as a student in South Africa, where he edited the newspaper at the University of Witwaters-rand, Johannesburg. After the apartheid government banned a number of editions, he was deported from the country.

He is married with two children and lives in Edinburgh.

Twitter @MarkDouglasHome

Facebook.com/markdouglashome.books

The Malice of Waves

MARK DOUGLAS-HOME

PENGUIN BOOKS

PENGUIN BOOKS

UK | USA | Canada | Ireland | Australia
India | New Zealand | South Africa

Penguin Books is part of the Penguin Random House group of companies
whose addresses can be found at global.penguinrandomhouse.com.

First published by Michael Joseph 2016
Published in Penguin Books 2016

003

Copyright © Mark Douglas-Home, 2016

The moral right of the author has been asserted

Typeset by Palimpsest Book Production Ltd, Falkirk, Stirlingshire

Printed in Great Britain by Clays Ltd, St Ives plc

A CIP catalogue record for this book is available from the British Library

ISBN: 978–1–405–92361–3

For Colette, Rebecca and Rory

Acknowledgements

For their time, knowledge or assistance, I am grateful to Bob McGowan, Senior Curator, Birds, at National Museums Scotland; Toby Sherwin, Emeritus Professor of Oceanography at the Scottish Association for Marine Science; Dr Gail Anderson at Simon Fraser University in British Columbia; Moira Forsyth, Pete Moore, Willa Straker-Smith and Vicki Clifford. Any factual errors are mine. I would also like to thank Emad Akhtar, my editor at Penguin; Maggie Hattersley of Maggie Pearlstine Associates, my agent; and Colette, my wife, and Rebecca and Rory, my children: all for their encouragement and help.

In my research, I read a large number of books. Among those that informed me were *Sea Room* by Adam Nicolson; *Atlantic* by Simon Winchester; *The Old Ways* by Robert Macfarlane; *The Scottish Islands* by Hamish Haswell-Smith; *The Raven* by Derek Ratcliffe; *The Birds of Scotland*, published by the Scottish Ornithologists' Club; the *Collins Bird Guide*; *The Egg Collectors of Great Britain and Ireland* by A. C. Cole and W. M. Trobe; and the Clyde Cruising Club's Sailing Directions to the Outer Hebrides. I also made use of the article 'Erythrism in the Eggs of British Birds' by The Rev. F. C. R. Jourdain and Clifford Borrer, which was published in *British Birds* in 1914.

As with the previous books in this series, the places I describe are mostly fictional. That includes the two islands which feature in this story – Priest's Island and Eilean Dubh. Although there are other Scottish islands with similar names, these are not them. My reason for inventing places is to avoid imposing a fictional plot on an island community that has a rich and interesting history of its own.

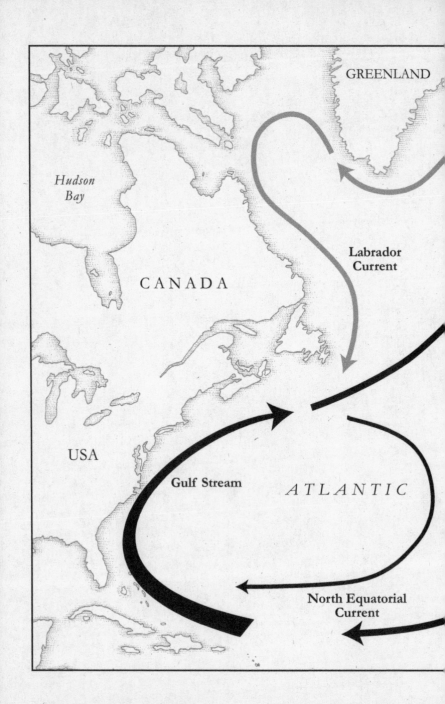

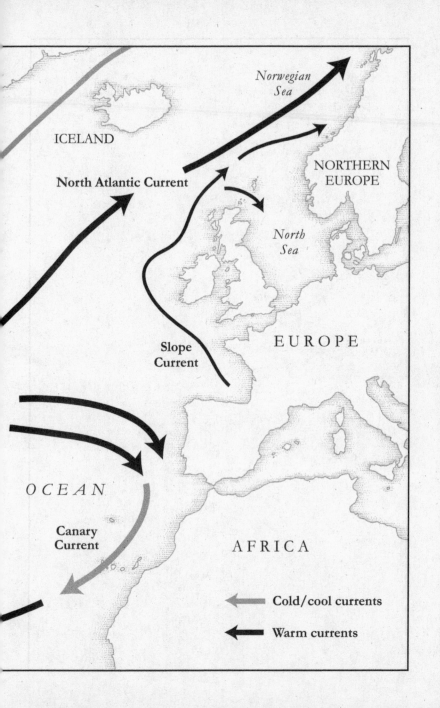

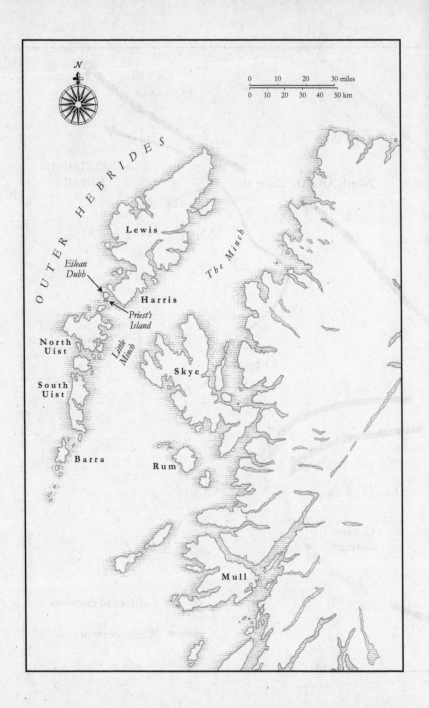

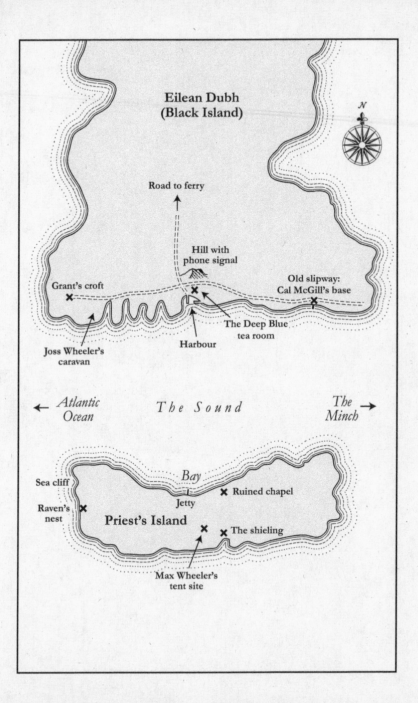

A few hours: wasn't that what Dr Lipman said? Cal McGill checked the time. Midnight had come and gone and Millie was still floating. 'Sink,' he said, 'for God's sake, sink.' He let out more rope in silent encouragement. Rather than settling lower in the water, she drifted away. Her skin turned sparkly and silver in the moonlight, making her bobbing motion appear nonchalant, even defiant. As if she was enjoying the attention. As if she was putting on some kind of valedictory show. 'Millie, sink.' Cal spoke softly in case his voice travelled over the water. In case anyone heard him talking to a dead pig. In case he was caught breaking the rules for disposing of dead farm animals. Some things were hard to explain even if the purpose was research.

Waiting for the tug of the rope to announce Millie's descent, Cal allowed himself a moment's annoyance at having to skulk in the night like a Victorian body snatcher. How often had he read about other researchers being feted for their work using pigs as human proxies? For instance, there was that Montana study where pig corpses were left to rot on land – on the surface as well as in trenches. Since the animals had similar organs to humans and similar bacteria in their intestines, the findings were considered significant for forensic science. More recently, Cal had seen a report in a scientific journal about pig carcasses being submerged and tethered in the Pacific off British Columbia. The purpose was to study how quickly sea lice, crabs and other scavengers dismantled the corpses and to provide accuracy in estimating time of death when human bodies washed ashore or were recovered at sea.

In Cal's opinion, there was other interesting work to be done, using pigs to measure how the rate of decomposition was affected by different wave and weather conditions and how rotting, bloating and predation affected speed or direction of travel. Since pigs were relatively hairless and their bodies often similar in size to human torsos, Cal thought they could be proxies in his area of investigation too.

The disappearance of fourteen-year-old Max Wheeler from Priest's Island in the Outer Hebrides was a case in point. According to the family's lawyer, the boy was small for his age. He was five-feet one and weighed in at one hundred pounds, give or take. So Millie was approximately right, at one hundred and fourteen. Anyway, at short notice, she was as near as Cal could manage. Available dead pigs of the right weight didn't come his way that often. Or ever before, come to think of it.

In life, Millie had belonged to Steve, a smallholder in Cromarty and secretary of a whale-watching group to which Cal emailed cetacean sightings. Occasionally, driving south from Sutherland, Cal would drop by with a load of beached timber for Steve's wood burner. In return he would be offered honey, bantam eggs or, in one unusual mid-morning barter, a muddy porcine corpse. Staring at it disconsolately, Steve described Millie as a good little pig and wondered if Cal might have a use for her in his research into how bodies travelled at sea. He'd prefer that to be Millie's fate than the knackers' yard or a maggot farm, two of the disposals ordered by regulation. Three and a half hours later Cal was back at his office-cum-bedsit in an industrial estate in Leith, the port district of Edinburgh. He had to eject various contorted and iced sea creatures from his chest freezer in the storeroom to make way for Millie's stiffened corpse. Waiting for the opportunity to deploy her, he had time for further investigation into her usefulness.

Would Millie's fat content and distribution make her more buoyant than a human body? If they did, the carcass would sit higher in the water and the wind would have greater influence on where she drifted. Exactly how Millie would float was another concern. Humans usually lay on their front, heads hanging and filled with blood from the pull of gravity. Were pigs the same? Cal searched the internet for pictures of dead pigs and found dozens showing bloated carcasses in the Huangpu River in China. They were lying on their sides. The sight of so many muddy-pink bodies stretched drum-tight prompted a further question, about bloating. After death, humans typically floated for a while, sank and resurfaced with the gases of decomposition. Would the same apply to pigs and in roughly the same time frame? He found the name of the researcher leading the British Columbia study, a Dr Ruth Lipman. A search of her institution's website yielded her email address. Cal sent a list of questions and, for academic credibility, also mentioned his PhD, attaching an abstract of his dissertation. It described his research into currents in the North-East Atlantic and the computer program he had devised for tracking flotsam, including bodies.

She replied promptly and briefly. 'I don't think pigs would behave in the water exactly the same as humans – due to body shape and distribution of fat – but it's hard for me to say since that's not my area of research. Pigs do float at first – there's a lot of fat in the butt area that holds them up. They sink after a few hours and, depending on depth, will bloat and refloat. When I've been working in shallow water I tether them so I don't lose them. In my present work, though, the depths are too great for bloat and refloat.'

Cal read the email again after the lawyer's call about Max Wheeler and studied charts of the sound between Priest's Island, 170 acres of uninhabited hill, bracken and rock, and its larger, inhabited neighbour to the north, Eilean Dubh or 'Black Island'. Driving to the ferry, the dead pig unfreezing under a tarpaulin in the back of his pickup, Cal decided he would start off by tethering Millie too. Given what the lawyer had said about the possibility of the Wheeler boy being weighted down, Cal would wait for Millie to sink then let her go. Otherwise, considering her buoyancy and the tidal forces in the sound, she could drift a long way on the surface before sinking. From what he'd read about the one-kilometre wide stretch of sea separating the two islands, currents of three knots were commonplace. At the biggest tides, called spring tides because they spring or rise up, they could reach five or even seven knots where there were constrictions. According to the historical data, spring tides occurred the night Max Wheeler disappeared.

Studying the charts, Cal saw constrictions and obstacles everywhere. He'd consulted a book of Hebridean sailing directions which warned against 'unwary yachtsmen being tempted by the prospect of a scenic interlude'. Not only were the sound's tidal streams prone to being diverted at right angles because of reefs, rocks and other obstructions, but there was also the danger of choppy seas or worse – large, standing waves – caused by the wind blowing against the tide. Apparently, this was a routine risk in the sound since the flood flowed into both ends almost simultaneously. If the wind was either easterly or westerly, difficult and often dangerous conditions could be encountered at one or other entrance. Afterwards Cal read a diver's blog for an underwater perspective. According to its author, the stretch of sea north of Priest's Island was unlike anywhere else he had experienced. Instead of the tidal stream increasing slowly, the flood started at full strength with the change of tide. Bang. One moment there was calm, the kelp upright; the next it was horizontal with boulders tumbling along the bottom. 'Not to be advised, especially when visibility is almost zero from the scouring of the sea bottom,' the diver reported.

Since it was night when Max Wheeler disappeared, Cal decided to put Millie in the main channel leading to the harbour at the southern end of Eilean Dubh. The current would be least obstructed there but it was also a likely place for a killer making an escape to have disposed of the teenager's body. At night, the channel was the safest and quickest route to navigate. According to the lawyer, Cal should work on the theory that Max's body was discarded in the panic of the moment and with materials to hand. He suggested the boy might have been wrapped up in netting filled with stones and tied with rope or some other improvisation. Cal said nothing but wondered if he should fit Millie with a tracker. On balance, given the legal situation, he decided it was better the pig didn't lead back to him. Trouble seemed to find him anyway. Wasn't waving it hello unnecessary?

Instead, he attached a small orange buoy to Millie's girth on twenty-five metres of rope. So long as she stayed in the relatively shallow water of the sound, Cal would be able to see where the underwater currents and eddies took her before she bloated; where, too, they might have taken Max's body. Cal expected Millie to experience the marine equivalent of being in a pinball machine, her pink body ricocheting from one obstruction to the next.

While Cal waited for Millie to sink, he made a bet. Three days, perhaps four, then she'd bloat and float and be washed ashore. In an area of sea like this, with islets, skerries and rocks, she'd find it hard to escape even with such strong currents. Why, he wondered, hadn't that happened with Max Wheeler? In shallow coastal waters, it was unusual for bodies to disappear, even those that had been weighted down. The reason was simple. From what Cal had read – his experience too – murderers and suicides underestimated how buoyant bodies became once decay set in. Stones dropped into pockets or even boulders put into sacks and tied to a victim's ankles would often be ineffective after a while. In the case of the stones, they might not be heavy enough once bloating began. With a sack or sandbag tied round an ankle, they could become detached by a process called disarticulation – not just the feet, but hands, even the head coming loose with decomposition. Then, having shaken off its ballast, the body would float and probably be washed on to land. Which made Cal wonder: since Max Wheeler was never found, why was the lawyer so certain he'd been dumped at sea?

The rope tightened and ran through his hands. Cal checked the time: another half an hour before the tide reached its low point. 'Good girl,' he said into the blackness where Millie had slipped out of sight without so much as a farewell gurgle. Cal held on to the rope until he heard the lazy slap of slack water against the RIB. It sounded like applause for Millie's good timing – knowing that just before the start of the next flood tide was when she was supposed to leave the stage. 'Brava, Millie,' Cal said, dropping the remaining rope and marker buoy overboard. 'Brava.' And, taking up the rhythm of the sea, he clapped.

The cold kept Cal awake. A north-easterly breeze penetrated the pickup's ill-fitting windows. He drank coffee for warmth and listened to a download of a radio programme from a series called 'Stranger than Fiction'. It concerned an incident that had happened three months after Max Wheeler's disappearance. A party of kayakers had visited Priest's Island and pitched their tents in the shelter of the ruined chapel beside the bay on the north shore. 'But they slept uneasily,' according to the programme's narrator, 'and, next morning, they paddled across the sound between Priest's Island and Eilean Dubh to visit the Deep Blue tea room by the harbour, where they asked Bella MacLeod, the owner, about a disturbance in the night.'

The oldest member of the group, a retired professor, recalled their conversation. 'Ha, ha, yes, I remember feeling rather awkward trying to describe the odd noise we'd heard. I think I called it "eerie" and my two companions, also retired academics, said something like "ethereal" and "rhythmic, kind of weird". You see, we didn't want to ask Bella outright about ghosts or whether the chapel had a reputation for being haunted because she might think we were drunk, mad, or, worse still considering our university backgrounds, superstitious.'

According to the narrator, Bella pressed them for a better description while she took their orders. 'Eerie, you say?'

'Yes, very,' the retired professor replied.

'Going louder and softer . . . vibrating . . . some squawking?'

'Exactly that,' said the professor.

Then Bella herself took up the story. 'Well, I recall saying, "No one's ever mentioned storm petrels being on Priest's Island before, but they're the only creatures that make a noise like that at night".'

The professor remembered 'my relief that rationality as well as ornithology had provided a solution.'

The narrator continued, 'After bringing coffee and orange cake, Bella returned with two guides to British birds, open at

7

the relevant pages. She proceeded to read out excerpts.' Then Bella's voice cut in: '"Only comes ashore in the nesting season and under cover of darkness . . . lays its eggs in burrows, among rocks or crevices of ruined buildings . . . makes a purring sound with interposed grunts, like stomach rumbling."

'When I put the books on the table for the men to read for themselves, the oldest of the three, the retired professor, asked me about the bird's size and I traced a circle with my index finger of my left hand on the palm of my right. I said a storm petrel was no bigger than a house martin and its plumage was similarly dark and with a white rump.'

'What did you do next?' the narrator inquired.

Bella had tapped the illustration. 'I said, "I think you'll find that's your ghost".'

After a pause, the narrator said, 'The kayakers departed to explore islands further north but, the following week, talk in the Deep Blue tea room turned again to storm petrels and superstition. Waiting for the mobile bank to make its weekly visit to the car park outside, Bella was talking to Ina Gillies, at seventy-nine the township's oldest inhabitant and self-appointed keeper of its history and folklore. Bella mentioned storm petrels being on Priest's Island . . . and this was Ina's reply.'

'I told her about my husband Neil's respect for the birds.' Ina's voice trembled with nerves and emotion. She cleared her throat before carrying on. 'He's no longer with us – God rest him – but whenever he came across storm petrels while out fishing he would stop what he was doing, raise his cap and say a few words. Storm petrels, he always used to tell me, were the wandering souls of sailors lost at sea. And then I said to Bella, "It would make you wonder why there are petrels on the island now when there haven't been any before . . . whether it's not the soul of that missing boy Max returning."

'Bella said she didn't think Max could be thought of as a sailor, but I said, "Indeed he was. Didn't the boy sail to Priest's Island with his father all the way from the south of England?"'

After another dramatic pause, the narrator told how a visiting expert on seabirds gave sustenance to Ina's theory later that summer. Investigating new storm petrel territories, he went to the island and reported only one occupied nest site in the ruined chapel. It was deep within the seaward wall, close to where the kayakers had pitched their tents. The expert, a Dr Harry Livesey from Edinburgh University, spoke with scientific precision, clearly as worried as the kayakers about appearing susceptible to Hebridean superstition. 'A solitary nesting pair is atypical for the species. Storm petrels usually nest in colonies, often hundreds if not thousands strong.'

The narrator again: 'The Deep Blue tea room was abuzz with the news. After one of the biggest police searches ever conducted in these far-flung islands, had Ina, guardian of the township's folk history, stumbled on a clue to the fate of young Max Wheeler? Could one of the nesting petrels – also known as water-witches – have been the boy's returning soul and did that mean he had not been murdered on the island, as the police believe, but had died accidentally at sea?'

Cal let the concluding music play out before switching on his torch. He poured more coffee from the flask and began to flick through a file of newspaper cuttings. He stopped at a first anniversary feature about the 'Max Murder Mystery' published in the *Daily Mail*, with a subsidiary heading: 'Boy's Fate Lost in Hebridean Fog'. Underneath was a report from the Deep Blue, 'the gathering place for the scattered township at the southern end of Eilean Dubh'. The writer described how the story of Max Wheeler's soul returning to neighbouring Priest's Island was dropped into tea room conversation 'as a matter of routine whenever strangers appeared'. It suggested the locals were 'naive, gullible or being wilfully obstructive'. But from Cal's reading another interpretation was likely. It was that the inhabitants had latched on to the only explanation available which pointed to the boy drowning and to his disappearance being a tragic if preventable accident. The alternative was to believe one of their own responsible for his death when, to a man and a woman, they thought culpability lay with the sea and, by extension, with the negligence of the boy's father. One anonymous regular at the tea room was reported as saying, 'What was David Wheeler thinking, allowing Max to spend the night alone on such a barren and wild place as Priest's Island? In all likelihood, the boy lost his way in the dark and stumbled over a cliff or took fright and tried to swim back to his father and sisters sleeping in the boat moored in the bay. Whichever it was, considering how fast the currents run in the sound and how cold the water is in March, it would have taken a miracle for him to survive. A miracle . . .' Another tea room interviewee in the *Scotsman* hinted at David Wheeler's southern ignorance of Hebridean conditions even though he owned Priest's Island. 'Thank goodness,' she said, 'the three girls had the sense to spend the night on board the boat. Heaven knows what disasters there would have been otherwise.'

Such township opinions, Cal discovered, were reported more briefly and grudgingly as time went on. The media fell in line behind the theory posited by the police and David Wheeler that the boy's disappearance and probable death were caused by criminality, not some unforeseen accident; a cold-blooded murder motivated by envy or unjustified grievance about land rights or a combination of the two and stoked by alcohol. Every cutting carried a photograph of Wheeler's thirty-foot boat, the *Jacqueline*, and of Max with his blond hair. The stories, captions and headlines described him as 'tragic golden boy', a catch-all reference to his colouring, looks and the death of Jackie, his mother, in a car accident when he was eleven. The *Jacqueline* was named after her.

By the time the kayakers arrived for late breakfast in the Deep Blue three months after Max's disappearance, the media had judged the inhabitants complicit in murder. Reading the stories, Cal understood why the township had turned in on itself – behaviour which was portrayed as a conspiracy of concealment. If he had lived there, Cal would have become hostile too. Every one of the twenty-seven houses scattered around the southern tip of Eilean Dubh had been searched. So had garages, cars and boats, some more than twice and, on occasion, in the middle of the night or at dawn, as though the police had been tipped off about the boy's body being moved or some other incriminating evidence being hidden. Dogs and mountain rescue teams had hunted hill, bog and coast. Divers had searched the many islets and skerries in the sound. Local men, including Donald Grant, the last tenant to graze his sheep on Priest's Island, and his teenage nephew Ewan Chisholm, had been taken in for questioning. B&B bookings had been cancelled. Eilean Dubh was consistently referred to in media reports by its English translation, Black Island, as though the historic name foreshadowed the later dark deed of its inhabitants.

The boy's disappearance blighted the township and continued to do so five years later. This was largely thanks to David Wheeler marking each anniversary with a memorial service on Priest's Island and commissioning a series of experts to review the evidence and to pursue fresh lines of inquiry since the police investigation had fallen dormant from lack of leads. According to the newspapers, this was Wheeler's way of letting the township know he would never give up and that his resolve to find his son's killer or killers was greater than theirs to keep him, her or them hidden. At first the experts excited renewed bursts of publicity but in the last two years they were limited to brief mentions of the person's identity.

There had been a retired chief constable from England; a US private detective referred to as T. C. Clancy; a forensic archaeologist who dug holes everywhere and was found in one of them, according to a mischievous diary piece, drunk and singing late at night. Then there was a botanist who studied both of the islands for unexpected plant growth or patches of fertility, and, last year, a former French intelligence officer whose speciality was taking and analysing high resolution aerial photography. His helicopter had clattered over the islands for days.

The last cutting Cal read was the most recent and longer than some. It was half a dozen paragraphs and tucked away on page eight of the *Herald*. It said that this year the inquiry would be conducted by Dr Caladh McGill, a thirty-year-old oceanographer with 'expertise in tracking objects at sea'. There was the usual complaint from the township about unwarranted persecution as well as linked speculation about Wheeler's worsening financial situation and whether this would be the last investigation. The family's home in Southampton was being sold to keep creditors at bay; his boat hire business in Southampton had gone into receivership with little prospect of resuscitation given the economic climate. According to an anonymous employee, the inattention of David Wheeler – 'his blind obsession with his son Max' – was to blame for the company's downfall. The remark exuded bitterness, implying Wheeler's duty was to the living and their families, not to the disappeared or dead.

~

Cal woke to the sun shining weakly through the opaque fug of the Toyota's windows. He yawned, stretched and upset the file of papers on his chest which set off an avalanche. A map, his laptop and torch slid on to the pickup's floor, joining discarded food wrappers and his wet boots. Cal swore and opened the door, his unintended and uncomfortable pillow during the four hours he had been sleeping on the pickup's back seat. His head fell into the gap. Outside, the air was fresh and still; the sky a hazy blue. Staring upwards, Cal wondered what time it was: ten, maybe eleven. Remembering the empty flask of coffee, he groaned and pulled himself up. His left hand gripped the headrest of the front seat while the right found his binoculars. Reversing out through the open doorway, he stretched one leg then the other. He squinted again at the sun. More like eleven, he thought, as he climbed on to the Toyota's back to get some height before scanning the sound. Although it was calm, Cal noticed flares of white water and swirls of turbulence which told of submerged rocks or reefs as well as of a restless energy, as if the sea could barely restrain itself from causing havoc, even on such a gentle spring day.

Cal spotted the orange buoy which was attached to Millie east and north of where he had left her during the night. She was still within the sound, between two skerries, and now probably sheltered from the ebb tide that was more than three hours old. Moving his binoculars along the coast of Priest's Island his attention was taken by a boat moored in the bay. It must have arrived that morning since nothing had been there the night before. The craft had a single mast and a covered wheelhouse. Even at that distance, the disrepair was evident. Cal saw dents and scrapes on its hull as well as paintwork damage, including the name. The tail of the 'q' and the final 'e' had all but disappeared from 'Jacqueline'. While he watched, a figure appeared at the entrance to the wheelhouse: a man. There was something about the way he held himself, a tension, which revealed his emotional torment. Like the sound itself, with its flares and eddies, he seemed scarcely able to maintain control. He stood for four maybe five minutes while Cal watched. Suddenly, he put his head back and his mouth opened into a gash extending across his face. Cal was too far away for any noise to carry but, a moment later, he heard a gull's call, a poignant sound; as if the bird was copying the anguished cry of a father making his annual return to the scene of his son's death. It was Cal's introduction to David Wheeler.

2

One by one Linda Pryke removed the labels from the back garden. Each was made of wood, painted white and printed in black with one of Stanley's codes, four letters followed by a forward slash and four numbers. Taxonomy, Stanley called it, whenever anyone remarked on how organized the borders looked. Typical of Stanley, she used to think. Finding a complicated word to pretend important work was being done when it was nothing of the kind. *Taxonomy*. She had never said the word out loud in case it encouraged him. Nor had she asked what the different letters and numbers of his various codes signified if for no other reason than she doubted Stanley would tell her. All she knew for certain was that somewhere in his room at the top of the house among his other card indexes would be one where her plants were recorded in meticulous detail. Stanley's passion was order and neatness – putting things in their proper place, as he would say. *Stanley's order*, as she referred to it with an upward roll of her eyes. Whether it was one of his collections, the books in the sitting room, the jams and chutney she made or the shrubs and roses in the garden, *her* garden, he labelled and recorded everything. The process was what provided his enjoyment, and the knowledge that only he could look at one of his labels and be able to identify the index to which it referred and the relevant data card.

Still, it was better than the alternative, or so she'd thought. Stanley fussing contentedly about the house, or in the garden, was the price that had to be paid for keeping him out of trouble. She remembered this tearfully while pulling another of his labels from the cold ground and dropping it into a carrier bag. She stretched her complaining back. All the bending was making it ache, a nagging pain to add to the discomfort of a penetrating easterly breeze. Yet she had to carry on. The garden had to be cleared. Since the telephone call at eight thirty that morning, each label appeared to Linda as a miniature gravestone under which a different part of her was buried.

Below that one lay the carcass of her marriage; below this, trust; below that, that and that, the now decomposing remains of her reassuringly nondescript life of suburban gentility, of being ordinary and unremarkable, like her neighbours.

She put her hands on her hips, arched her back and watched the clouds drift across the sky. How she hated March, with its nipping winds and threats. To everyone else, the month meant birdsong and longer days. But for Linda, they were harbingers of a season of uncertainty, of worrying about a knock at the door and the humiliation that might follow, of being anxious day and night. Almost from the start of her marriage, Linda had thought of spring as a snapping dog. Now she felt the creature's sharp little teeth, ripping away at the respectability she'd come to regard as her singular achievement, and her comfort. The adjustments she'd been forced to make after Stanley's transgression in that first year of their marriage! Hadn't she moved towns for him, set him up in business and given him her good name? Stanley's response had been as she'd hoped: over the next eight years he'd worked hard and done well for himself. Not that she would ever have said so to him, but the name Stanley Pryke had a certain ring to it. Honest. Solid. Trustworthy. Pryke: her father's name.

Better than the name she'd married.

From the beginning people reacted to Mrs Stanley Wise as if they knew something Linda didn't, as if it carried a bad smell, as if *she* carried a bad smell. Only when the police came knocking at their door that first spring did she discover what the smell was, what Stanley had been doing. Even in that short time she'd taken to being a wife. A round peg, it turned out, for a round hole. She couldn't imagine her life as anything else, not then. She'd done what wives have to do, but even now the memory of policemen searching her house could bring tears to her eyes and make her unsteady on her feet.

The humiliation she had suffered as they opened every cupboard and drawer and picked through her underwear! The indignity of being taken to the police station and questioned! Stanley's conviction and fine, the stories in the newspapers, the gossip among the neighbours and wherever she went in the high street!

She had coped, somehow. In hindsight, her dread at being alone again, aged forty-four, saved the marriage. Stanley's remorse had also helped, his confession bringing them closer for a while. He'd told her about his childhood, how he'd lived for those few unpredictable days when Tommy Wise, his father, would visit, when knowledge would be passed from one generation to another. They'd go on biannual expeditions, scouting in autumn, collecting in spring. The thrill never left Stanley, an addiction, he'd said. He'd been shaking too, just like an addict would, when he promised to change his ways. Never again, he'd said. Never again would he put everything at risk. Unexpectedly, she'd felt pity for him and, in time, an afterglow of satisfaction at having rescued him by setting him up in his own property management company and by buying a nice house for them both in a town a hundred miles away, where the name Stanley Wise was unknown, where Stanley Pryke could start again, where Mrs Stanley Pryke could go shopping without worrying about what people were saying behind her back, without anyone really knowing who she was apart from her name.

Until that terrible time, she'd felt beholden to him for making her, a plain woman nearing the end of her childbearing years, his wife. Afterwards, she took the view that if anyone had an obligation to the other it was Stanley. She stopped worrying about being older than him, her thinness or her flat bosom or her old-fashioned hair. Over time, she thought the two of them had found a happy enough equilibrium. Stanley had his interests and Linda, increasingly, hers. Being Mrs Stanley Pryke in a new town gave her the confidence to spread her wings. She attended charity events, played bridge or bowls with her women friends and often thought herself fortunate when she heard them complain about their demanding, unreasonable or unfaithful husbands. There had been none of that unpleasantness with Stanley. The worst she could have said of him (though, of course, she didn't to her friends) was that he was an absence rather than a presence. When he wasn't at work, he spent his time indexing, classifying and recording. Mostly he was shut away in his room upstairs. She'd tolerated it, or so she'd told herself, because it kept him from his old trouble.

Had he been deceiving her all this time? she wondered. Her hands shook as she plucked a label from beneath a viburnum plant. The thought of police coming again to the door was more than she could endure, or the horror of being taken in for questioning – the shame it would bring on her father's good name, on *her* good name; the gossip it would generate, the pitying looks, the exposure; that nightmare again.

'Where do you think he is, Linda?' the man had said when she picked up the phone by her bed.

'Where who is?' she replied, still half asleep.

'Why, Pinkie, of course.'

The sound of that vile name, after all this time. Now she was awake.

'Pinkie who?' she managed to say.

'Pinkie Wise, or perhaps I should say, Pinkie Pryke.'

Her family name, the name that had sounded so respectable to Linda's ears, now had the ring of a common criminal.

'Stanley Pryke,' she said, 'his name is Stanley Pryke.'

'Whatever you want, Linda,' he said.

'Who are you?' she demanded. 'Why are you ringing me?'

'It doesn't matter who I am. It's Pinkie we're discussing. Oh, my apologies, Linda, I forgot. His name's Stanley . . . Do you know where he is?'

'Of course I do,' Linda said.

'I don't think so.'

'He's in Carlisle.'

'Not even close,' he said. 'Not even the right country.'

'He is,' Linda insisted. 'He is.'

The man laughed. 'When last seen, Linda, he was on a ferry from the Scottish mainland. He was going to the Outer Hebrides, Linda. Do you know where they are? Not much property for Pinkie to manage out there.'

'What do you want?' Linda cried.

'Enough to stop me letting the police know about Pinkie being up to his old tricks again, something to stop your dearly beloved going to jail.'

Linda was too shocked to speak.

'Didn't you know that, Linda? The law's tougher now. For a second offence, he'll be put away in prison, no doubt about that, a man like Pinkie, with his reputation. A fine, too, I'd imagine, a big one.'

3

In 1898, the men of the township at the southern end of Eilean Dubh built a bothy. They chose a level site beside the new harbour and used the leftover stone to build the walls. The roof was covered with turf and tied down with ropes against Atlantic storms. In summer, after fishing the night tides for passing salmon shoals, the men bunked in its one gloomy room. At other times of the year the bothy was used for storing nets or as a refuge where whisky was drunk away from womenfolk and the minister's prying eyes.

A century later, a fisherman's wife by the name of Frances Mackinnon found another use for those same leftover stones. By then the walls and the roof had collapsed from neglect. She negotiated a loan and began the job of rebuilding and extending the bothy. Electricity, water and sewerage were installed. The roof was covered with corrugated zinc and painted blue. It stretched across a triple-glazed annexe where lattes, mochas, tea and cake were served daily from March to October, Tuesdays to Saturdays for the remainder of the year. An illuminated sign above the door announced 'The Deep Blue', though for a while, on account of the money that had been spent, the township's name for it was 'The Deep Red'.

Cal McGill arrived at the tea room with time to spare. After checking the harbour for David Wheeler, he parked and went inside. There were a dozen empty tables with blue-and-yellow gingham cloths and floor-to-ceiling windows which filled half the front wall and the entire west gable. A waitress was watching him from behind the counter. She was short with pinned-back black hair and startling white skin. An exercise pad was open in front of her. The top page, Cal saw as he approached, was covered with markings – lines, crosses and calculations. She turned the pad over. 'Can I get you something?'

'Coffee,' Cal replied, noticing the bib of her blue apron and the name that was written across it in yellow: Catriona.

'Americano,' he added. 'If you do such a thing . . .'

'Uh-huh, we do.' Her eyes flicked quickly to his face. 'Mug or cup?'

'Mug.'

'Came across on the ferry this morning, did you?' Catriona asked, busying herself at the coffee machine.

'Yesterday.'

'Almost a native, then.' She glanced at him again. 'Here long?'

'A few days . . . I haven't decided.'

'I wouldn't stay longer than two.'

'Why not?'

'A storm's coming.' The right side of her mouth pulled to one side, a gesture of resignation at the routine drama of island life.

'A big one?'

'That's what they're saying.' She laughed. 'Board up your windows, nail your sheep to the nearest fencepost.'

'That bad?'

'Aye, so they say.'

'I'll stay then.'

'Why?' Catriona frowned and shot him a sideways glance.

'I like storms.'

Catriona paid studious attention to pouring his coffee to conceal her amusement at the odd habits of mainlanders while Cal looked around the tea room. 'I wasn't expecting to find something like this out here. Nice place.'

'Aye, it's all right, I suppose.' She glanced at him again. 'It's been a bit slow this afternoon, but.' She put a napkin on the counter followed by the full mug. 'That'll be two twenty.'

Cal paid and dropped his change into a charity tin: holidays for the families of lost fishermen. 'Thanks. I'll let you get on with what you were doing.' He picked up the mug, leaving the napkin. 'Is it all right if I go outside?'

Catriona shrugged. 'Just mind you bring the mug back.'

Leaning against the bonnet of his pickup, Cal kept a watch on the sound for Wheeler's dinghy and recalled where he'd come across Catriona's name for the first time. It was in the office of Wheeler's lawyer. Cal had flown from Edinburgh to Southampton for the day. His plane was half an hour late and he'd been taken to a meeting room by a flustered PA. The lawyer, Mr Close (he didn't offer a first name) was waiting, sitting behind a desk. His hands were clasped in front of him and resting on a red file. Cal noticed the lawyer's fingers. They were stubby, an alarming purple colour, in contrast to his face which was pinched and a shade somewhere between grey and white. That washed-out look was accentuated by what the lawyer wore: rimless glasses, grey suit, white shirt and a diamond-patterned tie in two tones of grey. His hair was short and bristly, greyish too. Instead of standing to welcome Cal, Mr Close remained seated. 'Ah, finally,' he announced with a sigh, gesturing to Cal to sit opposite him. He waited for the PA to bring a glass of water.

'Can we proceed?' He took Cal's answer for granted. 'As I explained on the phone, Dr McGill, it's advisable for you to read this' – he indicated the file – 'before you meet Mr Wheeler.' He separated his interlocked fingers and laid his right hand flat on the file's cover. 'You won't be allowed to take notes of any kind or to make copies. Nor will you be able to refer to the contents. These are Mr Wheeler's instructions.'

He waited for Cal's response. 'Well?' he said. 'Do we understand each other?'

'Yes,' Cal said. 'I think we do.'

Mr Close pushed the file across the table. A damp imprint was left on the cover when he removed his hand. 'Very well, since we are late I suggest you start reading. I will stay to answer any questions.'

Cal thanked him coolly for his time and started at the first page. It told the chronological story of Max Wheeler's disappearance, beginning with the *Jacqueline* sailing down the Solent in late February five years before. Max, on an extended half-term break, had accompanied his father with two hired hands for crew. Their names were Colin Dunmore and his girlfriend Samantha Wallace, known as Sam. Three days after the boat party departed Southampton, Wheeler's three daughters, Joss, aged seventeen, Chloe, fifteen, and Hannah, eleven, left by road for Scotland. They were driven by Rosemary Coombs, their deceased mother's younger sister, her only sibling. They spent one night with friends in southern Scotland and the next in a B&B in the north-west. They caught the ferry sailing at mid-morning the next day. Approximately four hours separated the arrivals of the two parties of travellers at their final destination. The *Jacqueline* anchored in the bay on the north side of Priest's Island before ten a.m. on 2nd March. Rosemary Coombs parked her BMW by the harbour at the Deep Blue on Eilean Dubh, a kilometre away across the sound, soon after one p.m. Wheeler was waiting to pick them up in the *Jacqueline*'s dinghy having earlier disembarked his crew and their bicycles for a short Hebridean holiday. (By nightfall Colin and Sam would be thirty kilometres to the north, on the Island of Harris.)

At one thirty, the girls and their aunt went aboard the *Jacqueline* where Max greeted them. According to Rosemary Coombs, he was in high spirits and looking forward to camping alone that night on Priest's Island.

Around two, Wheeler took Max, his tent, sleeping bag and a backpack of food across the bay to the wooden jetty. Hannah went too after making a fuss about Max having more fun than her since he'd been helping to sail the *Jacqueline* when she had been stuck in a car for days. Later that afternoon, Joss and Chloe crossed to the jetty in the dinghy to check that Hannah was all right. They found her assisting or hindering (depending on whether Chloe's or Hannah's story was to be believed) Max to pitch his tent and to light a fire with driftwood. By evening Hannah was cold and wet having fallen into a sea-pool fully dressed. Since she didn't have dry clothes, she agreed to leave the island with her sisters. Max was happy on his own. As on previous occasions when he'd spent the night on the island, his tent had been pitched on the hillside to the west of the old shieling which was close to the southern shore. It was Max's favourite place. Out of sight of the *Jacqueline*, it allowed him to imagine he was in his own private domain. From his tent he looked out over an archipelago of islands.

At six thirty, as dusk was beginning to fall, Joss, Chloe and Hannah returned to the *Jacqueline*. Hannah showered and the family ate supper at eight. Hannah was first to bed before nine. Joss followed soon after – the three girls were sharing the same cabin. Chloe went on deck at nine thirty to keep an arrangement she had made with Max to signal him 'good night' by torchlight. Despite Chloe flashing for five minutes, Max didn't answer. Although Chloe was concerned, her father was reassuring, saying that Max had probably fallen asleep as he would have been exhausted after his journey by sea. At ten o'clock Chloe joined her sisters in bed. Wheeler and Rosemary Coombs retired soon after to the two remaining cabins.

The following morning, Wheeler woke early. At around eight, he went ashore with the intention of surprising Max by cooking breakfast on the fire. The boy's tent was empty. His sleeping bag was inside but still rolled up. The fire had gone cold overnight. After shouting for Max, Wheeler searched the island. At nine thirty, he returned to the *Jacqueline*. Twenty minutes later he dropped Rosemary Coombs, Joss, Chloe and Hannah at the island's jetty to continue the search. He crossed the sound to Eilean Dubh intending to ring the police on the Deep Blue's landline. Going ashore at the harbour, he found the island's resident officer, Constable Dyer, already there. He was investigating vandalism to Rosemary Coombs' car. The damage had been discovered by Bella MacLeod when she opened the tea room that morning. A photograph of the BMW was clipped to the page Cal was reading. It showed the windscreen shattered and a furrow gouged across the bonnet. Two of the tyres had been slashed.

By eleven, Wheeler returned to Priest's Island with Dyer. The island was searched again – Dyer, Wheeler, Rosemary Coombs and the girls walking in line. They carried out three sweeps, going along the south coast, back through the middle of the island, finally the northern shore. No further sign of Max was discovered.

At one thirty Wheeler took Dyer back to the Deep Blue so he could coordinate police reinforcements. Dyer also gave directions for boats to begin a search of the skerries and islets in the sound as well as the islands that lay immediately to the south of Priest's Island. By nightfall no clue to the boy's disappearance had been found. The following day, a police mobile operations room was brought to the parking area in front of the Deep Blue. A chief inspector took control. Fifty officers, including dog handlers, were deployed for two weeks. They were backed up by mountain rescue teams as well as police and navy divers. The boy had vanished without trace.

So much Cal knew already. He read on. The next pages included a general description of the township as well as mugshots, names, addresses and biographies of the residents. The individual entries varied in length and detail but most included information about work, family, circles of friendship and, on occasion, sexual relationships. At the end of each entry there was an assessment of who would lie for whom, who would protect whom, who would betray whom. Cal became more and more uneasy as he read the details.

'Where does all this information come from?' he asked Mr Close.

'It was Mr Wheeler's practice to send people to stay in the holiday accommodation, a chalet behind the Deep Blue, or to book B&Bs. They posed as visitors and mostly they gathered the gossip they heard in the tea room.'

'You mean he hired people to spy?'

The lawyer closed his eyes. Cal took the gesture as confirmation and a sign that no explanation would be forthcoming.

'This *was* his practice, you said. He doesn't do it any more?'

The lawyer's head shook.

'Just to make myself clear,' Cal said, 'I'm not going to spy for Mr Wheeler. OK?'

The lawyer's eyes closed again. 'That,' he said, 'will not be necessary.'

Cal returned to the file. Two names had been highlighted in red.

He showed the page to Mr Close. 'Suspects?' he asked.

'Everyone's a suspect, Dr McGill.'

'These two more than others?' Cal tried again.

'Those two more than others,' Mr Close agreed.

'One has a black dot beside his name. What does that mean?'

'It means that he's dead.'

The man's name was Donald Grant. He'd been the last tenant of Priest's Island and had died three years earlier, two years after Max's disappearance. According to the file, he had the strongest motive for wishing the Wheelers harm. His family had grazed cattle and sheep on the island for eighty-four unbroken years. The arrangement ended with David Wheeler's purchase.

Mr Close watched Cal. 'You should understand,' he volunteered, 'that Mr Wheeler made the cancellation of the lease a condition of sale. It wasn't the case that he terminated it himself. The vendor did.' The lawyer returned Cal's stare. 'In Mr Wheeler's opinion, it's an important distinction and one that has been overlooked by the township's residents.'

Cal thought the distinction a fine one but didn't say so. He studied the photograph of Donald Grant. It showed a weather-beaten man with white hair, bushy eyebrows and mottled cheeks; a kindly, fleshy face, one shaped by hardship and Hebridean winds. Cal knew the type well. He had never met a man like that capable of unkindness let alone murder. In Donald Grant's rheumy eyes Cal detected disappointment as well as the drink that killed him prematurely at the age of fifty-nine.

Cal let his eyes drift to the other chief suspect, Donald Grant's nephew, 'considered by the township to be the rightful heir to the grazing rights'. Ewan Chisholm was his name. His photograph showed a stocky young man with a flushed face and cropped fair hair. He was fifteen at the time of Max Wheeler's disappearance. However, the report cautioned, his youthfulness should not disqualify him as a suspect, 'in fact quite the opposite'. For his age, Chisholm was physically strong and he knew the sea around Priest's Island as well as anyone. He'd been crossing the sound with his uncle since he was seven. Navigating it at night, even in difficult conditions, would have been well within his capabilities. Also, he nursed a double grievance. Not only had the cancellation of the lease deprived him of the grazing rights in future – Ewan was Donald Grant's only male relative – he blamed his uncle's physical deterioration from alcohol on Wheeler's ownership of the island. By common account Donald Grant's spirit had been broken by the loss of the grazing rights which had been in his family for four generations. His nephew had motive as well as an instance of minor criminality in his record which pointed to him being capable of the other violent act committed that night, the vandalism to Rosemary Coombs' car. The police said the damage had probably been done with a knife.

Two years earlier, when he was thirteen, he had broken windows in a holiday home owned by a family from Newcastle. The house had been unoccupied at the time. 'It was, though, evidence of an activist attitude towards empty or under-used property belonging to those regarded as outsiders.' Another piece of circumstantial evidence against Chisholm concerned a visit by him to Priest's Island following his uncle's death. A rowan sapling had been found afterwards, planted close to the shieling where Ewan had spent summers with his uncle as they tended the sheep. The tree, which had later been uprooted on David Wheeler's instructions, was proof 'of Chisholm believing his family to have some continuing superior moral if not legal claim to the land'. In other words he had a grievance.

After his uncle's death, Ewan had settled in the township, having become the owner of the croft, a bungalow with two hectares. Apart from keeping six ewes and two dairy cows, he worked part-time doing odd jobs at the Deep Blue. He was saving money to increase his flock and to modernize his uncle's croft house. His 'protector' was Bella MacLeod, the owner of the tea room. His on-off girlfriend was Bella's niece, Catriona Mackinnon. It was considered unlikely that Bella would cover for Ewan if she had proof of his involvement in the disappearance or death of Max Wheeler. The same could not be said of Catriona, who had been uncooperative with the police inquiries.

Cal turned the page to the joint biographies of Bella and Catriona. Their photographs were side by side: a study in opposites. Bella was round-faced with a cheerful, animated expression – her portrait had been taken in a crowd and blown up. She was forty-nine, divorced and childless but made up for that by being 'a mother hen to strays'. Ewan Chisholm and Catriona were part of her brood.

Catriona's photograph showed a watchful teenager with dramatic jet-black hair and milk-white skin. Catriona's mother, Frances, had built and opened the Deep Blue though she hadn't lived to see its success. She died in a fishing accident with her husband Kenny, Catriona's father. The girl was three at the time and had been looked after ever since by Bella MacLeod. Bella had also taken over the tea room. It seemed the older inhabitants often found Catriona sullen when she served them in the teashop, even truculent. Catriona had been fourteen, the same age as Max Wheeler, and was known to be upset about the treatment of Donald Grant and Ewan. 'Although she claimed to have been at home that night – a story supported by Bella MacLeod – it's likely she was involved, if not in the murder of Max Wheeler, almost certainly in withholding incriminating evidence against Ewan Chisholm.'

After Cal had read the remaining potted biographies of the township's inhabitants, Mr Close slid a newspaper cutting across his desk. Under the headline 'Motive for Murder?' it showed a picture, taken the year before, of wooden posts driven into the ground at intervals around the perimeter of Priest's Island. The story talked of a symbolic act of protest inspired by celebrated land raids of the past. Particular mention was made of the seven men who staked claims to parcels of acres on the Knoydart peninsula in the late 1940s. It also reported a police press conference at which a detective inspector had spoken about a history of simmering tensions since David Wheeler had bought Priest's Island. 'Property ownership and land use,' the detective was quoted as saying, 'are strongly felt issues in a place like this.'

Mr Close explained. 'My client bought an island that Donald Grant and his nephew thought was theirs. The rest of the township supports that idea of moral ownership, and the result was a fourteen-year-old boy lost his life.' He looked at Cal. 'The position is clear. My client owns that land and now, after all that has happened, he is emotionally invested in it too. He will not give up ownership or his resolve to find out how his son was murdered and by whom.'

The lawyer's grey face had become quite flushed, almost the colour of his fat fingers. 'Your job, Dr McGill, is to examine the evidence and to suggest how the crime was committed and where Max's body was hidden. Mr Wheeler has looked everywhere. Only the sea is left. If you had to hide a body around Priest's Island, Dr McGill, where would you choose so that it would never be found again? You tell Mr Wheeler that and he'll find the murderer.'

The tea room door opened and Catriona appeared outside. 'Do you mind?' She held up a cigarette. 'Thought I'd take a break. I'll stand over here, downwind.' Then she said, 'Want one?'

Cal shook his head. 'I don't smoke.'

She pointed to Cal's pickup. 'That was you, was it, at the old slipway? Saw your pickup down there last night.'

'Yes.'

'The RIB too?'

Cal nodded.

'I wasn't being curious, mind.' Catriona dragged on her cigarette. 'I was walking. It's what I do in the evenings if the weather's OK. Once the tea room's shut, I climb up the hill to get a phone signal or I'll go by the old slipway because hardly anyone lives along there. Means I don't have to see people.' The way she said 'people', dropping her voice and elongating the word, suggested she needed her own company by closing time. She laughed. 'I think I'd go mad otherwise, stuck in here all day.'

'I didn't see you,' Cal said.

Catriona squinted at him. 'You're that Dr McGill everyone's talking about?' She seemed surprised by her own question, by daring to ask.

'Does it matter if I am?'

Catriona blew out smoke while she considered her answer. 'Not to me.' The inference was it would to others. 'Mr Wheeler's lawyer sent round a letter about you.'

'What did it say?' Cal asked.

'Just who you were and what you did,' she replied. 'Ach and there was the usual stuff about Mr Wheeler expecting privacy while he's here.' She put on a different voice, pompous and affected, her take on an English lawyer reading aloud the letter. 'In particular, Mr Wheeler would regard as unwelcome any attempt by the township to mark the anniversary of the disappearance of his son Max.'

Cal noted her use of 'disappearance'. He imagined Mr Close would have written 'murder'.

'Does the township mark it?'

Catriona nodded. 'When Mr Wheeler and the family say prayers on the island the whole township turns out. Every 2nd March, that's tomorrow, everyone'll be in their best clothes, paying their respects.' Catriona indicated the harbour wall with her cigarette. 'They'll be standing down there, sun, wind or rain, and usually there's wind and rain. If they stopped at home or treated it like any other day, the newspapers would call us callous and cold-hearted.'

'You'll be there too?'

'Not me.' Catriona shook her head. 'Anyway, someone's got to clear up the cups and plates in the tea room while they're all down by the harbour.' Cal had the impression of another, unstated reason, maybe something to do with Ewan Chisholm, her on-off boyfriend, being the main suspect. Cal would have asked her more but for a dinghy appearing in the middle of the sound.

'That for you?' Catriona nodded in that direction.

'I think so.'

Catriona sucked on her cigarette and stared at the boat. 'Wheeler, isn't it?'

'Yes.'

'He thinks one of us killed Max.'

'So I've heard.'

'Is that what you think?'

'I don't know,' Cal said. 'I've been asked to test some new theories. If Max did go into the water, where might he have ended up given the tides and winds that night and the next few days? If he was disposed of – let's say weighted down and dumped in the water – are there places where the body wouldn't be disturbed? I'm looking at different possibilities. It's not my job to say whether Max Wheeler died in an accident or was murdered.'

Catriona dropped her cigarette, squashed it under her foot and kicked the butt away from the door. 'Shall I tell you what people are saying about you?'

'Go on.'

'Well, some people think you might be OK because you're looking in the right place – the sea – and there's your background too.'

'What do you mean?'

'Your mother's family has island blood?'

'North coast, near Tongue, yes.'

'Your name's Gaelic?'

'Caladh, harbour,' Cal translated. 'But I don't speak Gaelic. I was born in Edinburgh, raised there too.'

'Aye well, there is that.' Catriona stared at him as if making up her own mind. 'My Auntie Bella says it doesn't really matter whether you have island blood since you'll be doing Wheeler's bidding.' She held out her hand to take his empty mug. 'And all that bastard wants is to put one of us away for murder.'

She went inside and Cal collected his backpack from the front passenger seat of his pickup. He walked to the harbour wall and waited by the stone slipway. He was surprised by Catriona's strength of feeling against Wheeler and wondered how long it would be before his conversation with her would be relayed through the township – a day at the most. She'd tell Bella MacLeod first, perhaps Ewan Chisholm. Soon word would spread. Within a day the township would know about him, how he would be investigating theories and possibilities. Would that be enough to persuade anyone to talk to him?

By now the dinghy was at the harbour entrance. Cal recalled Mr Close's telephone message of the night before. 'Mr Wheeler will collect you tomorrow at three. Be punctual. He will deliver you back at six. This will be the only meeting you will have with him. Afterwards, if you have any questions, you will deal with me. You must not contact Mr Wheeler or his daughters.' Then, as an afterthought: 'My client regards Priest's Island as a shrine to his dead son, Dr McGill. That must be respected at all times.'

4

Everything Cal had read about Wheeler portrayed a man of single-minded determination. Descriptions like obsessive or resilient frequently cropped up. Even his financial difficulties – the collapse of his company, his family home in Southampton being put up for sale – hadn't appeared to deflect him. By all accounts he was as relentless as ever in Max's cause, in his efforts to find his son's killer. The subtext in Mr Close's warning telephone call of the night before had been quite clear: Wheeler was not to be obstructed in his purpose or to be provoked. Yet the man Cal met barely forty minutes ago bore little resemblance to this caricature. Rather than being demanding and purposeful, as Cal had expected, David Wheeler gave the impression of being preoccupied. Only his general description fitted his advance billing. He was five ten or eleven and, by his clothes, a blue skiing jacket and cashmere scarf at his neck, still prosperous. His features told a different story. The ginger hair, always so perfectly parted in his photographs, was untidy, uncut and greying. The flesh of his face seemed drawn back and tight as though he was walking into a brisk wind. His eyes were dull. Wheeler might have the wardrobe of his previous life but somewhere along the way the personality that once inhabited the clothes had gone missing.

Why was Cal surprised? He had seen this often before. First the child was lost, then the parent. Only the shell, the flesh and bones, remained to carry on the life which had been lived before. Cal had been blinded by everything he'd read about Wheeler. The man himself was so changed he was almost unrecognizable.

After meeting at the harbour by the Deep Blue, they had crossed the sound in the dinghy. Only fractured conversation had been possible against the noise of the engines. Cal asked about the sea around them, its hazards and quirks, and Wheeler had shouted replies as they crossed to Priest's Island. Bypassing the *Jacqueline*, Wheeler landed at the wooden jetty. Their next destination, the chapel, was two hundred metres away. It took a while because Wheeler had a habit of stopping to recite another chapter in the building's history. He seemed eager to impress on Cal how important a structure it was, despite its semi-ruined condition. The chapel, Wheeler said, had been the work of a hermit priest in the twelfth century. Other priests on retreat had lived on the island since. The last record of the building having a roof was 1874, though irregular services had continued to be held there. Mostly they'd been organized by groups of pilgrims or baggers of remote and unusual churches. They'd come to a halt after 'my son's murder' – Cal noted the extra charge of emotion invested in the words. Afterwards, Wheeler said, the chapel became Max's memorial, his private shrine. The walls had been stabilized, a door of toughened glass fitted, a stone bench installed. Otherwise it had been left untouched. Twice a year – 2nd March, 'the day Max was taken from us', and 14th August, his birthday – a priest led the family in memorial prayers.

Wheeler became lost in thought. Cal tried to fill the gap by tactfully complimenting the chapel's positioning by the sea and its intimate size. But Wheeler made no attempt to respond. He appeared miles away. Cal doubted he'd even heard.

As they climbed the grassy mound to the ruin, Wheeler asked, 'What was I saying?'

'You were telling me about family prayers twice a year,' Cal prompted.

Wheeler nodded. The chapel, he carried on without embarrassment or apology, had become a place of solace for him and his daughters. It was where they felt Max to be, where they went to talk to him, where the family could be together again. The girls sensed their mother's spirit there too.

'The island,' said Wheeler, 'is the last place they remember the family being happy. The first time we came here, their mother was alive.'

Going there had been a spur-of-the-moment thing, an adventure for the children. They'd been cruising off the west coast of Scotland – Wheeler putting the boat through its paces after a refit – when a sunny morning and a stable high pressure system tempted them across the Minch. By chance they dropped anchor off Priest's Island, in the bay, and they stayed until the weather changed, almost a week.

'I remember Jackie watching Max and the girls swimming by the jetty and saying "David, wouldn't it be wonderful if they had somewhere like this, where they can be free?" Five weeks after we went home Jackie was killed in a car accident.'

Wheeler fell silent and Cal watched a raven tumbling above the hill at the island's western end.

'I bought the island,' Wheeler said, as though he was replying to an unspoken accusation, 'because it was Jackie's last wish for the children. Now, I own it because I have no choice.' He sounded as though he wished he had.

'Because this is where Max is . . .' Cal suggested.

'Yes.' Wheeler clasped one trembling hand to the other and looked to see whether Cal had noticed this frailty. Then he said, 'Is Max in heaven? Will we meet up when I'm dead? No, I don't think so.' A silence followed. 'That sort of after-life? I don't believe in it.'

'No, I don't think I do either,' Cal replied. 'Nor do most of the parents like you that I meet. If they had a faith before, they lose it afterwards.'

The mention of other parents had an effect on Wheeler. He searched Cal's eyes, as if he wanted to confide. 'They talk to you?'

'Some of them do,' Cal replied. 'When they're ready.'

Wheeler turned away and seemed deep in thought as he approached the glass door of the chapel and unlocked it. Before going inside, he started speaking as though making a confession. He addressed himself to the chapel but his words were intended for Cal.

'I misled you. Jackie wanted the island for all of the children, the girls too, but I wanted it for Max. If it hadn't been for Max I wouldn't have bought the place, no matter their happy memories. No, for me Priest's Island was for Max, for the boy to grow up with a free spirit, to be daring.' He turned to Cal. 'I bought it for Max's son, for Max's grandson, for posterity. That's the only afterlife a man can expect, to have a son and a grandson.'

Cal said nothing and Wheeler went inside. When Cal followed after a judicious delay – he thought Wheeler might prefer a few moments alone – he found him standing by a stone bench, his fingers searching the back for the engraving of Max's name.

'That's Max.' Wheeler nodded towards a small niche in the west gable. 'The photograph was taken the first time we came to the island.'

Behind a glass screen was a colour image in a silver frame of a fair-haired boy in a sea-pool bounded by rocks. He was treading water, splashing with his right hand and holding an upturned crab in his left. A face mask had been pushed back on to his forehead. A grin extended across his small face. Cal remembered that feeling of exhilaration. He had photographs of himself like that taken by his mother.

'I'm sorry for your loss.' Cal was angry with himself for sounding trite. He sensed Wheeler tensing, the slightest of tremors in the stillness of the ruined chapel, a flitter of irritation. How often must Wheeler have heard 'sorry'? How little it must mean to him, how inadequate an expression of feeling.

'He was eleven then,' Wheeler said. 'Look at his face, that's why I bought the island. What father wouldn't give that to his son if he could? That sense of life being something to live, of freedom and possibility.' He fell silent and stared at the photograph. Then he asked, 'Do you have a son?'

Cal took time to answer. He studied Max's face. 'No, I don't.'

'Then you won't understand.' Wheeler's tone was quieter and admonishing, sadder too, as if he was disappointed with himself as well as Cal, as if this was a lesson he should have learned by now, that nobody could properly understand, least of all someone without a son.

Cal said nothing. Better that, he thought, than saying the wrong thing. He'd met enough parents in Wheeler's situation to know how quickly the mask of emotional control could crack, how close pain lay to the surface, how it never went away. A dead child was the worst, a dead child whose body was lost the worst of the worst, an affront to parental instinct, the last rite of loving denied. Cal understood. What he could never know was how that *felt*. Perhaps he could have made the point, but would Wheeler have been listening? Although he was within touching distance, he seemed to be far away, beyond reaching. Without warning he walked out of the chapel.

Cal continued to study the photograph. A few minutes

later, he too went outside and found Wheeler still in a kind of trance and looking across the sound to Eilean Dubh. 'I'm going to find you,' he said, 'I'm going to make sure you're punished for what you've done.' Wheeler, Cal realized, was talking to the township, a father bent on retribution as well as redemption. Cal cleared his throat to let Wheeler know he was there. 'Would you like a few minutes alone?'

Wheeler stared at Cal. 'Why would I want that? Let's get on, shall we?' His voice and manner were brusque, the David Wheeler Cal had expected to meet. 'There's more of the island to show you and you'll have to come on board the *Jacqueline*. The girls will want to hear what you're going to be doing.'

A signal passed between the sisters, from Chloe to Hannah. *Don't*, it meant. Don't what? Cal wondered. Was Hannah upset? Was it something he'd said in his explanation of the natural forces at work in the sound? Perhaps Wheeler's youngest daughter had imagined Max's dead body being thrown about. Chloe had glanced angrily at her sister. *Don't make a scene, Hannah*: was that what it meant?

After Wheeler's introductions, Cal had spread a chart across the table in the *Jacqueline*'s cramped saloon. He'd talked about the reefs, islets and skerries, the tidal currents as well as Atlantic storms: the interplay between them, the power that would be generated. 'So strong the sea bottom will be scoured daily, the sand and silt will shift and churn. Even boulders will be dislodged.' He hadn't used Max's name or words like body, remains or corpse. That hadn't been necessary. The implication was clear enough: if Max had been dumped into the sea between Priest's Island and Eilean Dubh he wouldn't have remained where he was, even if he had been weighted down.

'Think of the sound as a washing machine,' Cal said, 'but many times larger and just as turbulent.'

On reflection he wished he'd been more circumspect. Had he been too graphic for sixteen-year-old Hannah? He glanced to his right, where she was sitting but no longer staring with an agitated expression at the chart. After Chloe's warning, she had turned away. All Cal could see was the back of her head.

'Should I go on?'

'Of course,' Wheeler said and Chloe gave Cal a reassuring smile as if nothing had happened, or nothing that should concern him. She pushed closer to her father until their shoulders were touching, the similarities between them easier to see: the same high forehead and wide-apart eyes, similar colouring too. Chloe's ginger hair was cropped short. 'It's interesting,' she said, 'isn't it, Pa, what Dr McGill has been saying?'

Cal was wary of blundering further into an unfolding family drama. If only there was a script he could have read. He glanced at Hannah again, her attention apparently caught by the aerial acrobatics of the raven Cal had seen earlier. It was flying over the bay, close to the *Jacqueline*.

'Well, if you're sure,' Cal said slowly, to give Hannah an opportunity to object. She didn't react. Feeling ill at ease, he hurried the details of his investigations. 'I'll map the sound's currents including the various eddies, and research its underwater structures. I'll be looking for hiding places, where a wall of rock or some other barrier to the currents prevent scouring, where the bottom is relatively undisturbed. In layman's language, I'll be trying to find an underwater hiding place.'

He'd glanced again at Hannah. She still appeared distracted by the ravens.

Cal continued. 'After five years all I can do is propose theories and suggest possibilities. On land, there might be some . . .' he hesitated, 'remains to be found. At sea, that's improbable. Especially as disposal . . .' Cal winced at the word, 'will have been rushed and likely to have been completed that first night under cover of darkness, before the start of the search the following day. Even if a makeshift container had been used it would have been broken open by the sea long ago.'

Cal looked from Wheeler to Chloe. He hoped the inference was clear without his language becoming too graphic: the body would have been broken too.

'One of the unusual features for me,' he carried on, 'concerns the flood tide which starts strongly straight after slack water and, after a ten-minute time delay on the Minch side, flows into both entrances to the sound. I'll be trying to work out what effect that has – whether an object would be contained within the sound or whether the earlier start of the flood on the Atlantic side would expel it into the Minch. That might be important, because there was a bigger than normal tide the night Max went missing.'

Cal was aware of Hannah moving. He turned to his right and found her staring at him. Her thin face and blonde hair reminded Cal of the photograph of Max in the ruined chapel. Instead of grinning with pleasure, as Max had been, her face was serious and wet with tears.

She looked at her father. 'I can't stand any more of this,' she shouted.

Cal noticed the set of Chloe's face, the way she pushed close to her father, as if shielding him from Hannah's attack, as if that was why she had drawn nearer to him before, to protect him from his youngest daughter.

Hannah shouted again, her voice trembling with emotion, 'Why . . . why do you make us go through this every year?'

She let out a cry of frustration and anger. 'Why?' She pushed past Cal to the door. 'Anyone would think Max is the only child that matters ... the only child you've lost. Oh, but I forgot, Joss, your other lost child, is only your *daughter*. She doesn't count. Only Max matters to you, your darling, angel *son* . . .' By now, her face was red with shouting. With a final cry of anger and frustration, she rushed outside.

Chloe put on a shocked expression. 'That was seriously out of order.'

Wheeler said nothing. As he stood up and followed Hannah, Chloe called after him, 'Pa, tell her she can't behave like that.' She looked at Cal, the shocked expression forming again. 'Well, she can't.'

'I'm sorry,' Cal said. 'The things I was saying. They would have been hard for her to hear, and for you.'

'Don't worry, it wasn't anything you said,' Chloe announced with certainty. 'It's just Hannah, the mood she's in.'

From elsewhere on the boat came the sound of Wheeler's insistent voice and Hannah's arguing back.

'What did your sister mean,' Cal asked after an uncomfortable pause, 'about Joss being lost?'

'Oh, Joss isn't lost,' Chloe said dismissively, as though Cal had just witnessed another of Hannah's affectations, one with which Chloe had grown impatient. 'Not in that way, not dead, not missing. She's living on Eilean Dubh, in the township, in some shitty little caravan.' Chloe rolled her eyes, as if both of her sisters had gone mad. 'Anyway, Joss is my big sister too, so I don't know why Hannah imagines she's the only one who's upset.'

'That must be difficult for you all, Joss living in the township.'

Chloe flashed a look at Cal. 'Living with the enemy, you mean.'

At half past five, thirty minutes early, Bella closed the Deep Blue for the evening. There was little point, she told Catriona, in the two of them waiting around for a customer when they had so much work to be doing. While Catriona set about cleaning the tea room, Bella propped open the kitchen door and rummaged in the cupboards for ingredients. In between lifting out packets and tins, she talked to herself. Where had she put the cocoa powder? What had she done with the sugar? Then she wondered aloud to Catriona about Max Wheeler's memorial in the morning. How many would turn out? Had Ina said anything about needing a lift? Had Isobel mentioned being able to take time off from the heritage centre? Surely she'd be able to swap shifts since she only worked there ten hours a week? Did Catriona think Joss would attend? Whether Joss stayed away or not, someone in the township would find cause for complaint. In case she did come, Bella had taken the precaution of having words with Fergie McCann from the north of the island about his son and the boy's good-for-nothing friends. She might as well have been speaking to a stone wall! Had Bella already told Catriona? Oh, she had, well, she wasn't going to stand for last year's behaviour again – the McCann boy driving along the coast road, car horn blaring, just as the memorial began, and on such a calm day too. The noise carried across the sound. Bella had been ashamed. Hadn't Catriona? Wouldn't it be awful if the same happened tomorrow? Bella sighed. Perhaps it would be better if Joss stayed away. She would ring the girl later. Could Catriona remind her?

Catriona's responses were brief or exasperated but Bella carried on as if she hadn't noticed. She laid down a smoke-screen of chatter and exclamations while waiting for Catriona to lower her guard. 'Should I make two date and banana loaves as well as two chocolate sponges? What about a fruit cake? I always think fruit cake's better for a sad occasion, especially as everyone will have spent an hour outside and a cold wind will be blowing. Shall I use brandy? The brandy! Oh, the bottle's empty. Well, that settles that. Whisky it'll have to be. Where is the whisky? Catriona?' She raised her voice. 'Was there any whisky in yesterday's delivery, because I'm certain I ordered a bottle but I can't seem to find it any-where?'

'Look behind the rolled oats,' Catriona replied. 'Anyway, whisky's better than brandy.'

'Found it.' Without pausing for breath, Bella said, 'I could do cheese scones in the morning when I'm doing rolls. What do you think?'

'OK.'

Bella waited a moment. 'Catriona, love . . .'

'What?' She was standing at the kitchen door, watching her aunt.

'Oh, it's nothing. Don't worry.'

'No, go on, what?'

Bella pulled a face as if Catriona was dragging it out of her. 'I was just wondering whether you'd been under the weather the last few days. You haven't seemed quite yourself.'

The ruse had worked once or twice before, Bella engaging Catriona in conversation as they prepared for a busy day and luring her into revealing something about her state of mind.

'I'm fine,' was all Catriona said.

It was a response that frustrated Bella, since a blind man could see the girl wasn't fine. At nineteen, Catriona's age, Bella had been out and enjoying her life, meeting boys, going to dances. Catriona, on the other hand, always appeared to be at odds with the world and unhappy. That afternoon Bella had tried to remember when she and Catriona had last laughed together, even shared a smile. How many weeks must it have been? How many months? Bella wasn't sure, nor could she remember when Catriona had last spoken to her in anything other than monosyllables or answered a question without a preceding sigh of exasperation.

She decided to persevere. 'Ewan will be coming round later,' she said brightly.

Catriona didn't answer.

Bella tried again when Catriona fetched some clean table-cloths from the kitchen table. 'Did I mention Ewan said he might drop round?'

'You just have, haven't you?'

'You'll talk to him?'

'Aye, if I want to.'

'Catriona, I don't just mean hello.'

'Yes, Auntie Bella, I know fine well what you mean.'

Bella put her hands on her hips and watched Catriona go back to the tea room. At least she didn't stomp, the usual warning for Bella to back off. Bella rubbed the back of her gloved hand against her hairnet, where it itched at the rim. She was a worry, that girl, always had been, ever since Bella had taken charge of the Deep Blue, and taken charge of Catriona too. Some three-year-olds were captivating, but Catriona hadn't been one of them. Even then she'd been a wraith of a child with her white skin and watchful eyes. Bella found her silent and withdrawn, untrusting. 'Who wouldn't have been after the shock of both her parents dying like that?' she used to tell herself. But, still, it hadn't been easy bringing up a child who was always just out of reach. People were forever telling Bella how good a mother she'd been to Catriona but they didn't know the truth. Nor had Bella told them; nor would she. Secrets weren't safe in a small community, and anyway, what good could it do?

Bella had been aware of her deficiency from the very beginning. At first she'd put her trust in the healing powers of time but now, after so many years, she knew things wouldn't change. She was a mother to Catriona in every way except one: she had no instinct of love for the girl. The lack kept her awake at night as she fretted about the accumulation of damage that was being done. Whenever Bella sought reassurance, listening to radio programmes on adoption or childcare, all she found was further cause for worry. How often had she heard some expert or other say 'A child who isn't loved won't be able to love'? That idea had long since invaded her like a parasite. In Catriona's on-off relationship with Ewan Chisholm, Bella thought she was witnessing the effect of her inability to love her niece as a mother would. What other explanation could there be, since Catriona and Ewan were made for each other? Bella blamed herself for their fractures and tried to help however she could. It was one instinct Bella did have, to want to compensate for her failing. Given the chance she would do anything to fix Catriona's life, if only Catriona would let her.

Bella started again on her checklist. Should they order more coffee for later in the week since tomorrow would be busy? Had Catriona remembered to take milk out of the freezer? Was there enough ham for the rolls and sandwiches, tomatoes too, come to think of it, and cheese? Oh, and while Catriona was checking the storeroom could she fetch some coffee and another jar of pickle?

It made no difference to Bella whether Catriona replied to every question as she was thinking aloud, putting up another smokescreen, waiting until she thought she could broach the issue again. 'You know,' Bella said as Catriona was wrapping napkins around knives and forks, 'Ewan always comes as close as he can. Boys are shy creatures. All you have to do is speak to him. It doesn't really matter what you say.'

Catriona snapped back, 'Leave it, Auntie Bella. Please.'

Bella replied with an 'I'd help you if you let me' expression but Catriona insisted, 'No, Auntie Bella.' She left the kitchen, stomping flat-footed away. 'Don't speak about Ewan,' she shouted. 'Nothing. Not a word. Ever again. All right?'

Bella bit her lip. It was a shame watching two young people making a mess of things, especially when they were so well suited. That wasn't just Bella's view: the township shared her opinion. Perhaps that was a pressure for them both, in such a small community, every glance or look causing comment, everyone knowing everyone else's business. What age was Catriona when she and Ewan became friends – eleven or twelve? Not boyfriend and girlfriend at that stage but boy and girl who explored together and found support in each other's misfortune. Ewan's parents had still been alive, unlike Catriona's, though they might as well have been dead for all the good they did him. The boy spent all of his holidays with his Uncle Donald at Grant's Croft to escape the violence and drunkenness at home in Fort William. What age was Catriona when she became Ewan's girlfriend? Thirteen, Bella thought, but because they were always breaking up and getting back together it was hard to keep track. The year of Max Wheeler's disappearance was when the relationship became serious. Donald and Ewan had been taken in for questioning, three times in all, and uncle and nephew had frequented the tea room with the rest of the township, working out what to do.

Catriona had listened in from the counter. Injustice had acted as matchmaker. When Donald drank himself into an early grave Catriona was sixteen and Bella thought she wouldn't be long in marrying. Ewan had inherited the croft and, though Bella hadn't told her, Catriona would become owner of the Deep Blue when she was twenty-one. Not only were Catriona and Ewan well matched, they would be as well set as anyone in the township.

In hindsight, Bella was sorry she had allowed herself to run ahead of the relationship. She'd been imagining a wedding at the Deep Blue, but then Catriona made an announcement she hadn't expected. Ewan and she were taking a break. They were young, she said. It was no big deal. She didn't love Ewan anyway. With each succeeding split – there were two more, as far as Bella knew – Catriona affected similar indifference and for weeks afterwards her white skin became pasty and lifeless. A tea room, Bella realized as Catriona put on weight, was hardly the place to nurse the end of a relationship. At every break-up Bella felt a skewer twisting in her heart. So, when Ewan started hanging around the tea room again, she offered him a part-time job as handyman. Maybe working together would make the difference, she thought. That it hadn't, yet, Bella blamed on Catriona and her ignorance of boys. 'Speak to him,' Bella had often hissed into Catriona's ear. 'Encourage him.' It was obvious to Bella what Catriona should do. It would have been obvious to a stone statue.

As Bella was sieving icing sugar, Catriona reappeared and stood in the door, her white skin blotched by tears.

Bella removed her gloves and apron and went over to her. She wrapped her in her arms. 'Oh, Catriona, love,' she said, 'don't listen to me.' She pushed Catriona's hair away from her face and kissed her on the forehead. 'I'm sorry.' She kissed her again. 'It's just that I'd like to see you happy.'

'It's not me Ewan comes to see.'

Bella leaned back and took a good look at the girl. 'Now you're being silly,' she said. 'It's always been you. This is Ewan you're talking about? Of course it's you.' She laughed at how ridiculous Catriona was being and immediately wished she hadn't.

'Why won't you listen?' Catriona struggled free. 'It's not me. I know it's not me. It hasn't been me since he started hanging round again.'

Later, Bella sat alone in the kitchen, the evening's work done, the cakes cooling and the dough ready for the morning. She sipped black tea. 'Please make her happy.' She looked at the ceiling, vaguely in the direction of God. 'Please, do that for me.' Outside an engine started and Bella went to the window to catch a glimpse of Dr McGill. 'What's he like?' Bella had asked when Catriona told her he was on Priest's Island with David Wheeler and that the Toyota pickup parked outside was his.

Catriona had been non-committal: 'All right, I suppose.'

'Not if he's taking David Wheeler's money, he's not,' she'd answered back. Afterwards, she'd apologized for sounding cross with Catriona when she was angry with Wheeler for turning their lives upside down every year, Ewan's in particular. 'That young man can never escape the suspicion of murder. What does that do to him?'

Catriona said nothing.

Now Bella wondered if that might be part of the problem, Ewan being uncertain about his future and as a result not being able to offer Catriona one.

~

How families disintegrated was on Cal's mind. The subject had a visceral curiosity for him. Most often it occupied his thoughts when he saw a disagreement of some kind between a father and child. It could be an argument in a street, a supermarket or on a train. Without intending to, he would find himself taking an interest, his subconscious always searching for an explanation. Why? Was that how it started? He looked for clues because the fracturing of his own family was still such a puzzle to him. David Wheeler's argument with Hannah had made him wonder if he and his father had ever been like that. But he couldn't recall any cross words or disagreements between them. Neither had there been underlying tension, or none of which Cal had been aware. Yet, as certain as he was of his memory, he was also aware that families didn't break into pieces for no reason. In the case of the Wheelers, it was easy to see what was forcing them apart: the father's obsession with his lost son had blinded him to the needs of his daughters. In David Wheeler's single-mindedness, in his carelessness too, Cal recognized something of his own father. Though, as always happened, when he looked to other families for insight into the fate of his, the circumstances were never exactly the same. The lessons were never quite applicable. The only thing that families seemed to have in common was how different they were. The puzzle remained unsolved and Cal grew irritated at raking over the same ground to no purpose. James McGill had forgotten Cal. Why couldn't Cal, a thirty-year-old man for heaven's sake, forget him?

For a long time Cal had thought the disintegration of his family was a process which began with the death of his mother from cancer. Cal had been seventeen at the time. Now, when he looked back across the thirteen years that had passed since, he saw the fracture as a single drawn-out event. When he lost his mother, he began to lose his father too. Following her funeral, James McGill suffered a mental collapse. His recovery was slow and appeared to be complete only when he removed himself from the context of his former life – the city in which Cal's mother and he had settled, the house where they'd been lovers, the son they had nurtured, the school where he worked as head of geography. He went abroad, teaching at charity-run schools for orphans (an irony, Cal thought), while assuring his only child of his firm intention to return, sometime. He never did. It was as if he was afraid of revisiting the scene of his collapse. Had he imagined proximity would trigger another breakdown?

Cal maintained fragile contact by irregular emails and, for a while, by flying once a year to visit his father in whichever country he was based. Papua New Guinea was succeeded by postings in Africa. In Mozambique, at a school in Maputo, his father met a fellow teacher by the name of Honesty Dlamini. She was a Swazi, twelve years his junior and mother of three daughters by a failed marriage. James and Honesty became man and wife at a hastily arranged (so Cal's father said) open-air ceremony attended by a handful of close friends. Cal received the photographs by email and, a few days later, a rare letter from his father announcing the sale of the family home in Edinburgh. It had been let for the previous nine years. The buyers had been the sitting tenants. 'Shouldn't it provide for the future instead of preserving the past?' his father had asked. Whose future? The answer was painfully obvious to Cal: his father's new family.

There was, however, one more rejection to come.

Now there was a son.

The child's name was Moses Ngwane McGill. He weighed six pounds, four ounces. Mother and child were doing well. The announcement had come by email two months ago, the first contact from Cal's father for more than a year. 'A son!' the email was headed. A photograph was attached. 'Dear All,' it began. There were nineteen addresses before Cal's, and more after: his father's contacts in alphabetical order. Cal didn't reply though others had, their effusive congratulations sent round robin and dropping into his inbox during the hours that followed. 'A boy at last!' one cheered. 'You must be thrilled after being surrounded by those girls.' Cal hadn't recognized the sender's name. Whoever it was didn't appear to know of a previous family's existence, of another son.

Ngwane, Cal learned from Wikipedia, had been the name of a Swazi king. James McGill had taken eleven years to replace Cal's mother, another two to replace Cal.

The argument between David Wheeler and Hannah had stopped with a final girlish cry of exasperation. Chloe had tensed in the silence that followed, becoming nervous and fidgety. Her unease, Cal realized, was not for Hannah but for herself, as though she feared a healing of the breach between father and sister, as if that might have implications for her. Her behaviour was more suited to a mistress agog at overhearing a disagreement between her married lover and his wife, the outcome of which would decide, one way or another, her fortune and prospects. When Chloe looked at Cal next, she did so with lingering curiosity as though she hoped to find in his expression some sympathy or reassurance, as if she now regarded him as her co-conspirator.

'I think I should be going,' Cal said abruptly and began to roll up the chart that was still on the table.

'Shouldn't you wait for Pa to come back?'

'No, I don't think so.'

Cal didn't say goodbye, nor did he speak to Hannah when he went outside. She was sitting on the deck, leaning against the stern rails. Her back was turned to her father who was close by, erect, looking in the direction of Priest's Island. Cal cleared his throat to let Wheeler know he was there. 'I should be going,' he said.

Crossing the sound, they didn't speak. Before stepping ashore at the harbour, Cal apologized to Wheeler for choosing his words badly, for upsetting Hannah. Wheeler looked somewhere over Cal's left shoulder. 'You're being paid to help me find a murderer,' he said, 'not to involve yourself in my family.'

After Cal climbed on to the harbour wall, Wheeler shouted after him, 'Make sure you stay out of the way tomorrow.'

6

Linda Pryke sat by the kitchen window, staring into the darkness of her back garden. Her eyes were wide and startled as if they recognized menace in the night's swirling folds.

The grating voice of Inspector Boyd Gillison echoed suddenly inside her head, the memory painfully vivid of the first time the police had come for Stanley, eight years ago.

'What do you think your husband does when he's away at the weekend?' Gillison had demanded.

'When Stanley's away he works.' She had appeared puzzled by the question, as though the answer went without saying. The inspector had replied with a cold glower.

'He's good that way, Stanley ...' Linda tried again, the inspector's silence making her gabble. 'Working to fit in with his clients ... when their offices are empty ... he'll keep going all weekend if he has to ... finish the job by Monday morning.'

Linda knew she sounded frantic, as if she was trying to persuade herself as well as the inspector of Stanley's industriousness. At that time, he was running his own painting and decorating business.

The policeman sneered. 'Likes to keep his clients happy, does he?'

Linda nodded.

Gillison reached for the file which was open in front of his colleague, a woman constable. He began to read – dates and places going back years, confirmed and unconfirmed sightings and records of Stanley being taken in for questioning. At the end of each page Gillison looked at Linda and Linda played with the watch on her left wrist, a gift from Stanley. After five minutes and twenty seconds Gillison stopped reading. That was the time it took Linda to realize she lived with a stranger.

'You've been married to him for four months,' Gillison said. 'You expect me to believe you know nothing about any of this, zilch?' Gillison glanced again at the file. 'Some of these sightings occurred since your wedding.'

He read those out again, six dates and places and commentary about Stanley. Suspect seen doing this, suspect seen doing that. Afterwards, Gillison said, 'Doesn't sound to me that your husband was doing much work, Linda. What about you?'

His sneering expression was all the more distressing because the policeman reminded Linda of her father. Arthur Pryke, like Gillison, had been a big, fleshy man with exaggerated features – wide mouth, splayed nose, broken veins on his red cheeks and dark hair shorn at the back and sides. Linda had imagined similar features forging similar personalities, but instead of being retiring and considerate – her father's attributes – Gillison was preening and snide.

Gillison repeated the penultimate date. 'For God's sake, Linda, that was only five weeks ago. A goldfish can remember that far back.'

Linda looked away in case Gillison saw the panic in her eyes. That weekend, Stanley had packed her off to London. He'd bought her theatre tickets for a musical, and booked her into a West End hotel for two nights. A treat, he'd said, for putting up with him working at such anti-social times. She loved musicals. She'd gone with Jenny, her friend who lived in Twickenham. They'd had dinner together and gone shopping.

Linda said nothing.

Gillison threw himself back in his chair in exasperation. 'Why do you think he's called Pinkie?'

Linda looked startled. She couldn't help herself.

'I don't believe this.' Gillison tossed his pen on the desk. 'Are you trying to tell me you don't know he's called Pinkie?'

'He's called Stanley,' she'd said. 'Stanley. His name is Stanley. Stanley. It's Stanley . . .' She repeated herself to stop the doubts filling her head, to cling on to the only remaining certainty about her husband.

Stanley had a ring to it. Like Arthur. She liked old-fashioned names.

The inspector persevered. 'Why do you think he's called Pinkie?'

'I've told you,' she said, 'his name's Stanley.'

'Is that so?'

Linda began to cry. 'I don't know what you expect me to say,' she mumbled, the tears obstructing her words.

'Well, let's try something easy,' Gillison said. 'Where do you think your husband was last weekend?'

'In Newcastle,' Linda replied. 'He was working.'

Gillison studied her before speaking. 'All weekend?'

Linda stared into her lap. 'Yes, he had a painting job, an accountants' office.'

'Pinkie was busy all right, but not painting.'

'Why do you call him that name?' Linda's eyes flashed up. 'He's Stanley, not Pinkie. Stanley . . .'

The day before the court case, Stanley had asked Linda if she would walk with him along the river path close to where they lived. He owed Linda an explanation. Walking would help the flow of words. He would feel less self-conscious.

So that he would have no reason for changing his mind, Linda had let him speak without interruption.

One by one the gaps in her knowledge of Stanley had been filled in.

Linda had known about Stanley being an only child, about his mother being called Irene and making her living as a self-employed seamstress. Linda had seen a photograph of Irene – a black-haired woman with a blurred reddish face. She looked kindly enough. Stanley had told Linda she died eight years before their marriage.

Now she learned about Stanley's father. He had predeceased Irene by three years. Tom or Tommy Wise had been an itinerant agricultural labourer, moving from farm to farm as work and the seasons dictated. Every two months or so, whenever his travels brought him close to the rented cottage where Irene lived with Stanley, he visited.

Linda bit her tongue. She longed to say: *You told me you didn't know your father; whether he was alive or dead. You told me a lie. How many more lies are there?*

She was glad she stayed quiet.

Tommy Wise, according to Stanley, was the product of an Irish mother, poor food and hard manual work. Although he was small, he was strong. His skin was leathery from being outdoors and he smelled of straw, hay or sawdust depending on the contents of the barn where he had slept. As far as Stanley could remember, his father never spent a night with his mother, even though they were married. On his occasional daytime visits, he would dig the garden or chop logs or any other jobs his mother wanted doing. By nightfall Tommy Wise would have gone, having given Stanley's mother money for her rent and housekeeping. While she counted the notes on the kitchen table, Stanley's father retreated towards the front door, as if he was frightened of the ceilings and walls enclosing him, as if the outside and freedom were exerting their pull on him. According to Stanley's mother, everything his father owned was in the pockets of his trousers or jacket or in the old army rucksack he carried.

Stanley came to learn of an exception to that rule. It was to be the bond between father and son as well as the explanation Linda was seeking.

When Stanley was nine, Tommy Wise said it was time for him to pass on his knowledge. Stanley imagined being taught about snaring rabbits or mending a stone wall. But the knowledge that passed between father and son was contained in a tin box that had been buried in the log shed. Inside was a hardcover notebook whose pages were filled with codes. Each referred to a point on a map and another similar tin box. By the end of that first day, Tommy and Stanley Wise had walked fourteen miles and visited twenty map references. Stanley had unearthed and reburied the same number of tin boxes. Each had been interred six inches or more below the surface and covered by a large stone, a marker as well as protection from burrowing animals. Each box had been sealed around the lid with waterproof tape and lined with cotton wool. And each contained a clutch of wild birds' eggs. That evening, after his father had departed, Stanley felt he had gained entry to a new and colourful world, of codes and secrets, of beautiful and often rare objects (his father called the rarest ones 'my gems'). Only two pages of the codebook had been turned that first day. There were forty-five more still to turn.

By the time Stanley was twelve years old, page thirty-nine had been reached.

Father and son were by the coast. The boxes they unearthed and reburied contained the eggs of birds that nested on cliffs or by the shore: gannet, kittiwake, fulmar, razorbill, Arctic tern and eider. A box containing a single guillemot egg decided Stanley on the direction of his own collection.

Although the egg's size and shape were normal, the background was an unexpected shade of pink. The markings, a scattering of blotches, were blood-red instead of being muddy to black. It was, said Stanley's father, an aberration thought to be genetic that occurred rarely in guillemots and some other species. Although he had only ever come across this one example, he knew that rook, magpie, house sparrow, grey wagtail, blackcap, whitethroat, black-headed gull and greenshank sometimes laid them too. The more his father talked, the more Stanley became entranced. 'Once a hen bird lays one of these eggs, it'll always do so, or that's what the experts think. Every clutch will have pink or reddish colouring.'

His father gave the rarity a name: erythrism. Then he presented Stanley with the guillemot's egg and, for his birthday, an identical but empty notebook. Stanley reburied the egg. His father helped him write the code.

Afterwards, his father sent him a copy of an article which had first been published in the seventh volume of *British Birds* in 1914. Its title was 'Erythrism in the Eggs of British Birds'. It listed all the known species which laid pink or red eggs. From then on his father called him Pinkie instead of Stanley.

Stanley showed Linda his codebook. It was the same one his father had given him all those years ago. Because of the rarity of erythristic clutches and the difficulty in finding them, it wasn't even half full: forty-three entries on nineteen pages, a different species to each page. Stanley's collection, like his father's, was buried. Like that first egg, each clutch had been hidden close to the nest. Stanley told Linda it was precautionary. Not only did it lessen the risk of him being found in possession; it reduced the likelihood of anyone – other collectors or the police – being able to find more than one clutch.

At the end of his story, Stanley tore up his notebook, page by page, each page being ripped in half and then in quarters, the codes and Stanley's collection of eggs lost forever – or so Linda had thought. He threw the fragments into a stream, but first he gave her the four quarters of one torn page, for her to remember this moment, for her to be certain of his desire to change. At that moment, against her expectations, Linda had never felt closer to Stanley and found herself making excuses for him.

It was an addiction, not a crime, she told herself as they carried on walking, now without speaking. What were forty-three clutches of eggs by comparison to burglary or stabbing a pensioner or interfering with a child? Stanley had been brought up to collect eggs. What choice had he? That night Linda lay awake and reminded herself of her lonely life before she met Stanley and of her marriage vow 'for better, for worse'.

In court Linda sat stony-faced at the back in an inconspicuous brown wool suit. She had persuaded herself to regard Stanley's hearing as a brief but necessary process, almost as a cleansing. From such a test, she told herself repeatedly, good would come. Stanley and she would emerge happier, their marriage stronger.

Linda's mistake was failing to consider the tactics of the prosecution and believing the assurances of Stanley's lawyer that his case would go unnoticed by the media.

By the time Stanley appeared in the dock and had entered his plea of guilty, the press benches were full. The county's newspapers and local radio stations had been alerted to expect a good and unusual story.

Rather than limiting himself to the detail of the charges – disturbing the nest of a sedge warbler and being found in possession of egg-collecting paraphernalia: a hand drill and a blow tube for expelling yolk and albumen – the prosecution lawyer painted Stanley as some kind of public enemy number one: 'a man who is far better known to the police than this, his first appearance in court, might suggest'. He glanced over at the press benches, making sure he wasn't going too quickly, and it dawned on Linda what was happening. Since a small fine was the only possible sentence for Stanley's offence, the prosecution appeared intent on imposing a greater punishment in the court of public opinion. Instead of the case going unnoticed, there would be stories in every newspaper, on every local radio bulletin. Stanley would be talked about in the supermarket, the hairdresser's and doctor's surgery. So would Stanley's wife. Linda's hands began to shake.

The prosecutor directed a self-satisfied smirk at Stanley.

'Mr Wise,' he continued, 'is well known in egg-collecting circles; in fact you could describe him as notorious, probably the most famous collector in this country. For example, it's common knowledge among experts on this subject that the first egg in his collection belonged to a guillemot. An egg like this one . . .' he held up a photograph of a rosy-pink egg with wine-red blotches, 'started Mr Wise on his illegal career. The colouring is untypical, a genetic oddity that occurs infrequently in a limited number of species. From that beginning, if the stories are to be believed, his collection of this rare type of pink egg has become the widest ever assembled, with clutches from at least nineteen species. Its existence is not in question. What is less certain is where the collection is hidden. Unfortunately, only Mr Wise knows that. Today, at least, we have the pleasure of seeing him in court after he was caught disturbing a sedge warbler's nest, a species known to produce these so-called erythristic eggs. The charges, which he has admitted, are in the name of Stanley Wise, but to most people who inhabit this world – other collectors, police wildlife officers and investigators for wildlife charities – he's known as Pinkie.'

Linda found herself shouting, 'Stanley, his name is Stanley.'

That night, the last of the reporters gone from their door, Linda announced they would be leaving home in the morning. They would go to a town where nobody knew them. They would make a fresh start. Linda would buy a house and Stanley would set up a new business. Linda would support him. They would change their name. They would become Mr and Mrs Stanley Pryke. Even at that first mention Linda liked how it sounded: decent, upstanding, her dead father providing for her as he had always done, with his money and his good name.

'Promise me,' she'd said to Stanley, 'this'll never happen again.'

Now it was happening again.

Linda drew the curtains across the kitchen window and shut out the night. She made herself another cup of tea and, while she waited, she did a google search for 'egg collectors'. Her anonymous caller was correct about people like Stanley being treated more harshly now – a second offence was dealt with by a custodial sentence. Thanks to wildlife crime officers trying to justify their existence, the media always seemed to be tipped off and waiting. What was more, Linda read with alarm, for some odd reason jailed egg collectors were regarded as low-life by other prisoners. They were often attacked.

At ten minutes to eight, ten minutes early, her phone rang. She picked it up.

'Thought I might be Pinkie, did you?'

Linda said nothing.

'Haven't heard from him, have you?'

The man waited for Linda's reply.

'If you mean, do I know where he is, the answer is I do. He's in Carlisle.'

'Didn't take his mobile, did he?' the man said. 'Never one to leave a trail is Pinkie. Anyway, I have a photograph that says he's somewhere else.'

'Where?'

'The Outer Hebrides, on a ferry.'

'I'm sure he's been to the Outer Hebrides at some time or other.'

'The photograph was taken early this morning. Give me your email address. I'll ring back in five minutes.'

The photograph was of Stanley on the deck of a large boat. Linda recognized the livery of Caledonian MacBrayne, the Hebridean ferry company. She saw that Stanley was wearing the trousers she had bought for him two days before.

The man's email address was 'jailforpinkie@hotmail.co.uk'.

'What do you want?' Linda said when the man rang back.

'Five thousand pounds or I'll tell the police, five thousand to keep Pinkie a free man.'

Linda said nothing. It wasn't that she was rattled. Just like the last time, her shame and anger at Stanley's betrayal was giving way to deliberation. But unlike the last time, she was thinking of her own escape, not Stanley's. She was not trying to rescue the marriage.

Five thousand pounds for Stanley's freedom, five thousand pounds for her father's good name and for Linda to buy time for herself, to work out what she would do, without the humiliation of the police knocking at her door and searching through the house: not so expensive after all.

'Get the money together and I'll tell you where and when,' he said and rang off.

Linda rang Stanley's mobile and left messages. Then she tried again when she was upstairs in her bedroom. She heard a noise in Stanley's room next door, a soft thud. When she went to investigate she found his phone on the floor. With all of Linda's calls it had vibrated across Stanley's desk and tipped over the edge. The ringtone, she realized, must have been turned off.

Later that night, Linda again addressed the question that had intermittently prodded at her since her wedding: why a thirty-seven-year-old man had married a woman seven years his senior; why Stanley had chosen Linda when he could have found a woman still likely to bear him children. She'd long ago ruled out love, given Stanley's reluctance even early in their marriage for intimacy, but what did that leave?

Sometimes, when her friends discussed their husbands, someone would comment that Linda didn't know her luck, not having to barter sex for a bigger allowance, new clothes or a car 'since you're well off, since you hold the purse strings'. Linda sensed their envy and something else that would be unspoken, as though money was Linda's compensation for an absence of beauty or children, the attributes that allowed a woman to negotiate life with a man.

No one ever said so but Linda was sure her friends thought Stanley had married for money. Occasionally, she thought that too, though he'd never shown any interest in her wealth – the residue from the sale of her father's engineering business. When she'd bought their house, after that first time, Stanley insisted the deeds were in her name alone. When she'd bought him the new business after changing their names to Pryke, he'd promised to repay her, and so he had.

Not love, not money. What?

Tears started rolling down her face as Linda realized that marrying her had been another example of Stanley's meticulousness, like leaving his mobile phone at home or devising codes and burying his clutches of eggs in different places. Linda was protection for him because she had been brought up to believe there was value in reputation and would do almost anything to protect her father's good name, her good name. Respectability had been her match-maker as well as Stanley's insurance policy.

7

The night was black, pitch, impenetrable. The only light that Cal could see was a weak glow from the saloon of the *Jacqueline*. It shimmered yellow on the sea, catching the top of one wave, seeming to jump to another. Cal watched from the old slipway, a mile east of the Deep Blue. He couldn't sleep nor, it seemed, could the Wheelers, the strain of the anniversary keeping them awake. Cal reflected on his encounter with the family the previous afternoon and contrasted the tension with his childhood experience. In Wheeler's temper, Hannah's tears and Chloe's jealousy he had seen emotion that had been absent from his relationship with his father. Was that the clue to the puzzle of their estrangement: had there been none of that strain with Cal, even in his teenage years, because his father hadn't cared that much?

Not for the first time Cal arrived at the only explanation that seemed to make sense: that James McGill had loved his wife, Eilidh, during her life but not his son, Caladh.

In the moment, the surrounding dark acted as sly encouragement for thoughts Cal would normally have kept unexplored. He found himself wondering why he'd agreed to work for an obsessive like Wheeler who spied on a township and was driven by a determination to blame someone, anyone, for his son's death. Might it be because Wheeler, for all his faults, regarded his son as an indivisible part of himself, even after death, and Cal had wanted to witness that? The thought suddenly irritated him: he was thirty, for Christ's sake, why couldn't he break the link as his father had done, jettison the baggage?

What was wrong with him?

As if to get away from the thought, he started to run along the shingle beach beside the slipway. The thump of his feet and the shifting of the stones cleared his head and provided a distraction. After a hundred metres or so he almost fell. He stopped and stared into the dark. As though the night had been to blame for his stumble as well as for raising the matter of his father, and his own motivation in taking on this assignment. No, he told himself defiantly, there was nothing complicated about why he was there. After five years the police and so-called experts had failed to find a solution to the mystery of Max Wheeler's death: didn't Cal always accept a challenge like that?

8

On Bella's urging, Catriona opened the tea room fifteen minutes early. 'They'll start arriving now that Wheeler's collected the minister from the harbour,' she said and so they did, turning out in their Sunday clothes. By ten twenty the tea room was full, the women seated at tables, the men standing at the window and keeping watch across the sound for the family party going ashore on Priest's Island. Better to be waiting and ready, they agreed, than run the risk of David Wheeler holding the memorial early to deny the township the opportunity of displaying its humanity in public. Implicit in every muted conversation, whether the women's or the men's, was steely defiance: how dare Wheeler continue his persecution; what evidence had there ever been of murder?

They talked too of their sorrow for the boy (the death of someone as young as Max always to be regretted) and with sympathy for Chloe and Hannah, the younger siblings. How hard must their adolescence have been, one loss following another, the mother then the brother. There was also curiosity about Joss, the oldest child, who had come to live in the township four months earlier, renting the caravan below the road on the way to Grant's Croft. Would she be attending the service? Had anyone seen her that morning? Curiosity was mixed with wariness: opinion of Joss divided the township, her actions and motives still matters for argument. Had she taken sides against her father by choosing to live in the township, as some believed, or had she, as many suspected, come to spy? Talk too of Fergie McCann's son: would the father pass on Bella's warning to him to stay away; would the boy, as wild this year as last, pay heed? There was no disagreement on whether a memorial service was the time or the place for protest: it wasn't. Attention next turned to Dr Caladh McGill, who had been seen that morning asleep in the back seat of his pickup. He was parked by the old slipway. Had McGill slept there all night? Was that where he planned to stay while he was on Eilean Dubh? As with Joss, there were questions but few answers.

At ten forty-five, discussion was interrupted when Wheeler's dinghy was spotted crossing from the *Jacqueline* to the wooden jetty on Priest's Island. The tea room emptied, followed by an orderly procession across the car park to the harbour's west wall.

Collars were raised against the chill breeze, feet shuffled in an attempt to find a comfortable place for standing, and then, like a ripple moving across water, heads dipped and rose as news passed from one to the other about Joss. Someone had caught sight of her on the slip road, walking towards the Deep Blue, tall and thin, hands thrust into the pockets of her jeans and blonde hair scraped back, her face cast down in anticipation of the attention she was now receiving. She arrived at the tea room door just as Bella was leaving.

Bella asked, 'Would you like to walk across?'

Joss glanced towards the harbour at the turned-up, white faces.

'Don't let them put you off,' Bella said. 'You'll be all right, if you're with me.'

Joss shook her head.

'You're sure?' Bella watched Joss's eyes and mouth and noticed the tightness with which her hair had been pulled back, the stretch of her skin, the strain.

'Oh, you poor girl, you don't know where you belong, do you, with us here or over there with your sisters?'

Joss shook her head again.

'Why don't you go inside,' Bella suggested. 'Make yourself some coffee and we'll talk later.' Going to join the others, Bella listened for a car horn. All she heard was the breeze. Thank goodness that McCann boy had stayed away.

<hr />

For a while, they were lost from view. The small chapel contained them. Joss watched from the tea room window and remembered the dankness of the place, the hollow, echoing sound of the minister's voice, the atmosphere of ruin and desolation, of Max being absent. She closed her eyes and when she opened them four figures were proceeding towards the raised spine of the island, on the other side of which Max had pitched his tent: Chloe and Hannah folded mournfully into one another, their father leading and the minister in close attendance.

A Wheeler family version of the stations of the cross.

Max a new messiah.

The thought made her angry. Enough!

She left the tea room and crossed towards the dark-coated huddle at the harbour wall. She stopped behind Mary-Anne Robertson, who was small, pinch-faced and at the back of the group, her lips moving as she said a prayer. The retired schoolteacher felt a hand on her arm and looked round to find Joss prising her away. Mary-Anne went without protest because of the strength of Joss's grip and because she thought Joss might be over-wrought and not entirely in control. When she was out of earshot of the others she asked what was wrong.

'Go, go away,' Joss replied as she turned back. Next to be prised away was Isobel Macrae, a fifty-year-old spinster who had a kindly manner and intelligent eyes. Joss took her to where Mary-Anne was standing, once again spinning away after telling her to leave. 'Just go away, please.'

By now the others were watching. Their staring, quizzical faces seemed to unnerve Joss. She looked from one to the other. 'What are you all doing?' she said. 'Why are you here?'

No one replied until Bella said softly, 'We're here because a boy has been lost, your brother. We're paying our respects.' Bella made it sound as simple as night following day or as unchanging as the rocks that formed the hills. There was a note of reproach in her voice. *Since you've been living amongst us, you should know that.* 'And we stand here every year,' Bella added, 'so people can see we're not as we've been portrayed.'

Isobel, in her practical way, gave the others a look to suggest they allow Joss and Bella some space.

A murmur of agreement was followed by a shuffling of feet and the wafting smell of mothballs from rarely worn old tweed coats. The group retreated along the harbour wall and gathered in front of the tea room. Once again heads lifted respectfully in the direction of the memorial across the sound.

'Are you all right, Joss?' Bella said. 'Is there anything I can do for you?'

Joss still seemed to be in search of an explanation. 'Why don't you people give up? For five years my family has accused you of murder.'

'Well, your father, but not you.'

'Every year it starts up again, the whole thing, another inquiry and another memorial.'

'And every year we stand here because we haven't done anything wrong and Max is still missing.' Bella took Joss's hand in hers. 'Would you have us behave as if this was any other day, go about our normal business and be accused of cold-heartedness on top of all the other names we've been called?'

Faintly, Joss shook her head.

'Well, then,' Bella said. 'Come here.' Joss leaned in and rested her cheek on Bella's shoulder. She was stiff and angular, Bella registered, the opposite of Catriona, who was small and rounded. Bella and her niece fitted together, Joss not at all. The same, Bella thought, could be said of Joss and the township. 'You're all mixed up, aren't you? Are you sure you've made the right decision?' she said. 'Coming to live here, with all the memories it has for you and your family, all these emotions? Not being able to stay away because it's where Max died, not being happy when you're here.'

Joss said nothing.

Bella tucked a wisp of blond hair behind Joss's left ear and glanced across at Priest's Island. Two small dark figures, Chloe and Hannah, were walking back to the jetty. The priest and David Wheeler were silhouetted against the sky, standing, rigid, like old-fashioned preachers calling down God's hellfire and damnation on sinners. Bella pressed Joss closer so she couldn't see her father. The movement acted as a prompt to Joss. 'Where else would I go?' she said.

'Anywhere,' Bella said.

'I can't. You know I can't.'

'Don't be so hard on yourself.' Bella had had this conversation with Joss before. 'You're not responsible. It's not your fault, whatever happened. It's . . .'

'I should have gone with Max,' Joss interrupted. 'I should have spent the night with him on the island. If I had, none of this would have happened.'

'The responsibility of the oldest child,' Bella said, 'the big sister . . .'

Neither spoke, the bond between them making words unnecessary. Bella's younger sister, Frances, had died too. Joss knew the story: how Frances had gone with Kenny, her husband, to lift his creels, how he couldn't manage the boat on his own because of an injury to his hand. Bella, visiting from Glasgow, had been babysitting the Deep Blue and Catriona when a storm had blown up. Kenny's upturned boat and two bodies had been found the following morning. Sixteen years later Bella was still looking after the tea room and the child. Every morning the sight of Catriona made Bella think, 'If only.'

If only she had listened to the weather forecast.

If only she had inquired more about Kenny's injury. If only she'd known how incapacitated he was.

If only she'd realized how short of money Kenny and Frances had been – the Deep Blue was a struggle in its early years, the prospect of a catch of lobster and crab the difference between paying the bills or not.

'If only,' Bella said. 'You can't live that way, Joss. Not at your age, not you.' It was Bella's way of saying it had been different for her. She had been older, thirty-three, divorced and childless. 'I had Catriona to look after and the Deep Blue. But you, this is tearing you apart, tearing you away from your sisters, living here, being with us. It's not right.'

Behind the Deep Blue a hill reared towards the sky. Its summit was a grassy knoll where, in another age, a lookout waited for a signal from the headland to the west. On seeing a white flag – a torn sheet tied to a boathook – he would shout to the fishermen in the harbour below, alerting them to a shoal of approaching salmon, flashing silver in the water. The boats would put out into the sound, the nets would be thrown and the fishermen would hope for a catch. For Cal, the hill also served as a lookout. He approached from the east, a walk of fifteen minutes from his pickup by the old slipway. Arriving early to avoid breaking the skyline while the memorial was underway, he searched with binoculars for Millie. He found the orange buoy near the middle of the sound, towards Wheeler's boat, further to the west than he expected, which indicated the strength of the west-flowing stream from the Minch.

Then, he watched the human drama of the memorial. Once the people of the township had gone inside the tea room, the only actors left on stage below him were Bella and a tall, blonde young woman – her looks and colouring identifying her as a Wheeler: Joss. After Bella had hugged her, the two separated, Joss walking slowly away, head down. For a while Bella watched Joss's back before going inside the Deep Blue. Cal thought it had been like attending the performance of a play in a vast natural amphitheatre and he was the only person in the audience.

Except he was an actor too, wasn't he?

Before going down the hill, he checked to see if his phone had a signal. There were two unread messages. One was from Mr Close early in the morning reminding Cal not to carry out any work on the sound that day because of Wheeler family sensitivity. The other was from Detective Sergeant Helen Jamieson.

> Hello, Cal, I haven't seen you for a while. Drink? There's something I'd like to discuss with you, ASAP if convenient.

Cal replied:

> I'm in north-west Scotland, on an island. Not going to be able to do much here for a while without causing offence. If I caught the afternoon ferry I could be in Edinburgh by nine. What about dinner tonight? Tell you about it then.

9

Stanley Pryke muttered and cursed as he hacked at the dried peat. What use was a garden trowel when he needed a spade or a peat-cutter with a sharpened blade, something he could put his boot on? Angrily, he stabbed at the peat and the trowel recoiled on impact. The heel of his hand was beginning to hurt. He stared at the reddened skin and cursed ill fortune. A blister would make the climb more difficult. Wasn't it dangerous enough already – a sheer sea cliff slicked and slippery with salt spray, the nest guarded by an overhanging sentinel of rock?

Frustration finally got the better of Stanley. He threw down the trowel. It made a clanging sound against the hardened peat, as though it had struck rock. Stanley muttered to himself about climate change deniers. Here was all the proof anyone needed, in this modest depression slung below an outcrop of Lewisian Gneiss. At no time in the past fifteen years, at no time in the past *hundred and fifty* years, would it have been as dry as this, the ground as hard, as impenetrable.

It seemed to Stanley that bad luck was dogging him at every turn.

The stubbornness of the peat, his nascent blister and his unsettled state of mind made him wonder whether he'd paid too little regard to the passage of time and to the extra inches around his girth. For a year or two he'd noticed a decline in his strength and his stamina, some breathlessness in ascending steep flights of stairs. In this, his forty-sixth year, having been out of practice for so long, was he past it?

An incident on the early morning ferry had started this corrosive train of thought.

Stanley had been on deck when an older, balding man and a younger blonde woman approached. Like him, they were foot passengers, practised walkers by the look of their worn boots and weathered backpacks. The woman said 'lovely day' and Stanley thought he saw recognition in the man's eyes, an involuntary double-take. 'Yes, isn't it?' Stanley replied with enthusiasm before wandering further along the deck. When next he glanced in their direction, the man, Stanley saw with alarm, was hurrying away in the direction of the bridge. The prospect of the police waiting for him when the ferry docked, of being detained or questioned, brought on a kind of panic attack. He thought he might collapse, but to avoid drawing attention to himself, he sat on a bench, hoping the impression he gave was of a traveller letting go of life's stresses, gulping invigorating Hebridean sea air. The next he knew, the woman was standing over him, her face set in a worried expression. 'Are you all right?' she asked.

'Yes, quite well, thank you, and you?'

Stanley managed to sound breezy and the woman said with an apologetic laugh that her children were always telling her off for interfering, but wasn't it better to be safe than sorry? When he saw her again, she was reunited with her male companion and he was taking a camera from his backpack. Stanley turned quickly away and spotted a seal basking on a rock thirty or so metres from where he sat. As soon as he saw it he realized he'd probably jumped to a wrong judgement. Instead of the man trying to sneak a photograph of Stanley, wasn't it more likely he was taking one of the seal?

The couple's subsequent behaviour supported this idea. As the ferry steamed on, they walked quickly towards the stern, trying to keep abreast of the creature, the man taking photographs as he went. Earlier, instead of the man recognizing Stanley, perhaps he had been registering an urgency in his bladder. The toilets, Stanley now saw from the sign, were through the door that led to the stairs to the bridge. Self-recrimination followed. Stanley hated uncertainty even if he was right to be wary. The first time he'd been caught, hadn't the police acted on information supplied by an informant who'd been paid after Stanley's conviction? The memory was a worm that wriggled around in his head after the ferry docked and as he walked inland.

So by the time he was hacking impotently at the peat, he was in an odd mood. One moment he would convince himself there was something suspicious about the man on the ferry (had he rushed off to fetch a camera to snatch a picture of Stanley?), the next he would be adamant that everything was all right. The man was going to the toilet! Stanley's outburst of temper at the bluntness of his trowel was a sign of this crisis of confidence, not just about the events on the ferry but about the rest of the trip. He accused himself of having gone flabby and soft in his years off, like his stomach. He kicked at the heather, frustrated at his fearfulness about the climb as well as the returning thoughts that he had been identified on the ferry and there were people who would know how to make money out of such information. There had been eight years before. Prison loomed in his imagination, black, terrifying and echoing, the metallic bang of a cell door shutting.

Stanley's face was clammy with cold sweat. He wondered if he should bow out, admit defeat, live off his memories. What, after all, did he have to prove? His collection was better and had a wider range of species than any of those mentioned in Cole and Trobe's book, *The Egg Collectors of Great Britain and Ireland*. Stanley had multiple clutches from successive years of rook, blackbird, magpie and rock pipit and single clutches from fifteen other species. One more would make it twenty, and raven was the gap he still dreamed of filling. He'd waited years for this moment to arrive, an investment of effort and money. The weekends he'd spent scouting in Cumbria or the Highlands and Islands of Scotland; the risks he'd taken as a young man scaling cliffs and tall Scots pines to check ravens' nests – all too many to count.

Here he was on the brink of greatness, of achieving his life's ambition, and look at him, a bag of nerves at the thought of being caught, at the prospect of the climb he had to do.

Stanley stopped kicking. Now he berated himself for letting his nerves get the better of him. Wasn't he Pinkie Pryke, the field man? No matter the obstacles didn't he always collect his own eggs? Wasn't it his badge of honour? Not for him the lazy ways of those Edwardian 'Cabinet men' who sat in their drawing rooms showing off their collections and paying others to take the risks.

Stanley calmed himself by closing his eyes and imagining the raven's eggs. Each would have a background washed in a shade of pink, some as delicate as a young woman's lips, and the markings would be darker, richer. He hoped for blotches of hellebore red. The more he considered their beauty, their sensuous shape and colour, the more they pulled at him. Of course he had to go on: wasn't this his crowning achievement, his last adventure?

He kicked at the ground again, no longer a gesture of frustration but one to stiffen his resolve. In another year, the ravens might have been shot or poisoned and he would be older and fatter, the cliff even harder to negotiate. There were those who accused him of leading a charmed life, having been convicted only once, but charm had nothing to do with it. No one had seen his preparations, the mapping of nests, the excursions in autumn and winter or the effort he had put into finding informers who were knowledgeable as well as loyal.

No one realized the work involved in identifying erythristic eggs and not getting caught in the process.

He stared at the trowel and the shallow scrape he had made in the ground. He began digging again, working methodically. Rather than stabbing wildly, he inserted the blade of the trowel into the cracks in the peat, prising them wider. Fragments broke away, then lumps, and soon he was staring into a hole at the bottom of which was a large square biscuit tin. Stanley took it out and stripped away the waterproof tape. Inside were packages of varying sizes. Each was wrapped in sealed food bags secured with rubber bands.

The first contained a cardboard box with reinforced metal corners. Stanley lifted off its lid, examined the six compartments inside and squeezed the felt padding between his thumb and forefinger. His father last used the box twenty-eight years ago. On that occasion it held four kestrel eggs. Stanley, aged sixteen, had been there. In fact, Stanley, being lighter than his father and able to climb higher, had scrambled up the tree to collect the clutch.

The second polythene bag Stanley opened contained a drill. It was four inches long, with a wooden handle. The metal shaft had a cone-shaped corrugated tip. Stanley pressed the point against his hand. The prick was sharp enough, he thought, to chip an eggshell. The corrugations also appeared sufficiently well defined for the grinding process to make a neat, small hole.

The blowpipe was unpacked next. It, too, was about four inches long and made of brass tubing. One end was curved for inserting into the hole made by the drill. In the same bag was the hook. Wooden-handled like the drill, it had a thin metal shank bent at the end into a not-quite-closed circle for dragging out an embryo bit by bit. Stanley regarded the hook with distaste, seeming to be in two minds whether to take it with him or not. His father always carried it, a reminder, he always told Stanley, that 'no field man worthy of the name should ever resort to one of these diabolical things'. Stanley put it into his backpack for the same cautionary reason, knowing he would not need it since incubation had only just started.

The fourth bag contained six padded pouches in a mossy-green material. They were stitched together and configured like a whorl so that each one resembled an opening petal of a large flower. A loop of material was fastened to the centre like a grossly enlarged pistil. Stanley pulled at it to test its strength. Then he held it between clenched teeth and imagined climbing the cliff, both hands holding on to the rope, the dangling pouch keeping the raven's eggs safe. His worry was a strong wind – one was forecast. Would the pouch swing too much? He inspected the loop again. Making it shorter might reduce its free movement but would mean it hanging right under Stanley's chin. If for some reason he jerked his head down, his chin could break an egg. Stanley decided to leave it as it was. It had stood the test of time with his father.

The last bag he opened contained three rolled-up bundles, all of fifty-pound notes.

Stanley put the money into his backpack with his father's equipment. Then the empty biscuit tin was returned to the hole. Stanley buried it with as much of the crumbled peat as he could gather. Soon there was nothing to see apart from a depression and a scrape that an animal's hoof might have caused. Stanley slung his backpack over his right shoulder and returned the trowel to the base of the boulder a few metres up the hill. He'd put it there the previous November after an unusual meeting with a prospective tenant at one of the flats he managed in Glasgow. Would Mr Pryke, Mr *Pinkie* Pryke, like to know where he could collect a clutch of erythristic raven eggs? she'd asked. The price for the exclusive option would be one thousand pounds, in cash.

Bella MacLeod had come smartly dressed in a camel coat and patent shoes, apparently to view a flat. In her gloved hand, she held some letting particulars, a nicely authentic touch, Stanley thought later. In the passage between the lounge and the kitchen, Bella stopped and asked whether he had received some photographs in the post. Stanley pretended puzzlement. Not that he could remember, he said. Were they photographs of a property, a flat perhaps? Photographs of eggs, Bella prompted: particularly rare eggs. Stanley said he hadn't, or didn't think he had. Maybe she had the wrong man. Bella asked if she was speaking to Mr Pryke, Mr Stanley Pryke, Mr Pinkie Pryke? Stanley agreed that Pryke was his surname but it wasn't uncommon. He was sure there would be another Stanley Pryke. Maybe she had the wrong one. He didn't know of a Pinkie Pryke. Without further sparring, Bella showed him her driving licence. 'This is who I am,' she'd said. 'This is how this deal is going to get done. We're going to have to trust each other.'

'What deal?' Stanley asked.

'How would you like to buy an option?' Bella asked.

'On what?'

'A clutch of raven eggs to be laid next spring. They're pink eggs with red markings. You would call them erythristic eggs. The photographs I sent you show this spring's clutch. They've hatched now but, as you know, once a raven lays one clutch of pink eggs it will do so again.'

Stanley had received the photographs, of course. As soon as he had opened the envelope his mind had been racing. He'd waited years for something like this. Inside were two photographs of the same clutch of five raven eggs. In the days before the meeting in the flat, Stanley had examined the photographs over and over, cross-referencing their colouring, size and markings to his records of erythristic raven eggs in private or museum collections. He was alert to a hoax or a trap, but a grand passion, awakened, had him in its grip. Of all birds, the raven!

Now, standing in a damp passage of a third-floor tenement apartment (two beds/one reception/GCH), he was lost again.

Bella told him the story of the eggs' discovery. They had been found by two young Australian climbers holidaying in the Hebrides. Their interest was scaling sea cliffs and stacks, not birds. They didn't know that raven eggs were usually shaded green or blue with brown or black blotches, though Bella did. When they showed her their photographs of the large nest platform, which she recognized to be a raven's, she asked if she could have copies. Although she had known something about erythrism before, she had learned more since: how extraordinarily rare such eggs were, and how collectable, how valuable.

Stanley listened and said little. Bella proposed a deal: since it was October, she was offering Stanley first option for the following spring. He would have to pay one thousand pounds. It was not returnable in the event of one or both of the ravens being killed. If they nested again he would pay another thousand for being delivered to the site. Once he had the eggs in his possession he would pay two thousand more: four thousand in total, in cash. Apart from the eggs, the money would buy him confidentiality. Bella was the only one who would know his identity and it would stay that way. There would be no further auction of eggs in subsequent years, the risk of gossip reaching the police or wildlife charities too great. This was Mr Pryke's opportunity, his only opportunity. There could be no negotiation on terms. The money would 'set up a young man who had had something unfairly taken from him . . . put him back on his feet'. In a manner of speaking, Mr Pryke would be contributing to a deserving cause.

If he wished to go ahead, they would meet again at the same flat in two days, enough time for him to check out Bella and to withdraw the first instalment.

At the next meeting, Stanley watched from the flat above. Bella arrived alone. No one followed her or looked on. After letting her in, he asked a number of questions and set conditions before handing over the thousand pounds. He needed to know where the nest site was so he could move equipment to within a day's walk the following month, November, when no one was looking out for collectors. Bella gave him a map reference that was within six kilometres of the site; there were at least seven nests in that area or close by. If Pinkie – by then she had dispensed with Mr Pryke – tried to find it on his own, she would be informed. The deal would be off. Pinkie would lose his money.

In turn he insisted there must be no disturbance of the nest site. When had the photographs been taken? The second week of March, Bella replied.

'Contact me again when the ravens are back at the nest in the spring. Let me know the first day the female starts sitting. Then I'll come immediately.' He emphasized the point. 'The clutch must be complete. You must call me as soon as incubation starts so that the embryos don't grow.'

'Yes, I understand.'

'And no witness, no assistance after I've been taken to the site.'

Bella agreed.

All winter Stanley dreamed of the ravens being poisoned or shot, of his opportunity being lost. Bella made contact in the middle of February to report the ravens putting on aerial displays, flying side by side and making synchronized rolls above the nest site. Two weeks later she reported the hen raven sitting for longer periods: incubation seemed to have started, although it was at least a week earlier than the previous year. The bird had not been disturbed. Stanley could be reassured of that. The observations had all been made from a boat.

After walking in the wrong direction for half an hour, his usual precaution, Stanley found a rock for cover. He waited and watched until he was certain he had not been followed. Then he relaxed his guard and unpacked his father's egg-collecting equipment from his backpack. As he inspected it again he thought how fitting it was that it would be used for his last clutch, for his final expedition. With evening, the clouds picked up speed. The wind would follow. The air seemed to come alive with anticipation of the storm, and a change of mood came over Stanley too. He thought of his rendezvous with Bella MacLeod the following afternoon and felt a surge of exhilaration.

No, he wasn't too old and unfit for this after all.

10

With men, a fear of running out of conversation unnerved Detective Sergeant Helen Jamieson. She would cast around for something interesting or witty to say and wonder afterwards why she'd bothered. In her bruised experience, *they* hadn't.

With Cal, it was different. *She* was different.

Take this moment, for example. Here she was sitting in Cal's pickup while he drove her across Edinburgh to Leith, the port district. Neither had said anything for a while, yet Helen wasn't experiencing a compulsion to speak. Nor did she regard his silence as an unspoken accusation about her looks or some other personal failing. As she watched the streets go by, she wondered why this was. Why was she so comfortable with Cal when, if anything, she should have been more on edge, since with him she had a *thing*? She played around in her head with that word: thing, *thing*. She decided she liked its lack of definition. She enjoyed its utilitarian quality.

Often when she was at work or lying awake at night she would wonder what Cal was doing or where he was. Usually, a question would pop into her head, as it did now: *Wouldn't it be nice?* She wasn't clear what *it* involved: sex, marriage, a date or even a kiss? *It* could include any or none of these, or a combination. Helen thought the reason *it* remained as undefined as *thing* was because Cal had the role of ideal male in her life; anything or nothing was possible with him.

Sometimes, for example, she would pretend he was accompanying her to functions where she expected to feel insecure – because of her size eighteen figure, her hair which was thin and unruly, her face which was prone to flushing at awkward moments. Mostly these were police events or conferences where male officers routinely regarded her appearance as an affront, as if being in the company of females prettier than Helen was one of rank's privileges. With Cal her invisible companion, she managed to endure their slights and condescension. Occasionally, she'd look up and imagine Cal across the room, the two of them exchanging conspiratorial glances. It was, she acknowledged, a little peculiar and not something to be confided in her best friend, if she had a best friend, but surely harmless enough, a survival mechanism. Though sometimes she wondered at herself: a detective sergeant with an IQ of 173, a first-class law degree and a Masters in criminology – behaving like a social incompetent. What was *that* about?

With Cal, she felt accepted. Solitariness and silence were his everyday companions. Helen regarded it as a compliment when she was invited in.

Crossing Newhaven Road in east Edinburgh, Cal spoke again. 'Would you mind if we went to my office? Just for five minutes. The restaurant's nearby, walking distance.'

'Why should I mind?' Helen replied, being curious to see where he was living. Usually, when they met, he would pick her up as he had tonight and they would go to a bar.

'Are you still trading under the same name?' Helen asked, remembering the first time she'd come across his company, Flotsam and Jetsam Investigations, and imagined Cal to be some odd eco-nut. Then, he'd worked for environmental organizations or charities, hunting down polluters. At that time tracking missing or dead bodies, calculating where – if

– they might come ashore, had been his area of specialist research, his hobby. Later on, from what she'd heard and from the bits and pieces he'd told her, he did little else. The drawback, she supposed, of Cal's media profile and the desperation of families. He was their last chance of finding their son or daughter, their father or mother. Helen knew it was difficult for Cal, a dilemma of his success. He'd talked about it the last few times they'd met, how he didn't think he could take on any more cases involving recently lost children. He'd described the parents' appalled expressions on those occasions when he'd found a washed-up body, a sweet son or daughter rendered unrecognizable, a horror story of decaying flesh, not 'closure' but the stuff of continuing nightmares.

'No,' Cal replied. 'I've changed the name to the Sea Detective Agency.'

'I remember you saying something about that.' She nodded with approval. 'The Sea Detective Agency, that's good. It does what it says on the tin.'

At the next junction Cal turned into an industrial estate. They passed a picture framer, a company offering industrial lighting solutions and a laser engraver before the pickup stopped by a single-storey unit which appeared to be unoccupied.

'This is it,' Cal said.

'Headquarters,' Helen suggested.

Cal smiled. 'I suppose so.'

He parked and Helen said, 'No sign outside?'

'I prefer not being known by my neighbours. Anyway, most of my clients contact me through my website or by email. I go to them – they don't visit me.'

Cal unlocked the door and preceded Helen inside. The strip lighting flickered on and off at first, providing Helen with a snapshot impression of familiar objects: maps and charts covering the walls, a table filling the middle of the room. Helen had seen them before, two years ago, when she'd raided his flat with Detective Inspector Ryan. Despite the circumstances being inauspicious, she'd taken to Cal from the start. Cal's 'offence' had involved night-time excursions into the gardens of politicians and leaving behind a plant that survived the last ice age as a warning of climate change. To Helen's amusement, Cal ran rings around Ryan before the case collapsed. Even the Environment Minister, one of Cal's 'victims', had refused to give evidence for the prosecution because he was worried about enraging the green lobby.

Ex-Detective Inspector Ryan, Helen grinned. How she had disliked him, another one of those officers who judged a clever woman by her looks and tried to put her down.

'Since we're here,' Cal said, 'would it be all right if I had a shower and found something clean to wear?'

'Sure,' Helen smiled. 'Of course, go ahead.' She wafted her hand across her face, as if dismissing a bad smell. 'Sooner the better, if you want my opinion.' She shouted after him: 'No need to hurry, either.'

While Cal showered, Helen looked around the office at the brick walls, at the gantry of metal shelves along one wall, at the disarray. Everywhere was a chaos of books and files and charts. She read some newspaper cuttings stuck to a noticeboard, reports of deaths and disappearances at sea, missing bodies. Beside the cuttings was a display of photographs. Helen scanned them quickly: bodies lying bloated on sand; bodies broken-jointed and sprawled on rocks; stripped bones protruding from white, bulging flesh. She had been involved in murder investigations where the condition of the victims had been more palatable.

The photographs reminded her of two investigations

where Cal and she had cooperated: the discovery of disarticulated feet encased in trainers which had washed up on beaches in Orkney and East Lothian, and the murder of Preeti, one of two Indian girls trafficked to Scotland.

Turning her back on the photographs, Helen regarded the table. She remembered its disorder from the raid on his flat. Now the mess was worse, another two years of accumulation on display. Books and files were in leaning piles across its length and breadth. Helen thought it resembled a model of some endlessly expanding shanty town that had run out of available space and could only grow by extending upwards. Everywhere were jutting or leaning towers of paper in danger of partial or complete collapse. Some had already fallen, only to become the foundations for the construction of yet another unstable edifice.

How could Cal work in such a mess?

Towards the back of the room, away from the fluorescent glare of the overhead lights, she noticed a kitchenette in an alcove, with a kettle, a camp stove and two mugs on the sink drainer. Below, on the floor, were a camp bed and a sleeping bag. A large rucksack was propped against the wall. Clothes spilled from its open top. Helen registered the details one by one, like gathering the clues to a crime. Cal hadn't brought the rucksack with him from the pickup. 'God, Cal,' she said in an undertone, 'is this where you're living?'

A book was open in Helen's hands when Cal returned from the shower. Its title was *Waves, Tides and Shallow-Water Processes*. 'Finally,' Helen said, looking up, noticing Cal's wet hair, his white shirt outside his jeans and his bare feet. 'I've found an explanation I understand.'

'For what?' Cal asked.

'For waves, how the movement we see is energy passing

through the water. How, overall, the water itself stays more or less in the same place.'

Cal rubbed at his hair with his towel before hunting through the rucksack. 'Like wind ruffling a barley field,' he said.

Helen returned the book to Cal's table. She studied the room again, a look of concern on her face. 'You don't live here, Cal, do you?'

'This place suits me,' he said. 'Anyway, it's cheap. I can lock it and leave it.'

'Really, Cal? This is home?'

'When I'm in town, I stay here, yes.'

'How often is that?'

'Five or six days a month.'

'When you're not in town, what then? Where do you sleep?'

'If the weather's bad, in the pickup.'

'If the weather's good?'

'A beach, the dunes, in a tent or my sleeping bag.'

Helen laughed as though she didn't know living that way was possible. 'I thought you must be renting a flat.' She looked around the room again. 'I didn't realize. Some friend I am.'

Cal said, 'It's fine. I'm comfortable.'

'When did you last sleep in a bed – one with a sheet, a pillow and a duvet?'

'God, I don't know.'

Helen raised her eyebrows. 'Try.'

'A year ago, maybe more. A client booked me into a hotel.'

'And the time before that?'

'I can't remember.'

'Why didn't I know?' Helen said.

'Not much of a detective,' Cal countered.

'No, hopeless, obviously,' Helen said. 'After all this time, I find out you're living like a serial killer on the run.'

~~~

The restaurant, an Italian, was bright, friendly and warm, the opposite of Cal's office. The owner, Luigi, took Helen's coat and winked conspiratorially at Cal.

'Usually, I come here alone,' Cal explained to Helen, after Luigi had shown them to a table.

'Usually?' Helen asked.

'When I'm in Edinburgh. I have lunch or dinner here.'

Helen said, 'I can see why; it's nice,' but she was thinking how sad that he ate alone when more often than not she did too. And she felt a pang of guilt at why she had asked to see him. Cal, typically, had not mentioned her text message or wondered at her urgency. He had driven all that way and now he was allowing her to choose her time. As if Helen wasn't a bad enough friend already.

After Luigi had brought their drinks – white wine for Helen, beer for Cal – she decided to broach the subject. 'What are you working on?' she asked, hoping that Cal would think her awkwardness was caused by another of Luigi's winks. 'Didn't I read in a newspaper somewhere that you were looking into the disappearance of Max Wheeler?'

Cal looked up. 'Do you know the case?'

'Everyone knows that case,' Helen said quickly and remembered what her boss, Detective Chief Inspector Richard Beacom, had told her. *You're not lying to him, Helen, and your intentions are honest.* And so they were, she thought. Maybe she shouldn't be feeling so bad.

Cal looked surprised. 'I thought that would be one case the police would want to forget.'

'No,' Helen said, 'not a bit of it.' She felt herself flushing again. 'I read the case file a few weeks ago, my boss too. It's always brought out at every anniversary.'

'Anything you can share with me?' Cal asked.

'I don't suppose it would do any harm to tell you the general conclusion.'

'Which is?'

'Nothing much you can't guess at: that Max Wheeler either died because of an accident or he was murdered. Escape has been ruled out – he wasn't that strong a swimmer – and anyway he wasn't the kind of boy who would run away. He wasn't a misfit, moody or rebellious. Nor was he suffering from some teenage angst about the future.'

'So he didn't throw himself off a cliff but he might have fallen off one?'

'Yes.'

'Is that it?'

'Not quite.' Helen seemed to be making up her mind whether to tell him. 'It's about the motive, why anyone would have wanted to kill Max Wheeler.'

She hesitated, and Cal said, 'I know there's a theory that Donald Grant killed the boy to take his revenge on David Wheeler for buying Priest's Island and bringing an end to the grazing lease.'

'That's what the senior investigating officer believed at the start.'

'He changed his mind?'

'Yes, after questioning Grant and talking to people in the township, at least those who would speak to him. Donald Grant being a killer just didn't stack up.'

'Why not?'

'He didn't bear a grudge,' Helen said. 'He wasn't angry with the Wheelers.'

'He had cause to be.'

'The loss of the grazing rights affected him in a different way. It broke him. In the end, the only person he was capable of killing was himself.'

'He drank himself to death.'

'Yes, eventually.'

'So what happened to Max? If he was murdered, who killed him?'

'Most likely it was Grant's nephew, Ewan Chisholm.'

Cal thought for a moment. 'Ewan had to watch his Uncle Donald's destruction, so he decided to take revenge, to destroy something that was as precious to David Wheeler?'

'Forty per cent right, the other sixty per cent is where it gets interesting. A psychologist listened to Ewan Chisholm's interviews. Remember, he was fifteen then. His emotional age was younger.'

'Tough family background, parents always fighting . . .'

'Yes,' Helen said. 'How do you know?'

'Oh, Wheeler has information on everybody. He used to send people to spy on the township, proper little intelligence operation, who's sleeping with whom, everything.'

'Honestly?'

Cal nodded. 'I've seen the file.'

'What did it say about Ewan Chisholm?'

'Probably the same as yours. Ewan had means and motivation. He was strong for his age, was able to use his uncle's boat and knew the sound well enough to navigate at night. There was also mention of an earlier incident where he'd been caught damaging a holiday home owned by a couple from Newcastle.'

'I read that too,' Helen said. 'Chisholm resented people from England buying into his adopted home. Wheeler's treatment of his uncle turned that into something more dangerous.'

'That seems to be Wheeler's theory too.'

'Well, the psychologist had a more interesting take on Ewan Chisholm,' Helen said. 'As you'd expect, he found the boy to be angry, but more to the point he also discovered him to be jealous. This wasn't your usual green-eyed monster stuff but something more worrying. According to the psychologist, Ewan's rage wasn't directed where he expected, at David Wheeler. It was at Max, the boy who would grow up to take over Priest's Island, the boy that Ewan had expected to be when he succeeded his Uncle Donald.'

'Angry and jealous enough for murder?'

'Yes, possibly. But in the psychologist's opinion it wouldn't have been tidy. Ewan wouldn't have thrown Max into the sea. No, his was the kind of jealousy that would have been messy. There would have been blood. That's what he wrote in the report. Don't look for a body. Look for blood. Somewhere on the island there will be blood, lots of it.'

'Not now, there won't. Not after five years, not with that rainfall.'

'No, but this was in the early days of the inquiry.'

'So Ewan Chisholm was capable of murdering Max. It's just that there isn't any evidence that he did.'

'That's about it. The psychologist was persuasive about Ewan's state of mind. Potential for great violence and a surfeit of grievance where Max Wheeler was concerned. Those were his comments.'

'A dangerous boy?'

'For Max Wheeler, potentially, yes.'

'Did the psychologist have an opinion on whether Ewan would grow into a dangerous young man?'

'Not really, though he said that Priest's Island might continue to be a trigger for his anger. At a moment of stress, it could throw him back.'

'Whoever replaced Max as heir apparent should watch out?'

'I suppose that's a conclusion you could draw,' Helen said. 'The psychologist doesn't?'

Helen shook her head. 'Is there an heir apparent?'

'I don't know,' Cal said. 'It's not exactly happy families on Priest's Island. Joss, the oldest daughter, has separated out. She's living in the township. Chloe and Hannah are still with their father but I don't know how long that will last. Hannah's relationship with him is tense.'

He considered Helen's question again. 'Wheeler's so obsessed with avenging Max's death and honouring his memory that I wonder if he's given any thought to the future of the island. Maybe he'll leave it to one of his daughters. Maybe he'll hand over the ownership to a Max Wheeler memorial trust or something like that. Who knows?'

'Well,' Helen said, 'that could be a good thing – the uncertainty, I mean. Perhaps that's what keeps the girls safe.' She paused. 'What's your opinion about the township? Are the residents protecting Ewan Chisholm? The senior investigating officer had been certain they were.'

'Do I think there's a conspiracy?'

'Yes.'

'Not to kill Max Wheeler,' Cal said, 'or one to cover up for Ewan Chisholm, no. It's not like that. My sense is that there's a circling of wagons, of the township protecting itself and one of its own.'

'That person being Ewan Chisholm, the adopted son?' Helen said.

'Yes.'

'And Catriona Mackinnon, Bella MacLeod's niece?'

'What about her?' Cal asked.

'Does Wheeler's report say anything about her?'

Cal thought back. 'It doesn't rule out her being actively

involved in Max Wheeler's death, but it's certain that she's been covering up for Ewan.'

'She was known to be upset about what had happened to Donald Grant and, by extension, to Ewan,' Helen told him.

'Upset enough to have killed Max with Ewan?' Cal sounded doubtful.

Helen leaned forward. 'For the sake of argument, let's say they didn't intend to kill Max. But once he was dead, if two of them were involved, disposing of the body would have been easier and quicker.'

'Bella gave a statement that Catriona was at home all night,' Cal pointed out.

'Yes, she would, wouldn't she?' Helen said dryly.

'Wheeler's report says the same,' Cal continued. 'It doubts whether Bella would hold back evidence about Ewan's involvement in Max's death, but not if Catriona was involved.'

They were interrupted by Luigi bringing their food: spaghetti and scallops for Helen, artichoke risotto for Cal. Once he had gone, Helen said, 'The Wheeler case is the reason I sent you that text message.'

'Really?'

'Yes. Beacom asked me to meet you.'

Cal nodded. He knew Beacom. He'd run the operation to round up a human trafficking gang – the case involving the two Indian girls that Cal and Helen had worked on together. 'What's on his mind?'

Helen sensed Cal's wariness. She kept to Beacom's script. 'He'd like to see if we could work in tandem.'

'I don't like doing that. It's not good for my reputation.'

'You've done it before.'

'Because a fourteen-year-old girl's life was in danger.'

Helen nodded. 'And yours, if I remember rightly.'

'Are you saying I owe you one?'

'No, Cal, I'm not saying that.'

'But Beacom is?'

'Something along those lines, yes. He's been given the Wheeler case to review because of the anniversary. He's put a team together.'

'And he wants me to help him out.' Cal shook his head. 'Fuck, Helen. There's no proof that Max Wheeler was even murdered.'

'There's no proof of anything. That doesn't mean we should stop trying to find some. All we're asking you to do is share information. Just do what you normally would – work out the currents, drop hints about progress, upset some people, stir things up.'

'Where will your boss be?'

'He'll be here.'

'So he expects me to do all the work?'

'No, we'll have our own eyes and ears on the ground. We'll be watching and listening . . . *I'll* be watching and listening.'

'You.' Cal seemed nonplussed.

'Well, thank you for being so pleased.'

'How will that work?'

'I'm going to be staying at the Deep Blue's holiday chalet. But don't expect me to say hello when you drop by for coffee. I'm booked in my own name but they don't know I work for the police. Bella MacLeod took the reservation. I told her I had to get right away from everything after the break-up of a long-term relationship and all I wanted was somewhere with sea views and to drink tea and eat cake.'

'What did Bella say?'

'She was very welcoming. She said I was coming to the right place. Cal?' Helen tried to catch his eye. 'Will you help?'

For me, she added silently.

Wouldn't it be nice?

Helen wished Cal would look at her in a different way. Sometimes. Even once. As though *it* was a possibility, whatever *it* was. Still, she couldn't have everything. At least Cal didn't put her down and she could talk to him. Before going to bed, Helen texted:

> Well?
> *Well, what?*
> Have you decided?
> *Yes.*
> Well?
> *It's up to me what information I share . . .*
> With you, Cal, is there any other way?!

There was a gap before his next message.

> *OK, will head off now. Sleep at the ferry*
> *terminal. First sailing's at seven thirty.*

Helen read his text twice, trying to work out whether he was being brief or terse, whether he felt manoeuvred. She decided on brief and replied:

> I'm heading up tomorrow afternoon. Where
> are you staying?
> *Along the coast, east of the Deep Blue, not*
> *far, by an old slipway. It's marked on the*
> *Ordnance Survey map. Don't miss your ferry.*
> *A storm's forecast for later.*

For Cal, that was fulsome. After all, he'd told her where to find him. She replied:

> See you there.

She signed it HXX and, on reflection, deleted one X.

Then she rang DCI Beacom. 'Cal's going back,' Helen said as soon as he answered.

'Good. That wasn't so hard, was it?'

'Sir, that doesn't make it right.'

'What doesn't?'

'Not telling him about the money . . .'

'We've discussed this, Helen. If you tell McGill the police are paying his bill he'll walk, won't he? Isn't it more important that we find out how a fourteen-year-old boy disappeared?'

'Of course, sir, but . . .'

Beacom interrupted. 'When we're done, Wheeler's lawyer will hand over his fee and McGill will be none the wiser. He doesn't need to know it wasn't Wheeler's money.'

'With respect, sir . . .' Helen found she was speaking to an empty line.

She was asleep that first night, when the rocking started. The caravan tilted one way then the other, the frame creaking and the rope hawser rubbing against the roof. It was like being in a storm, except that in a storm the wind usually pushed and pushed from one direction before relenting. The motion was so violent and the noise so loud she almost wondered whether the hawser holding the caravan down had snapped and the wind had carried her away, whether Atlantic rollers were crashing about her.

Joss fumbled in the dark for her phone. She was about to turn on the light when the rocking stopped and the shouting began: 'Slag, clype!' How many voices? Two or three. She found Constable Dyer's number when, suddenly, there was silence. Had they gone? She waited, hardly daring to breathe, wondering whether she should ring and deciding she wouldn't. Not if it was all over. Not if they'd gone. She was shaking so much she had to lift her thumb away from the phone, in case she pressed ring by mistake. If she did, everyone would know. In the township, everyone knew everything.

Everything except how Max died.

Hours later, she went to sleep.

The next night Joss took precautions. She roped the door and covered the windows with cardboard. She checked the phone signal. Two bars. Then she waited. The longer she sat the more she worried. She'd made a prison for herself, one that didn't offer easy escape. If they broke in through the window, she wouldn't be able to run out the door. If they kicked down the door, she wouldn't be able to jump from the window. What if they threw in a burning rag doused in petrol? She thought about removing the web of rope by the door, but wouldn't that make it easier for them to break in?

Indecision meant she did nothing, and then it was too late. She hadn't heard a sound when the rocking started, the caravan tilting back and forth. Then there was shouting. 'Bitch, whore!'

When it stopped, Joss found she was breathless. She calmed herself by saying it was all over. She lay back against her pillow and closed her eyes. Sometime later, how long she wasn't sure, there was a bang at her door, a single rap. 'Next time,' a male voice said. Then silence. She didn't hear him going away.

She screamed into the dark, 'What?'

And again, '*What*, next time?'

She tore at the ropes and opened the door. Outside, she shouted again '*What*, next time?'

A sharp breeze was blowing and everywhere Joss looked there was movement: the clouds, the sea, the grass. Were they still out there? Was *he* still out there? Next time: when would that be? She hurried back inside and roped up the door. Being inside a prison would have felt safer.

At daylight she ventured out, sitting on the step of the caravan. She remembered Max, how nasty, brattish and spoilt he'd been. Usually, thinking of him left her confused and guilty. But this morning, it made everything clear.

It had to stop.

Everyone's lives had been blighted.

She didn't blame those who were trying to frighten her away. She would have done the same, rock a caravan in the night, if she thought the person inside was passing on information.

Those who did that to her were scared too, terrified her father would find his culprit irrespective of guilt or of what had happened to Max. Everyone was caught up in the same nightmare.

Even little sister Hannah, her adolescence ruined.

Everyone's lives affected by her father's obsession for gilding Max's memory. In death, Max had become the perfect boy, a cherub, whereas in life he'd been unpleasant and disobedient. My fault, she reminded herself sharply. She should have gone to the island with him.

Later, she collected wood from the shore. There and back she kept on looking at her mobile. Two bars. One bar. Two bars. Three bars where the ground rose. She didn't stop in case someone was watching but she counted her steps back to the caravan so she would be able to return to the same place that night. She spent the rest of the afternoon indoors. At dusk, her nerves started again. She checked her phone. No bars. No bars anywhere in the caravan. She panicked. Were they coming? Were they watching? But, she told herself, she had to wait until it was dark before going outside. If she went now they might see where she went.

'Next time,' he'd said.

Next time, what? The question kept going through her head. Would they attack her? Would they kill her? Would they rape her? Would they burn her?

At last it was dark enough. She took a brown rug from her bed and slipped from the caravan. She closed the door quietly behind her and held the rug to her face to prevent her skin flashing white. Her hiding place was eighty steps away. At sixty, she felt safer. At seventy, she hurried. At eighty, she found a dry place to sit, a patch of heather. She checked her phone, shielding the screen with the rug. Three bars. She looked in her contacts for Constable Dyer's number and waited. The shingle track to the caravan made a pale pathway through the night. The road beyond was invisible, though not the headlights. One moment they were there, blazing, the next they were gone. Was the car free-wheeling in the dark to the parking place by the track? Soon after, Joss saw a movement – or thought she had. Next she heard someone knock at the door of the caravan. Like the night before, the knock came first. 'Are you there?' It was a male voice.

'Joss.' He opened the door and went inside.

She heard him say her name again. A flickering light went on, a match or a lighter, and she watched him moving around inside. 'Thank God,' she whispered to herself. 'Thank God. Thank God.' Anything might be happening to her now.

After a few minutes, he appeared in the door. 'Joss,' he called. He went back into the caravan. The light went out and Joss saw him again, now an indistinct outline. 'Joss, are you there?'

He closed the door and waited, as if he could sense her. Why else would he keep repeating her name?

'Joss, if you're there, it's OK.' He took a few paces towards her. 'Joss?'

She stopped breathing. Now she thought his voice was familiar. But whose?

'They'll not be coming tonight.'

Joss saw his shadow move towards the track. She dared to take a breath. Had he heard her because he waited and spoke again?

'They were some young guys from the north of the island. They won't be coming back. I've warned them off.'

After a while she saw the car lights going away. How did she know it wasn't a trick? Was he one of them? Were others watching, waiting for her to break cover?

At dawn, she looked for unfamiliar shapes or movement. She stared at darker patches of heather until she was sure they didn't conceal a threat. Eventually, shaking with cold and fright, she went back to the caravan. She checked her phone. Two bars. Her thumb was on the call button. She opened the door and on the floor inside was a note.

Joss, I'm sorry. It won't happen again. Ewan.

He left his number.

Ewan, of all people. Ewan.

She ate some dry bread and drank a mug of tea while she stood in the doorway of the caravan, looking across the sound at Priest's Island and the *Jacqueline* at its mooring in the bay. Her jaw tensed as she thought of Hannah, how unhappy she would be. She took her anorak from its hook and closed the caravan door. 'This has to stop. Today.'

It was past ten in the morning when Cal drove up to the Deep Blue. After his early start from Edinburgh, he longed for coffee. Three cars were parked outside the tea room and a white minibus by the harbour. A group of hikers was milling about, putting on coats, boots and backpacks. Cal noticed the flap of sleeves and the flutter of maps, the stirrings of a light wind. He looked at the sky, at the clouds to the west, at the sea. There would be time, he thought as he got out of the pickup, a few hours yet before the storm.

Inside the Deep Blue, two tables were occupied, seven people in all. Cal was aware of heads rising, of conversation stopping as they saw him.

Catriona, who was standing behind the counter, caught his eye. *What did you expect*, she seemed to be saying, *a welcome?* What she said was, 'Same as last time?'

Cal nodded. 'I'll take it with me.'

'Large or medium?'

'Large.'

While Catriona busied herself at the coffee machine, a man shouted out, 'Ye're never serving that man, are ye?' When Catriona paid no attention, he shouted again, 'He'll be paying with Wheeler's dosh.'

Cal didn't turn round, nor did Catriona. 'So long as he pays,' she said in a soft voice, as though she didn't care whether anyone heard her or not.

She put Cal's coffee on the counter. 'Thanks for that,' he

said, handing her a five-pound note. 'Wheeler hasn't paid me yet. This isn't his money.'

She shrugged. It didn't matter to her.

He picked up the cup. 'Anyhow, I haven't taken sides. I'm doing a job for the man, that's all.'

'Is that so?' Catriona said. 'Split any rock on Eilean Dubh and that's not what you'll find written there.'

'Yeah, I know,' Cal said before turning for the door.

Outside, the walkers were moving away. Only when they'd gone did Cal notice a young woman standing on the harbour wall. She was tall and wore an anorak with a fur-trimmed hood. Her back was to him. She seemed to be looking across the sound, towards the *Jacqueline* and Priest's Island. He paid her no more attention until he was by his pickup. A movement caught his eye. He looked round and saw she was walking towards him. Her hood had fallen on to her shoulders and he recognized her from the day before, her scraped-back blonde hair, her thin face and high forehead. Up close she reminded him of the photograph of Max Wheeler. The way she moved was familiar too: the turn in her hip, the twist to the right when she placed her left foot on the ground. Hannah, her younger, prettier sister, also walked that way.

His immobility seemed to spur her on. Her walk turned into a run.

He supposed he could have prevented what happened next. He could have held Joss Wheeler's arms by tightly wrapping his own around hers. He could have ducked or pushed her away. Instead he let her punch him and claw at him with her nails. He did little apart from parrying some of the blows to his face. He recalled his own rage, the times when he would have punched anyone who took his father's side; how he might still. And he waited for the tempo of Joss's attack to slow, until all she could do was to beat feebly against his chest, one clenched hand following the other. Then he held her by her wrists. 'Stop,' he said. 'That's enough.'

Her head hung, her arms went limp, pent-up rage spent.

'I can explain why I'm here,' he said, 'if you'll let me.'

Her arms tensed and she tried to break away. When she found she couldn't, she screamed, 'Get off me.'

As Cal held her, he became aware of people behind him. The tea room's customers had come out to watch. Catriona was standing at the window. A car drove up, a white Ford with rust around the wheel arches. A stocky young man with a florid face and stubbly blond hair got out. Cal recognized him from Wheeler's dossier.

'Leave her,' Ewan Chisholm said. 'Let go of her.'

A woman shouted. Cal turned to see Bella MacLeod at the tea room door. 'Take your hands off her.' Cal remembered the description of Bella, 'a mother hen to strays'. Now, as she hurried towards Joss, her cardigan ballooned like half-raised wings and her skirt billowed as though extravagant leg feathers were being ruffled by a gust of wind.

'Get off her,' she shouted at Cal. 'Leave her alone.'

He released Joss's wrists and stepped back.

Bella wrapped the young woman in her arms. Fussing over her, she took her towards Ewan. 'Take her home, will you?' She hugged Joss again, then waited for the car to drive off before turning to Cal. 'You're not wanted here, Dr McGill.' She went towards the tea room. 'No, you're not wanted at all.'

For a while, Cal sat in his pickup, the door open. The tea room's customers waited inside and watched through the window. His neck and arms were sore from Joss's blows. He touched the nail scratches on his face, feeling for blood. He found himself thinking of Rachel, his ex-wife. She was the first woman who had clenched her fists in rage at him. Unlike Joss, Rachel had hit him softly on his arm. He'd felt no more than a push or a nudge. But in the restraint of that blow he knew the force of her anger. It was typical of Rachel's control, her way of letting him know how disappointed she was with him, for running away to the coast so often there had been no marriage left to save, and for his infidelity. If she'd punched and clawed at him like Joss he would have let her. It would have been his punishment. He'd been in the wrong then and he wondered if he was now, whether he was on the wrong side.

Mary-Anne Robertson was the first to speak after Cal had driven away. She had the oddest feeling, she said. 'Something else is going to happen, something awful.' She said it again when Bella sat down with a cup of tea. Didn't Bella sense it too? Mary-Anne pressed her lips together, making her face look more pinched. 'What do you think it could be? What can we do to keep out of harm's way?' Bella found herself disagreeing if only to inhibit her friend's imagination.

'Don't you think we've had enough excitement for one day?' Bella replied, wishing Mary-Anne had more to occupy her mind since her retirement from teaching.

At least Mary-Anne didn't respond indignantly. Sometimes she did, implying that Bella didn't have her sensitivity because it was God's gift to those who were regular in their church attendance and in saying their prayers. Bella was irregular at best, but Mary-Anne still made a habit of sharing her premonitions with her. It was as if she thought that Bella, being without divine protection herself, required help, otherwise she would stumble blindly into danger. For Mary-Anne, giving Bella warning of future events was akin to an act of charity, one for which she expected gratitude rather than a put-down. For Bella, it was becoming rather tiresome.

Having finished her tea, Bella went round the tables taking orders. She sensed a peculiar atmosphere. At first she thought the low murmur of conversation was a delayed reaction to the shock at Joss's attack. Later on, the tea room still subdued, Bella detected a hushed expectancy as though something worse was about to happen, just as Mary-Anne said. Did the tea room's regulars imagine that by speaking quietly they would draw less attention to themselves and so place themselves less at risk?

From what? Bella wondered.

Bella also found herself being unsettled by another discovery. Going from table to table, she was concerned by how often she overheard insulting or antagonistic comments about Joss. The young woman was being blamed for having set in train a sequence of unstoppable events, though what they might turn out to be no one was sure beyond the general mood of foreboding. There was also scepticism about her assault on Dr McGill – a put-up job, some said, to make it appear she was on the side of the township when she had been spying for her father all along. Thank goodness, Bella thought, she had asked Ewan to take Joss home. Better a cold caravan than expose Joss to hostility in the tea room.

After her rounds, Bella realized Joss had few supporters left. Once or twice she heard people express concern about what the young woman might do next. Bella silently agreed. That was her fear too. How often had she warned Joss about drawing attention to herself? Fit in, don't stand out and you'll be accepted. Be patient; let the township come to you. Bella and Mary-Anne had both advised discretion but Joss had displayed the opposite since the arrival of her father's boat. Everyone was tense. Joss's behaviour at the memorial service, dragging Isobel and Mary-Anne away, hadn't helped. Now this.

Bella glanced through the window at the lowering bank of black cloud on the Atlantic horizon – a storm was building – and then at Catriona's glum face as she served behind the counter. Problems always come in threes, Bella thought. 'Didn't anyone tell you a smile is worth more than a month of scowls?' she remarked to Catriona on her way to the office to check on the forecast. No sooner had she sat down and opened her laptop than Catriona was standing in the doorway.

'Why did you do that?'

If she wasn't mistaken, Catriona seemed close to tears.

'Do what?' Bella replied. 'Tell you off for looking miserable?'

'No, asking Ewan to take Joss home . . .'

Bella watched Catriona pick at her fingers. 'For goodness' sake,' she snapped. 'You can't be serious.'

Catriona stomped away and Bella wondered at her niece. As if she didn't have enough worries without concerning herself with Catriona's notions. Ewan and Joss? She couldn't imagine a more unlikely combination.

Force ten. Gusts of eighty mph. Torrential rain. The storm would reach landfall after dark. It would moderate around dawn before another storm blew in, the wind switching from west to north-west. Severe weather warnings had been declared for the Hebrides and north-west Scotland. Bella read the highlights and wished she had time to fill her head with nonsense like Catriona. Instead she had two storms to worry about and a female raven that had laid her eggs more than a week earlier than the previous year, which meant the Wheelers were moored in the bay, a complication she hadn't anticipated.

Now she had a meeting in a quarry with a man called Pinkie Pryke.

13

Ewan lit a cigarette, his sixth. The stubs of the others lay discarded at his feet. As soon as one had been reduced to a stained filter, he began the next. Doing something, *anything*, was his way of keeping his thoughts and emotions under some kind of control. It was why he preferred being occupied. Whether feeding his sheep, mending his uncle's old tractor or carrying out odd jobs at the Deep Blue, his mind was on his work. Having time for other thoughts made him jangly, the way he was now.

Lighting and smoking the cigarettes stopped him from knocking on the door of Joss's caravan, but they hadn't taken away his desire or his turmoil. If anything, since he'd been standing there, the feelings had become stronger and so had the contradictory voices. *Do it; don't do it. She'll want to know; she'll laugh at you.* Each emotional call to action was followed by a warning of bad consequences as well as that most insistent and immobilizing of questions: *Who do you think you are, Ewan?* He was confused about why he felt this way. Why was it, why was *he*, so complicated, when all he planned to tell Joss was that he would keep an eye? His croft was close by. They were on the same road. It made sense, Ewan watching out for her as he'd already done.

It would be no bother, no bother at all.

What would Joss hear: a neighbourly offer or an unspoken declaration of something else, and recoil from it?

Ewan was still in a muddled state when Joss appeared in the doorway of the caravan. 'Can I join you?'

'Suit yourself,' Ewan replied, too quickly. 'Free world.' He was irritated with himself. He sounded as if he didn't care, when the opposite was the case. *Free world*. What was he thinking?

As she reached him, she said, 'I don't want to be shut in.'

He offered his pack of cigarettes. 'Thanks,' she said, taking one. He lit it for her, noticing the length of her fingers and the colour of her skin. Catriona's were stubby like his own and her skin was pallid. Joss's were slender, her skin honey-coloured.

'You OK?' He looked shyly at her before dragging on his cigarette.

'Yes,' she said. 'I think so. Now.'

For a while they smoked. Ewan was oblivious to everything apart from Joss and the battle going on inside him. *Tell her; don't tell her. You'll never get a better chance.* The right side of his face, the side on which Joss was standing, felt as if it was burning. He was sensitive to her every movement, the lift of the cigarette to her lips, her inhalation and exhalation, the arc of her arm, her lips, wondering how it would be if he kissed them.

'Thank you, by the way,' she said and laughed nervously. 'Not by the way at all. Thank you. I don't know what I would have done otherwise.'

'It was no big deal driving you back,' Ewan answered. 'Beats working at the Deep Blue . . .'

'No,' Joss said, 'I meant last night. It was a big deal, really. Thank you.'

'So you were here,' Ewan said.

'Yes, over there.' She nodded towards the dark patch of heather which had hidden her in the dark.

'I thought so.' He stopped himself from going further in case he alarmed her with a tumble of words that he couldn't control. He'd known she was there, somewhere. He'd been so certain he'd spent the rest of the night in his car so that if the McCann boy and his pals had tried something on he would be nearby.

'Who were they?'

'One or two of the boys ... balloons.' His expression made it clear she was better off not knowing names. 'Idiots,' he translated, 'from the north of the island. I had words with them. They won't be back.'

'I owe you.' Her voice wavered and she touched him on the arm. 'Thank you.'

The contact was enough to stop the warning voices. The words blurted out just as he feared they would. 'I'll look after you if you let me.' He didn't look at her. He addressed the distant horizon. He was shaking with emotion.

'Why would you want to look after me?' she asked. 'Me of all people?' It was a reference to everything that had happened since her father bought Priest's Island: the ending of the grazing rights, Max's disappearance, Ewan's arrest, Ewan's uncle drinking himself to death, the unpleasantness. 'I thought,' she hesitated. 'Well, I thought you didn't like me very much.' She made a snorting sound. 'Who could blame you?'

Before he could stop himself he said, 'I've always liked you, Joss, always. What's happened, that wasn't your fault, none of it.' Then he paused and looked at her. 'You're special, different. I don't want to see you hurt any more. Let me protect you.' Each word was clumsy but a declaration of something more eloquent and emotional than he could express.

'You and me,' she said, 'against the world.' She smiled but Ewan heard her with renewed confusion. Was she laughing at him now? If only he could explain himself better.

'Max and me . . .' He had her attention again. 'We were friends.'

'Were you?' She sounded surprised. 'I didn't know that.'

'I used to go to the island in my uncle's boat. We would meet up.'

'Did you? Really? Were you Max's age?'

'I was older.'

'What are you now?'

Rather than admit to being two years younger than her, he carried on talking about Max. 'We spent days together, exploring the island. Sometimes I'd sleep over in the shieling, sometimes in Max's tent. Nobody knowing was part of the fun, nobody suspecting.'

'The night he went missing?' Joss asked. 'Were you on Priest's Island?'

'No. The tide was strong that night. My uncle caught me leaving the house and stopped me. For once he wasn't drunk.' Ewan sounded regretful about that.

'Max was expecting you?'

'No, I'd just turn up when your father's boat was there. It wasn't regular.' He paused. 'I wish I had been with him.'

Surely now she could see the bonds between them. Max connected them. Each knew he might still be alive if one or other had been with him that night. Both had paid the penalty for the last five years. Joss had lost a brother and now her family; Ewan, his friend and his uncle, the only family he recognized. People might look at him and Joss and see differences but he saw similarities, coincidences. Their lives had been brought together by fate.

'You're the only one I've told,' Ewan said.

Joss nodded. 'I'm glad you were Max's friend.' She touched him again on the arm. 'And now you're mine.'

'Yes.' He dared to look at her. She smiled at him, quickly,

reassuring him. He felt light-headed. The sensation was as unexpected as it was liberating. Joss hadn't laughed at him. She had touched him. At last he could talk about Max. The words rushed out. 'Max and me used to make a bonfire and then catch food to cook – prawns, velvet crab and pollack. I showed Max where to fish and taught him about the tides, when it was safe to walk at the bottom of the cliff. I showed him how to climb . . .'

Ewan's voice cracked, the unspoken guilt of five years and these new emotions undoing him, the impulse to tell Joss everything overcoming his reticence. 'Max and me didn't start out as friends. To begin with I'd been angry about what had happened, the loss of the grazing, your family owning the island, but I knew its secrets, the hiding places, the best pools for swimming, where to catch fish . . . Max wanted to know all that.'

He stopped and Joss said, 'Go on.' She touched him on the arm again. 'It's interesting.'

Ewan stared at the ground. 'I'm so sorry.'

'You've got nothing to be sorry about. I should be the one apologizing for my father accusing you of murder . . .'

'No, you don't understand.' Ewan seemed cross, frustrated, as though there was something he had to get off his chest now that he had the opportunity and Joss was encouraging him. 'The inside of my head was all wrong. I took it out on Max . . .'

'Why, what did you do?' Joss asked.

Ewan heard the alarm in her voice. Had he ruined everything in his tongue-tied way, when all he was trying to do was to show Joss how intertwined they were?

'I made him do things in exchange for teaching him about the island.'

'What sort of things?'

'Stuff . . . like climbing down to a ledge on the cliff and swinging on a rope over the sea. I wouldn't let Max back until he'd swung ten times.'

'That was you,' she said accusingly. 'You made him do that.' Her voice was brisk. The softness, the gratitude, had gone. 'You.'

Confusion rushed back in where certainty had so recently been.

'*And now, you're mine.*' Ewan and Joss: weren't they friends, more than friends? Hadn't she said so? Yet he was losing her, had lost her, in the time it took to take a breath, and he wasn't sure why.

Nor did he know what to do, so he gabbled, 'I was a mess . . . my uncle losing the island . . . his sheep being sold off . . . It wasn't Max's fault . . . I was angry . . . I lashed out and Max was in the way . . . I'm not like that now . . . Give me a chance and you'll see that I've changed.' He looked into her eyes, saw them slide away and the next thing he knew he was holding her, pulling her to him. His hand touched one breast, then the other. His lips pressed against hers. His tongue searched for a way inside. Instead of warmth and wetness, he met hardness. Her teeth were closed against him. It was the same wherever their bodies touched. Instead of the give of flesh, Joss was bones and hard edges. Every part of her seemed to resist him. When she twisted her head away he panicked and put his hand over her mouth. Then, as suddenly as he'd grabbed her, he let her go. He was aware of her moving away, of the door of the caravan closing, of the awful mistake he had made.

'I'm sorry,' he moaned. 'I've waited so long. I couldn't help myself.'

Linda Pryke rested at one of the benches by the pond. Yesterday, she had done the same, and the day before. It was a habit of hers, whenever the weather was fine, to go for an afternoon walk across Meadow Park and to sit for a while. She would watch the children playing, dogs chasing balls or mothers talking. She liked to see the world go by, or the part which strayed inside the park railings. Always, before returning home, she would feel more at one with life, as though something missing had been replaced. Today, however, was different. Today, she sat uncomfortably on the edge of the bench, as if at any moment she might jump up again. Today, when anyone new came through the gate, someone she hadn't seen before, she gave them an accusing look before dropping her eyes or turning away. Today, she didn't watch and wonder about the lives of the people who passed her by. Nor did she say hello or exchange comments about the weather. Today, it was all she could do to sit still for twenty minutes.

Today, she wasn't the watcher but the watched.

Somewhere, in the park, at one of the windows of the surrounding houses, in a passing or stationary car, he would be observing her. 'Get there at four,' he'd said when he rang her back, 'like you did yesterday. At four twenty, the same time as yesterday, get up and put the bag into the bin beside the bench. Then go home and think about what you'll cook when Pinkie arrives back from Carlisle or Glasgow or wherever he told you he was.' She hadn't really listened as the man reminded her about the consequences for Stanley if she didn't follow his instructions. All she could hear was 'like you did yesterday'. Yesterday, she thought she'd been alone watching others. But he'd been watching her.

Watching as she locked her front door.

As she went down the lane.

As she entered by the park's gate.

As she walked across the grass.

As she rested on the bench.

What had happened yesterday was why she was frightened today. She'd had no idea, no sixth sense of being observed.

'No doubt we'll talk again,' he'd said, 'the next time Pinkie goes on his travels.'

At four nineteen she stood up. She dropped the bag of money in the bin beside the bench. She walked quickly towards the gate. She didn't catch anyone's eye. She didn't look up until she was at her front door and then only to insert the key.

After locking up behind her and attaching the security chain, she hurried first into the sitting room then the dining room, closing curtains. The front having been secured – she imagined him circling the house looking for a corner of a window through which to spy on her – she hurried to the kitchen. She lowered the blind, tugging at the right-hand side where it snagged, before drawing the curtains. Afterwards, she stood in the windowless hall and listened to the wind outside. Where was Stanley?

The question was a reflex. Now she didn't care.

14

Cal splashed his face with water. The salt stung where he had been caught by Joss Wheeler's nails. Twin lines of torn skin ran down the right side of his nose. Two more extended from his right ear along the curve of his jaw. He felt for their rough edges with his fingertips while he studied the sea's surface. It appeared restless, as if the water was anticipating the storm and limbering up, as though some charge was travelling unseen through it. A few moments ago the waves had seemed to be regular, rhythmic: lulling. Now they were shifty-looking, unreliable. There was that sense of something about to happen, a foreshadowing. Even the land, Cal noticed, exuded an aura of preparation. Whereas the sea seemed to be readying itself to react to the wind's power – to churn, rear and plunge – the land appeared braced for defiance, for stubborn, unmoving resistance. Wherever he looked Cal had an impression of impending violence. As he pushed the RIB into deeper water, he thought about the Max Wheeler case and the people who were caught up in it – Joss Wheeler, Catriona, Ewan Chisholm and Bella. Unlike the sea, they would not all be able to bend. Unlike the land, they would not all be able to brace against its force.

Cal climbed into the RIB and started the motor. Looking out for Millie and her buoy, he set course for the middle of the sound before veering to starboard. In the half-hour it took him to reach the ocean edge, passing the *Jacqueline* at anchor, the sky at the horizon became lowering and black. Opposite the west of Priest's Island, where a soaring cliff fell sheer into the sea, he throttled back and turned to port. The RIB rose and dipped while he emptied the contents of a canvas bag at his feet. Three packets spilled out. They were identical apart from their colour. Each pack contained twenty cards made of thin wood. Each card was eight centimetres by thirteen, individually numbered, covered in non-toxic paint, and bore an identical message addressed to the finder.

Thank you for recovering this biodegradable drift card and for helping with important research into the movement of ocean currents. Please email Dr Cal McGill at theseadetective@gmail.com to let him know the following information:
Where you found this drift card
On what date
Its colour
Its number
Thank you for your assistance.

Cal took a card from the yellow pack. He checked its number – twenty – before dropping it into the sea. Throttling ahead, he dropped the other cards at regular intervals until he was below the cliff. The last card in the sequence was numbered one. Before distributing the next batch – they were painted red – Cal steered the RIB along the north coast of Priest's Island to the bay where the *Jacqueline* was moored. From a distance, he saw figures moving around the deck. As the RIB drew closer, the boat started to move, going towards the harbour on Eilean Dubh. Cal guessed Wheeler was seeking shelter while he still had daylight and time, while the sound was calm enough to navigate with safety. He slowed the RIB until he was behind the *Jacqueline*. Then he dropped the first of the red drift cards overboard. It was numbered one. Keeping his distance, he tracked the *Jacqueline* across the sound, releasing cards as he went.

After watching the last red one – the twentieth – become caught in the RIB's bow wave, he looked up to find David Wheeler standing at the stern of the *Jacqueline*. He was staring in Cal's direction but seemingly blind to his presence. His gaze, Cal realized after a while, was fixed on Priest's Island and the chapel, the pain of separation evident. The greater the distance between him and his son's shrine, the more he appeared to lean towards it. Even though Cal disliked the man, he found his agony compelling. Not once did Wheeler acknowledge Cal as the two craft crossed the sound. Nor did Cal acknowledge Wheeler. It would have been like intruding on private grief.

For a moment, because of Wheeler's behaviour, Cal wondered whether news of Joss's attack on Cal had reached the *Jacqueline*. Was Wheeler deliberately ignoring him? What version of the story might Wheeler have heard – that Cal provoked the confrontation? But no, Cal decided, Wheeler's obsession with Max was sufficient to make him blind to the world around him. Would Cal be the same if he lost a child? Would he be as damaged, as oblivious to the needs of his other children, even after five years? He hoped not, though maybe Wheeler had been right. Perhaps Cal didn't understand, since he didn't have a son. He turned the RIB to starboard, going along the south coast of Eilean Dubh towards the old slipway. In the distance were the grey waters of the Minch. He turned to starboard again at the eastern entrance to the sound. As before, he began dropping off cards – this batch was orange. Number twenty went into the sea closest to Eilean Dubh; number one by the eastern end of Priest's Island. After watching the final card float away, Cal steered into a sheltered inlet. With the *Jacqueline* departed, he could explore Wheeler's island undisturbed and enjoy being alone and storm-bound for the night.

He tied up the RIB before walking the island's south coast which sloped from the central ridge down towards the sea. He found the shieling a few hundred metres away, situated at the bottom of a widening gully above a sandy beach and a small, horseshoe-shaped bay. The building's atmosphere of desolation was familiar to Cal. The west coast and the islands were disfigured with dozens similar. They were abandoned or ruined, the lives that were lived there, the stories told, long forgotten. Cal always found the experience affecting, the emptiness of the building resonating with the loss of his own connection to an island way of life. His grandfather on his mother's side had been born to that tradition off the north coast. Eilean Iasgaich or Fishing Island had been abandoned after World War Two, the village deserted. The house where his grandfather was born had become roofless and ruined, occupied only by sheep taking shelter from storms or by roosting jackdaws. In that respect the shieling was different. It was wind- and weather-tight: the roof still intact, the windows boarded and secured with metal bars. The door was solid and nailed to the frame. Attached was a printed notice enclosed in a box of toughened glass. The shieling was private property, it proclaimed. Anyone attempting to gain access for whatever reason would be prosecuted. The notice was signed by J. Close – 'Mr David Wheeler's legal representative'.

To Cal, such a forceful reminder of individual property rights somewhere uninhabited seemed out of place. He thought of Ewan Chisholm and imagined how much more objectionable the warning would be to him. The shieling was where he had spent his summers, where he had been taught shepherding by his Uncle Donald. Somewhere close by, Ewan had planted a rowan tree in his uncle's memory. David Wheeler had torn it from the ground, *his* ground. Cal felt indignation on Ewan's behalf, as he always did when confronted with similar examples of a southern and urban mentality in a place where wildness and sharing – community – was more appropriate. The island had been turned into a memorial for one family, for one life, when multiple other lives had greater claim.

It was the conundrum of possession in Highland Scotland – did this landscape rightfully belong to Wheeler or to those like Ewan and his uncle who worked it and had become captivated by it? Whether that provided the motive for Max Wheeler's death, as Mr Close claimed, had still to be proved. But, in Cal's opinion, it explained everything that had happened since: the alienation of the township and its hostile reaction to David Wheeler.

Climbing the slope behind the shieling, he tried to work out where Max had pitched his tent. He knew the site was on higher ground somewhere to the west but couldn't find exactly where it had been. Then he watched a raven soaring above the island ridge and envied its free spirit. On the plateau he leaned into the freshening wind and walked towards the sea cliff. Ahead of him was an elemental scene: a sky daubed different shades and textures of black and, below, a sea of leaden grey, rushing on ahead, as if now in competition with the wind to wreak havoc. Cal relished moments like these with the wind thuggish and bullying, the sea sliding and treacherous, its relentlessness of purpose masked by the magnificence of spectacle. After descending to the island's northern shore, he watched the unfolding drama and marvelled at nature's ability to deceive: how the beauty of waves hid their destructive force.

It was just after five forty-five by the clock in Bella's car. She had almost fifteen minutes to herself, time to think at last. So many problems were demanding attention. Driving to the disused quarry, her rendezvous with Pinkie Pryke, she fretted about Joss's state of mind – the attack on McGill showed how emotional and disturbed she was. After listening to the animosity against her in the tea room, Bella also feared for her safety. Should Bella offer Joss her spare room until tempers cooled? Bella could imagine Catriona's reaction. She'd sulk around the house, her face like thunder. Heaven knows where Catriona got the idea that Joss was interested in Ewan, or that Ewan was interested in Joss for that matter. Bella bit her lip. What a mess everything was!

It was Bella's bad luck the holiday chalet was booked for the next few days. Otherwise she could have put Joss there. Bella sighed. Nothing could be done. Helen Jamieson had emailed to say she was on the ferry. Bella had told Catriona to expect her between six thirty and seven, and to be sure she was in and not on one of her walks.

As Bella drove on she wondered whether she gave Joss too much attention. Was that the cause of Catriona's jealousy? Maybe it had nothing to do with Ewan. Was her niece feeling short-changed? She shouldn't be, because Bella had dedicated her life to Catriona and to making sure the Deep Blue was a thriving business for her to take over. There was no winning with the girl. Bella thought of her white face, how lifeless it was, how lifeless *she* was. If only Bella could magic up some fun for her, but the township was hardly Glasgow. Dances as well as boys were few and far between, and Catriona had been careless to let go of a good one. What *had* gone wrong between her and Ewan? This time the split looked permanent. Catriona had even talked of leaving the township to study in Aberdeen or Edinburgh. She'd announced it as though she intended to punish Bella. After all Bella had done for her! The girl had been born ungrateful.

As Bella was feeling thrown off course by events, so a gust of wind buffeted the car, making it veer across the narrow road. Now there was another problem: the storm was arriving sooner than forecast, the wind already strong. By nightfall, it would be blowing a gale and the crossing to Priest's Island in the dark would be dangerous even for someone who knew the safe channels as well as Ewan. Bella decided on a change of plan. Instead of crossing the sound as soon as it was dark, Ewan would take Pinkie across at dusk. The gathering gloom would provide some cover but there would be sufficient light for Ewan to find his way. Every imaginable disaster passed through her head – Ewan capsizing, the police waiting at Ewan's mooring when he made the return crossing. What was it that Mary-Anne said about a foreboding of something awful about to happen? Bella took a deep breath. She had to hold her nerve. What she was doing was right. Ewan should have the grazing rights on Priest's Island. Morally, they belonged to him. If one crop on the island couldn't be exploited for his benefit, another should be. Selling four or five eggs would do no harm. Chances were the ravens would lay again later that spring, since Pinkie would be removing the clutch before incubation was properly underway.

The money would make all the difference to Ewan. Four thousand pounds would set him up nicely. He'd be able to enlarge his meagre flock of sheep and pay for improvements to the croft house. Bella had also hoped the money would make it possible for Ewan to propose to Catriona. In that regard he was a traditional young man, the type who wouldn't take on a commitment like a wife until he could offer her a decent house. He was still sleeping on Donald's single mattress and the kitchen was only an old range and sink. There was no proper bathroom. The house wasn't in a state Ewan would wish for his bride, or so Bella thought. Still, they'd broken up now, and that had happened after Bella told Ewan about the money. She allowed herself a twinge of regret. Was there something different she could have done to help the course of love?

Bella parked in the disused quarry, as arranged. She hadn't been there more than a few minutes when a gentle tap at the window made her jump. Pinkie Pryke was outside, wearing waterproofs and a brown corduroy cap. Bella beckoned to him to come round to the front passenger door. She glanced at the clock as she leaned across to unlock it: six precisely. Pinkie Pryke was as good as his reputation. Bella's admiration was short-lived. The stickler in Pinkie's personality made him question every detail of Bella's new plan.

'Crossing the sound at dusk increases the risk of being seen,' Pinkie said.

'It's either that or you won't get across. This storm will have passed by tomorrow morning and there'll be an hour or two before the next one arrives. That's when you'll be brought back. But if you don't go this evening there might not be another opportunity to make a return crossing for a couple of days.'

Pinkie snarled, 'This wasn't what we arranged. I don't like surprises.'

'Tell that to the weather,' Bella replied.

Pinkie banged his hand against the dashboard. 'I don't like it.'

Bella said nothing. Out of the corner of her eye, she noticed Pinkie reclining his seat. 'I don't want to be disturbed until it's time to go,' he growled. While Pinkie rested, Bella watched the clouds racing across the sky and suffered in silent exasperation. Why did Pinkie, like Catriona, blame her when all she was doing was trying to help?

At six thirty, she woke Pinkie and handed him a balaclava

to replace his cap. She waited while he put it on. 'On second thoughts,' she said, 'you'd better duck below the dashboard when the car leaves the quarry. If anyone sees me with a male passenger, there'll be gossip. I assume you'd prefer to avoid that. I most certainly would.'

Bella detected reluctance on Pinkie's part, as if she had sprung yet another surprise. She wondered whether he was married. If he was, she pitied his wife. Bella couldn't imagine having to tiptoe around a man as fastidious as this. Soon she was passing Joss's caravan. Round the next bend, Grant's Croft came into view, the house and the side barn jutting against the sky. Ewan, as instructed, was waiting by the rough path to his jetty. A balaclava was pulled over his face. Bella checked her mirror before telling Pinkie he could sit up again.

'Did you see that?' Ewan pointed behind her, 'Wheeler's yacht is in the harbour. He's sheltering from the storm.'

'That's marvellous,' Bella said before explaining to Pinkie the chances of them being observed were negligible now. 'A weight off my mind, I must say.' The news about the *Jacqueline* made her realize how stressed she had been, how worried. 'Thank goodness, no danger of witnesses,' she said.

Pinkie looked at Bella as though she was untrustworthy. 'I thought that was the arrangement.'

'Why don't you tell that to the ravens?' Bella snapped. 'It's not my fault they finished laying their eggs early, when the owner of the island was still here.' She took a deep breath. 'The arrangement,' she said, 'was that you would pay one thousand pounds before you were taken to the boat.'

Pinkie stuck his hand in his pocket and put a roll of money on the dashboard.

Bella counted twenty fifty-pound notes and gave them to

Ewan. 'That leaves two thousand to pay when you've got the eggs.'

~

Cal checked the time. It was almost seven. Soon it would be dark and the squalls would start. He imagined the thump and crash of wind and waves, the sound and fury of unrestrained power – and felt the pull of it, the certainty that came over him at such times, that this was where he belonged, the only place: alone, on some wild coast in a storm. He listened for the sea breaking on the shore, for the rattle and shift of stones. Then he heard a different noise: rhythmic, like the stones, but mechanical. In the gloom, he saw a boat heading towards him. It bounced and tossed in the waves. Two hunched figures were aboard, one by the stern, the other at the bow. Cal shrank into the shadow of a rock. Thirty metres from him, the engine cut out and the boat pushed ashore. Both men got out. The one from the stern appeared agile and stocky. His companion appeared older and walked stiffly, a large backpack in his right hand. Both had their faces covered. The younger man pulled the boat higher on the shingle beach before tying it up. After a brief exchange – Cal could hear indistinct voices – they set off together, going uphill, the younger man leading, the older unsteady, his legs seeming still to be at sea. Cal watched them until they were lost in the evening. He shuffled further back in the shadows of the surrounding rocks.

What had Mr Close said? 'The island is a shrine to Max Wheeler. It must be respected at all times.' Someone didn't seem to know.

~

It was just as the man on the ferry said. 'Take the road south – there's only one,' was his reply to Helen Jamieson's question about directions. 'At the first junction – again there's only one – you'll see a wee slip road straight ahead. You can't miss it.'

She hadn't missed it, though she had parked outside the Deep Blue with a sinking feeling. The tea room was in darkness, the door shut and locked. There didn't seem to be a bell and night was falling. 'My niece Catriona will be there to let you in and take you to the chalet,' Bella MacLeod had re-assured Helen after apologizing for her own absence. Though Helen hadn't said so, she'd been pleased. Having Catriona to herself would allow her to make the nineteen-year-old's acquaintance, woman to woman, broken heart to broken heart. Where was she, though? As Helen knocked on the door and called Catriona's name, a voice behind her said, 'I came as quickly as I could.' Despite the distorting effects of the wind, Helen detected truculence. The girl's face matched the voice, as Helen saw when she turned round. Catriona was standing a few paces away. She seemed fixed as though she had been there for a while, watching.

'Oh, thank heaven,' Helen exclaimed. 'I thought I was going to have to spend the night in my car. Catriona ... you are Catriona?' From her description in the case files, Helen knew it was her. Even so, the girl's white face was a shock, a pale moon.

Catriona stared as if she too was matching a description to the person in front of her. Helen knew what it was – the pot-ted biography she had deliberately let slip to Bella MacLeod when she was booking the chalet: thirty-two years old, no boyfriend, holidays alone, likes eating cake. After a moment's consideration, Catriona said, 'You're Helen Jamieson, right?'

Even though she was probably the only visitor expected that evening, the question disconcerted Helen. Did she look like that kind of woman?

'Yes, I'm Helen.' She was careful to drop the surname. The sooner Catriona and she were on first-name terms, the better. 'I hope I didn't interrupt anything. Your aunt – Bella, she is your aunt, isn't she? – told me to ask for you.'

'I was looking out,' Catriona said defensively. She pointed above Helen's head, over the Deep Blue, to a looming, shapeless blackness against the dark sky. 'Up there, on the hill. I came as quickly as I could when I saw your headlights.' Helen registered the change: truculent one minute, almost apologetic the next.

'That's a hill, is it?' Helen said doubtfully. 'What were you doing, walking?'

'There's reception up there,' Catriona said, 'three, sometimes four bars.'

'Ah, phone reception,' Helen said. 'I was wondering whether my phone would work.'

'There's no reception down here. That's why I go up the hill when the tea room's shut, or over that way.' Catriona pointed to Helen's right. 'The hill's better, though.'

'Better reception?'

'More bars and no one can see me from the road when it's daylight.'

'Well, Catriona,' Helen said, 'your secret's safe with me.'

In the car, Helen had devised a plan of attack. *Call her Catriona whenever you can. Let her know she can trust you. Pay her a compliment. Build a relationship around coincidental similarities.*

The opportunity to compliment the teenager presented itself when Helen moved aside to let Catriona unlock the door. 'It seems to me, Catriona, that you're an important person to know.' She made it sound casual, light.

Whether that made the difference, Helen wasn't sure. But she noticed a change in Catriona. As she led Helen through the tea room and out of the back door – 'a short cut to the chalet, you're welcome to use it when the tea room's open' – she appeared less watchful. She pointed out the side gate where Helen could come and go without everyone inside knowing her movements and where she could park her car. At the door of the chalet, Catriona was apologetic. She hoped it didn't feel unlived in – it had been shut up during the winter. Helen was the first visitor of spring.

'A swallow,' Helen ventured.

Catriona gave her a funny look.

'Hmm,' Helen said, 'I see you don't think I'm exactly built for flying between continents.'

Catriona laughed, Helen too.

'When I leave here you won't recognize me. A new me . . .'

Catriona opened the chalet door, turned on the light and stood back to let Helen precede her into a large square room. The walls were pine-panelled, a warm orange-yellow. Two tweedy sofas were on either side of a wood burner by the left-hand wall. A silver-coloured flue extended up to the ceiling. A rocking chair was by one of a pair of large windows. The sills of both were lined with books. 'This is perfect,' Helen said, 'I won't want to leave.'

'You wouldn't say that if you lived here.'

Helen waited before answering, making sure the pitch was just right. 'No, it's always different when you've grown up somewhere. It seems to close in on you, doesn't it? Even a place with wide horizons like this.'

Catriona looked wistful. 'Where do you live?'

'In Edinburgh.'

'Maybe we can change places.' Her voice trembled a little with nerves.

Helen pretended not to notice. 'That's an idea. You can have my flat and my ex. That sounds like a good deal to me.'

Suddenly the tension left Catriona. She laughed. 'And you mine. My ex, I mean.'

'No! You too?'

Catriona nodded.

'How long?'

'Two months and four days.'

Helen replied, 'Six days, five hours . . .' She looked at her watch, 'and twenty minutes, give or take. That's why I'm here. You see, we live across the street from each other. I couldn't get away from him.'

Catriona said, 'Mine was cheating.'

'Mine too,' Helen said, 'although he told me he needed to take time out, to find out what he really wanted. It turned out to be a blonde called Phoebe.'

'Same,' Catriona said, 'except she wasn't called Phoebe.'

'Well,' Helen said, 'I think we're going to have to look out for one another.' She made a point of glancing around the sitting room. 'Would you give me a tour?'

Catriona started opening doors and turning on lights. 'In here is a bedroom. In here is another. In here is the bathroom and toilet. And here . . .' the last door swung open, 'is the kitchen.' Helen followed behind, looking into each room and enthusing about the size or the furnishings.

'If there's anything you need, just come over to the tea room when it's open – ten to six – or ring on the landline. There's an honesty box.' Catriona walked over towards a side table beside a sofa and picked up a blue ring file from the bottom shelf. 'There's lots of information about the area, things to see, the best beaches, walks.'

'What about the flattest places to run?'

Catriona seemed amused.

'I told you, it's the new me,' Helen said. 'A run before breakfast, a walk after lunch . . .' She put on a serious face.

'And cake for tea … Well, it's all right for a slim wee thing like you. But I need an incentive, something to look forward to after all that healthy exercise. No hills, though. Which way would you suggest?'

Catriona said, 'It's about two miles before the end of the road whether you go east or west.' She pointed east. 'But it's flatter that way.'

'So, east it is,' Helen said and thought ruefully: it was one thing Catriona being amused, quite another Cal. She imagined his surprise when he realized who was running along the road towards him, then his mocking smile: Detective Sergeant Jamieson, in tracksuit, trainers, fleece and bobble hat. It had been DCI Beacom's idea. On an island, he'd said, everyone was expert in furtive behaviour and concealment. Being upfront was less suspicious, he'd said to Helen.

'Mind,' Catriona said doubtfully, 'I'd see what the weather's like. It's already quite wild outside. There's a storm coming in tonight and another one forecast for tomorrow.'

Linda knelt beside the open suitcase and looked around the hall floor at the possessions that would accompany her. Practical items were to her right – her clothes, shoes, make-up and wash bags, a light raincoat, a hand towel and a collection of important documents, among them her passport and birth certificate. Items of emotional significance, those from which she could not be separated, were to her left. There were only four: a framed photograph of her father at her graduation day, in his good blue suit; a gold crown coin her grandmother had pressed into her hand the day before she died, when Linda was six; a Meissen porcelain figure of a monkey playing the violin which had belonged to her mother; a small wooden boat Linda had made in carpentry in her primary school. Even as she was going round the house, gathering up what she would need and those things she could not bear to leave behind, she was uncertain whether she would be able to walk out of the door, whether she had it in her. But when everything was assembled in the hall and she saw her few emotional possessions, how little the house contained of her, she realized she would have to go, that she had no choice. As she packed, she surprised herself again. Rather than being regretful or torn, as she had expected, she became impatient to leave. How much longer would the taxi be? Should she ring and ask for it to come earlier? She could always spend a few hours at the airport, drinking coffee, reading a book or a newspaper. Instead she wrote Stanley two identical letters. One she put into her handbag in case time made her forget her reasons. The other she put on the kitchen table.

> *Stanley,*
> *I'm going away. I don't know where. I'm taking a taxi to the airport*
> *and I will make up my mind then. I have to get away from this house,*
> *from you, from your deception and from the shame you have brought to*
> *my father's good name. I gave you that name so that you could start*
> *again, so that WE could start again after the last time you let me*
> *down. You are welcome to go on living here. If not, the house will be*
> *sold and I will give you half of the proceeds. My only condition is that*
> *you stop calling yourself Stanley Pryke and that you revert to Stanley*
> *Wise. Do not try to find me. I do not want to see you again. Linda*

Afterwards, she sat on the chair in the hall with her suitcase beside her. She watched the hands of the grandfather clock mark out the early hours of the morning. At five minutes to four, she stood up, put on her gloves and went to the front door. She opened it and stepped outside. She banged the door shut, double locked it and put her keys through the letter box. It was dark, the new day still to dawn. Suddenly Linda found it hard to take another step. But she managed one, then another, then another. By the time she arrived at the pavement, the taxi was pulling up. 'To the airport, is it, love?' the driver said, opening his door to help with her bag. 'Going somewhere nice?'

~

Joss paid attention to every sound, to the thuds and thumps of the wind, to the rattle of a squall of rain, the hawser rubbing against the roof, the creaks and growls of the caravan being lifted and dropped by a passing gust. She listened too, in terror, for those small noises, the roll of a stone, the snap of a stalk of heather, the fall of a foot by the caravan's door, for an approach stealthier than the storm's. She sat upright and tense on her bunk in the dark. Her right hand gripped her mobile phone – the last time she looked it had no signal. Still, what else did she have to cling on to? What other hope did she have of calling for help when, if, they came? Her left hand covered her mouth, as though clamped to a wound. She breathed in the soapy smell from her fingers to banish the taste of Ewan's tongue, to drive from her memory its warmth and wetness, stubbing against her teeth, demanding to be let in. Every so often she would shudder and imagine it being in the caravan with her, disembodied and dog-penis pink, waiting to slip itself silently into her mouth if ever she took her hand away. Invasion of one kind or another played on her mind. She imagined the shrieking of the wind being baying voices, her enemies emboldened by the knowledge that Ewan would no longer protect her. In alarm she checked the windows to make sure the cardboard reinforcements were still in place. Then she pulled at the rope tying up the door, testing its strength.

When she was back in her bed, the wind blew stronger than before, eighty, ninety miles an hour. Joss listened for the rubbing of the hawser, for the roof to compress under its pressure, for the caravan to tip and become level again as had happened a hundred times already that night, a thousand times since she'd taken up residence.

This time was different. As the caravan was being lifted, it slewed broadside to the wind. Joss waited for the sound of the straining hawser, for the recoil of the caravan, for the bump as it settled back on its chassis. Instead the caravan kept on rising and then it rolled, a white shadow tumbling through a black night, the crash and screech of metal buckling and, faintly, the high note of a young woman's scream.

The storm had roared and raged, depriving Stanley of sleep. His arms and legs shook from cold. His shoulders and back ached from lying on rocky ground with barely a centimetre of covering soil. Every part of him felt battered and bruised as if some mindless thug had punched and kicked him. His spirit was leaking away, like blood from a gash. Even with the wind drumming in his ears, a small voice made itself heard above the din. *Are you up for this, Stanley? You've let yourself go – you're past climbing cliffs. You're only fooling yourself, Stanley.*

In the hour before dawn, he attempted to bolster his morale, what little was left, by recalling the honourable tradition to which he belonged and the sacrifices it demanded. More than belonged, he told himself, to emphasize his particular responsibility. Wasn't he the last of the field men? Wasn't he the best of the breed? As if reciting a poem learned in childhood, he made a mental list of those like him who had endured discomfort for their calling. They were egg collectors with names that resonated with resilience and character, men like the Rev. F. C. R. Jourdain, Dr Stennett Sloan Chesser and Edgar Percival Chance. Some, like Major Charles Bendire, had taken mortal risks to add to their collections, in his case joining the US cavalry and reportedly removing a zone-tailed hawk's egg while being attacked by Apache. He kept his prize safe by putting it in his mouth.

As the wind and rain gnawed at Stanley, he rehearsed other similar feats of derring-do, how his forebears conquered the highest crags and cliffs with only an old length of rope, a walking stick, a sturdy pair of boots and a bottomless well of courage. Which of them would have allowed such weather conditions and a sleepless night to sap his indomitable spirit? Yet here he was, on a metaphorical cliff edge of self-pity, with weatherproof clothing, a good climbing rope and a safety harness. Had he gone soft? The question was implicit in his self-doubt, the answer too. Chastened, he lamented his lack of fortitude on this, his last expedition, the one that would place him above all those others whose names he'd heard first from his father.

Stanley Wise (also known as Pryke), field man: he would be proud to own this simple epitaph.

At last, with dawn, the rain stopped and some light and bravura returned. The nagging worries about his bulk and fitness – would he be able to control his descent, would he be able to haul himself back up the cliff? – were all but forgotten as Stanley allowed himself to be diverted by the sensuous allure of those rosy-pink eggs.

Like a young woman's soft lips.

So near.

The expectancy of imminent possession buoyed him. So did an easing of the wind. Sitting against the boulder that had provided inadequate shelter during the night, he was optimistic enough to consider the weather his assistant instead of an implacable foe. The notion offered a solution to the problem that had worried Stanley since his second meeting with Bella MacLeod. Although she would not tell him the location of the nest, she'd described its general disposition so that he would know what to prepare for, what equipment to bring. It was, she said, a substantial structure of branches and twigs on a ledge some ten metres from the top of a cliff and concealed beneath a sheer overhang of rock. This last detail had sent Stanley into a sweat. But the weather seemed to present an unexpected solution. He would abseil down the cliff face, drop below the overhang until he was opposite the ledge. Hanging in mid-air, he'd wait for a gust to blow him towards the nest. The wind was westerly, ideal for his purpose, and no longer so strong he risked being dashed against the rock face.

Walking stiffly and hunched towards the cliff, Stanley found that, though his mind was willing, his body was proving less adaptable. It was as if all his joints had fused, so still had he lain and so paralysed by cold and wet had he been during the night. Also, his earlier estimation of the wind's strength now seemed inadequate. The gusts were so forceful he was taking one step back for every three forward. But those tweedy gentlemen of the past spurred him on again as did the sight of a single raven flapping by him – the cock. The hen would be on the nest, protecting her eggs, protecting *his* eggs.

The thought helped Stanley to feel his old enthusiasm for the challenge, man against nature. Even if there was a flickering flame where once there had been a raging fire, it was sufficient to goad him on. He looped the rope, a familiar and trusted friend, around a boulder close to the edge. Making sure it was secure, he attached the rope to his harness. Then, after leaving his backpack in the shelter of a depression, he stepped off the cliff and experienced a rush of exhilaration, even joy: an addict rediscovering his drug of choice. Though the wind was strong and waves crashed about with a thunderous sound below him, he felt alive, a field man again.

Pausing for a moment, he warned himself against over-eagerness when he was close to the nest, when he first saw the eggs. Then he lowered himself, working the belay, waiting for the wind's lulls, his body at an angle of forty-five degrees, his boots pressing against glistening black rock.

Soon he was on the overhang and preparing to descend to the recessed ledge hidden somewhere below. All he had to do was push off with his feet, let out rope and gravity would do the rest. It was a simple manoeuvre, one he had done before, but neither his hands nor his feet would do as he asked. His courage had taken flight. He couldn't go down. Nor, he realized, could he go up. He was stuck. All his doubts clamoured for attention. *You're too fat, Stanley, past it, gone soft.*

A powerful gust dislodged him and, in panic, he let out too much rope. As he dropped, he was aware of a large platform of brown sticks and black raven wings brushing against his shoulder.

And the colour pink.

Four, was it five eggs?

One moment Stanley was hurtling past the nest towards the sea, the next he jolted to a halt. Swinging in the wind above rearing waves, his nerve was shot and his limbs shook. It took a while for him to regain his breath and a few minutes more to control his arms and legs. Even the proximity of the raven's nest failed to rally him. Each time he looked up he saw the overhang looming above, black, forbidding and dripping with salt spray. But, before his strength departed, he had to attempt to haul himself up. Two heaves brought him to the ledge; another and a gust of wind took him to within reach of the nest, which was more than a metre high and as much across, the accumulation of so much material evidence of many years' occupation. He grabbed at the base. His fingers closed round a tangle of heather branches. Some snapped, others broke free and he grasped again at the nest as a drowning man pulls at the hand of a rescuer. The structure shifted towards him just as he lunged upwards and another gust of wind caught him. He crash-landed on flat rock.

He vomited. He pissed his trousers. He called for Linda.

The ledge, as Stanley blearily saw, was almost three metres long. It stopped where a wide diagonal crack cut up beside the rock overhang. Stanley raised himself on trembling arms to view the eggs. They lay on top of the nest platform in a concave bed of sheep's wool, the narrower ends pointing towards each other so that the eggs described a circle. Three were pale rosy-pink with hellebore-red blotches, just as he'd hoped. The other two were blush-white with a variety of pink and red blotches and spots.

Stanley stroked each one, feeling the leftover warmth of the hen raven on his fingertip. He took his father's pouch from his anorak pocket and picked up each egg as though they were precious beyond price. One by one he slid them into the individual padded cells. The excitement of possession gave him courage for the ascent. He bit against the pouch's cloth handle, the eggs contained and swinging safely below his chin. With both hands free to hold the rope, he shuffled to the edge of the ledge and dropped off. Between gusts, he pulled himself slowly up.

Fortune was on his side, he thought, when the wind veered suddenly to north-west. It blew him along the cliff face, where the overhang was less pronounced. But another, stronger blast started him spinning. He yanked on the rope and arched his body. He tried to use his weight to return to the ledge. Instead, he spun faster and faster until he was so dizzy he didn't realize his mouth was gaping wide, or that he'd let go of the pouch or that his trusty rope was fraying against jagged rock at the edge of the overhang. Nor did he register, a split second later, the difference between light-headedness and weightlessness. The instant before he splashed into the sea, he saw his father's pouch on the crest of a wave. It was rising towards him. Stanley reached out but the wave swirled and dipped, holding the pouch just beyond his outstretched fingers, as if taunting him, as if enjoying a moment of malice.

Ewan Chisholm was agitated. He paced the shingle beach. Cal had watched him since daylight started to drape the day in colour – steel-grey and spindrift-white for the sea; pale yellows, duns and black for the land. For half an hour, more, Ewan had put on a display of impatience. Sometimes he threw out his arms. At others he kicked in temper at the shingle or gazed out to sea. Cal knew what was going through his head. The same was going through Cal's. The wind was moderating and changing direction. One storm was departing and another was about to arrive. A window of opportunity to cross the sound would soon close. Then there would be no escape for twenty-four hours, perhaps longer. In another, more violent gesture of frustration, Ewan kicked again at the shingle. He swore – Cal saw the accompanying grimace; heard the delayed bark of his voice – before striding off the beach, apparently going to chivvy his companion. As Ewan began climbing the hill, he put on a balaclava. Cal wondered why. After all, his face had been uncovered since daylight. Why hide it now?

When Ewan went behind the skyline, Cal broke cover, running, keeping to the short grass that fringed the shore, passing the jetty and the chapel. It took him ten minutes to reach the other end of the island, another two to untie the RIB and to edge out into the sound. Soon he was rolling and pitching among waves three, four metres high, steering a course along black canyons of water with white spray scudding above. Cal kept to the troughs and watched to port for billowing waves threatening to crash over the RIB. Narrowly avoiding one by accelerating, he glanced up at its breaking crest and saw a carcass. It was barrel-bloated, rotating as if on a spit, four stiff legs slicing the sea: Millie, still putting on a show and looking for applause, was floating.

Cal whooped as the wave plunged behind him. 'Good pig, Millie.'

And then, suddenly, he was in calmer, more sheltered water. Eilean Dubh's shoreline was close by, the old slipway two hundred metres to starboard. Cal turned the RIB and throttled back, allowing the wind and waves to carry him. A figure was standing by the slipway, in tracksuit, trainers and a woollen hat. 'Jamieson?' Cal looked again. 'Helen?' He turned the RIB towards her.

'Don't,' she warned.

'Don't what?'

'That,' she said, 'that smirk.' She'd seen it before, a flicker of amusement at the edges of his mouth, one moment there, the next gone. When the RIB nudged against the slipway, Helen said, 'Your face, what happened, Cal? It's all scratched.'

'A disagreement with Joss Wheeler . . .'

'Some disagreement.'

'She was doing all the disagreeing.' Cal stepped ashore. 'She was waiting outside the Deep Blue; launched herself at me, no introductions, nothing.'

Helen looked closer at the wounds, twin welts running down his nose, more along the line of his jaw. 'Nasty.'

Cal shaped his hands into claws, his fingers pretending to rake at his face. 'She's got sharp nails.' He shrugged. 'Being unpopular seems to be an occupational hazard of working for David Wheeler.'

'Well,' Helen said, 'you always did make friends easily.'

After tying up the RIB, they sat with their backs against

Cal's pickup so they were hidden from the road. Cal told Helen about his night on Priest's Island and the arrival of two unexpected and masked visitors and how, at daybreak, he had recognized Ewan Chisholm, the principal suspect in Max Wheeler's disappearance. 'What puzzles me,' Cal said, 'is why he put his balaclava back on when he went up the hill to look for the other man.'

'Maybe he was cold,' Helen suggested.

'No, I don't think it was that. He didn't want the other man to see his face. That's what it was.'

'They didn't know each other?'

'They didn't speak much when they came ashore. They didn't behave as though they were friends.'

'You think there's a connection to Max Wheeler's disappearance?'

'Everything and everyone is connected in a place like this.'

'But you don't know how?'

'No,' Cal said. 'But Ewan Chisholm wouldn't go back to Priest's Island under the noses of the Wheelers unless it was something important. The way he was pacing up and down the beach, waiting for the other man ... he was worried about being caught there by the storm.'

Helen stared again at the sea. Then she said, 'Cal, there's something I have to tell you.'

'Go on,' Cal said.

'Wheeler isn't paying you. Beacom is.'

Cal swore.

'He didn't want me to tell you.' Helen waited a beat before starting her explanation: how Wheeler was as good as bankrupt, how the *Jacqueline* and Priest's Island were all he had left, his house in Southampton was on the market to pay off his creditors, and Beacom had seen an opportunity in his ruin. 'Cal, Wheeler doesn't have the money to commission another investigation – he hardly has enough to keep the *Jac-queline* in fuel. Beacom posed as a rich benefactor who had lost a son. He contacted Wheeler's lawyer, saying he would pay for another investigation. The condition was the person would be selected by Beacom. And not one of the deadbeats and charlatans that Wheeler allowed to rip him off in previous years.' Helen took a deep breath. 'Beacom wanted someone who would stir things up. You, Cal – you were perfect because Wheeler hadn't ever commissioned anyone to look at the sea. It was the only place left.'

For once Helen found Cal's silence uncomfortable.

'Cal,' she pleaded, 'a fourteen-year-old boy is dead. A father has lost his son. Three girls have lost their brother. The township won't cooperate with the police. Beacom's got the job of finding out what happened. He saw an opportunity to try something new. He thought you'd like to help.' She paused.

'Good of him to let me know.'

'Well, he did save your life.'

Cal lobbed a stone into the sea, then another. 'So you reminded me last night.'

'Will you stay?' Helen asked. 'No one else needs to know.'

'Tell Beacom I don't want his money.'

'But you'll help?'

Cal threw another stone. Abruptly, he stood up and opened the driver's door. The engine coughed and started.

'Wait, Cal.' Helen stood too. 'Cal?'

17

Whenever a storm blew in, Bella would lie awake listening to its delinquent rampaging and she would congratulate herself on her foresight. Thank goodness she had built her house and the chalet side by side in the shelter behind the Deep Blue. Old friends from Glasgow would come to stay in summer and express tactless disappointment at her sitting room's restricted sea view but Bella would reply, 'You wouldn't say that if you were here in autumn or winter.' She might also attempt a description of the weather's capacity for violence once September turned to October. Usually, her guests would counter with their own experiences of ruined family holidays on Bute or Arran, as though they too had suffered the elements at their fiercest. Bella would bite her tongue before attempting to explain the difference between islands lying 200 kilometres to the south in the relative shelter of the Firth of Clyde compared to her northern exposure. Then she might recall her first December at the Deep Blue, how shocked she'd been by the weather. When she lived in the city, she regarded gangs in the same way as she now did storms: both capable of mindless acts of vandalism and of terrorizing entire neighbourhoods.

Once light began to infiltrate her bedroom her thoughts would turn to the prospect of a busy day ahead. In wild weather, the Deep Blue was where the township gravitated. Crofts went untended, boats stayed at their moorings and washing lines flapped bare as the tea room filled and became fuggy. Before getting up, Bella would conduct a mental stock-take. Was there enough coffee? Would she run short of cake and biscuits? Should she leave a message for Jimmy the postman to pick up milk from the store by the ferry pier, in case sailings – and supplies – were disrupted for more than a day? With her 'to do' list already written in her head, Bella would put on her dressing gown and head downstairs to her own kitchen rather than brave the weather and cross to the tea room's. She would make bread rolls and brownies. While they cooled, she would drink tea and listen to the radio, the presenters' voices contributing to a restoration of calm after Bella's burst of industry, as well as providing a contrast to the turbulence outside. Having washed, dried and tidied away the pans and trays, she would go back upstairs for her shower, leaving Catriona to sleep on – after all, why provoke another storm?

This morning, however, Bella paused by Catriona's room and decided to go in. It had an unhindered view of the sound, the only one in the house. She was agitated about Ewan, feeling she should have heard from him by now. He had promised to drop by or to ring once he'd brought Pinkie back from Priest's Island. Parting the curtains, Bella watched Wheeler's boat straining at its mooring by the harbour wall and, beyond, a hazy tumult of waves and spray. The sight made Bella feel sick. The thought of Ewan being out in that! Surely he had the sense to stay put, to wait for the next depression to clear, even if that wouldn't be for another twenty-four hours. After all, with the *Jacqueline* held captive by the weather on this side of the sound, the risk of Ewan being discovered was slight. Bella clung to the notion as though to a life raft. Of course, she told herself with a certainty she didn't really feel, wouldn't that explain why Ewan hadn't been in touch?

Since it was past eight, she decided to open Catriona's curtains. Perhaps the light would rouse the girl slowly and render her more or less civil when Bella knocked on her door at eight thirty, Catriona's usual wake-up time. That would make a pleasant change. Bella studied her niece's face, admiring her perfect milk-white skin – so like her mother's and grandmother's. She wondered how she was so peaceful in sleep yet so spiky and contrary awake. It seemed as if there had never been a time when Bella hadn't worried about her. If there was, Bella couldn't recall when. Every day arrived with a new concern: was Catriona depressed, was she on drugs, might she be suicidal? Bella was exhausted trying to find explanations and solutions. Perhaps she was guilty of over-analysing. All teenage girls were mysteries, her best friend Isobel had said with her usual common sense: 'Weren't you? Didn't you have moods and secrets just like Catriona?' Bella agreed she had, but her mother had possessed an instinct for her two daughters, an intuitive understanding. She would always know if Bella or Frances, Catriona's mother, were in serious trouble, when interference was required, when it wasn't. Bella lacked that unconscious knowledge of Catriona. She was always trying to work her out. Over-analysis was one description, being in a constant state of defeat was another and the one that better described Bella's experience.

As if subconsciously protesting at being observed by Bella, Catriona began mumbling and flailing her arms. Her sudden restlessness dislodged the duvet, exposing bare shoulders, a black camisole and an exercise pad. It was lying on the bottom sheet close to Catriona's right thigh. Bella rescued it in case her niece rolled over and crushed it, though when she saw the open page her brow furrowed in puzzlement. It was covered in pencil lines of different lengths, all fanning from the same point. Catriona had written letters and numbers at the beginning and end of some of the lines. Perhaps they were calculations, Bella thought, as she put the pad on the bedside table and sent a hair clip skittering across the floor. Bella flinched. How clumsy she was! She glanced fearfully at Catriona, hoping to find her undisturbed, but two open and hostile eyes were staring up at her, just what Bella had been trying to avoid. She steeled herself for Catriona's usual complaint about being woken too early but her niece's first words were an accusation: 'You looked.'

Bella felt her face reddening. 'Aren't you always so sweet and charming in the morning?'

'You did, I know you did.'

The usual wilting feeling of failure crept over Bella. 'Anyway,' she said, trying to summon up a put-down before Catriona warmed to hers. 'Even if I did look, I wouldn't have a notion of what I was looking at, all those lines, squiggles and numbers.'

Rather than stay to be Catriona's punchbag, Bella went along the landing to her room. She showered, dressed and, on her way down the stairs, knocked at Catriona's closed door and shouted: 'Are you up yet, my sweet-natured darling?' She didn't wait for an answer, another verbal assault. Back in the orderly surroundings of the kitchen, Bella felt less defeated. At least the baking was ready; she had done something right. When did Catriona ever thank her for that, for making a success of the Deep Blue, for being the caretaker of Catriona's interests, of her future? She put the rolls into carrier bags, and the brownies into tins. Then she draped a coat over her head and, arms laden, hurried from the front door. Although the distance to the tea room was no more than a few steps, one tin was blown from her grasp. When she bent to pick it up, the wind almost knocked her over.

'Mercy, what a day,' she exclaimed when she was safely inside the tea room and shaking the wind from her hair.

After checking the contents of the dropped tin for damage – thankfully, there was none – she turned on the main lights and wiped down the tables. At nine, she opened up the office and switched on her laptop to check on the weather. According to the BBC, wind speeds would be seventy miles an hour, gusting to ninety. The severe weather warning was expected to remain in force for another twenty-four to thirty-six hours. Travel disruption should be expected, especially in the Highlands and Islands. The Meteorological Office warned of a threat to property and life. She closed her eyes and thought again of Ewan, willing him to be safe on Priest's Island. She went into the tea room and stood by the big window. Since she last looked, visibility had worsened, Priest's Island reduced to a blur through the rain and spray.

At least Ewan was used to riding out such weather. But Pinkie: how resilient was he? Just as Bella was scolding herself about taking on the worries of the world – Pinkie was not a legend for nothing; the man could look after himself, flabby waist or not – a running figure in a tracksuit, fleece and woollen hat crossed in front of the Deep Blue. Bella exclaimed out loud and watched as the figure – it was hard to tell whether male or female – went round to the side of the tea room. 'Of course,' she said under her breath. 'Helen Jamieson.' She'd forgotten all about her. What was the woman thinking, running in weather like this? Bella would give her a talking-to when she saw her later. The islands weren't Edinburgh! Though, on reflection, having seen Helen in her tracksuit, she thought it would take an unusually strong gust of wind to knock her off her feet.

Feeling at a loose end in the forty minutes before opening time, Bella returned to the office. She did her accounts, caught up with letters and left two messages for Jimmy to pick up some milk, the first on his phone and the second with Gill at the store by the ferry pier at the north end of the island. By nine thirty, her thoughts turned again to Catriona.

The first customers would be waiting at the door in twenty minutes. Where was the girl? Bella toyed with chivvying her but decided not to. It would only cause more unpleasantness and give Catriona an excuse to be in a mood all day.

Not that she ever seemed to need an excuse. No wonder Ewan had had second thoughts about her!

Instead, Bella rang Joss to make sure she and the caravan had survived the night. The call went to answer and Bella left a message: 'It's Bella. Ring me.' Where could Joss have gone? Surely she couldn't be out in these conditions. Though there could be a simple explanation for her not answering. As with most of the island, phone reception at the caravan was at best temperamental.

Bella wondered why she invested so much emotional energy in any of them: Catriona, Ewan and, lately, Joss. She was never done worrying. If it wasn't one, it was another. This morning it was all three.

As if to prove her wrong, Catriona appeared in the tea room, wearing a clean apron but, as Bella expected, a defiant expression. Rather than risk an argument, she asked about Helen Jamieson. What was she like? Catriona rolled her eyes and Bella found herself gabbling. 'Was that her out running? I'm sure it was – about half an hour ago, going towards the chalet gate. She had a hat pulled down on her head so I couldn't even see her hair. It must have been her, don't you think? No one from the island would run in this weather, not if they were in their right senses.'

Catriona snapped, 'So I'm not the only one you're spying on.'

'I wasn't spying,' Bella said wearily. 'I thought the exercise book might be precious. I was concerned about you rolling over and crumpling it.'

'Oh, right,' Catriona said. She stared at Bella, a withering look, as if examining some alien and disgusting life form. 'What did you think you were doing, coming into my room when I was asleep?' Catriona shuddered and put on an expression of disgust. 'Watching me . . .'

'I wasn't watching you,' Bella said. 'If you must know, I was seeing whether the sound was rough.'

'What did you think it would be like?' Catriona slapped the heel of her hand against the side of her head. 'Duh, there's a storm, isn't there?'

Bella's relief at Catriona going next door to the kitchen was short-lived. As usual, it turned to guilt, followed by a nagging desire to make things better between them. She went after Catriona. 'I could help you with the napkins or put out some cakes.'

'No.' Catriona banged down a knife on the counter. 'No.' A fork clanged next.

~

Cal clenched his left hand and hit the steering wheel. Once, twice and again, and each time he swore between clenched teeth, his lips stretching into a grimace. He braked before the turning to the road north which would take him to the ferry. Then he glanced in his mirror as if looking for Helen. A moment of decision: should he go or should he stay? Just when he wanted to indulge his anger at Beacom's deception, he found Helen was on his conscience.

He didn't want me to tell you.

If Cal drove north, would Helen be in trouble? Would Beacom blame her?

'Fuck.' He banged the steering wheel again, both fists.

Instead of going north or turning round and driving back past Helen – he wasn't in the right frame of mind for that –

he went straight on, towards Grant's Croft. He'd do what he always did when he was angry. He'd walk, let the wind blow his temper away and, since he was going in that direction, he'd check on Ewan Chisholm. Had he been able to leave Priest's Island? Cal thought not. The next storm was closing in, the wind blowing hard, Ewan's opportunity gone unless he'd found his companion soon after Cal made his escape. Driving along the single-track road, the sound a blur of spindrift and spray to his left, Cal realized he would soon pass Joss Wheeler's caravan. Should he try to make peace?

He was still undecided when he turned a corner, expecting to see the caravan two hundred metres ahead – an off-white eyesore with a thick rope hawser stretched across its dinged roof.

Instead it was just below the road, lying on its side, buckled and broken, and being lifted up with each gust of wind.

Cal braked hard and the caravan reared again, flipped over twice and crash-landed across a flooded stream, straddling the gully. He imagined Joss stumbling about inside the caravan, dazed, or too badly hurt to get away. He ran down the slope, his momentum carrying him on to the caravan's upturned side. Cal grabbed at the rim of a broken window as another gust of wind lifted it and him up. Looking inside, all he could see was a splintered table, a jumble of bedding, clothes, books, tins and bottles from a store cupboard; no sign of Joss. Below him, across the caravan, was another window, similarly misshapen and with the glass missing. The stream rushed past below with a roar. Had Joss fallen out into the torrent?

Cal shouted 'Joss' and was about to drop inside when the wind caught the caravan again. It reared up, almost toppling, before crashing back. Cal was thrown on to the ground. His flailing left hand glanced off a rock. His shoulder jarred against wet peat. His head pushed into heather. He was winded and for a moment he lay where he was. A metallic shriek sounded behind him. He turned to see the caravan standing on its end, and just then the gust of wind passed and it fell back. Cal climbed on again only to slide off as the caravan bucked. He fell into the gully, almost into the surging stream. He glanced up through the underside window. The caravan lifted again and Cal, fearing he would be crushed, scrambled out of the gully.

Now he looked around, in case Joss had been thrown out earlier. And it occurred to him, as he followed the trail of debris, that the hawser must have snapped at the height of the gale during the night because the clothes and paper that were strewn about were all water-logged. It hadn't rained for a while. As he walked he kept checking his mobile phone. No signal. After a hundred metres, he turned back in time to see the caravan tumble over again. Now it was clear of the gully but there didn't seem to be anything to stop it rolling all the way to the Deep Blue. Tying it with ropes secured to a four-wheeled drive or tractor was the only solution. But one of Cal's ropes was attached to Millie, the other was in his RIB.

He had to get help.

Bella longed for ten o'clock and opening time. 'Won't it be nice to be among friendly faces?' she said to Catriona who was refusing to talk. Catriona said nothing. 'For goodness' sake, Catriona, what do you expect me to say? You're not exactly a joy this morning.' By ten thirty, every table was occupied and Bella thought how cheery everyone seemed to be and lighter in spirit compared to the foreboding of yesterday. Perhaps she was aware of the change because of the contrast with Catriona's sullen glances, but Bella thought it more than that. Going from table to table taking orders, it was as if a weight had been lifted from the township now that the memorial service was over. Everyone seemed to be chattier and more relaxed and optimistic. Even Joss's assault on Dr McGill was dissected for its possible and beneficial consequences.

To Bella's surprise, Mary-Anne Robertson, normally to be relied on to see hell and damnation around the next corner, was also guardedly optimistic. Wouldn't McGill be dismissed after the incident with Joss? 'Since Wheeler's running out of money, that might be the end of it – no more investigations.'

Isobel looked startled at the prospect. 'Imagine that! We'll be able to get on with our lives.'

'Oh, I don't know,' Bella said. 'Wheeler's nothing if not single-minded . . .' Straight away she wished she'd kept her mouth shut. Although just trying to stop hopes becoming too high, her remark had more of a dispiriting effect than she intended.

Alistair Morrison, a square-built thirty-five-year-old on leave from his oil job in the North Sea, said, 'McGill won't be going anywhere for a while – the ferry won't be running for a day or two.'

Then Graham Stewart, known as 'Grey' on account of his first name and being the township's oldest working crofter, added to the gloom. He'd got up at first light to check his sheep on the east of the island. 'McGill's pickup was by the slipway but I didn't see him or his RIB.'

Ina Gillies put her hands together as though praying, taking a leaf out of Mary-Anne's book, and cast her eyes up. 'If there's a God at all, he'd have seen to it last night that McGill was blown right across the Minch back to the mainland . . .'

Mary-Anne pursed her lips in disapproval at God's name being taken in vain. Grey sat in his usual hunched way, chair pushed back from the table, forearms resting on his legs. 'He'll be out there somewhere . . .' He shook his head in resignation.

Isobel added to the gathering despondency by finishing his sentence '. . . doing Wheeler's work.'

The swing in mood depressed appetites. Bella took advantage of the lull in orders to take the weight off her tired feet.

'Five minutes,' she told Catriona as she went to the office, 'then it'll be your turn for a break.'

Catriona gave her another of her sour looks. At least silence was better than the alternative, Bella thought as she collapsed into the chair by her desk. No sooner had she closed her eyes than she heard shouting coming from the tea room. What now! Hurrying back, she was surprised to see McGill standing by the noticeboard, having just come in the door. She was about to throw him out when she realized most of the noise was coming from him. Something had happened but she wasn't sure what. Was it something to do with the storm – had his pickup been damaged? Her curiosity turned to dismay when she heard him say, 'The caravan's going to roll into the sea if we don't do something now.'

Isobel saw Bella's distress. 'It's Joss,' she said to her across the tea room. 'The caravan's been blown over and she's missing.'

Bella slumped against the office door frame to keep her from falling. 'Oh no, I can't bear it,' she moaned.

Cal said, 'The hawser holding the caravan must have sheared during the night. The wind's blown it quite a long way and it's been badly damaged. The inside's a mess but I couldn't see Joss, not that I had much time to look. The wind lifted up the caravan while I was on top and I was thrown off. It'll have to be roped down and tied to a tractor or four-wheeled drive.'

As if in reply to the shock on Bella's face, to the question that she was asking herself, Cal shook his head. 'Joss is going to be injured if she was in the caravan when the hawser broke, all that bouncing around and sharp edges.'

Bella gasped, 'Oh, heavens, oh no.' She looked at McGill, then at her regulars. Why weren't they moving? She saw suspicion in their expressions, as though this was some kind of trap of Wheeler's, setting off the same thought in her mind too. 'Dr McGill,' she said, 'I'd be obliged if you'd leave my tea room.'

Cal looked exasperated. 'I'm telling you what's happened. There isn't time to fuck around.'

As soon as he was out of the door, Bella studied the faces in front of her. Once again none met her eyes. What was wrong with them? 'We must find her.' She watched for a reaction but no one moved. 'Hurry, Joss's life is in danger.'

'If you take McGill's word for it,' someone muttered.

Bella saw how they gave each other awkward glances as if waiting for someone else to volunteer. 'I don't believe this.' Bella's voice cracked. 'At least go and see what's happened. Are you really going to take a chance with Joss's life? Are you going to leave her there, let her be swept into the sea because of McGill and because her name's Wheeler? Heaven knows what state she's in.'

She looked again from face to face and found the same reluctance to meet her eye. 'Shame on you! Where's your humanity? Don't let David Wheeler turn us into monsters. If that young woman dies because none of you would save her, there'll be no forgiveness. Everything that he's ever said about us, everything that's been written about us – our cold hearts, our murderous, vengeful natures – will be true.'

Alistair Morrison raised a hand. 'I'll go and have a look.' Others followed with murmured apologies. The shock of McGill bursting in and his report about the caravan had immobilized them, they said, rather than any reluctance to help Joss. Six of the fittest men agreed to go with Alistair. Grey would go to his croft and bring his old tractor. They passed Cal who was waiting outside the door. No one spoke to him until Alistair turned back and pointed. 'McGill, this doesn't change anything. You keep out of our way.'

18

Helen was sure she hadn't been seen. She'd entered the tea room from the chalet by the back door, as Catriona said she could. She'd hung back when she heard Cal's voice, knowing by his raised tone that something was seriously wrong. When Bella offered the rescue party waterproofs and boots from the tea room's cloakroom, Helen left by the back door. She hurried to the chalet and rang Beacom, praying that the line hadn't been blown down in the night.

'Oh, thank goodness, sir,' she exclaimed when Beacom answered. 'There's a bit of a situation here – Joss Wheeler's caravan has been blown over. She's missing. Even if she's not injured I wouldn't give much for her chances. There was a bad storm last night, another's coming in now. Some men from the township are heading out to search for her. Should I take charge? It'd mean abandoning my cover.'

Beacom thought aloud. 'What can you do that they can't? They know the area. If the weather's as bad as you say, it might be better leaving it to the locals. What's the alternative? You saying you're a detective, won't that just be a distraction when you want everyone focused on the search for Joss? No, for the time being, just listen in. If you think the search isn't being done properly, let's talk again.'

'OK.' Helen tried to sound more certain than she was. 'I'll go back to the tea room and see what's going on.'

Once the rescuers had gone, Bella rang Constable Dyer at the police house. According to his answerphone message, he was off the island for a couple of days. She dialled the number for divisional headquarters to which Dyer's calls were being referred. An operator took the details. Bella doubted there was much anyone off Eilean Dubh could do. Even the neighbouring islands were cut off. The police wouldn't be able to bring in search teams from the mainland for a day, probably more. Back in the tea room, Bella organized Isobel, Mary-Anne, Ina and the rest of the women to make sandwiches, soup and flasks of tea and coffee. While they cleared tables for worktops, Bella asked Catriona to take charge of the Deep Blue because she was going to drive to Joss's caravan with a first-aid box and dressings – in the panic of the moment she had forgotten to give them to Alistair. At least she would be doing something practical even if it might be inadequate and too late. Catriona's reaction, appearing cooperative, was a relief to Bella but soon forgotten in her anxiety about Joss.

On the narrow coast road, the wind buffeted Bella's car with such force she feared she would crash. She imagined flipping over, the car rolling with her inside. The thought made her feel sick for Joss. If the poor girl had been in the caravan when it was bouncing around, she was bound to be badly injured. What hope was there for her?

The shock of arriving at the scene only increased Bella's alarm. The caravan was lying on its roof. One rope had been put around it and tied to Alistair's Land Rover. Even so, the wind kept lifting the caravan as though it was readying for another somersault. Three men were trying to attach a second rope to Grey's old tractor. At times they could barely stand against the wind and Bella wondered if she had been right to dragoon them from the tea room. They were risking their lives, the caravan threatening to crush them all. How would she forgive herself if anyone was hurt? Why hadn't she gone to Joss last night? Why hadn't she gathered her up and let her stay in her spare room? The answers piled guilt upon guilt. She had been too preoccupied with Pinkie and Ewan, too concerned about Catriona being unwelcoming. If something awful had happened to Joss, wasn't she to blame? Approaching the cars parked on the road above the caravan, Bella recognized Grey by his crofter's stoop. She stopped beside him and opened her window.

'Is there any news of Joss? Is she all right?'

Grey's big mouth twitched. 'No one's been able to get in yet.' He stared at the knot of men struggling to keep the caravan tethered.

Bella closed her window. How long she sat there, she didn't know. She was in a daze, unable to see anything but Joss's bloody and broken face. Sometime later she registered the caravan being secured with two, three, four ropes and watched a figure with Alistair's squat build going inside. A few minutes later, Grey knocked on Bella's window.

'Joss? Has she been found?'

Grey opened the car door and knelt beside her. 'Joss wasn't in the caravan.'

'Oh,' Bella exclaimed. 'Oh, thank goodness. Then she'll be safe.'

But Grey was avoiding her eyes.

'What's wrong?' Bella asked. 'You said she wasn't in the caravan.' She let out a nervous laugh. 'Didn't you?'

Worry creased Grey's leathery face, the words hard to say. 'She could be hurt, Bella, badly hurt, and heaven knows how long she's been out in this weather.' He reached for her hands, holding them tight. 'Alistair found blood in the caravan, quite a lot of blood. I'm sorry, Bella.'

Helen broke off a corner of date and walnut cake before returning the rest to the side of her plate. 'I'm just not hungry.' She glanced around the tea room, at the township women sitting at tables. Like Helen, they were picking at biscuits or cake, or sipping at tea. If they talked, they did so in hushed voices and sporadically. How apprehensive everyone seemed, Helen thought, and beaten down. What a difference in such a short time. Before, she'd been impressed by the women's organization, at how speedily they'd set about making sandwiches and ringing round the island recruiting volunteers for the search. The reaction, Helen assumed, of coastal people practised at dealing with emergencies and responding with minimum fuss and an absence of emotion. Now, with nothing practical left to do, waiting for news, the women appeared shrunken and frightened, a mess of emotions. 'They're like different people,' she said, 'like they've retreated into themselves.'

Catriona didn't answer so Helen placed another sandwich in the box that was to be taken to the rescuers.

'But if worrying could make a difference,' she went on, 'there's enough in this room for Joss Wheeler to be found alive.' She glanced at Catriona. 'Wouldn't that be wonderful?'

Catriona started wrapping film around more sandwiches. Her hands stopped before she'd finished and she glanced up at Helen. 'That blonde girl I was telling you about . . .'

'The one your ex was cheating with?'

Catriona nodded. She leaned towards Helen. 'That was Joss Wheeler.'

'No way,' Helen cried out, forgetting herself. Lowering her voice, she said, 'The Wheeler girl? That was her, the blonde you mentioned?' She was conspiratorial now, whispering, 'So I don't suppose you mind much if she disappears?'

She watched Catriona, how young she seemed, how hurt.

'Well,' Helen said, 'time for me to confess too.' She frowned

164

as if hoping Catriona wouldn't think the worse of her. 'I suppose I've had the odd bad thought about my ex's Phoebe: buses running her down, lightning striking her, Islamist militants kidnapping her.' She was aware that Catriona was studying her. 'But I wouldn't want her dead, not really. Anyway, I wouldn't give her the satisfaction of hating her that much.' Helen paused for thought. 'That wouldn't be dignified.' She pulled herself upright, as if ascending to high ground. Then she said, 'How about you and Joss? You wouldn't want her dead, would you, not really?'

Bella saw the upturned caravan bucking and heaving. In her feverish state, it seemed to resemble a wild animal straining against the ropes of captivity. A piece of Joss's clothing – flimsy and dull red in colour – blew from the wreckage. Bella imagined the wind as a scavenger, making off with ripped flesh. Her eyes flitted from one scene to another, as if other horrors were waiting unseen, as if vigilance was the only deterrent, the only way of keeping Joss alive. She daren't breathe or blink for fear of some new threat to Joss taking advantage of her inattention. Now Bella watched the huddle of men in front of her car. A face lifted and turned towards her – Grey's. Even through the smears of rain on her windscreen she understood that expression of dread. As soon as she saw it, she shut her eyes. Now warding off evil was a matter of blinding herself. When the car door opened and she felt the rush of wind she kept her eyes closed and offered up a prayer. But when Grey spoke she couldn't stop herself looking and listening. She noticed every little detail, how he crouched beside her, how his face was tight with strain, how her duty was to make it easier for him, as he was trying to do for her. 'What is it, Grey?'

'Bella.' He shook his head. 'It wasn't the wind. Someone did this.'

'Did this?' Bella said. 'Someone?' she added in puzzlement as if such chaos and distress were beyond the power of one person, as if Grey must have been invaded by the derangement which had overtaken everything else. 'All of this, Grey?' she asked. 'Are you sure? How?'

'Bella, the hawser was cut.'

'Oh.'

'It was cut at the base, Bella, where it was fixed to the ground.' He spoke slowly, repeating her name, as if trying to summon her into the present, into reality. 'It wasn't the hawser fraying in the wind against the caravan roof as we thought. It was cut, deliberately. Someone did this, Bella.'

They watched each other: Grey's rheumy, small eyes working out whether Bella understood, Bella wondering what other shocks still had to be revealed.

'What is it?' she coaxed when his eyes avoided hers. 'Grey, tell me.'

'Bella, the caravan door had been secured on the inside with ropes. Joss must have been worried about someone breaking in during the night.'

Bella heard herself exclaim 'oh' and 'oh' again as Grey described how the door had been torn from its hinges – by the wind, by something or someone – and how the rope had been severed. 'Bella, they found traces of blood on the door frame.'

'Oh.'

Grey's large, rough hands took Bella's. 'Either Joss got out by herself or someone took her out. Whoever cut the hawser would have been there when the caravan turned over. In that wind, it would have been instantaneous.'

'Who, Grey?' Bella asked. 'Who? Who could it be? Not one of us?'

She noticed how his eyes still wouldn't engage hers, how he stuttered but didn't answer her question. Instead he told her Alistair had rung the police from the landline at Grant's Croft, and that a senior officer had given instructions on conducting the search. A detective chief inspector and three other officers would be arriving by helicopter as soon as the worst of the storm had passed, and reinforcements, including PC Dyer, would arrive later tomorrow by ferry – weather permitting. Suddenly, he stopped and held Bella's right hand. 'We'll find her,' he said. 'We'll find her.' Alarm crossed his face when he saw Bella's expression.

'Who, Grey?' she insisted. 'Which one of us would have done that to Joss?'

Grey exhaled, a long, deep breath of resignation. 'Ewan's missing, Bella. He wasn't at Grant's Croft when Alistair went there to use the phone. His boat's gone too. Alistair checked.' Grey shook his head, 'I'm sorry. I didn't want to worry you any more than you are already. No one's seen him. No one knows where he is.' Bella realized they were both thinking about history repeating itself, Max now Joss, the nightmare never ending.

'Another of Wheeler's children has gone missing,' Grey said, 'and Ewan's going to be blamed.'

Bella saw in Grey's anguish a conscientious man beginning to wonder if the township had been hiding a killer all this time, if the police and the media had been right, if Wheeler had been justified in his long persecution.

'Ewan,' she stammered. 'No. Not Ewan. No ... It was McGill, don't you see, McGill, after Joss attacked him. It must have been him.' She wasn't sure she believed the accusation but she was in a panic to stop suspicion spreading about Ewan.

She saw Grey's puzzled expression and heard him say, 'I

must be getting back, to help Alistair with the search.' And in the abruptness of his leaving she realized he must have understood her motives. What else could she have said? Panic gripped her. She looked out through the windscreen at Grey's retreating back and felt a lurch in her stomach at having let down Ewan, at having given Grey more grounds for suspicion. Should she call him back, should she confide in him, tell him about Ewan being on Priest's Island with Pinkie? She daren't. Nor could she let him leave like that. She had to do something, but what? In her confusion and worry she became aware of a red pickup ahead of her on the road, of Grey stopping briefly at the driver's window and pointing. The next thing she knew she was leaning into the wind, the rain stinging her face, her skirt becoming heavy and clinging wet to her legs.

She arrived at the pickup when the driver's door opened and Cal McGill got out. She heard herself screaming. 'You did this, *you*. You cut the hawser in revenge.' She jabbed at him with her finger. Two arms closed around her from behind. 'You, Dr McGill. You're to blame. You. You're responsible. See what you've done.' Her legs gave under her and Grey caught her as she fell. 'It wasn't Ewan.' She stared up into the old crofter's face. 'Is Joss dead? Is she?'

19

Cal watched the men's solemn faces and recalled Mr Close's account of the investigation into Max Wheeler's disappearance. The township had put on a public display of grief that the police believed to be an elaborate deception. He wondered if they had been right about that, and if they would think so this time as well. Cal glanced at the clock on the pickup's dashboard: forty minutes already gone. '*Come on.*' The weather was closing in: the sea and land turned brooding, visibility and hope slipping away. In two hours, less, the wind would be so strong the search would have to be abandoned, the risk to other lives and limbs too great.

Cal thought: if not the community in conspiracy against Joss Wheeler, then the elements. What chance did she have? He closed his eyes. '*You're to blame. You. You're responsible.*' Nor was Bella alone in regarding him culpable. By their hostile glances, the township men did too. He'd stood among them after Bella's departure, seeing surly accusation in their eyes. Even if he hadn't cut the hawser, hadn't he caused trouble enough by his unwanted meddling, by stirring up old tensions? In Alistair's chilliness – 'Dr McGill, it'd be better if you remained in your vehicle' – he identified the same quick reflex to blame. It was why Cal still waited. Better not argue when searching for Joss was the priority.

'You got four-wheel drive?' Alistair's head suddenly appeared at Cal's open window.

Cal nodded.

'That thing works, does it?' Alistair spoke out of the side

of his mouth. His head jerked upwards. Still, he didn't look at Cal.

'The spotlight?' Cal said. 'Yes.'

'We'll need this vehicle down at the search area.'

'OK. Tell me where to go.'

'Not you, leave your keys in the ignition. I'll take it down. You're to inform the family, Wheeler and his daughters. You'll be taken to the harbour – your lift's three cars back. The driver's called Helen Jamieson.' Alistair banged on the side of the pickup: end of discussion.

Cal swore.

He did so again as he got into Helen's car.

'Short straw?' Helen said.

'You've heard.'

Helen nodded. 'I've been hearing quite a bit about you – about Bella MacLeod blaming you.'

She started the car and waited for four men to cross the road. Each held a black bin bag which jerked and flapped in the wind. Helen remarked on their resemblance to dogs straining at their leashes. 'The bags are Beacom's idea,' she said. 'He's told Alistair to instruct the search parties to collect up anything that's been blown from the caravan because it won't be around for much longer.'

'Christ, Alistair's slow,' Cal said. 'Why don't you take charge?'

'Beacom doesn't want me to.' Helen pulled out into the road and changed gear. 'Not if Alistair's got things under control. Which he has. He's methodical. What's more he knows the men who are doing the searching and the ground that's being searched. I don't.'

A gust of wind shoved at the car. 'Anyway,' Helen said, 'keeping a car on the road seems to be about the limit of my abilities.' She glanced at Cal: 'What will you say to Wheeler?'

'What can you say to a man who's already lost a son?'

'Will you tell him about the blood in the caravan?'

'I don't know,' Cal said. 'Why don't you come with me?'

'To see Wheeler?'

'Why not?'

'Alistair's asked me to go to the Deep Blue. I've to collect a kettle, coffee, tea, milk and some cups.' She peered through the windscreen. 'I've to leave them before the turn-off to the harbour, a council depot of some kind.'

Cal pointed ahead and to the left. 'Just round the next corner. It's a bit off the road.'

'Apparently it's got a phone, water, a toilet. Beacom's going to base himself there when he arrives. There's a key at the Deep Blue. I've to pick it up from Catriona and leave it in the lock so that Alistair can drop off the bin bags later on.' She paused: 'Interesting young woman, Catriona.'

'In what way?'

'She doesn't like Joss Wheeler very much. In actual fact, she doesn't like her a lot.'

'Why?'

'She thinks Joss stole her boyfriend.'

'What, Ewan Chisholm?'

'Catriona's certain of it.'

'So certain that she'd do something about it?'

'Oh, every night she'd be slashing away at that hawser with a knife. In her dreams she would. In the mornings she must be surprised her bedroom isn't a caravan scrap yard.'

'Only in her dreams?'

'I think so.'

Helen turned down the slip road towards the harbour. The Deep Blue's windows were bright with light. 'Speak of the devil.' Helen looked into the tea room. The women were still sitting at tables, waiting for news. Catriona was standing at the counter. But Cal was looking in the direction of the harbour, at the *Jacqueline*.

Helen noticed the movement of his head. 'I'll wait for you,' she said.

'Thanks,' Cal said.

～

The hood hid her face, sheltering from the wind by the wheelhouse, a cigarette in her right hand.

'Hannah?' Cal asked.

The hood moved. 'No, Chloe.' The cigarette burned red as she put it to her mouth.

'Chloe, I need to speak to your father.'

'He won't want to talk to you.' She flicked the cigarette into the gap between the *Jacqueline*'s hull and the harbour wall, then she lit another. 'You still here?' She dragged on it twice. 'Weren't you told not to bother my father? You're supposed to contact Mr Close.'

Cal pushed past. 'For God's sake, Chloe.'

The girl's disdain turned to fearfulness as Cal went into the wheelhouse. 'Tell him I told you not to disturb him,' she shouted after him, as though concerned she would be blamed.

Cal found Wheeler in the saloon. He was sitting at the end of the small rectangular table. His shoulders were slumped. His hands gripped a half-empty bottle. His head hung over it, swaying with the movement of the whisky and the boat. 'Come back, have you?' He cleared his throat, a cough which extended into a snarl of rage. 'My favourite darling daughter, come back to pity me . . .'

'I'm not Chloe, Mr Wheeler.' He waited for Wheeler to react. 'I've got some bad news about Joss.'

Wheeler's head stopped moving. 'What about her?'

'She's missing. The township's out looking for her. Her caravan overturned in the gale. She was inside when it happened.'

Wheeler started swaying again and Cal waited for him to speak. He noticed the framed photograph on the wall above Wheeler's head. It was of the family on the *Jacqueline*. In happier times, Cal thought. Wheeler and his wife stood at the prow; their children, like half-folded wings, in front and on either side, Max and Chloe by Wheeler, Joss and Hannah by their mother.

'Mr Wheeler,' Cal tried again. 'Do you understand? Joss, your daughter, she's missing.'

The swaying stopped. Wheeler growled, 'I don't have a daughter called Joss.'

The cabin door behind Wheeler opened. Hannah's thin face appeared. 'Are you talking about Joss?' She seemed disorientated, woken from sleep. 'What's happened? What are you saying about her?' She looked from Wheeler to Cal. 'Well, what?'

Cal waited for Wheeler to speak.

'Tell me.' Hannah looked at Cal. 'One of you.'

'I'm sorry, Hannah,' Cal said. 'Joss is missing. There's a search going on.'

He saw Wheeler's hands move. Cal jerked to his right. The bottle struck wood panelling to his left. It fell unbroken on to the bench seat below and made a glugging noise as the remains of the whisky spilled out. 'Get out,' Wheeler shouted. He thrust his head forward. His eyes bulged. 'Get out, damn you. Get out.'

Cal went back through the saloon's double doors. Chloe was inside the wheelhouse. By her shocked expression, he thought she'd overheard.

'What's happened to Joss?'

'Make your father understand, Chloe. Tell him it's serious.

Joss is probably hurt. She's been missing since last night. Her caravan overturned. The township's out looking for her. If she's not found soon . . .'

Chloe gasped, 'How, how did it happen?'

'The hawser was cut. It was deliberate.'

Her eyes closed. Her head shook. 'Why? Why Joss? She was on their side. Why would they want to hurt her?'

'I don't know,' Cal said. 'No one does. The police will be here tomorrow. They'll find out.'

Chloe stared into Cal's face, still searching for an answer.

Cal said, 'Tell Hannah, will you? Tell your father.'

Chloe smiled weakly. 'My father doesn't care, not about any of us really, not at all about Joss, not since she went to live in the township.'

Going back across the parking area between the harbour and the Deep Blue, Cal wondered if the Wheeler family had ever been happy. He said the same to Helen when he got into her car.

'How did Wheeler take the news?'

'He said he didn't have a daughter called Joss.'

'You're not serious?'

Bella wished Catriona would go to bed. It was night, probably ten o'clock, and here she was back in Bella's room. Instead of saying anything, Bella kept her eyes closed and her breathing slow and rhythmic. She was alert for every movement Catriona made. When her niece put her face close to hers, Bella felt the lightest touch of warmth against her cheek. When Catriona stood up, Bella heard the rustle of her clothes. When she stepped back, one footfall, another, Bella followed Catriona by the creak of the floor. But when

Catriona was still, when she stood and watched, Bella found the pretence of sleep difficult. Not only did her lids begin to twitch and her breathing become irregular and fast (or so it seemed to Bella) but her mind started to race. Was Catriona concerned for her – after confronting McGill she'd become faint and rather confused – or was she troubled about Ewan? Was that the reason she was lingering?

What more could Bella say to the girl other than the re-assurance she'd given her earlier?

'It's not true what they're saying about Ewan, is it?' she'd asked Bella as she put a cup of tea on her bedside table. 'He wouldn't be involved, would he?'

'Of course not,' Bella replied. Then, in case Catriona thought Bella knew something, she added, 'Don't we both know Ewan well enough to be sure he wouldn't do anything violent like that?'

Catriona nodded.

'Well then.'

'How do you know Ewan's not involved?' she asked quiet-ly when she returned to Bella's room. But Bella couldn't answer. Nor could she lie. Pretending to sleep was the only deception possible while making silent declarations to Catriona, affirmations of love. While Bella willed her mental messages to vault the space between them, Catriona took a step away, another and another. Bella listened – now she heard the click of the door closing and she opened her eyes. Her breath came in gasps after the effort of keeping it slow and rhythmic while Catriona was close by. She made a prom-ise. In the morning, she would hug Catriona and say aloud everything she'd thought in silence. How much she loved her. How precious she was.

Bella rearranged her pillows, sat up and watched the night sky. The wind chased black clouds fringed in white past her window – they looked like priests fleeing from the devil. Bella repeated the bargain she had struck with herself. Until she knew Joss and Ewan were safe, she wouldn't sleep. She would watch over them. Though, in all honesty, what choice did she have but to stay awake? Bargain or no bargain, her eyes would be open wide, as they had been when she watched the caravan, when she saw it bucking and rearing.

An hour passed, another and another. Bella got out of bed, put on her dressing gown and went to the landing. She looked for a light under Catriona's door. Seeing none, she allowed herself some small relief from her guilt. Perhaps, by feigning sleep, a responsibility had been lifted from her niece, allowing her to rest. At the bottom of the stairs, she removed her coat from its hook and went to the front door. She waited for a lull in the wind before opening and closing it quietly behind her. The wet and cold made her shiver, a shudder of fear for Joss. Would she have had time to put on her boots or even a coat? Inside the tea room, she turned on the lights. Instead of the chaos she expected, it was as neat and orderly as if she had tidied it herself. Everything was as it should be; tables cleared and wiped, clean napkins and cutlery on trays at the counter, ready for that morning. The kitchen was the same, nothing out of place. The pans were stacked, the teapots upside down on the drainer.

A single sheet of paper was on the table, a pen on top as if to prevent it, too, blowing away.

Everything's been tidied away and ready for tomorrow, love you, Catriona. PS Helen helped, a lot!

The writing went smeary as tears filled up Bella's eyes.

Helen, she wondered: who was Helen? Of course, the chalet! Bella had quite forgotten they had a guest. She boiled the kettle, made herself a mug of instant coffee and went back to the tea room. After turning out the lights she sat at a table by the large window. She stared unblinking into the darkness until dawn, when she hunted the emerging landscape. Her eyes flicked and flashed from place to place, going wherever light began to fall, as though by willpower alone it was possible to fashion a happy ending to this drama. Believe and it will be so, she told herself. Believe with every fibre, every muscle and every thought. She imagined Joss stumbling into view, making her way towards the tea room and to Bella.

There!

There!

Someone was there! Joss!

She hurried across the tea room floor, her legs and feet so cold they were numb apart from a pain in her toes. From the coat hook by the back door, she removed a pair of binoculars and returned to the window. Where was she? Bella couldn't see any movement or any shape that looked like a person. Had she imagined Joss? Her hands shook when she lifted the binoculars to her face. She fiddled with the focus.

There!

There she was!

Bella let out another cry of elation followed by one of disappointment. Her arms fell as though the binoculars had become too heavy. She sank into her chair and watched the moving figure now silhouetted against the sea: not Joss but McGill.

20

Past the harbour, the shoreline changed. From open bays, it became gap-toothed with deep inlets. Instead of waves breaking on gravel or sandy beaches, they dashed themselves against jutting headlands. Each impact was like a detonation. To Cal, it seemed as though he walked among a battery of guns; now this one firing, now that. Their reports roared in his ears. Salt spray stung his nostrils and eyes. For respite from the wind's astringent blasts, he cupped his hands over his nose and narrowed his eyes to slits while he hunted exposed rocks and ledges in case Joss was already lying broken-backed and discarded. Then, before moving on, he searched the breaking waves, expecting some part of her, an arm or a leg, to breach the surface and to flop lifelessly into view. Walking between inlets, he turned his left shoulder to the wind and let his eyes stray inland, if only for relief from the storm.

On one of these times, he saw a helicopter. It flew low, appearing to clip the horizon before dipping out of sight: Detective Chief Inspector Beacom's arrival. On another, wondering if the upturned caravan was yet in view, he looked to the north-west and saw a group of men. They were three hundred metres away and standing so close that Cal supposed they were discussing where next to search and using each other for shelter while they decided. He carried on to the next inlet, a gash of heaving sea, and only when he was climbing on to the next promontory did he see the men again. They had not moved and now that he was closer he noticed something familiar about their manner, how erect they were despite the ferocity of the conditions (why didn't they crouch rather than stand?), how agitated they seemed to be.

Cal had seen similar behaviour before. Whenever he found a body and his clients had insisted on joining him in the search, there would be that same instinct to stand apart, the living finding reassurance in the living, as if putting death on watch and keeping it at some remove delayed its next visit. And in the men's faces, as Cal approached, he saw that same mixture of awe and fear, as though the discovery of a body on a beach, or here on a barren landscape, posed a particular threat that one found in a house did not, as if it was unnatural, disturbing. Instead of going up to the men, he went to where they had been looking, an area of grass and rock among heather. The colours were pale yellows, greens and black, similar to Joss's clothes, so it took Cal a few moments before he saw her.

She was lying on her front, away from him, her body shaped by the scoop of ground on which she had fallen. Her neck was stretched, her blonde hair still tied, her arms splayed in front of her, as if she had stumbled and attempted to break her fall. Cal went closer and saw a cut on her shoulder, a rip in her green shirt and bruised flesh showing through the tears in her black jeans – wounds inflicted by the caravan, he thought; all that sharp metal. He imagined the terror with which she must have fled from one assailant – whoever cut the hawser – only to encounter another, a merciless and cold wind. No one, not even the hardiest of islanders, could have survived in so few clothes. He pictured her falling, frightened, weak, soaked through and frozen. She wouldn't have had the strength or the will to lift herself. Even if she had, she would have fallen again. If not here, ten, twenty, thirty metres further on: there was no escape; not dressed like that, barefoot, in that storm, that night.

Cal noticed her fingers. They were bent and shaped like claws, just as they had been when she raked his face. He saw how her nails had scored the ground. If that was her last act, it was one of fight, not exhaustion. If she had strength, why hadn't she got up? He knelt beside her and began talking while he looked for other clues. It was what he did when he found bodies on the shore. Usually, he would introduce himself, describe his work, his methods, and say how long and hard had been the search, how missed the person had been, and how pleased the family would be at the prospect of reunion. To Joss, he said, 'Joss, we've been looking for you. Everyone's been worried.' Then, leaning across her torso to inspect her other side, he put his hands close to her and felt a sticky wetness that was neither rain nor sodden earth.

His fingers were stained dark red with blood. Cal looked where his hand had been, and where her shirt had snagged on heather he saw exposed flesh. There was a gash four centimetres long. The rim was red and purple. Cal glanced at the men, who seemed to shrink away because they too had made the same discovery and understood its meaning. One by one, they looked into the heather closer to them and Cal saw the knife. It was wooden-handled with a rusted blade that had been worn away by sharpening and use. At first Cal noticed how clean of blood it was – the rain had washed it. Then, when he went closer, he saw the initials carved on to the handle, DG.

'Who's DG?' he shouted.

None of the men replied. They shrank from him again and Cal thought he knew why.

'Donald Grant,' Cal said. 'DG: does that stand for Donald

Grant?' The men stared back blankly. 'He was Ewan Chisholm's uncle, wasn't he?' Cal asked. 'Well, wasn't he? Can't any of you speak?'

After despatching two men to the road, to find DCI Beacom, he waited beside Joss. He sat at arm's length from her, with his back to the wind as well as the four remaining men, and talked to her again. He said he was sorry about 'that flare-up' between them outside the Deep Blue. He wished they could have met in different circumstances. He told her about Beacom and the case they had worked on before. 'A good policeman; saved my life,' Cal said. 'If anyone can find out what happened to Max and who attacked you, he will.' He told her too about Helen Jamieson and her undercover role, how she had won the confidence of Catriona and how the immediate puzzle concerned Ewan Chisholm. 'The chief suspect in your brother's disappearance,' Cal said, 'and now, the chief suspect in your murder too.' Not only had he gone missing on the night her caravan turned over but she'd been killed by a knife belonging to his dead uncle. 'But I'm sure he was on Priest's Island so I don't see how it could have been him.' He stopped speaking as though giving her the opportunity to tell him who had stabbed her.

A voice behind him said, 'The dead don't talk, Cal, more's the pity.'

Cal turned to see a slight man with a sharp face and small mouth standing and looking at Joss's body. He wore a blue baseball cap, a flapping raincoat, a hood and black wellington boots. Cal nodded: acknowledgement as well as agreement. DCI Richard Beacom squinted into the wind, the direction from which Joss had come. 'Have you ever had one of those nightmares?' he asked, turning back to Cal. 'It's dark and there's a storm and you're running, running for your life.'

Although Beacom said, 'Don't go away', Cal would have stayed anyway. It was too soon to go, to leave Joss. This feeling, if hard to express, wasn't unfamiliar. Cal experienced it whenever he found a body. Sometimes, he wondered whether his own subconscious didn't force him to stay, whether a hidden fear of dying alone was the cause. Was this his way of stacking the odds in his favour of having people around him when it was his turn? But mostly he thought the body itself exerted the pull. It wouldn't let him go. It wanted him there and took the decision away from him, not just whether to stay but when to go. That was his common experience of bodies that had suffered violent deaths. In Cal's work, that was them all. The bodies pulled him to them and then, suddenly, they didn't, like a gravity field being switched off. When the release came it was total. There was no indecision, no lingering doubt. Cal could and did walk away, always. It was as if the body had no more use for him. Then, just as it had been wrong to leave before, it would be wrong to stay. Where each body was different was in the time that Cal was detained, from an hour to as much as a whole night. The body, in that case a child, released him when it was daylight again.

Though Cal didn't believe in any god or an afterlife, he had come to think that a person's spirit might live on for a while after death and if that required him to stay close, while the process of dying was completed, body and soul, he was prepared to assist. Anyway, it wasn't as if he felt he had a choice. In that respect, he disagreed with Beacom. In a manner of speaking, bodies could talk and Joss Wheeler was asking – no, insisting – that he stayed.

A uniformed policewoman was at one side of Joss, that closest to the road, Cal at the other, towards the sea. While he waited for his release, he watched the comings and goings of the township's inhabitants; men who had been searching the night before and that morning. They approached in ones or twos, their heads bowed until they were close enough to see the flap of Joss's clothing or the dark straw colour of her wet hair against the grasses that had been drained almost white by the Hebridean winter. Then, they shook their heads or mouthed a prayer and departed. None lingered. None ventured close enough for the policewoman to warn them away. They stood apart, each stopping a similar distance from the body. If Joss would not let him go, not yet, neither would she let them close, only near enough to witness the consequence of their community's hostility towards a young woman and no further.

Chloe and Hannah Wheeler arrived to a different choreography. Instead of walking from the road, they were brought by Land Rover. Instead of drab greys and greens, the neutral tones of the township men, the Wheeler girls were dressed brightly, a red anorak for Chloe, electric blue for Hannah. The nautical wardrobe, Cal supposed, of two young women in shock and ill prepared for death. In another way, too, they differed from the previous visitors. The township men had walked slowly, respectfully, looked and gone away. Chloe and Hannah approached with faltering resolution. Only when they became used to seeing their sister's body from one point did they draw closer. To begin with they held hands but, after, they folded into each other, the ordeal too much for them singly. The closer they approached, the tighter they held on so that when they sank into the grass as close as Beacom would allow, they seemed to be conjoined. From inside her anorak, Hannah removed a framed photograph. Together, using one hand each, they propped it against a stone to face Joss. Cal recognized it from the *Jacqueline*'s saloon and he wondered again at the Wheeler family's habit of using photographs as memorials – Max Wheeler's smiling face in the ruined chapel, now this. Did the photographs lie, were the memories false? Cal questioned again whether this was ever a happy family. While the sisters sobbed and comforted each other, Beacom stood by Cal. 'Wheeler wouldn't come.' Beacom spoke from the side of his mouth so the sisters couldn't hear. 'Can you believe that?'

Cal said, 'He told me last night he didn't consider Joss his daughter.'

Beacom didn't react and Cal added, 'Mind you, he was drunk, on whisky. He threw the bottle at me.'

'He's sober today – no excuses.'

When Chloe and Hannah got to their feet, Beacom made to leave. 'I'll pick you up on the road. We need to talk.'

'You might as well put a notice in the Deep Blue and tell everyone I'm working with you,' Cal told him.

'Or,' Beacom said, 'that we're just doing our job.'

'How?'

'From what I hear we'll find your skin under Joss Wheeler's fingernails. That's motive. Didn't you find the caravan overturned? Doesn't that make you a suspect, someone we have to eliminate from our inquiries? Apparently some people in the township think you're guilty.'

Beacom followed Chloe and Hannah. Cal said to the body, 'Who did this, Joss? Who?'

He didn't ask again or stay any longer because there wasn't that pull. Joss had released him.

Beacom's makeshift headquarters was the size of a large garage. Inside was a pile of grit, bags of salt and, against a wall, half a dozen shovels. A sign at the entrance announced that it was a property owned by the 'Community Roads

Department'. Another inside warned of the danger of letting engines idle with the depot door closed. Laid out on the concrete floor were the contents of the searchers' bin bags: two white plastic cups, a piece of orange fabric, the ripped pages of a book that had become translucent in the rain, a towel, a jersey, a pillow, a box of matches, the torn cover of a magazine, assorted broken fragments of the caravan's bodywork, a strip of chrome, a sock, a bottle of shampoo, an empty carton of milk, a black bra, a sodden and misshapen box of tissues. 'The usual detritus,' Beacom said. He sounded disappointed at the familiar routines of murder even in so remote a place, at the poking and lifting through the victim's effects. He bent down: 'Apart from this.' It was a piece of lined paper, a crease where it had once been folded, and wet through. It was torn on its left side. Cal bent too, to read the faded writing.

Joss, I'm sorry. It won't happen again. Ewan.

There was a phone number underneath.

Beacom said, 'That's the landline for Grant's Croft, Ewan Chisholm's place.'

He stood straight, and Cal did too. 'Here's the difficulty,' Beacom said. 'There's a young woman lying dead out there. She's been stabbed with a knife that bears the initials DG – Donald Grant. Detective Sergeant Jamieson has been told by Catriona Mackinnon that Ewan Chisholm had the hots for Joss Wheeler. "Joss, I'm sorry. It won't happen again." What was Ewan referring to? A row? Had he lost his temper? Maybe she'd turned him down and he'd been violent, slapped her. What if it happened again? What if Joss had told him where to go? Wheeler's oldest child: imagine the effect on Ewan and that grievance of his about Priest's Island being stolen from him. What if he thought she was his chance of being able to have sheep on the island again and suddenly it was snatched away? The psychologist that assessed him as part of the investigation into Max's disappearance found Ewan had a potential for violence and that a moment of stress, particularly if it involved the Wheelers or Priest's Island, could be a trigger.'

Cal said, 'Except . . .'

'Except,' Beacom interrupted, 'there's that difficulty I mentioned. You say he spent the night on Priest's Island.'

'I think he did.'

'All of it? You saw him?'

'No, not once it was dark.'

'So you didn't *see* him?'

'Not all night. But he was there. He must have been.'

'So, for most of the night you didn't actually set eyes on him?'

'No.'

'He could have crossed the sound, killed Joss Wheeler and returned.'

'The sea was too rough,' Cal said. 'He'd never have made it in the dark. Not even crossing it once, let alone twice . . . Anyway, his boat hadn't moved by the morning. He'd pulled it up the night before. It was still in the same place at daylight.'

'And you'd say so in court?'

'If I had to.'

Beacom grimaced, a police officer preparing for trouble. 'Here's my problem, Cal. The first ferry from the mainland will have police reinforcements but also the media. They'll rip me apart if the killer hasn't been arrested by the time they get here. I've put in a request for the first ferry to be commandeered by the police and for the media to be held on the mainland and briefed there for a day or two, until I've been able to interview everyone in the township and carry out searches.'

He shook his head.

'No go?' Cal asked.

'No. After the fiasco over the Max Wheeler case, all the damage to the police reputation, the chief constable is concerned about the perception if we try to keep the media away.'

'They'll accuse you of a cover-up . . .'

'Yeah.' Beacom swore. 'I've got till this evening then this island's going to become a fucking circus, with media everywhere. The population's going to double. I've got four officers – myself, Willy Clarke, a DI, who's out searching for Chisholm, and two constables to guard the body and the Wheelers. There's Helen, but I want her to stay under cover.' He looked at his watch. 'That's six, maybe seven hours, if the forecast's right and the ferry sails on time. Who gives a damn about transparency and media access when there's a murderer on the loose and a family being picked off one by one?'

'Did you say that to the chief constable?'

'Don't get me started on that man.' Beacom walked across the depot and back, his chin on his chest, deep in thought. 'So, let's stay with Ewan Chisholm. Say sometime during the night when you were asleep . . .'

'I didn't sleep much.'

'But you did sleep?'

Cal shrugged. 'On and off.'

'How close were you to the boat?'

'Once Ewan and his companion had gone inland I moved further away. I didn't want them coming back in the night and falling over me.'

'Could you have heard if Ewan had taken the boat?'

'In that wind, I don't know.'

'So, for the sake of argument let's say Ewan did cross the sound during the night.' Beacom held up his hand to stop Cal's objection. 'He went to Joss Wheeler's caravan but he found she'd barricaded herself in. She wouldn't let him in, so, in anger, he cut the hawser. When the caravan turned over, she managed to escape. That's why she ran in the direction she did, *away* from Grant's Croft even though it was the nearest house. She ran towards the Deep Blue because she was running *away* from Ewan. He killed her and crossed back over to Priest's Island.' Beacom threw up his hands and pretended to be Ewan: 'Who, me? Kill Joss Wheeler? I was on Priest's Island. And I have a witness.'

'He didn't know I was going to be there.'

'I mean his companion.'

'Ewan put on a balaclava in the morning when he went to look for the guy. Why would he do that?'

'He was cold.'

'Or they didn't know each other and wanted to keep it that way. If that's the case, Ewan doesn't have much of an alibi.'

Beacom screwed up his face. 'The knife worries me too.' He thought again. 'Let's stay with Ewan being the killer. OK, so Joss pulled away from him with the knife still sticking in her. She ran off and it fell out, or she pulled it out, just before she died. He didn't run after her because he couldn't see her in the dark.' Beacom kicked at the wall. 'Fuck. Why would he use a knife inscribed with his uncle's initials? He has a croft. He'll have other knives.' He kicked again. 'So who, if it's not him?'

'The ex-girlfriend Catriona?'

Beacom tried it out. 'She kills her rival and takes revenge on her ex-boyfriend by stabbing Joss with his uncle's knife and leaving it behind. Well?'

'It's possible.'

'I'd say it was.' Beacom stared at Cal. 'But why did she tell Helen about Ewan breaking up with her because he fancied Joss? That doesn't make sense if Catriona's the murderer. Why would she let it be known she had a motive?'

The chief inspector paced back and forth. 'It's one or other of them.' He stopped. 'This is what we'll do . . . When we pick up Ewan we won't tell him we know he was on Priest's Island that night. We'll see if he tells us.' Still thinking aloud, Beacom said, 'Yes, that's it. We'll pretend we don't know. We'll arrest Ewan and hold him as the suspect for murder. We'll do what the township expects us to do. Meanwhile Helen will stick close to Catriona – and we'll see what happens next. We'll have a conspiracy of our own.'

For a while neither spoke. Then Cal glanced at Beacom. 'By the way, I don't want your money.'

Beacom nodded. 'Helen mentioned it, did she? I thought she might.'

'For the record, I should have been told at the start.'

'Would you have agreed to work for Wheeler if you had?'

Cal shook his head.

'You owed me.'

'Yeah,' Cal said.

21

Bella had to be doing, had to be busy. Shock took her that way. She couldn't sit. She couldn't be on her own. Nor could she be spoken to. Staying polite was the hardest thing. The expressions of concern as she went around the tea room were getting to her. Was she sure she was well enough, strong enough? Shouldn't she be in bed resting? Couldn't someone else help Catriona behind the counter? At every table some-one or other mentioned Joss's murder, how shaken and upset Bella must be. Her reactions varied from gratitude to cold civility. Eventually, her irritation showed. 'Isn't there enough to worry about without me being added to the list?' she said tartly. 'Anyway, I'd prefer to be working and busy than doing nothing and fretting.'

Still they wouldn't take the hint.

Later, she snapped back. She couldn't help herself. She shouted, 'Stop looking at me, stop talking to me!' The tea room went pin-quiet. 'Please.' At least her voice was calmer now. 'Please, can't you let me go about the tea room without commenting? Can't I just get on and do my work?' When she noticed the shock on their faces, she added, 'Sorry. You mustn't mind me. I'm upset about Joss.'

Of course, the cure was worse than the disease. Instead of people staring at her less, they did so more, though warily, when they thought she couldn't see them. Instead of talking to her – since they expected their heads to be bitten off if they did – they worried about her when she was out of earshot. It all became too much, so she escaped to her office. The silence there made her even more ill at ease, that and the lack of room to move around. Tears filled her eyes and her hands shook. What a disaster it all was, so much misery and sadness. Why hadn't she taken Joss in the first night of the storm? So many regrets and worries crowded in she began to feel dizzy. Just when she needed to think straight she found she could hardly think at all. One moment she imagined Joss running frightened in the dark, the knife plunging into her side, blood gushing from the wound; the next she felt weak at the talk of Ewan being her killer. Where was he? If only she could speak to him. Should she go to the police and tell them about Pinkie, about Ewan taking him to Priest's Island? Should she confess the lesser crime to exonerate him from the bigger? She didn't know what to do. She'd interfered too much already, taking both Joss and Ewan under her wing. Look where that had got them.

Bella was so muddled even she wondered whether Ewan was guilty. Everyone else thought so, which made her stop and think. She'd been wrong about so much else. Had she been wrong about Ewan? At first, she batted the notion away. Wasn't McGill a more likely suspect? Why didn't anyone else think so? Of course it wasn't Ewan. At the time of Joss's death he'd been with Pinkie. Only Bella knew that. But her conviction slipped the more she turned the last two days over in her mind. Ewan was expert at navigating the sound, even in the dark and in bad weather. What if he'd returned to the township during the night? What if he'd killed Joss and gone back unseen to Priest's Island? If Bella told the police about Pinkie's boat trip, would that be enough to clear Ewan of Joss's murder? Perhaps not, and she might just be guaranteeing a jail sentence for Pinkie and a day in court for herself. There was nothing to be gained by confessing. She should wait to see what transpired when Ewan reappeared, if he reappeared.

The scrap of paper Alistair had found blowing away from the upturned caravan had also unnerved Bella. The tea room had been agog at Ewan's message to Joss. Obviously, something had happened between them. Why else would he have apologized to her in a note? Bella had never known Ewan put pen to paper, so it must have been important. Whatever it was, it must have been bad.

If only she could look into Ewan's eyes. If only she could talk to him. Of course Ewan didn't kill her. What was she thinking? Oh dear. Oh dear.

'Stop it,' she said out loud. 'Stop it.' She was becoming hysterical. In such a mood, she wasn't any help to herself or to Ewan. Taking a deep breath, she decided to return to the tea room. The distraction of other people, even their unwanted attention, was preferable to spending more time on her own.

Just as she was steeling herself, Catriona came into the office. She started to cry as soon as she closed the door. Bella held out her hands and, when Catriona took them, Bella said, 'You've been so good. Everyone's said so. You've worked so hard, done everything right.'

Catriona knelt and rested her head against her aunt's knees.

Bella stroked her hair. 'I'm so proud of you, Catriona. Just like your mother, calm in a crisis.'

Catriona looked up into Bella's face. 'Ewan didn't do it, did he, Auntie Bella?'

'Of course he didn't.'

'Then where is he?' Her voice rose with emotion. 'Why isn't he here?'

Bella put her hands over Catriona's. 'Perhaps he's just gone somewhere in his boat and got caught by the storm. There'll be an explanation. There's bound to be.'

'But what?'

'I can't say, darling.' She ran the back of one of her fingers down Catriona's right cheek, wiping away a tear. 'I wish I could.'

For a while, neither spoke. Then Bella said, 'You didn't take to Joss, did you?'

Catriona shook her head.

'I thought not.'

'Ewan liked her. That's why we broke up.'

Bella let out a long sigh. 'And you'd think in a small place like this you'd know everything that was going on.' She kissed Catriona's forehead. 'I'm sorry. I didn't realize.' She closed her eyes. 'You won't tell anyone else.'

Catriona mumbled, 'No.'

'I mean no one, Catriona.'

'Not even if it helps Ewan?'

'It won't.'

'Why not?'

Bella watched her niece, as though making up her mind to confide in her. 'Joss was too messed up to have any kind of relationship – she said so to me a number of times. She didn't want a boyfriend.'

'I didn't know.'

'She'd have turned Ewan down. Perhaps that's why he wrote the note because he'd reacted badly. It won't help Ewan if the police know he liked her.'

Catriona buried her head into the folds of Bella's apron.

'Say nothing,' Bella insisted. 'Promise me.'

'It just doesn't seem fair,' Catriona said. 'What they're saying about Ewan.'

'I know.'

Bella found a paper handkerchief in her sleeve and blew her nose. 'I haven't cried so much for . . . years.' She almost said since Frances, Catriona's mother, died. 'I'm not going to be able to get back through that door into the tea room with all those people looking at me unless you come too.'

'OK,' Catriona said.

'Here, dry your eyes.' She gave Catriona another handkerchief. 'And let's go before we change our minds.'

As it happened, she was wrong. Only one person looked up: Helen Jamieson from the chalet. While Bella went to table one to start taking orders, she noticed Catriona going to table six, where the Jamieson woman was sitting. They exchanged a few words before Catriona returned to the counter.

'What was that about?' Bella asked.

'What?' Catriona replied. 'Oh, Helen, she wants a skinny latte.'

Although Bella was pleased that Catriona seemed to have made a friend, she was also uneasy. Who was Helen Jamieson? All she seemed to do was hang around the tea room, listening in, and go for runs. The thought was interrupted by Mary-Anne saying in a loud voice, 'Look, they've stopped moving.' Everyone turned and Mary-Anne pointed at the bushes on the bank above the harbour. 'Look,' she said.

'What?' Bella asked.

'The bushes,' Mary-Anne said. 'They're still. The wind's gone.'

There was a pause while everyone looked.

'So it has,' Bella said.

The tea room became noisy with similar exchanges and exclamations. Why had no one noticed? How caught up in their worries they'd been. How distracted. Afterwards, the stillness outside seemed to affect the mood inside. If anyone talked it was in an undertone or in whispers. Mary-Anne muttered a prayer, another one, while Bella went to stand by the window. 'The calm before the next storm,' she said.

Heads nodded in understanding. By evening the ferry would be operating again. By nightfall the township would be invaded. The parking area between the Deep Blue and the harbour would be where the media gathered, as it had been the last time. For a while no one would be safe from the prying of police or reporters.

'Whatever happens,' Bella said in a louder voice, 'we're a community. We're stronger when we stick together. That's what we did when Max disappeared. That's what we'll do again. If you're worried about anything, come here. We'll open late until this is over. Between six and seven every night will be for residents only.' A murmur of gratitude was followed by relief that the tea room would again be the township's evening rallying place in a time of crisis and that its matriarch's strength had been restored.

Helen apologized. She thought she would never be able to get away. Ina Gillies had been telling her stories about the township — 'Like a story for every one of the eighty-four years she's been alive! I'm not exaggerating.' She glanced at Catriona, who was standing against the tea room door frame, holding a cigarette and staring dismally at the harbour wall and at a policeman keeping guard on the Wheelers inside the *Jacqueline*. 'What is it, Catriona?' Helen touched the girl's arm. 'Tell me. You said you had something to show me.'

Catriona removed a folded sheet of paper from the pocket of her apron and handed it to Helen.

'Can I?' Helen opened what seemed to be a page from an exercise pad. It was covered with pencil lines. She looked up, asking for an explanation.

'See the three crosses,' Catriona said.

'Yes, yes, I see them.'

'The top one is Ewan. The two at either side of the bottom are me and Joss.' Catriona waited before carrying on. She let Helen study them again. 'See how many marks there are here.' She pointed at the neat lines between Ewan's cross and Joss's. 'And how few there are here.' She pointed at the left-hand side of the page, between her cross and Ewan's. 'Recently, Ewan only hung out in the tea room when Joss was here. I kept a log of how often he looked at her and how often he looked at me. Just to know where I was. Sometimes he'd look at me, but he'd look at Joss six, seven times more often. Most of the time he looked at me he was just checking to see if I was watching him.'

'Oh, I'm sorry, Catriona,' Helen sympathized. 'It's hard when you catch them out.'

'But I didn't, that's just it.' Catriona closed her eyes and tears squeezed out between her lids.

Helen studied the page in case she had missed something. 'If he'd been my boyfriend, I'd have thought the same as you. I'd have wanted an explanation. Any girl would.'

Catriona breathed in deeply. Her whole body lifted and fell with the effort. 'Joss didn't want a boyfriend. She was too messed up. Auntie Bella told me.' She stared at Helen.

'Did Ewan know?'

'What does it matter? He didn't cheat on me.'

Helen thought the girl was clutching at straws. 'Catriona, cheating doesn't only mean going to bed with someone.' She held up the page. 'By the look of it, he wanted to cheat. Isn't that what matters?'

Catriona's face was puffy, her eyes red.

'You poor girl,' Helen said. 'You're miserable. I'd have done the same as you. I'd have asked Ewan to explain himself.'

Catriona closed her eyes as if she couldn't bear to think about it.

Helen continued, 'What do you think happened, that Ewan tried it on with Joss again, and she rejected him and he lost his temper?'

Catriona didn't reply.

'Did he ever lose his temper with you?'

She shook her head.

'Never? Were there ever times when you said you didn't feel like it – sex, I mean – when you said no?'

This time, a nod.

'And that didn't make him angry?'

The head-shake again.

'Do you think he might have been angry with Joss if she said no?'

Catriona spoke in a whisper. 'I don't, but everyone will say she was prettier than me and he wanted her more.' Her voice trembled. 'But Ewan isn't like that.' Saying it aloud used up the last of her self-control. 'Even if he did love Joss and not me,' she wailed.

Helen touched Catriona's hand. 'You're a good friend to him, aren't you?'

The door opened behind her and Helen found she was being pushed aside. Bella put her arms round Catriona. 'What's wrong, my darling? What's wrong?' She glowered at Helen. *What did you do to her? What did you say?*

Helen replied coolly, 'She's upset over that young man everyone's been talking about, Ewan Chisholm.'

But Bella wasn't listening. She was fussing around Catriona, taking her inside.

~

Isobel Macrae, returning from the heritage centre at the north of the island, brought news of the mainland ferry. It was already at sea, she said, aghast. The tea room reacted with similar shock, as though something precious had been taken away. 'Two hours before its scheduled departure!' Isobel exclaimed. 'When has that happened before?' No longer would the invasion of police and media begin in three or three and a half hours; it might be outside the Deep Blue in one. Not even a last afternoon of being able to look out on to the harbour and pretend that nothing much had changed.

Mary-Anne waited for Isobel to sit beside her before expressing her opinion. She spoke into her friend's ear. 'The captain will have been under terrible pressure to sail.' She looked nervously around, wondering whether her habit of trying to understand the other person's point of view, her Christian duty, was on this occasion misplaced. On every face was the same expression of apprehension. 'Oh,' Mary-Anne said in a tremulous voice. Now she understood. 'Oh.' Even the ferry company was against them now. Was anyone left on their side?

She was about to ask Isobel that question when Bella clapped twice and called for silence.

'Would you like the tea room to close early before the police and media arrive? Everyone here is welcome to remain inside.' She looked around. 'A last afternoon to ourselves, well, what do you think?'

There were noises of appreciation at Bella's suggestion but Grey rose unsteadily to his feet and gave voice to another point of view. 'We can't expect Bella to turn away customers. None of us wants these people but they're on their way. Who knows, they might leave in a day or two. The Deep Blue is important to the township but we spend little enough here. Bella has a business to run. If she stays open, then someone will benefit.'

'Aye, it'll be the only windfall that'll do any of us any good,' Alistair put in.

There was a murmur of agreement. 'Well,' Bella said, glancing around. 'Are you certain? That's what we'll do then.'

It was like waiting for the arrival of bad news, no one being able to think of anything else but no one wanting to discuss it either. Ina took advantage of a gap in conversation to ask Helen, 'Have I told you about Max Wheeler's soul returning to Priest's Island three months after he disappeared? I haven't? Well, it was brought ashore by a seabird called a storm petrel. And, wait till you hear what my Neil always used to say about storm petrels . . .'

Fortunately for Helen, Ina was distracted by the arrival of the first cars. There were three of them followed by two vans, then two more. Soon there were two dozen vehicles of different shapes and sizes including six, Isobel counted, with satellite dishes. Police, photographers and reporters milled about. A flow of strangers made their way to the tea room, starting with a woman radio reporter. Ordering coffee, she held her microphone towards Bella. 'How worried are you,' she asked, 'about the killer being free?'

Bella replied, 'You'll get nothing out of me except this.' She put a take-away cup of coffee on the counter.

'What about anyone else?' The woman surveyed the tea room tables. 'I mean, is there anyone here who would like to say sorry?'

'Sorry for what?' Bella said sharply.

'Why,' the reporter looked at Bella as if she was simple, 'for protecting a murderer for five years, for making it possible for him to kill again. Don't you feel guilty? In your shoes, I know I would. Don't you think an apology is owed?'

Bella pursed her lips and watched two more reporters going from table to table. 'Come on, just a few words,' one said in exasperation to the whole tea room. 'Didn't you know he was violent?' At every table, heads went down or backs were turned. 'Do you sleep at night knowing what he's done, knowing you've protected him?'

'I get it,' the radio reporter said to Bella, 'the natives are hostile.' Picking up her cup of coffee she went to the door.

For half an hour or so that was the pattern of Bella's exchanges with new arrivals: sparring at the counter around orders for coffee and cake. When respite came, Bella crossed to the window to check what was happening outside. The reporters and cameramen were waiting in a group. Although they were talking, they were also glancing towards the slip road. 'What do you think's going on?' Bella asked Isobel, who had quietly been taking everything in.

'They're expecting something,' Isobel said.

'Yes, but what?' Bella replied. 'What could it be?'

'*Who* could it be?' said Isobel as she caught sight of a man walking down the road. He was small and wore black wellington boots and an olive-green raincoat that appeared too long and too big for him. A blue baseball cap covered the top half of his face. 'Who's that?' Isobel asked when the reporters began to move towards him.

Grey, who was the other side of Bella, replied, 'That's Detective Chief Inspector Beacom.'

This exchange was followed by the sound of chairs being pushed back. The tea room's regulars went to stand at the window. 'Well,' Isobel said, 'he doesn't look like a chief inspector or even a policeman, come to think of it. He looks more like one of that lot.' Everyone watched as Beacom held up his hand to the approaching reporters. Microphones were extended towards him. Cameras flashed. 'He's talking to them,' said Mary-Anne.

'No, he's going to the *Jacqueline*,' said Isobel as Beacom kept on walking.

'Something must have happened,' Mary-Anne said, offering up a silent prayer.

When Beacom reappeared after what seemed an age, the media again gathered round him. As before, his hand went up. He said a few words. 'What's going on?' Ina demanded.

Beacom pointed towards the Deep Blue. 'He's coming in here,' Isobel said.

Everyone turned to the door.

'It's Ewan.' Bella's hands went to her face. 'They must have found him.'

'You don't mean he's dead, do you?' Mary-Anne gasped.

The door opened and there was a distinct movement in the tea room air: a recoil, a pulling back, or shrinking away, as Mary-Anne would later describe it. Beacom stopped after a few steps inside. He planted his feet apart and pushed back the peak of his baseball cap. His raincoat fell open to reveal jeans and a leather jacket buttoned across. He coughed and introduced himself. 'I'm sorry about all this,' he went on to say. 'I'm sure it's upsetting and disruptive for you. But a young woman's been murdered so it's necessary.' He paused and looked around. 'Nice place . . . I hope you won't be disturbed for too long.' He shoved his hands into his raincoat pockets. 'I'll do what I can to keep you informed. That's why I'm here now. You probably know I've visited the Wheeler family. After this, I'll be holding a news conference outside. But it's important that you're the next to know.' He looked from face to face. 'At three forty-seven this afternoon a single male aged twenty was arrested in connection with the murder of Joss Wheeler. That's all I can say at the moment. Thank you.' He nodded, pulled down his cap, fastened a button of his raincoat and went outside.

Silence.

Everyone in the tea room had the same shocked expression.

Words were unnecessary. They were all thinking the same thing. Isobel, being practical, said, 'He'll need a lawyer.' There was an exchange of looks: *a lawyer and a miracle*.

Mary-Anne said, 'Look, he's talking to them,' and drew attention back to the scene outside. The reporters were gathered around Beacom. Cameras flashed.

Isobel said, 'He's answering questions.'

Grey complained, 'He didn't let us ask questions.'

A murmur of discontent. More shared glances. *The police aren't to be trusted. They weren't when Max Wheeler disappeared. Nothing has changed.*

According to the Deep Blue's clock, seven minutes passed before Beacom walked back in the direction of his makeshift headquarters. A uniformed policeman stopped some reporters from following. One, a fair-haired young man, peeled away from the pack and entered the tea room.

Isobel was at the counter with Bella, trying to cheer her up. The young man – Dominic, he said his name was, from the *Sentinel* – ordered coffee, large and black.

Isobel said, 'Let me do this one, Bella. Why don't you go into the office and put your feet up?'

When Isobel turned to attend to the coffee machine, Dominic said to Bella, 'How about we swap. You tell me what Beacom said to you and I'll tell you what he said outside?'

Bella didn't reply.

Dominic shrugged. 'I'll go first.' He glanced over his shoulder to check no other reporters were queuing behind to hear what Bella or Isobel might say. 'OK.' He lowered his voice. 'They've arrested this bloke everyone's been talking about, Ewan Chisholm. The cops were waiting for him up at a place called Grant's Croft. They got him when he was tying up his boat.'

Bella asked, 'Was he alone?'

The reporter raised his eyebrows. 'Dunno, to be honest, but that's what the detective chief inspector told us: one bloke, one boat.' He took out his notebook and checked. 'Yes, that's what he said all right. Now, it's your turn.'

Isobel said, 'He didn't even tell us that much.' She looked at Bella, who was looking most peculiar. Isobel put the coffee cup on the counter. 'Bella, are you all right?' She put her arms around her friend, as if ready to hold her up. 'You've been on your feet too long.' Isobel turned to Dominic. 'I'm sorry, it's been a difficult day. It's all been a great strain.'

'Another time then.' He put a five-pound note on the counter. 'Keep the change.' He winked. 'Maybe it'll buy me some goodwill.'

Isobel took Bella into the office, tutting at her stubbornness. 'You look terrible. Let me take care of the tea room while you and Catriona rest.' She frowned. 'Bella, why did you ask that reporter if Ewan was alone?'

Afternoon sun slanted across Priest's Island. It crept over a hillside. It penetrated a gully. It lit up a rock. It appeared to be making suggestions: *here is where he might be hiding, look here or here.* Cal swore. He'd searched everywhere. He'd checked the ruined chapel and the shieling. He'd covered the high ground from east to west. He'd walked the south shore and now he was walking the north. Was there another living creature on the island? It seemed inconceivable that someone could hide in this landscape, flattened by storms and stripped of cover. How could two people simply disappear there – first Max, now Ewan's companion?

Among torn-up kelp and wrack at the tideline, a carpet of

purple-brown, Cal spotted a flash of yellow. It was one of his drift cards – numbered four, he saw when he bent to pick it up. He'd dropped it north-west of Priest's Island on the Atlantic side. Straightening up, he spotted another in a pool of sea water nearby. Approaching across a shingle beach, he stepped over some washed-up moss or seaweed and saw a line of stitching. He bent to discover a cloth bag. On further investigation, he found it was separated into compartments set in a circle. The first four contained broken pieces of eggshell. The fifth was empty. From the sixth and last he tipped an intact egg into the palm of his hand. The shell was clammy cold, light pink and covered with red-brown blotches – the same patterning as some of the broken pieces. Because of the size, about five centimetres by three, Cal thought the egg a seabird's, perhaps a kittiwake's or guillemot's. On reflection, he couldn't remember seabirds being on their nest sites as early as March. Usually, when he saw them, it was late spring or early summer. He returned the egg to the pouch and collected the second drift card – it was numbered one and had been dropped below the sea cliff. Then he thought of the ravens he had seen flying above the island, of the ravens' nests he had seen on other sea cliffs and, in the past, being surprised to find ravens at their nests as early as February. Had the bag and the drift card been driven ashore from the same place?

He returned to Wheeler's jetty where his RIB was tied up. For safe-keeping, he put the bag and its undamaged egg in a locker. From another, he removed a rope and set off across the island towards its western buttress. Ten minutes later he breasted the plateau, and two ravens lifted into the air. They wheeled to watch him. When he was at the cliff's edge, they settled and began a chorus of rasping, croaking calls. In protest, he thought, at his being on their territory. He stopped by a wide crack – a diagonal gash in the cliff face – and studied the rubble of rock which filled it. At some time in the past it might have been climbable; not any more. Then, a short distance ahead, he saw a place where the grass looked freshly worn and flattened. He knelt to press his fingers against a patch of scuffed earth. Next he went to the boulder that was perched back from the edge, as if in some distant time a giant had lugged it towards the cliff edge to repel seaborne invaders only to run out of strength. The boulder was more cylindrical than round. Cal noticed more signs of friction about the base. He unwound his rope, tied a large loop at the top and fitted it over the rock. When it had slipped down, he yanked the loop tight before tying another, with an overhand knot, further along the rope. He tested the loop for size with his foot, untied it, made it bigger and made more of similar size about forty centimetres apart.

When he was finished there were forty-three loops. He went to the cliff, knelt and gripped a loop in each hand and pulled the rope tight against the boulder. Then he scrambled inexpertly over the edge until he was hanging. He put one foot into a loop, then the other and began to descend. He went slowly, releasing one hand at a time and looking down to find the next foothold. The wet rock face grazed his knuckles as he gripped tight to the loops. He kept on going until the rope below him seemed to be hanging in mid-air. When he looked down, he found he was at an overhang. Hand, foot, hand, foot, one loop after another. Now he could see a ledge below him. On it was raised a large platform of sticks and branches, a raven's nest. In the middle, as though shaped by a bowl, was a lining of sheep's wool. The nest was empty.

Suddenly he started spinning.

On his first turn round, he saw what looked like a crust of human vomit on the rock beside the nest.

He spun again. Cal saw how some branches hung over the

ledge. Others looked as though they'd been torn away. Then, on his next spin, he noticed how the nest platform had been pulled away from the back of the ledge where it abutted the rock face and, dimly, in a crevice there, he thought he saw a wood-handled boathook.

Helen's eyes flitted from Ina's bony fingers digging into her arm to the sideways slump of the old woman's head. 'Sorry,' she said to Mary-Anne at the next table before glancing at the clock. The minute hand was at two minutes to six. Helen pulled a face which meant she knew the tea room should soon be left to the locals, but what could she do? If she got up to go she would waken Ina.

'Oh, don't worry, you're fine,' Mary-Anne smiled in understanding. 'Isn't that right?' She addressed the question to Isobel, who was returning from checking on Bella. 'Nobody's going to fuss if Helen stays on after six, are they?'

'Please. Stay! You must.' Isobel lowered her voice. 'If Ina wakes up and you're not here she'll want to tell us one of her stories.' Isobel rolled her eyes.

'I could listen to her all day,' Helen said. 'What an amazing life she's led.' She glanced at Ina before opening her book, a Hebridean travel guide. 'Trying to work out where to go next.'

She made a show of reading while Isobel and Mary-Anne talked about Bella.

'She's determined to come back to the tea room,' Isobel said. 'You know Bella when she's made up her mind. Stubborn isn't the word.'

'She's her own worst enemy. She'll make herself ill.'

'She's ill already if you're asking me. Grey had to drive her home last night because she was so exhausted. This afternoon, with that reporter, I thought she was having a stroke. Honestly I did. She didn't look right.'

'I know,' Mary-Anne replied. 'What an odd question to ask – was Ewan alone?'

'You should have seen her afterwards. She couldn't move. She looked dazed, far away. Do you know what she said? "Oh Isobel, I don't know where I've been." And I said, "Bella, if you don't look after yourself you won't be coming back the next time".'

'Watch out,' Mary-Anne whispered, 'here she's coming now.'

Helen turned the page of her guidebook.

Isobel asked, 'How are you feeling, Bella?'

Helen heard Bella's footfall and felt a movement of air against her neck.

When she turned and looked up, Bella was standing with her hands on her hips, staring down at her. 'It's after six,' she said. 'You shouldn't be in the tea room.'

'Oh, that's our fault, Bella.' Mary-Anne sounded nervous. 'We didn't think anyone would mind. After all, Helen's done so much to help, making sandwiches and sitting with Ina.'

'Well, she can't stay.'

Helen noticed Mary-Anne and Isobel exchanging glances. 'We thought an exception could be made,' Isobel said.

'It's all right,' Helen interrupted. 'Bella's quite right. I shouldn't be here . . .' She looked at Ina's collapsed and sleeping face and then at Bella. 'I didn't mean to cause any trouble.' She put her book in her bag and loosened Ina's grip on her arm. The old woman's eyelids sprang open. She looked around her with a bewildered expression. When she saw Helen, she said, 'Have I told you about the time my Neil's boat ran aground in a storm?'

'Not yet, you haven't, Ina.' Helen patted her on the hand.

'There's always tomorrow.' She looked out of the window. 'Before it gets dark, I think I'll take some exercise. Run off all that cake.'

~

Helen wondered at herself. What *was* she thinking? A young woman had been murdered. Not just killed, but terrorized at night in a storm and stabbed, and Helen was worried about her face becoming red. But she couldn't stop jogging because she was still in view of the Deep Blue. Bella could be watching. That was Helen's job, watching people. Now it seemed *she* was being watched.

'Nosy old besom,' Helen said out loud. She stopped running and bent over as if catching her breath so that Bella could see how unfit her holiday tenant was. Helen walked for a bit before carrying on jogging. As soon as the upstairs windows of Bella's house were out of sight, she stopped. Now her cheeks felt burning hot and Cal's pickup was only a couple of minutes away. There was no chance her face would subside. She walked disconsolately on and issued silent warnings to Cal if he dared mention her grey tracksuit, if she detected the beginnings of a smile. 'Huh, after all that . . .' she complained when she arrived at his pickup. He was nowhere to be seen. His RIB was gone. 'Typical.'

She wrote in the dirt on the side of his pickup:

NEED TO TALK. I'LL TRY AGAIN IN THE MORNING.

She didn't write her name in case anyone passed by and read it. But it looked a bit odd on its own. So she wrote 'H'.

'Cal, where have you gone?'

Sometime, she thought. Even once would be nice.

22

Bella was making scones and biscuits, baking determinedly to distract herself from thinking about Joss. Tears dropped on to the hot trays and made a sizzling sound. Joss dead and Ewan arrested for her murder! She couldn't accustom herself to what had happened no matter how often the words turned around in her head. Every time was still a shock.

The phone rang, causing her to start. What now? She remembered her mother's adage about no good news ever arriving before breakfast.

It was Isobel.

'Bella, I thought I should ring you straight away so you were warned. A body's been washed up on East Skerry. Another body, isn't that terrible? Who could it be?'

It was like a punch to Bella's ear. She fell against the dresser and dislodged one of a set of floral cups from the top shelf. It smashed on the kitchen floor and Bella found herself kneeling among the fragments. A pale yellow primrose was on the piece nearest to her. She stared at it with a bewildered expression. Such a pretty thing, she thought, and broken too. Just like Joss. Like everything. Shattered.

'Are you all right, Bella?' Isobel sounded alarmed. The phone lay on the floor among china fragments. Bella picked it up. 'Bella?' Isobel inquired. 'Are you all right? Bella, speak to me.'

'A body?' Bella managed to say, but her head was spinning so much she could only hear Isobel's reply in fragments: 'Appears to be human . . . fleshy . . . pale skin . . . not had a close-up examination ... police going out ... no one local reported missing.'

Bella laid the phone beside the broken pieces of cup while Isobel was still talking. She went upstairs to Catriona's room.

When she looked from the window and saw skuas, gulls and crows wheeling and quarrelling above the skerry, she knew it was Pinkie. The symmetry of that distant scene made perfect sense. The creatures that Pinkie had preyed on in life were tearing him apart in death. In Pinkie's fate, she saw a glimpse of her own. Her flesh would be stripped for bringing him to the islands. Other sharp beaks would expose her bones for being Ewan's protector, for being Joss's. Bella surrendered to self-pity – had good intentions ever been more cruelly rewarded? Everything was spoilt and broken. Nothing could be mended. Now Pinkie too! How was he dead? What could have happened? If only she could talk to Ewan.

The next she knew, Catriona was getting out of bed and standing at her side, dark eyes peering into Bella's face. 'Auntie Bella, what are you doing in my room?' She looked out of the window to where Bella was staring. 'Are you watching the birds?' she asked doubtfully. 'Why? There are always birds out there. Why are you looking at them this morning?'

Bella said, 'They're feeding on a body.'

Catriona glanced at the birds and back to her aunt. 'Are you sure? A body?'

'Isobel's been on the phone,' Bella said. 'I'm sorry, Catriona. I'm so sorry.'

'What did Isobel say? You're sure she said a body?' Catriona jerked back her head in puzzlement. 'Really?' She watched her aunt's face. 'Whose body?' She took her aunt's hands in hers. 'Why are *you* sorry? What have you done?'

As she always used to when Catriona was a child and she

would be too inquisitive or nosy, Bella pulled her niece towards her and held her tight. She rested her chin on Catriona's head so she could no longer search into her eyes. Then she said, 'You're better than all of us, Catriona. You've never thought Ewan capable of murder, have you? Not once.'

'Auntie Bella!' Catriona said. 'Why are you saying that? Has Ewan got something to do with that body? *Tell me.*'

But Bella held her tighter and said nothing.

Helen peered round the side of the Deep Blue. News of the washed-up body had not yet reached the media encampment – the only sign of conscious life was a policeman standing on the harbour wall by the *Jacqueline*. If Helen had to put on tracksuit and trainers to go running in the early morning, she'd rather do so without an audience of reporters and photographers. For that small mercy she gave thanks. She did likewise when she saw the tea room was dark and empty. Thank goodness Bella wasn't up and watching. The woman had a suspicious nature. Helen jogged across the tarmac towards the rocky pathway leading uphill to the road. As before, she kept on running until she was out of sight of the upstairs windows of Bella's house. Life was unfair, she thought: with Cal, events or time were always conspiring against her looking her best.

There were compensations for being up early, she told herself. The morning was glorious – the air cold and the light so clear that every detail of the landscape was illuminated. Wherever her eyes fell there were contrasts of colour: here, grasses so pale they looked translucent; there, a patch of rushes the darkest of dark greens; there, across the sound, Priest's Island, all browns, blacks and soft yellows and textured like tweed; and in between, the sea a shade of pale azure that Helen had only seen in holiday brochures. It was as if a shroud had been lifted during the night and dawn had revealed heaven on earth, Helen realized in sudden and unexpected wonder. Had she ever had such an experience before? Not when she was a child: her memories were of cold rooms, of foster parents with worried faces, of wanting to be loved. Not in adolescence when she lived through books, finding within their pages her only friends and her first romances (her later romances too). Nor in early adulthood: then, she dedicated herself to reading of a different kind, law for her first degree, criminology for her second. At every stage, she lived in a city. Not in all those years did she have a memory of being as she was now: alone, out of doors, among beauty, being dazzled by it, living in the moment. It was as if a private exhibition had been staged especially for her. She spun around, taking it all in, before carrying on along the road. At last she thought she understood why Cal lived as he did.

When she saw his pickup, she laughed. Instead of him sitting cross-legged on the bonnet appreciating the early morning, as she'd imagined, the windows were steamed up. He was inside, asleep. She knocked on a window and, when she heard a grunt, she knocked again and said, 'Cal, I thought you'd be out in the fresh air.' She breathed in and exhaled loudly. 'Mm, it's good! Better than where you are, that's for sure.'

Cal mumbled sleepily from inside.

Helen heard him grunt something about her message. She looked at her finger scrawl in the dirt on the pickup's near side. Underneath Cal had written,

DO NOT DISTURB UNLESS YOU'RE BRINGING COFFEE.

'Sorry, you'll just have to go to the Deep Blue like everyone else,' Helen said. 'Anyway . . .' She banged on the pickup's door. 'Beacom's been on the phone. A body's been washed up on East Skerry, don't know what yet. The fisherman who reported it thinks it could be human but he couldn't take his boat in close enough to be sure. Beacom reckons it might be Ewan's mysterious companion. Could be why Ewan hasn't been talking except to say he didn't kill Joss.'

The back door on the other side of the pickup swung open. Cal's fingers gripped the edge of the roof. His head appeared, followed by his torso. He was wearing a creased black tee shirt and jeans, and held binoculars in his right hand. After looking at the sound for less than a minute, he said, 'I thought so.' It was as if he was speaking to somebody else.

'Thought what?' Helen said testily.

'See those circling birds.' He handed her the binoculars. 'That's East Skerry.'

'Are they feeding on the body?' Helen sounded shocked.

'Don't worry, it's a dead pig.'

Helen stared at Cal. 'How do you know?'

'Look about twenty metres to the left of the skerry . . . in the water, see the orange buoy.'

'Why does that make it a pig?' Helen asked.

'It just does.'

'What's going on, Cal?'

'You're better off not knowing – let's say the pig has been assisting me with my inquiries. She's been helping me work out whether the currents would have washed Max Wheeler's body out of the sound. It appears they might not, in which case I wonder why Max didn't end up on a skerry too.'

'She? I don't suppose the pig has a name.'

'Millie. The pig's called Millie.'

Helen shook her head. 'Beacom's not going to be happy.'

Just then a RIB with two police officers came into view. 'I think I'll let them break the good news about Millie.' Helen handed back the binoculars. 'Anyway, where were you last night?'

'Out there . . .' Cal nodded towards the sound and Priest's Island.

'Well, that's specific,' Helen said. 'While you were out there, I heard something interesting. Bella MacLeod asked a reporter whether anyone was with Ewan when he was arrested.'

'Did she?' Cal stretched and yawned.

'The reporter said Beacom told them Ewan was alone. Bella reacted in a very odd manner. One of the women in the tea room thought she was having a funny turn or a stroke.' Helen paused. 'Cal, Bella must know about Ewan being on Priest's Island. She must know who he was with. But why doesn't she say anything? Why doesn't Ewan?'

Cal said, 'I've got something to show you.' He lowered himself into the pickup and reappeared holding a small cloth bag. 'Here . . .' He stretched across the roof. 'I found this washed up. Be careful, it's fragile.'

As Helen examined the bag, Cal said, 'Open up the pouches. Inside you'll find four broken eggs and one that's intact. That's what Ewan was doing – stealing eggs or helping someone else to take them. There's a raven's nest on the sea cliff. I climbed down and had a look. It's been disturbed.'

Helen screwed up her face. 'He's a suspect in a murder investigation. Why doesn't he say that's what he was up to?'

'His companion could be a difficulty. Ewan would have to produce him,' Cal said. 'Maybe he can't. The man might not want that.' He squinted at Priest's Island. 'Maybe something has happened that makes it impossible. Whoever was with Ewan isn't there now and the eggs were dropped into the sea. When I climbed down to the nest I started to spin round. If there had been a strong wind, as there was when Ewan's friend was there, I doubt I'd have been able to regain control and climb back up.'

Helen said, 'You think he fell into the sea?'

'The bag did.'

'Can I take it away?'

Cal nodded.

'I'll photograph the contents when I'm back at the chalet and email the pictures to our people in wildlife crime. See what they say.'

'Then what?' Cal asked.

Helen thought for a moment before answering. 'Why don't you give Bella a shock – say you know she's withholding information about Ewan? See how she reacts.'

Cal jabbed his finger towards Helen and mimicked Bella: '"You're responsible, Dr McGill." If she says anything, that's what it'll be.'

Helen continued, 'Also talk to Catriona. Scare her. Tell her the police aren't looking for anybody else. Tell her they'll make the evidence fit. Mention Ewan being jailed for twenty-five, thirty years. Say you know Ewan didn't murder Joss but you can only prove it with Bella's assistance. Make Catriona think you're Ewan's last chance.' She paused. 'Tell her you don't work for Wheeler any more.'

'Don't I?'

'Beacom thinks it's time you went independent.'

'Does Wheeler know about that?'

'His solicitor will be told this morning. He'll be provided with the text of a statement which he'll release in David Wheeler's name. "Following the tragic death of Joss Wheeler, the investigation by Dr McGill has been overtaken by events . . . danger of duplication, possible confusion with the police inquiry . . ." – that sort of thing.'

Cal nodded. 'I'm comfortable with that.'

Helen removed a piece of broken eggshell from the bag. 'Show this to Bella. It's time to shake her up a bit.'

Soon after opening, the tea room was full. The inhabitants of the township crowded inside as though a storm had driven them from their crofts. In a manner of speaking, it had. Every few minutes a new rumour blew in. If it wasn't about the body on East Skerry it was about the investigation of Joss's murder.

The police were searching Grant's Croft.

Ewan was being kept in custody on the mainland.

A large sum of money had been found in Ewan's possession when he was arrested.

Alistair arrived with a similar story. 'Three thousand pounds in fifty-pound notes,' he said. PC Dyer told him about it when they met on the road. The money had been in a bag on Ewan's boat. Although Ewan was refusing to answer most questions, he told DCI Beacom the money had been his uncle's. Donald Grant had buried it on Priest's Island because he didn't trust banks.

Dyer had asked, 'Where did Donald get money like that?'

Like Alistair, the tea room thought Donald Grant might have buried whisky bottles for safe-keeping because he didn't trust his neighbours. 'He never had any money.'

Then someone wondered in Catriona's hearing whether Joss had hidden money in her caravan. Had Ewan taken it from there? Catriona became so upset that Bella took her home and Isobel stood in behind the counter.

By mid-morning the tea room was in a state of heightened anxiety; it felt less like a place of refuge, more like a waiting room. Mugs of coffee and tea went cold. Cake was picked at or left uneaten. Isobel rang Bella from the office and told her to stay at home with Catriona. Since a few reporters were about and no one else was ordering anything, she could manage on her own. 'Put your feet up.'

No sooner had she replaced the phone than a BBC cameraman asked for coffee and said Isobel should prepare for a rush. Everyone was coming back from watching the police RIB at East Skerry. 'That body,' he said, 'was a pig's.'

Isobel asked Mary-Anne to look after the Deep Blue while she went to Bella's house. She found her in the kitchen. 'It isn't bad news,' Isobel said in reaction to Bella's worried expression. 'The body on East Skerry is a pig's.'

Bella picked up her apron and put it on. 'How's the chocolate cake, Isobel? Is it running out? I thought I'd make another one.'

Isobel stuttered, 'I don't really know.' She watched her friend pick up a baking tray. 'Bella, you did hear what I said about the pig?'

'Oh yes.' Bella seemed surprised at the question. 'I'm not deaf, you know.'

Once Isobel returned to the tea room, Bella went upstairs to Catriona's room. She stood outside the door. 'Catriona, love.'

'What?' Catriona sounded angry.

'I don't know what came over me earlier.' Bella's voice was hesitant, doubting. 'I haven't been sleeping very well. Maybe that was it. That and everything else.' She paused. 'They've found a dead pig on the skerry. Did I tell you that already? I can't remember what I said. Didn't I tell you? I'm sure I did.' And again: 'I'm becoming so forgetful.' She let out a little laugh. 'I wonder where a pig drifted in from. Whatever next?'

Going back downstairs, Bella doubted she'd managed to fool Catriona, but that thought was chased away in the rush of other worries. Where was Pinkie? Had something happened? Why didn't Ewan tell the police what he was doing? Better to be charged for stealing wild birds' eggs than murder, surely. Should she make a statement about Ewan being on Priest's Island, say she'd organized everything and that Ewan's role was limited to being a boatman taking a passenger to the island. What stopped her was Pinkie – where was he, what could have happened to him? Was Ewan in some other trouble which Bella would make worse by talking? She'd contact Ewan's lawyer and ask him to pass on a message: was there anything Bella could do to help? Ewan would know what she meant. As she was going into the kitchen, the bell rang. If it was Isobel or Mary-Anne they would have opened the door and called out her name. The doorbell rang again, longer and louder.

Cal stretched out his hand. On his open palm was the broken shell of an egg. It was convex, washed pink with red-brown blotches. Bella was about to speak but the words seemed to stick in her throat. Her mouth hung open.

'I think we should talk, don't you?' Cal took a step towards her, pushing his hand closer. 'Here, take it. I don't need it. I've got other pieces. I found them washed up on Priest's Island.'

Bella kept on staring at the shell and Cal said, 'You look like you've seen a ghost.' The door banged shut and Cal pressed the bell again. 'You know what Ewan was doing and who he was with, don't you?' His voice was measured, as though he was concerned about Bella, as if he wanted to help. 'I think you know he didn't kill Joss Wheeler.' He jabbed his finger against the bell, a short, loud blast. He heard voices inside – Catriona's and Bella's. They were arguing but he couldn't make out what they were saying. Catriona sounded angry and accusing; Bella alternately exasperated and pleading. Cal shouted, 'Ask your aunt where Ewan was. Ask her, Catriona.'

The door opened again. Catriona was staring at Cal. She was barefoot, in jeans and a green dressing grown. Her hair was wet. Cal saw Bella standing behind her. In the gloom of the hallway, she now looked like a ghost.

'What do you want?' Catriona asked.

Cal offered the eggshell. 'Take it. Ask your aunt what it is. Make her tell you what Ewan was doing the night Joss Wheeler was murdered.'

Catriona looked at the egg and then at Cal. 'What *was* he doing? Do you know?'

Cal nodded. 'I think your aunt knows more.'

Catriona looked behind her. 'Is that true?'

Bella hurried towards the door. 'Don't listen to him,' she said, 'he works for David Wheeler. He murdered Joss.'

Cal went on talking to Catriona. 'The police aren't looking for anyone else. Ewan will get life for a crime I don't think he committed.' Before the door slammed shut, Cal threw the eggshell inside.

Not moving, he said loudly, 'I don't work for Wheeler, not any more.'

❧

The eggshell lay crushed on the hall floor. After Catriona had run upstairs, Bella knelt and touched the fragments with the tips of her fingers, as if feeling for answers. Where was Pinkie? What had happened to him? Was he broken, just like the raven's eggs? She gathered up the pieces of shell and took them to the kitchen. After washing them away under the tap, she went to the foot of the stairs and called up. 'Catriona, love, that's me away to the tea room.' She listened for a response and, when none came, she went to the door. Before opening it, she was struck by a thought. From now on she would be at the whim of the sea. The pig was a forewarning. Any morning she might wake up to Isobel ringing with news of another body being found on East Skerry or West Skerry or one of the islets. She would go to Catriona's room and see the birds wheeling and fighting, their sharp beaks stabbing at Pinkie, ripping away at his flesh.

23

Mary-Anne was dithering. One moment she thought chocolate cake would be nice with her cup of tea; the next, a lemon muffin. 'How very indecisive I'm being,' she said apologetically.

'Why don't you take all day?' Bella snapped. 'It's not as if I've anything better to do.'

Mary-Anne looked like she'd been shot. She managed to say, 'Aren't you a bear with a sore head?' Afterwards she became flustered telling Isobel about the exchange. No one had talked to her as sharply for years. Nor could she recall when she'd last been so outspoken in reply. 'Oh dear,' Mary-Anne said, 'I do hope Bella will forgive me.'

'Forgive you?' Isobel raised her eyebrows. 'She should hope you'll forgive her. It's not your fault. She *is* like a bear with a sore head. Look at her now with Catriona. Those two haven't said a civil word to each other all afternoon.'

But Mary-Anne was staring out of the window at the cars and vans by the harbour, the huddles of reporters and photographers, the uniformed policemen on duty. 'Oh, don't you wish we could go back to the way we were?' She glanced at Isobel, looking startled. 'Was that me speaking? Oh dear, I think it was.' The right side of her throat flushed red and her head shook a little.

Isobel smiled consolingly. 'I'm sure things will return to normal, aren't you? When everyone's gone and it's just the township again.'

'How? We're all so changed. Haven't you noticed?' Once

again Mary-Anne looked surprised at having spoken her thoughts aloud. 'I don't know what's got into me.' She laughed nervously. 'Perhaps I should have a piece of chocolate cake after all. Maybe that will settle me. You mustn't pay me any attention.'

While Mary-Anne was at the counter talking to Catriona, Isobel thought about her odd behaviour, how out of character it was for her to disagree or to argue. Normally she wouldn't say boo to a goose. Like Bella, she must be feeling the strain. Weren't they all showing it one way or another? Later on, Isobel thought Mary-Anne had a point about there being a change.

She noticed it when Beacom walked past the Deep Blue on his way to the *Jacqueline*. As on his visit the day before, the township was already assembled in the tea room. Everyone gathered at the window to watch. The talk was of Beacom's shabby appearance – old leather jacket, white shirt unbuttoned at the neck, black jeans and scuffed white trainers – and of the bad impression it made. His swept-back greasy hair which was overdue a cut also caused comment. So did his sharp face. Didn't he look disreputable, even dirty and sly, not at all as a senior police officer should? Isobel thought so too. But as she drifted from one vantage point to the next, she overheard her neighbours speak to one another in asides. They sounded fatigued. Like Mary-Anne, they longed for the township to return to normal and they wondered whether it ever would. Isobel also picked up resentment which was expressed quietly, privately, unlike the loud complaints about Beacom. It was directed against Ewan. The bitterness surprised Isobel. Where did Ewan come by three thousand pounds? He must have been up to no good. If he didn't murder Joss, why didn't he talk to the police? It wasn't surprising that Beacom thought Ewan the killer. Wouldn't anyone?

Ewan had brought trouble on himself. The township would be better off without him.

Isobel was unsettled by what she heard and went to stand by Bella. She thought she would show solidarity, since Ewan was one of Bella's brood. The two women were together when a call went up that Beacom was walking towards the tea room. Unlike the day before, the movement inside – the pulling back, the shrinking away – happened before the door opened in anticipation of bad news. By the time Beacom entered, the tea room was hushed, everyone still, waiting. As before, Beacom planted his feet and told them he had a brief announcement to make.

'I would like you to know that our inquiries are continuing and a twenty-year-old man has been charged with the murder of Joss Wheeler.' Beacom dipped his head as if to indicate that was the end. 'Thank you, that's all I am able to say at the moment.' He turned and went out of the door.

Afterwards Catriona became tearful and was comforted by Helen. Isobel helped Bella behind the counter and listened to the chatter of the reporters and photographers who formed a queue after Beacom's media briefing outside.

Max Wheeler's death was to be reinvestigated, she heard them say. All the evidence, including witness statements, would be double-checked.

Everyone in the township would be interviewed again.

Every property would be searched.

There was also mention of a statement from David Wheeler's lawyer. Dr Caladh McGill's investigation into Max Wheeler's murder had been stopped because it might interfere with the ongoing police inquiry.

Only later, when she was asked by Bella to collect dirty mugs and cups from the tables and to take orders, was Isobel able to tune back in to the mood of her neighbours. As she expected, people were alarmed at their houses being searched and at being questioned about Max Wheeler's disappearance. What would happen if there were discrepancies between their previous interview and the next one? And there was dismay at Beacom again telling the media more than the tea room, a sign that he thought someone else in the township apart from Ewan was guilty. He wouldn't treat the residents that way unless he was deliberately trying to unsettle them. Once again, there were quieter comments. Isobel heard enough of what was being said to realize the murder charge against Ewan had hardened opinion. Not only had Ewan murdered Joss and taken her money, but he had probably killed Max too. His upbringing was to blame: the violence, the drunkenness of his father; what goes around comes around. Ewan was a weak character. It wasn't right that the township should be turned upside down again because of him. It was as if they were casting off Ewan as a way of cleansing the township of the unspoken guilt at having sheltered him for so long and for having obstructed the police's inquiry into Max Wheeler's disappearance.

Isobel went over to Mary-Anne who was sitting alone. 'You were right,' Isobel said. 'We have changed.'

'You see what Beacom's doing, don't you?' Mary-Anne said. 'He's destroying the thing that kept us safe the last time. Day by day he's breaking us down. Already we're abandoning Ewan to him. Who will be next? Who knows what we'll be capable of?'

'I don't know,' Isobel said.

Mary-Anne shook at the thought. 'Then God forgive us.'

Passing by the window, Isobel was aware of a quick movement by the harbour. She stopped to look and saw a young woman running. She was wearing a red jacket or anorak. Reporters and photographers were converging to block her way. Isobel recognized Chloe Wheeler just as she disappeared from view, surrounded by all the other bodies. Another figure appeared on the deck of the *Jacqueline*. A young woman with blonde hair: Hannah Wheeler. She scrambled off the boat on to the harbour wall and began running too. The policeman on guard duty was gesticulating as Hannah pursued Chloe and also became lost in the media scrum. Isobel was about to tell Mary-Anne when both young women reappeared, Hannah gripping her older sister's arm. They were arguing. Chloe pulled away and began walking towards the Deep Blue. Hannah stayed where she was, the reporters pushing past, the policeman walking in front holding out his arms as a barrier.

'Chloe Wheeler's outside,' Isobel blurted. 'I think she's coming in.' Isobel might as well have said a runaway lorry was about to crash into the tea room. Everyone stopped talking. Some stood. There was a shuffling sound, a general bracing against the inevitability of impact.

When the door opened, two dozen pairs of eyes were watching Chloe. She stopped just inside.

'What kind of people are you?' She stared at them and now two dozen pairs of eyes avoided hers. 'You protect my brother's murderer and you allow him to kill my sister. What would make you do something like that? My beautiful sister . . .' She put her hands to her face. 'Have you any idea what you've done?' She laughed bitterly. 'As if people like you could have any idea. You've ruined my father's life . . . my life . . . Hannah's life.' She blinked away tears. 'What did we ever do to you?' No one answered. 'What?' She directed the question at Catriona, who was closest to her.

The two young women looked at one another.

'Ewan didn't kill anyone,' Catriona said quietly. 'I know he didn't. He couldn't have.'

Chloe's expression changed. 'So, you're the girlfriend.' Now she looked at Catriona with disdain. 'How can you stand there when you know what he's done?' She screwed up her face. 'You people.' She looked at them all again, slowly, before turning for the door.

Catriona went after her and grabbed her arm. 'It wasn't Ewan. I'm sorry about what's happened but it wasn't him.'

Chloe shook her off with reporters and photographers pressing at the open door. 'Don't,' she shouted at Catriona. 'Don't you touch me. Ever.' Cameras flashed and Chloe pushed her way outside. The reporters fell back: more camera flashes, cries of 'Chloe'. Catriona watched at the doorway. She turned back towards the tea room. Her expression was pained. 'It wasn't him.' Her voice was pleading. 'You know it wasn't.'

As with Chloe, Catriona found the tea room reluctant to look her in the eye. No one said anything. People went back to their seats.

Isobel wasn't sure whether the silence was an aftershock caused by Chloe's outburst – an understandable reaction – or whether it was brought on by something more worrying, a further hardening of mood. She carried on clearing tables and taking orders. At first she overheard comments about Chloe, how hurt she must be, how distressed, what terrible tragedies she had suffered. Her mother, Max and now Joss were dead, each one killed violently, a car crash and one, if not two, murders. No wonder she was beside herself with grief. Wouldn't anyone be?

After a while, Isobel began to pick up criticisms of Catriona. Piecing it together from a snatch here, another there, she was taken aback by the strength of resentment. Catriona had been wrong to speak up for Ewan. The pictures of her arguing with Chloe would be everywhere, in the papers, on TV, the township's name blackened again. Couldn't she have kept quiet? Didn't she have any sense?

~

'I thought you might be here,' Helen said when she found Catriona later on the hill behind the Deep Blue. 'I've been looking everywhere. Then I remembered this was where you went to find a phone signal and to get away from people.' Catriona was smoking a cigarette in that nervy way Helen associated with runaways. Drag, exhale, fast and shallow. When Helen was a police constable, she would often come across kids smoking like that. They would be twelve- or thirteen-year-olds who were being abused or whose mothers had moved in a man who was violent or sleazy. She would discover them in derelict flats or abandoned outbuildings, shivering in some damp corner, lost. Helen would arrive with a flask of sugary tea she kept in the car for that purpose. With something sweet and warm inside them, they would become less jumpy. They might even talk.

'You must be frozen,' Helen said when she saw how little Catriona had on – blue shirt, apron, jeans and trainers, just what she'd been wearing at the Deep Blue. 'Here, I've brought you some tea.' She put the take-away cup down within reach of Catriona, then sat on a rock just below her. Another thing she learned from runaways: if you want them to talk, sit, don't stand, don't watch. She said, 'I thought that was brave of you.'

'What was?'

'Sticking up for Ewan like that. He's lucky to have such a good friend.'

'He'd do the same for me.'

'Would he? Not many men would. Not the kind of men I meet. I suppose that makes you lucky too.'

Catriona lit another cigarette. Drag, exhale, in, out. 'What will I do?' Her voice was plaintive, despairing.

Helen glanced round and found Catriona watching her. 'What?' Helen asked. 'What is it?'

'You'll tell no one.' Drag. Exhale.

'Course I won't.'

'Auntie Bella knows Ewan wasn't on Eilean Dubh when Joss was murdered.' Drag. Exhale. 'Cal McGill came to the house and said so.'

'Did you ask Bella about it?'

'She wouldn't tell me. She said I shouldn't listen to McGill because he worked for Wheeler. He was a liar, a troublemaker who was protecting his own skin because he killed Joss.' Catriona looked panicked. 'McGill said the police weren't looking for anyone else. He said Ewan would go to prison for, God, life.' Drag. Exhale. 'Why won't Auntie Bella tell me?'

'Why don't you ask McGill what he knows?' Helen suggested. 'Why not? If it could help Ewan.'

Catriona stared at her.

'What's the problem?' Helen said. 'People were talking in the tea room about his investigation ending. He's not on Wheeler's side now.'

Catriona's mouth pulled.

'Not that easy, huh?' Helen asked. 'The township doesn't let people change sides, is that it?'

Catriona nodded.

'So you don't want to be seen with McGill, is that what you mean?'

She nodded again uncertainly and Helen thought aloud. 'You come up here after the tea room has closed to check your phone, don't you?'

Catriona said she did, some days, depending on the weather.

'Well,' Helen said, 'it's going to be fine tonight. I'll find McGill and bring him to you. I pass his pickup when I go running. I'll ask him this evening. OK?'

Drag. Exhale.

Bella replayed the message from Ewan's lawyer. 'Mr Chisholm has asked me to thank you for your inquiry and to tell you he is well, under the circumstances. There is nothing you can provide by way of practical support at the present time but if that changes he will give his instructions to me and I will pass them to you.' Bella listened to the affectation in the lawyer's voice and his formal choice of words. Ewan's meaning was clear enough. Bella should say nothing.

If only she could speak to Ewan – then she would know what was really happening.

She checked her emails and clicked for the second time on the automatic reply from Pryke Property Management. It said that Stanley Pryke would be out of the office on business until 5th March. Yesterday – Pinkie should have been back by now. In case of emergency a mobile phone number was supplied. As before, when Bella rang, it went straight to message. She composed another email, saying she was worried about missing out on a flat for rent advertised on the company's website. She would like to arrange a viewing, so could Mr Pryke get in touch as soon as possible? She clicked 'send' and waited. Another 'out of office' reply appeared in her inbox. She checked his return date: yesterday, still yesterday. Where *was* Pinkie? She went to the office door. 'Still no Catriona?' she asked Isobel.

Isobel wiped up a puddle of coffee. 'Not that I've seen.' She glanced around the tea room. 'Helen doesn't seem to have returned either.'

Frowning, Bella asked Isobel to look after things for a few minutes while she went home to check for Catriona there. After opening her front door she called her niece's name. She shouted it again going upstairs and, softly, outside her niece's room. 'Are you there?' She knocked. 'Catriona?' She looked inside. The bed was unmade. Catriona's clothes were scattered around the floor. A towel was thrown over the chair in front of her dressing table. Bella picked it up and sat down. In the mirror, an old woman looked back at her.

She was disturbed by sounds from downstairs. With dismay, she realized that any moment Catriona could catch her in her room. What excuse could she give? Then she heard Isobel's voice, calling for her. Bella hurried out on to the landing and arrived at the top of the stairs as Isobel was coming out of the kitchen.

'Ah, there you are,' Isobel said. 'Catriona's back. She'd just gone for a walk. She asked me to tell you she'll work through until closing.'

'Is she all right?' Bella asked.

'A bit upset after what Chloe said to her but she says she'd rather be busy.' Isobel smiled. 'And you think she's not like you!'

24

That evening, they arrived separately on top of the hill, Helen ascending the stony path from the road, Cal approaching by way of the long slope of its eastern shoulder. As they walked along a narrow sheep's track, Helen told him Catriona would join them when the Deep Blue closed. She would be another half an hour.

'Which is just as well,' Helen continued, 'because I've got news. An inspector in charge of wildlife crime has been in touch. He's confirmed the egg was laid by a raven, but not just any raven. The egg's a genetic freak, a collector's item.'

She explained the difference was in its colouring, in the pinkness of the background and the redness of the blotches. Normally ravens' eggs were drabber, their background colour blue-green or grey-green, the blotches and streaks in greys, browns or blacks. The abnormality, called erythrism, had been documented in a number of different species. It was rare in ravens, a fact illustrated by the scarcity of records. The inspector had consulted a number of ornithological experts, who had been able to find only occasional references in more than a hundred and fifty years. They included a clutch found in Shetland in the middle of the nineteenth century and another taken from a nest near Tyndrum in the Scottish Highlands by a collector called P. Meeson on 6th April 1938. At various times during the twentieth century erythristic ravens were known about in Westmoreland, Cumberland, Wales and the Southern Uplands.

'They're potentially very valuable to an illegal collector,' Helen said.

'Which might explain how Ewan managed to have three thousand pounds when he was arrested,' Cal replied.

'Wait till you hear this.'

The inspector had provided a list of a dozen known collectors. All but one was active or had been active in the past five years. The exception was a man called Stanley Wise or Pryke, nicknamed Pinkie because of his particular interest in erythristic eggs. He was in his mid forties and was thought to have retired from collecting. 'But he continues to be a legend among egg collectors,' the inspector reported. Even a museum curator who was in charge of one of England's largest collections of eggs admitted to having a sneaking regard for the man. Wise or Pryke (he took his wife's maiden name after a minor conviction) was reputed to have the largest variety of erythristic eggs ever assembled in a single collection. According to rumour, it comprised nineteen different species and, in some cases, multiple clutches. Although the RSPB and the police had targeted him when he was younger, his collection had never been found. After he pleaded guilty and was fined for disturbing a sedge warbler's nest and being in possession of equipment to blow eggs eight years ago, he disappeared from view. Stories about him continued to circulate. Some said he had grown fat on his wife's money, others that he continued to outwit the law by using his property management company as a front for his activities. Whatever the truth, he hadn't come to police attention for a while.

'The inspector said two other interesting things,' Helen said. 'It seems to be common knowledge that the species missing from his collection of eggs is a raven. If anything would bring Pinkie out of retirement, an erythristic raven's clutch would. Also, it would be out of character for him to be careless. Both the inspector and the curator stressed the point. Pinkie is renowned for his meticulous fieldwork, for never breaking an egg and for taking only a clutch at the start of incubation so that the parent birds were more likely to breed that same year. The curator was surprised when the inspector informed him that four other eggs in the clutch had been broken. His view was that something must have happened if that was Pinkie. Something must have gone wrong.'

'Whoever the man was with Ewan, he wasn't fit,' Cal said. 'He could have been in his mid forties. He didn't look like he could climb down a cliff in a strong wind.'

'Pinkie would have insisted on doing the climb himself,' Helen said. 'According to the inspector, he was well known for that. It was a matter of honour for him, being a collector who did his own fieldwork.'

'Something did go wrong,' Cal said. 'Ewan thought so – that's why he was pacing up and down at first light. That's why he had to go back up the hill.'

'There's more,' Helen said. 'The inspector sent an officer to Pinkie's house and to his company, Pryke Property Management. There was no answer at either. The company's phone has a message saying that Stanley Pryke expected to be out of the office until yesterday. A constable will call at the house again tonight. The inspector also showed the curator a photograph of the bag you found. He said it was something a collector might use during a climb. But afterwards the eggs would be transferred to a secure container, typically a tin or reinforced box. It would be separated into compartments and lined.'

'So Pinkie or whoever it was got into trouble on the cliff. That's when the eggs were dropped.'

Helen agreed. 'We know he reached the nest and removed the eggs. Something bad must have happened when he was trying to climb back up. So what did Ewan find when he went searching the next morning?'

'A body, a rope, a backpack, or maybe only a backpack if the rope hadn't been secured properly.'

'The man you saw had a backpack?'

'Yes.'

'Whatever was there, Ewan must have cleared it away. Apart from the money – he took that. When Ewan returned to Eilean Dubh, he had no idea what had been going on because visibility had been bad and he was out of phone contact. When he was arrested for Joss's murder, what could he say? "I've been on Priest's Island with an egg thief who might or might not be dead." What would you do if you were Ewan? You'd think you were in serious trouble. You'd come up with some story about the money being hidden away by your uncle because he didn't trust banks. After that, if you were twenty years old and you thought the police had a score to settle, you'd sing dumb. You'd deny everything and wait to see what happened.'

Night crept in and they talked quietly, intermittently, as if conversation was dying with the day. Finally, they waited in silence for Catriona, and Helen watched Priest's Island become indistinct and black. How different to that morning when she had seen it so richly textured, a fine weave of subtle colours. With anyone else she would have talked about her experience, how affected she had been, still was. With Cal, she hesitated and wasn't sure why – intuition, the fear that she might spoil something. Instead she wondered if this was *it* with Cal: being with him on a hill, looking out on to an archipelago of islands, night

233

falling, the darkness binding them together in silent companionship. How unexpected, she thought. Having day-dreamed about *it* being sex, marriage, a date or as little as a kiss, she didn't think she minded the alternative a bit.

So quiet was the settling night that they heard Catriona's footfall when she was still some distance away. Helen said, 'I'll go to meet her. You stay here.' A few moments later Cal heard voices – mostly Helen's, as though Catriona was having second thoughts.

When Helen reappeared, Catriona was hanging back and Cal decided to start talking. 'Helen's been telling me you're the only friend Ewan's got left. I can help him if you'll let me. Why don't we sit down and I'll tell you what Ewan was doing the night Joss was killed?'

Catriona remained standing.

Cal stood too and carried on. 'Round about this time two nights ago I was on Priest's Island watching a boat crossing the sound. There were two men in that boat. One of them was Ewan. Later that night Joss was killed. But I saw Ewan early the next morning. He was still on Priest's Island.'

Now Catriona appeared rapt, her face like a moon illuminated by hope. But, as Cal continued, it dimmed as if the light inside her was sputtering. 'If only it hadn't been night-time,' Cal said. 'I would know for certain that Ewan never left Priest's Island. But I couldn't see when it was pitch-dark, and the wind was so loud I might not have heard if he'd taken the boat. Also I slept on and off. But if you want to know whether I think Ewan stayed on Priest's Island all night, yes, I do, and I think I know what he was doing there. He was taking a collector of wild birds' eggs to the raven's nest on the cliff. That broken eggshell I brought to your house this morning – it came from that nest. The eggs were a very rare type, a genetic abnormality, and prized by collectors. That's why the police found all that money on Ewan's boat – I think it was a payment.'

Catriona gasped, 'Is that where Ewan got it?' As though she, too, had been having private doubts.

'The egg collector could be a man called Pinkie Pryke. He's well known for his collection of this type of rare egg,' Cal continued. 'The question is, what happened to him? He wasn't in the boat when Ewan returned to Eilean Dubh.'

'Do you know what happened?' Catriona asked.

'I can guess. I found the eggs yesterday. They were in a cloth pouch and washed up on the shore. Only one egg was unbroken. I think there had been an accident and Pinkie Pryke fell off the cliff after climbing down to the nest. That's why the pouch ended up in the sea. Ewan probably got rid of anything else that was evidence of Pinkie having been on Priest's Island – the other man had a backpack when I saw him. That's why Ewan hasn't told the police where he was or what he was doing, because he's implicated in covering up another death and another crime.'

Helen went closer to Catriona. 'Are you all right?'

She nodded. 'Have you told the police about this?' She was addressing Cal.

'No, a statement from me wouldn't help Ewan because Beacom, the police, are only interested in proving him guilty. They'll find an expert to say the sound was passable that night for someone with Ewan's knowledge and experience and I can't swear on oath that he never left Priest's Island.' Cal paused, as though thinking it through. 'They'd make out the other evidence – the note, the knife – was so compelling it proved that Ewan had gone back to Eilean Dubh to murder Joss. They'd say he planned the raid on the raven's nest the night a storm was forecast to give himself an alibi. They'd say Ewan got caught out by events. He hadn't anticipated an accident or his witness disappearing. That was why he hasn't said he was on Priest's Island and admitted to a different and lesser crime. No, whatever I told the police, Ewan would still be charged with murder and Bella would be implicated for withholding evidence and obstructing a murder investigation. She knew what Ewan was doing, ask her.'

Catriona lit a cigarette. She seemed deep in thought.

Cal added, 'I don't think Ewan's a murderer. That's why I went to speak to your aunt. I need someone to tell me what's going on. He doesn't stand a chance otherwise.'

For a while Catriona carried on smoking. Then she said, 'I'll tell you what I know.' She took another drag on her cigarette. Her voice was quiet and jerky, as though sharing a difficult private memory with the night. 'These two Australians arrived in the tea room. It was last spring. They'd been on Priest's Island, climbing the sea cliff, and they showed Auntie Bella and me their photographs. They'd taken some of the raven's nest. Auntie Bella must have known the eggs were unusual because she asked if she could have the pictures emailed to her.' Then, with frustration, Catriona exclaimed, 'What was she thinking!'

The tip of her cigarette flared red. 'Ewan doesn't know about birds but Auntie Bella does.' After a moment she went on. 'Ewan won't say anything to the police, not if there's a risk of Auntie Bella getting into trouble. Not unless there's no other way.' Not even then, her tone seemed to suggest. She exclaimed again, another realization. 'So that's why she was being weird when the pig was found. Auntie Bella was standing at my window looking at the gulls on East Skerry and saying she was sorry. I said, "Sorry for what, what have you done?"'

Catriona laughed in a single short breath, like a cough.

'She wouldn't tell me. Now I know why. She thought it was that man Pinkie.'

Cal said, 'It's complicated for Ewan, if there's been an accident, if there's another body.'

Catriona stubbed out her cigarette and lit another. 'It's so unfair!'

Helen asked, 'What's unfair?'

'Ewan never said before . . .' Catriona spoke warily, uncertain about carrying on. 'It's like now . . .' She dragged on her cigarette. 'When Max disappeared . . . Mr Wheeler, the police were saying it was murder, and Ewan couldn't tell the truth.' She exhaled, her cigarette smoke escaping along with a secret. 'Ewan and Max . . .' She sounded nervous about mentioning their names together. 'They used to hang out. Nobody else knew, apart from me.' A pause. 'Ewan will kill me . . .'

Cal said, 'He won't have to know.' He waited so she didn't feel pushed. 'You'd better tell me. If you think it could help him . . . otherwise he's going to be in prison for thirty years.'

The cigarette flared red while she made her decision: 'I didn't like Max.'

'Did you know him too?' Cal asked.

'I met him a few times. He wasn't a nice boy.'

'But Ewan and Max got on?'

'I suppose. They did stuff together.'

'What sort of things?'

'Hanging out on Priest's Island. Max used to sleep there in a tent and Ewan would go over in his uncle's boat and join him. Boys' stuff . . .'

'Did Max's father know?'

'No. Neither did Ewan's uncle. After Wheeler bought the island, Donald Grant was always drinking.'

'You and Ewan were together then?'

'Sort of, it wasn't like we *did* anything.' She hesitated. 'I was young. Anyway, we had a big row.'

'About what?'

'About Max. Ewan was making Max do all these things, taking it out on him because his father bought the island.'

'What sort of things?'

'Fighting, making Max go on a death swing, horrible things ... Ewan thought I'd be impressed but I told him I wasn't. I said I didn't want to be with him if he was going to be nasty to a smaller boy, even if Max was a Wheeler. We broke up, but afterwards Ewan said he'd made friends with Max. He asked if we could be together again and said he was sorry about the things he'd done. He hadn't been himself, he'd been angry about the island. But he'd changed and he wanted to prove it to me. Would I go with him to Priest's Island when Max was there? He kept going on about it so I said OK, if he wanted. Ewan said I would enjoy it. Max would be my friend too.' She snorted. 'But Max wasn't expecting me. He didn't want me there. He started talking about the island being *his* and said I could only stay the night if I passed a test. It was a rule, *his* rule. He said he'd learned it from Ewan.'

'He said that, *his* island?'

'Yes, like he was a little king or something.'

'What did he expect you to do?'

'Go on the death swing.'

'What was that?' Cal asked.

'It was on the cliff, where the ravens nested, on that ledge. Either you climbed down on the rope which was tied round a rock at the top of the cliff, or if you were small like me and Max you could climb down a deep crack in the cliff face. It was just wide enough and went all the way to the ledge. Once you got there, you had to catch the rope with a boathook.

Because of the overhang above the ledge the rope hung out of reach unless there was enough wind to blow it in. Ewan had made Max swing ten times over the sea and under the ledge without putting his foot down. That was what Max wanted me to do.'

'Did you?'

She snorted again. 'As if. I told Ewan he had to take me back to Eilean Dubh. But he was cross with me. He said I should have gone on the swing and I'd let him down. We had another row. I said I wasn't surprised Ewan and Max were friends because they were the same – Ewan had taught Max to be a bully like him. After he dropped me at the harbour, he went back to Priest's Island.'

'When was that?'

'The summer before Max disappeared.'

'They remained friends?'

'Yes, but Ewan told me the police mustn't know. He was frightened they'd find out about Ewan and Max fighting when they were younger, that I might tell them.'

Catriona stubbed out her cigarette in a spray of burning tobacco.

Cal asked, 'Ewan wasn't with Max the night he went missing?'

'He wanted to go but his uncle stopped him taking out the boat. The one night his Uncle Donald wasn't drunk was the night Max disappeared! Ewan says Max would still be alive if his uncle hadn't run out of whisky.'

'Why?'

Catriona hesitated. 'I said I wouldn't tell anyone.' Then, nervously, 'After we broke up that time, he told me he'd taken Max to this place he'd discovered. Nobody knew about it apart from him and Max. Once you went inside no one could find you. It wasn't possible to go there all the time, it depended

239

on the moon. I thought he was making it up, to let me think I'd missed out on something. But sometimes I wonder if Ewan is worried that's where Max went when he disappeared.'

'Did he say where this place was?' Cal asked.

'By the shieling, that's what he said when he told me that first time. But now if I mention it he says he was just winding me up.'

Cal said nothing.

'They were friends, Ewan and Max,' Catriona said after a long gap. 'They *were*,' she insisted, as though the night air had been whispering its doubts or that Cal's sudden silence had unnerved her.

~

Catriona and Helen left together. Cal waited. When he could no longer hear the skittering of the stones they dislodged, he followed them down the hill. At the road, he turned right. At the turn-off to the Deep Blue he went left. When he saw the back door of the chalet was open and the light on – the signal that Helen was alone – he jumped the fence, crossed the side garden and went inside. Helen was waiting for him in the kitchen, drinking coffee, another mug waiting on the table for Cal.

'Right at the end, why were you like that?' she asked him. 'You were so quiet. Catriona thought she'd said too much or the wrong thing. She was very unsettled. She thought she'd got Ewan into trouble. I tried to reassure her. I've seen you do that before, go AWOL.'

He sat down. 'I was thinking.'

'I know that,' Helen said. '*What* were you thinking?'

Cal's lips compressed. The gesture meant he was still

thinking; he wasn't sure about the conclusion. 'When Max Wheeler disappeared, there were big tides, called spring tides. Spring refers to the sea rising up. They happen after every new and full moon.'

Helen nodded. 'I read about there being a spring tide in Max Wheeler's investigation file. The currents were stronger than normal, weren't they?'

'The currents would have been strong but I expect they were normal for spring tides.'

Helen smiled at his fastidiousness. It had always amused her – Cal, who lived like a vagrant, being so particular about odd things. As she sipped her coffee Cal explained that spring tides were the biggest tides – high tide was higher than average but low tide lower than average. 'When Max disappeared, the low tide was almost as low as it would ever be.'

Catriona's reference to the moon had made him think. Was the place Ewan had found on Priest's Island only accessible at a spring low tide, the lowest tide? Instead of Max stumbling into the sea at night or being swept away by the tidal currents in the sound, as the township liked to think, maybe Max's death had something to do with the low tide, how low it had been and what it exposed. 'Low tide was at four minutes past two in the morning when Max disappeared. Perhaps he'd gone to this place Ewan had discovered and became trapped when the tide turned.'

Helen said, 'So Catriona was wrong about Ewan – he wasn't just winding her up when he said he'd found a secret place?'

'I don't think so. Why else would he have mentioned only being able to get to it if the moon was right?'

'I could ring Beacom, get him to ask Ewan.'

'Won't he deny it, say the place didn't exist? Wouldn't you? If you thought that was how Max died, if you thought some of his bones might still exist and the police would suspect you of trying to conceal his body there? Ewan hasn't mentioned it to the police or to Catriona for the last five years. Why should he now?'

'Yes, you're right,' Helen said. 'And if Beacom asks Ewan about it, he'll know that Catriona's been talking. We can't do that to her, not if we don't have to, not yet.'

Cal agreed. 'It was spring tide today. Low tide tomorrow afternoon is also pretty low, half a metre higher than it was when Max disappeared, but it might still be low enough. I'll be able to see what's exposed, where Max could have gone, if that's what happened.'

Helen reached a decision. 'I'll brief Beacom by phone, tell him not to mention it to Ewan.'

Cal nodded. He got to his feet. 'I've got charts and maps of Priest's Island that'll give me an idea of where to look.'

Helen went to the back door with him and he said good night.

As she closed the door, she felt oddly disappointed by his abrupt departure. Yet what else did she expect?

25

Cal woke to the whop-whop of propeller blades. He wiped his hand across the pickup's side windows and looked out through the smear. In the grey of early morning, a red and white Coastguard helicopter was hovering above the sound. Cal glanced at the clock: seven forty-five. Now the Sikorsky was turning, going towards Eilean Dubh, flying slowly, searching. Cal closed his eyes, a pause to a day that was starting too quickly. Whop-whop. The noise roused him again and he opened the door. A small boat with a puttering outboard was circling an islet. A RIB was speeding west of the harbour. Another was leaving the jetty at Priest's Island. He yawned, then stumbled from the door of the pickup and walked to the slipway. Taking off yesterday's clothes, he waded into the sea and ducked his head. Returning to the pickup, he collected his jeans and dried himself quickly with his discarded tee shirt. He dressed – black jersey, dirty jeans and walking boots – and brushed his teeth, rinsing his mouth with water from a bottle.

On the road he passed two police cars and a police RIB patrolling the shore.

Arriving at the Deep Blue, he felt that he'd been the last person left sleeping. A dozen people were standing outside the tea room, stony-faced and watchful. More were gathered by the harbour – the media, milling. Cal saw Beacom. He was with other police by the *Jacqueline*; pointing, issuing orders. Cal parked close to a group of reporters and listened in.

'Is she blonde like Joss?'

'What age was she?'

Cal noticed the past tense. Was someone else dead?

'Does anyone have a picture?'

'Who are you talking about?' Cal asked, but they had started to walk away because Beacom was moving. Cal tagged along and caught Beacom's eye. Though the contact was fleeting, Cal's impression was of a man knocked off balance and unsure how to get back. That wasn't like Beacom. Whatever had happened must be serious.

Beacom held up his hands, calling for quiet. 'Everybody, please.' He sounded impatient, which was also unlike Beacom. Cal associated him with coolness, subtlety, having a plan, playing a long game.

Beacom was talking again. 'Hannah Wheeler was reported missing at five ten this morning. The *Jacqueline*'s dinghy had also gone. It has since been found west of here, floating and upright, but Hannah wasn't on board. Everything possible is being done to find her. Our thoughts are with her father and sister. Our efforts, energies and resources are focused on finding Hannah alive.' He listed the manpower, boats and equipment deployed. Another Coastguard helicopter would be arriving soon. 'We're investigating a number of possibilities, one of which is the dinghy ran aground on a skerry or rocks during the night and Hannah was thrown out.'

A male voice shouted out: 'Is there any hope?'

Beacom replied, 'Of course there is. Hannah is a good swimmer. She's young and strong. She could have reached shore. At this stage we have every expectation of finding her alive.'

What else could Beacom say, Cal thought – that searching for Hannah was complicated by her swimming ability? He imagined the Coastguard's search and rescue experts would have been pessimistic. Beacom would have been briefed about people becoming disorientated when they were in the sea in the dark. They might strike out in the wrong direction, away from land. The current was another factor complicating the search. Low tide had been at two in the morning. Later on, the flood tide could have run at between three and seven knots in different parts of the sound. Even at three knots the current was travelling at five and a half kilometres an hour; at seven knots, almost thirteen. If Hannah had swum with the current she could be a long way beyond the present search area. Beacom was missing two other important pieces of information. He didn't know when Hannah had gone into the water or where. Cal was less optimistic than Beacom of finding her alive.

A woman reporter said, 'Can you tell us what happened last night? Was there an argument? Do you know of any reason why Hannah should go off like that?'

Beacom consulted a female police officer who was standing behind him. When he turned back, he said, 'There was no argument or disagreement. Hannah's father went to bed at about ten. Hannah and her older sister Chloe stayed up to talk. As you can imagine, it was an emotional conversation about Joss and Max. Although it was private, I can tell you that Hannah expressed a desire to return to Priest's Island. She told Chloe she wanted to visit the chapel. Hannah and Chloe agreed they would ask their father this morning. Then Chloe retired to bed and Hannah went on deck. In Chloe's opinion, Hannah must have felt impelled to attempt a crossing of the sound on her own during the night.'

The same reporter asked, 'Didn't the police officer on guard duty try to stop her?'

But Beacom didn't appear to hear. Instead he was taking a question from behind Cal. 'Why have you stopped the township from helping in the search?' Cal turned and saw Alistair, his square head thrust forward in anger. The people who had been standing outside the tea room were clustered behind him. Alistair appeared muscular and self-important, as though he was leading a delegation. 'It's Wheeler's doing, isn't it?' Alistair demanded. 'He doesn't want the township involved.'

Beacom replied that the police had sufficient – 'in fact, more than enough' – resources because of the large deployment for the investigation into Joss Wheeler's murder. 'Mr Wheeler has other important and distressing matters on his mind, but I'm sure he would be as grateful as I am for any offers of help. That's all, thank you.'

Afterwards, Cal hung around while Alistair held court, accusing Wheeler and the police of blacklisting the township because of the wrong-doings of a disturbed young man who had grown up on the mainland. Cal noticed Helen. She was walking round the back of the group. She turned to look at the helicopter when she was beside him. 'The boss wants you to go to Priest's Island, look for this place that Ewan mentioned to Catriona.'

Cal replied in an undertone. 'Low tide is at two eighteen. I'll be back later if you're thinking of going for a run this evening. I'll let you know if I've found anything then.'

Mary-Anne picked at Ina's uneaten chocolate cake and agonized about Hannah, whether there was anything the township could do to help.

'I've been praying for her,' she said to Helen. 'Would it be a good idea if I stood up now and asked everyone to join me?'

Seeing how agitated she was, Helen tried to reassure her.

'I'm sure everyone is praying already. Probably best if people do it privately.'

'I suppose you're right,' Mary-Anne sighed.

Later, when Mary-Anne was calmer, Helen asked, 'Was Hannah closest to Max, do you think, since she was next to him in age?'

'Oh, I don't really know,' Mary-Anne replied. 'Bella said Joss was always worrying about what happened to Max. She blamed herself for not being with him on the island. Maybe Joss, not Hannah, was closest emotionally to Max because she was the oldest and felt responsible for him. I've known that before in families.'

'Really, how interesting,' Helen said. Then, a few moments later, 'I wonder why Joss blamed herself for that night in particular.'

Mary-Anne looked puzzled.

'Well,' Helen said, 'Max spent other nights alone on the island. Joss didn't go with him any of those nights. Isobel told me that. Or was it you? I forget who.' She paused but Mary-Anne didn't answer. 'Why do you think Joss felt guilty about not being with Max that night?' Helen persisted.

'I don't know.' Mary-Anne looked alarmed. 'You won't say anything to Bella. She'll think I've been talking.'

'Of course I won't,' Helen reassured her. 'I'm just curious. Are you a fan of detective fiction? Well, I am. I like the old-fashioned ones when all the characters gather at the end and the murderer is revealed. Don't you think that being in the tea room, hearing all the chat, is rather like that, being in the middle of a murder mystery?' She made a guilty face as if she couldn't help herself.

Mary-Anne was about to speak but Helen gushed on. 'It's been so interesting, trying to work out the clues, what's important and what isn't. You see, I was thinking . . . there

247

was one thing different about that night.' She leaned close to Mary-Anne, becoming conspiratorial. 'Hannah.' She raised her eyebrows as if prompting Mary-Anne. 'Hannah was the difference. Every other time Max had camped alone. Wasn't that night supposed to be Hannah's first? Why did Joss and Chloe go to see whether she was all right when she was safe with Max and they were only a shout away?' Now Helen put on a frustrated expression. 'Some detective I'd be – too many questions without answers.' She ate another crumb of Ina's cake – Ina was once again asleep in her chair, clutching Helen's arm. 'Still, it's interesting that Joss blamed herself. Her fault, since she's the eldest. Isn't that what you just said? I wonder what she meant by that: a responsibility to Max or to Hannah?' Helen looked defeated, as if it was a mystery that would never be solved. 'Or to both.'

After a moment she added, 'Another thing, was it you who told me about Max being not a very pleasant boy? I'm sure someone did but I can't remember who. I wonder if Joss couldn't trust him to be nice to Hannah and if that's why she and Chloe went to the island?'

Mary-Anne appeared put out, as though Helen had gone too far. 'Well, it certainly wasn't me. Nobody's ever told me that. This isn't a crime novel, Helen.' She lifted her head towards her God. 'Real people have died. I think you'd do well to remember that.'

Afterwards, she was silent, Helen assumed in prayer for Hannah and probably asking forgiveness for her flash of temper.

26

Wherever Cal looked, machines and people were on the move. Police cars drove along the shore road on Eilean Dubh. An assortment of small craft kept watch along the north coast of Priest's Island and around the islets and skerries in the sound. One helicopter patrolled to the east, towards the Minch, and another to the west, on the Atlantic side. The restlessness that Cal saw around his RIB was matched by his own unease – the recurring thought that he was an actor in the Wheeler family tragedy. Crossing the sound, he regretted ignoring the warning signs of tensions, especially when he thought back to his first meeting on the *Jacqueline* when Hannah had become distressed.

Cal remembered Hannah's parting remark to her father, the frustration and distress with which she said, 'Anyone would think Max is the only child that matters . . . the only child you've lost.' Like Hannah, Cal also felt discarded. What was he thinking, interfering in the affairs of a fractured family? Of all people, he should have known better. Then there was Joss's attack on him. He touched the scabs on his face, finding them hardening, changing – almost *living* – when Joss was dead. If he hadn't taken on the role of Beacom's *provocateur* would Joss be alive? Would Hannah be missing? Even when he reached the south shore of Priest's Island, away from the cars, boats and helicopters, he questioned why he was still there. Inquiring into Max's disappearance and death had led to more blood being shed. Shouldn't he leave?

So it was in a troubled frame of mind that Cal hunted the

shore below the shieling, looking into the hollows and fissures left exposed by the falling tide. Not only a troubled conscience but a sense of futility: what was the purpose of trying to find out where Ewan and Max used to hide away when Hannah was the Wheeler child who mattered now? Cal should be involved in searching for her. After all, bodies in the water and where they travelled were his areas of expertise. Cal's feeling of uselessness increased as the gaps and openings revealed by the retreating sea all seemed to be too narrow, not sufficiently enclosed or too shallow.

Once you went inside no one could find you. Wasn't that what Catriona had said?

Then, at low tide, just as he was about to give up, he noticed a rectangular dark area at the base of a large perpendicular slab of rock across the small bay: the emergence of an opening of sorts. On closer inspection, Cal saw the gap extended beneath the slab and water was draining from it in a fast stream, a sign that much more was inside. That it *had* an inside. He shone in his torch and lit up a rock passageway which led into a flooded chamber: the torch beam lit up a back wall.

Cal crouched and crawled on his hands and knees through the stream. After three metres, a cavern opened and he was able to stand. The floor was ankle-deep in water and covered with stones, weed and silt. The walls were rock. The atmosphere was cold and dank. Cal shone his torch around and was surprised by how high the roof was above him, twice the height of a normal room, and how wide and spacious the interior. He formed the impression of an accident of geology having created this large chamber rather than it having been gouged out by the scouring of the sea. It was as though at some time in the distant past a vast stone slab had slipped from the land – a natural portcullis dropping – and had enclosed this space. Eventually, over decades, even hundreds of years, the sea had undermined the area below the rock and had created an entrance. Cal thought of Ewan showing it off to Max and of Max going there on his own and becoming trapped. Was that what had happened to the teenager?

Cal shone his torch on to the back wall and saw that the high-water mark was higher than he was. Looking around for the possibility of escape – somewhere the rock could be climbed to get away from the incoming tide – he noticed a rectangular shape dug into one of the side walls. Above was a rusted iron ring and another and another, an ascending procession of what appeared to be footholds and handholds leading to a deep recess or alcove that could have accommodated a medium-sized man or a teenage boy who was small for his age. A cross was carved above the recess. It was crude but unmistakably done by human hand.

As Cal crossed the chamber intending to climb up to the alcove, there was a stirring of a shadow at the edge of his vision, similar to when he was at sea and a dolphin or porpoise breached nearby. There would be a split-second awareness of movement and, once Cal had turned his head to see what it was, it would reappear a little further away, a sleek black back arcing through the water. On this occasion, he went to the far side of the chamber to be able to shine his torch further into the alcove. He imagined the movement to be one of the odd dancing effects caused by the beam reflecting off wet rock. But no: again he saw movement, this time more definite, a pressing into the rock, as though he had disturbed a terrified night-creature which was cringing from the light. He made a noise, a cough which changed into a shout, not sure what he expected to frighten, perhaps a bat. Instead he saw blonde hair and the side of a face.

'Hannah,' he said, 'is that you?' His voice lifted in surprise and relief. 'Thank God, you're alive.' He noted the slump of her shoulders, a physical dejection to match the lifelessness of her face. 'Hannah,' he tried again. 'It's me, Cal McGill. We met on your father's boat. Are you all right?' Again she didn't respond or react. Cal moved the torch in case its blinding light was disorientating her. 'Everyone's been so worried about you,' he said. 'How long have you been up there? Your legs must be stiff. You'll be cold. Shall I climb up and help you down?'

He splashed as he went back across the cave and Hannah cried out, 'Don't.'

Cal looked up and saw that she had stretched out her left arm. The torch caught a flash of silver, a blade. She held a small knife at her exposed wrist. 'I'll do it. I'll cut myself.' She jabbed the point closer. 'I will, if you come any closer.'

———

Soon there was another incident to intrigue the detective in Helen. Catriona came into the tea room from outside, an unfinished cigarette in her hand. 'The *Jacqueline*'s moving,' she announced. 'She's leaving harbour.'

The tea room erupted in noise and movement – chairs scraped as people hurried outside to watch. The commotion disturbed Ina. She woke with a start, gripping tight on to Helen's arm. 'What's that racket?' she asked.

'The Wheelers are leaving,' Helen answered. 'You stay here and I'll find out what's going on.'

Following the others outside, she heard snatches of conversation, speculation that David Wheeler and Chloe had decided to join the search for Hannah or that they had been advised by the police to take the *Jacqueline* out into the sound, for their own safety.

When the boat was beyond the harbour wall Chloe

appeared on deck and stood at the stern watching the township watching her. Helen thought her demeanour was defiant, almost accusing. The tea room's regulars must have thought so too because they fell silent and became restless. One by one they returned to their tables, but Helen watched the *Jacqueline* until she was halfway across the sound. Going back inside, the tea room was buzzing again.

'Has something else happened while I was away?' Helen asked when she sat down beside Ina. 'Some use I am, Ina. I was supposed to be telling you what was going on.'

Mary-Ann replied for Ina. 'Bella rang Constable Dyer and he told her that Chloe had persuaded her father to carry out Hannah's wish. They're going to the chapel on Priest's Island to remember Joss and Max. They're going to wait for Hannah there.'

'Not look for her?' Helen stared through the window towards the sound. 'That's odd, don't you think?'

Mary-Anne appeared irritated at Helen playing detective again. 'Constable Dyer also said that Chloe planned to light a fire and keep it burning so her sister would be able to find her way home. The smoke would guide her during the day and the flames at night. He didn't seem to think there was anything curious about that.'

Helen said, 'Well, he's the policeman . . .'

'It's OK, Hannah.' Cal backed away.

Slowly, her arms dropped to her sides.

'I won't come up there if you don't want me to.' He moved back again and the light of the torch moved with him. 'But I'm not going to leave you.'

She didn't react and Cal asked whether she minded him

talking. There was something he wanted to tell her; a confession, he supposed, an apology too. She didn't reply but sat back and leaned her left shoulder against the rock wall – signs, Cal thought, of her being prepared to listen.

'I was thinking of you when I found this place,' he began. 'We've all been dreading the thought of you being pulled out of the sea, dead. I'm so relieved you're alive. Everyone else will be too – there's a big search going on for you.' He paused, trying to gauge her reaction. 'I have a confession to make. It was a bad idea coming to work for your father. My mistake – I'm sorry. All I seem to have done is to make the tension between the township and your family worse.' Still she didn't move. 'When I saw how upset you were that time on the *Jacqueline*, I should have walked away.'

He stopped speaking. The only sounds were of running water and the rhythmic plop of drips falling from the rock ceiling. 'You going off like this will have made everyone understand how hard these last few years have been for you.' Hannah seemed to slump a little further and Cal tried a different tactic. He had to get her talking. 'Did your brother Max show you this place?'

She didn't answer.

Cal carried on, 'I don't have brothers or sisters, so I can't imagine what you're going through. But I did lose my mother when I was seventeen – she died from cancer. And my father had a breakdown and went away to another continent, so I lost him as well. I'm alone too and quite a few times in the last few years I would have wanted to hide away in the dark, somewhere like this, where no one might find me. But I'm glad I didn't.'

Still Hannah said nothing.

'What you're feeling now is the worst it will be. In time, the pain will be dulled. It will be bearable. It's different for me, I know, but that's been my experience. I'm sure it'll be yours too.'

Again he paused.

'I can promise you – you won't always feel like this. You will be happy again.'

He hoped he wasn't saying the wrong things. 'Hannah, would you like me to switch off my torch – would you rather be in the dark? Promise me you won't hurt yourself when it's off.'

Still silence and Cal said, 'I'll take that as a promise.'

Now he couldn't see her. A low, weak light came from the cave's entrance. It made shadows inside like grey ghosts. Cal listened for Hannah moving but all he heard were drips falling and the lapping water which was starting to flow into the chamber. For the moment his concern was Hannah – the water level would take time to become critical. He wondered what she was thinking, what she was doing. Was she cutting herself? He imagined the drips might be blood, not water. He wanted to turn on the torch. Instead, he said, 'Hannah, say something so I know you're all right.'

He heard her move. She coughed to clear her throat.

'You don't understand. It was me . . . I killed Max.'

27

A thin column of smoke rose above Priest's Island. Lower down, against the russets and pale yellows of the land, it appeared greyish. Higher up, contrasting with the black clouds approaching from the south-west, it seemed cleaned and cotton-wool white.

'Look.' Helen nudged Catriona as they leaned against the front wall of the Deep Blue. 'That must be Chloe starting her fire.'

Catriona glanced up briefly before settling back and turning towards Helen, deliberately averting her eyes. She put her cigarette in her mouth.

Helen said, 'You don't like Chloe, do you?'

'What's to like?'

'You don't even feel sorry for her?'

'Why should I?'

'I'm not saying you should.' Helen gave Catriona a quick reassuring smile. 'I'm asking because I'm interested that you don't, because I trust your instincts about people, because I don't either. I'm wondering why that is, why we don't feel sympathy for her, considering what she's gone through.' She watched the column of smoke. 'I wonder if it's her or if it's us.'

'It's her,' Catriona replied immediately.

'Because of what she did, coming into the tea room like that, saying what she said?' Helen glanced back at Catriona. 'Why do you think she did that?'

'Make everyone feel sorry for her, I suppose.'

'That's the funny thing,' Helen said. 'It didn't, though, did it?' She paused to consider the answer to her own question. 'It should have done, but it didn't. I wonder why that is.'

'Because,' Catriona said under her breath, 'she's a bitch.' She glanced at Helen guiltily.

'That's it,' Helen laughed. 'You're right. Queen Bitch.' Then, on reflection, focusing again on the smoke, 'But why would she want us to think that? We were sorry for her because Joss had been killed – at least I was – but not after that performance in the tea room. What impelled her? It's odd, that's all.'

Helen watched the fire smoke and cloud creeping over the sky, darkening the late afternoon. 'If it was your sister who was missing,' she said, 'is that what you'd do? Light a fire . . .'

'Dunno.' Nor did Catriona care, her tone implied.

Helen carried on regardless, tantalized by the mystery of Chloe's behaviour. 'What's a fire got to do with Hannah being missing? If she's alive she would have seen the helicopters or the boats searching for her. If she wanted to be found, she would have shown herself to them. If she's injured or dead, the fire isn't going to help her at all. She's hardly going to swim towards it. In fact, that's exactly what she shouldn't do since the tide's coming back in and the currents will be strong. No. That's not Chloe's purpose in lighting a fire. She's showing off, just like she was in the tea room. Chloe wants the township's attention.'

'I told you,' Catriona said, 'bitch.'

Helen nodded and, in a quieter voice, said, 'No, not like the tea room. Not like the tea room at all.'

'What isn't?'

'I said Chloe is showing off, like in the tea room. But, on reflection, that's not what she's doing. In the tea room she

257

wanted everyone to look at her. Tonight everyone will be looking at the flames.'

Catriona shrugged. 'So?'

Hannah's voice was weak and trembling, as if it was travelling into the chamber from a darker place where there was not even a ghostly light.

Although a short distance separated them, Cal felt Hannah was slipping from him. 'Hannah,' he said. 'Listen to me. You were eleven years old when Max disappeared.' He was careful not to say died or killed. 'You were a child.'

'I killed him.' Her voice was matter-of-fact and flat. There was no trace of recrimination or regret.

'Tell me what happened. Was it an accident?'

Hannah said nothing.

'If it was an accident, there'll be an investigation, but you'll come through it, everything will be all right in the end – you'll rebuild your life, go to university, have an interesting job, travel, marry if that's what you want to do, have children. You'll be like everyone else.'

Silence.

Cal said, 'Isn't that what Joss would have wanted – for you to get on with your life and leave the past behind?'

Silence.

'Did Joss know how Max died?' Cal asked.

Another clearing of the throat: 'Yes.'

'Hannah, will you make me a promise? If you tell me about Max you won't cut yourself, will you? Promise you won't hurt yourself.'

'Tell my father,' she said after a while.

A cold chill came over Cal. Suddenly he knew what she

planned to do. She wanted him to tell Wheeler because she would be dead. 'I'll go with you to see him,' Cal said. 'We'll be together. If you like, I'll do the talking, but he won't believe me if you're not with me.'

Silence.

'Hannah, are you all right? Listen to me, you can do this. We can do this. I'll be with you. I'm not going anywhere.'

Her quietness unnerved him. Was she cutting herself? When Hannah started talking again Cal wasn't sure whether to be relieved or alarmed. Was this her suicide note?

'I was so happy when Max brought me here . . .' She spoke so softly Cal could hardly hear her. 'I thought I was being grown-up.'

Again Cal registered the lack of emotion, as though she had already lost feeling and all that remained to be spent was her blood. He had to keep her talking, even though he felt the sea water rising towards his knees.

'Was that when you asked if you could spend the night with Max on the island?'

She let out a brittle laugh and became animated. 'I was so excited when my father said I could go. I should have known Max was lying when he said he'd look after me. I should've known it wouldn't be straightforward.'

Now softer again, as though she was talking to herself: 'Nothing with Max ever was.'

Another laugh.

'What happened?'

'After we were dropped at the jetty, Max said we had to hurry. He wanted to share a big secret with me and I had to promise not to tell anyone. I agreed. Why wouldn't I? It was an adventure, sleeping out, being with Max on the island.'

Then, a pause: 'This cave is where he brought me.'

Another: 'This is where it started.'

'What happened, Hannah? Tell me.'

'Max said he'd only let me into the cave if I promised to do something afterwards. He didn't say what, except that it was a rule of his, a test that everyone had to pass before they were allowed to stay a night on the island. I had to give my word.'

Her voice wavered at the memory.

'If I didn't, he said he'd take me back across the island; he'd leave me on the jetty to be collected; he wouldn't let me see inside this cave or let me spend the night in his tent. If I refused, it would prove I wasn't grown-up enough.'

A longer gap.

'I promised and Max showed me in here. He said hermit priests had used this place as a hide-away hundreds of years ago and that a storm had covered the entrance, which was why its existence had been forgotten. Another storm had recently cleared away the rocks. I wanted him to tell me more – how did he know about the priests and the storms; how had he found the entrance? But Max said we had to hurry. The tide would be coming back in. We mustn't delay, and anyway, I had to keep my side of the bargain. I had to pass the test before he would let me spend the night in his tent.'

'What did he make you do?'

'He took me to the sea cliff . . .' She hesitated, the memory too hard.

'Why?' Cal prompted.

'He wanted to see how frightened he could make me. That was how Max was – he was always nasty. Why did I think he would be any different?'

'What happened?'

'He made me climb down a big crack in the cliff. It was just wide enough for us because we were small. He went first. I didn't say anything because I didn't want Max to think

I was scared. I followed him to a ledge where there was a big nest – Max said it was a raven's nest. A rope was hanging from the top of the cliff and swinging just out of reach. Max caught it with a boathook.'

A long sigh: 'He swung out over the sea and on the way back he opened his legs and tried to grab me. He said he would drop me into the sea if I didn't get on the swing with him.

'Tell my father that,' Hannah said, suddenly loud, angry. 'Tell him Max was mean like that. Tell him he didn't know Max, and the Max he remembers is made up.'

Once more softly: 'He never had a son like that.'

Cal said, 'I'll only tell him if you're with me.'

'No,' Hannah said, now firmly. 'You'll tell him because you'll have to. There'll be no one else who can.'

She was right, of course. For a moment Cal began to wish he hadn't found her. Then she wouldn't have had a messenger. Perhaps she might have decided to deliver the message herself and to stay alive.

Hannah was speaking again, quickly. 'I was so scared. Max was swinging towards me, grabbing at me. I said I wanted to go back to the *Jacqueline* and I didn't want to spend the night on the island. But Max just kept on at me, trying to pull me off the ledge. He was swinging in so fast and I picked up the boathook . . .'

Cal listened to the water and didn't dare to make another sound.

'. . . I was just trying to protect myself. I didn't mean to harm him. The boathook went into his eye. The speed of his swing drove him on to the spike.'

Hannah stopped. Then, her voice trembling, she said, 'Can't you see, I was just trying to keep him away.'

Then: 'I can still feel his weight . . .'

Cal waited for her to continue.

'I let the boathook go and Max swung past me and hit the back wall. After he fell, he didn't move. I didn't know what to do. I thought he might still try to grab me. I kept on kicking at him . . .

'. . . My shoes and gloves were covered in his blood. I killed him.'

Silence.

'Hannah, are you all right? Hannah?'

He switched on his torch and Hannah covered her face with her hands. She was kneeling, sitting back on her legs, her left side leaning against the alcove wall. 'I'm sorry,' he said as she twisted away. 'I had to make sure you were all right.' After he turned off the torch, an impression remained of Hannah being caught in the light and never being able to escape. He considered the glare that would be waiting for her outside, whether his reassurances about her being young enough to make a new life were misguided and whether, in Hannah's place, he wouldn't choose the dark.

After a while, he apologized again. There was another silence before he said, 'Did Joss find you on the ledge? Is that what happened next?'

Helen excused herself when Catriona finished her cigarette. After so many dramas, she felt wrung out. 'I think I'll put my feet up in the chalet and maybe go for a run later.'

'OK, see you sometime,' Catriona replied before going inside.

Back at the chalet, Helen read the case file on Max Wheeler then rang Beacom on the landline. Would he mind listening while she worked out some thoughts? She was coming round to the opinion that the investigation went wrong at the beginning. Why were the three Wheeler girls always questioned together? And why was their father allowed to sit in on the first interview? No attempt had been made to test the stories of the three girls separately.

'I might have done the same,' she said, 'since the girls were young – Joss, seventeen, Chloe, fifteen and Hannah, eleven. But knowing what we do now about Max's character – him being turned into a bully by Ewan – I can't help feeling the investigation was overly influenced by the family's show of grief, in particular Hannah's distress. If they hadn't been teenage girls – pretty, middle-class girls – would the investigation have been conducted that way? I don't think it would. From the beginning they were regarded as the victims and the township as the villains.'

'That's not surprising,' Beacom said, 'given the history of antagonism between the family and the township. Also, the aunt's car was vandalized that night. At the time, would I have thought there was a connection between that and Max's disappearance? I'm sure I would, and David Wheeler was talking abduction or murder right from the start; so were the media, putting pressure on the police.'

'Yes, I can see that,' Helen said. 'Now, sir, would you mind going outside and telling me what you see.' She waited on the phone.

'Smoke, a fire,' Beacom said when he returned. 'Is that the right answer?'

'Yes,' Helen replied. 'I think that's what you're supposed to see. Are there any police on Priest's Island overnight?'

'There's a constable on the *Jacqueline* but no one on the island.'

'In that case is there a RIB I could use, sir?'

'Should be one.'

'And two officers?'

'OK.'

'Can you ask them to bring the RIB to the old slipway, where McGill's pickup is parked? Give me half an hour. I'll change into my tracksuit and make out I'm going for a run.'

A few minutes later, Helen called Beacom again. 'Did anyone think to bring some night-vision equipment?'

<hr>

To Cal the sea lapping against the chamber's walls was the sound of the tide flowing in as well as of time running out. The water was at his thighs. Soon it would reach his hips and, in time, he would have to move. But, for the moment, he stayed where he was in case he disturbed Hannah. Perhaps it was Cal's imagination but he thought she was speaking faster as though the tide was carrying her along, hurrying her towards the conclusion. 'Yes,' she said, in answer to his question about Joss finding her. 'And Chloe was with her.'

'Did they climb down to the ledge?'

'No, I must have crawled back up the crevice to the top of the cliff. I don't remember anything except Joss and Chloe finding me there. I couldn't speak. They saw my shoes and gloves, and asked why they were covered with blood. They thought I was hurt.'

'Did they ask where Max was?'

'Yes.'

'Did you tell them?'

'Not straight away. I couldn't. Then Joss sat behind me and held me and asked, "Is Max all right?" and I started crying. Joss said, "What happened?" and I told her about the swing and Max trying to pull me off the ledge and me trying to stop him with the boathook. Joss asked, "Where is Max now?" and I said he was still on the ledge. He wasn't moving. I was crying all the time, begging Joss and Chloe not to tell my father.'

As if wondering to herself: 'Isn't that mad? I was more worried about my father knowing than about killing Max.'

To Cal: 'Be sure to tell him that, will you?'

Cal said nothing.

Hannah had flashes of memory after that. 'Joss taking off my shoes and socks though not my gloves – I don't know what happened to them. I remember Joss going away, then Chloe. When they came back Joss sat on one side of me and Chloe on the other. They talked in turns, saying they'd removed the rope hanging down the cliff and dropped it into the sea. They had also dislodged rocks to block the crevice that ran down the cliff, making it look like Max had caused the fall and had become trapped on the ledge. Joss said people would think Max had impaled himself trying to lever the rocks out of the way with the wooden end of the boathook.'

Cal was encouraged by how easily she was now speaking, as if the memories were no longer as painful. 'What did they do with Max?'

'They left him where they found him, up against the rear wall of the ledge by the back of the raven's nest. That's where I'd kicked him. The boathook which had fallen out of his eye was beside him. They said our father would never have to know how Max died so long as we all stuck to the same story. I had to tell him I'd changed my mind about spending the night with Max because I was cold and wet after falling into the sea and Max was being horrible and wouldn't let me borrow his spare clothes. Joss and Chloe would back me up and say Max was putting up his tent when they last saw him. In fact, Joss and Chloe had done that and lit his fire.'

Before going to the jetty, Joss and Chloe had taken off all

Hannah's clothes and washed them and her in the sea. She was shivering when she returned to the *Jacqueline*, which backed up her story about being cold and wet. 'I dried myself with a towel, changed into my pyjamas and had supper. I went to bed by eight thirty. Joss followed me soon after but Chloe stayed up later, going on deck at nine thirty with her torch, pretending to our father that she had an agreement with Max to exchange "good night" signals after dark. None of us slept that night because we were dreading the morning when Max would be found dead.'

Silence, apart from the drips and the lapping tide.

'In that situation, at your age, I'd have done the same as you,' Cal tried again to keep her talking. 'I'd have been frightened to have gone on the swing. I'd have tried to stop Max grabbing me, any way I could. I'd have panicked just like you. It must have been awful for you, an experience like that and your brother dead.'

'Chloe said I shouldn't feel guilty.'

'Did Joss say that too?'

'Yes.'

'They must have been upset ... seeing Max's body like that.'

Silence.

Cal said, 'Weren't they?'

'They didn't like Max.'

'Are you saying they weren't upset?'

'None of us minded not seeing him again.'

'None of you?'

'Yes.'

'You too?'

'Yes.' Her voice dropped.

The water was now at Cal's waist.

'But Max wasn't found the next morning?'

'No. The ledge was the only place that wasn't searched. The police didn't know about it since they'd been brought in from other islands. The crevice running down the cliff was examined, but as it was blocked with rock, they thought it had been impassable for a while. By the next morning, people in the township were being questioned and houses searched. I heard my father and the police discuss possible suspects. Joss and Chloe said Max was bound to be discovered soon and I mustn't forget the story no matter what anyone said. But he wasn't, and Joss started to say the police would lose interest. In other cases of people who had gone missing, the searches lasted a week, sometimes two. Soon it would be over. But it wasn't!'

A note of desperation reverberated in the cave.

'After the first year we realized the search for Max would never end, because my father wouldn't let it. Last year Joss asked him to stop bringing in experts and holding a memorial service. She said it was time for Max to be laid to rest and for my father to pay attention to his other children. But he shouted at her, saying he would find Max's killer if it was the last thing he did.

'That's why Joss went to live in the township. She thought that might make him stop hiring another investigator. But she was wrong. Staying there she realized how much damage was being done by our father's obsession. The last time we spoke she said she thought all three of us should go to him and tell him the truth. Joss said that would stop him – having accused the township of murder for so long, how could he go to the police and hand over his three daughters for covering up Max's death?'

'What did you think of that idea?'

'I didn't support it at the time, nor did Chloe. We asked Joss for more time to think. We hadn't been able to discuss it with her again before she was killed.'

She fell silent and all Cal heard was the sound of rising water. It was now at his ribs. Hannah said, 'I was wrong, wasn't I?'

'You've changed your mind?'

'Yes. Joss was right – the only way this is going to end is if he's told what happened to Max.'

'Does Chloe agree?'

'No. We had an argument last night.'

'Is that why you're here?'

'Yes.'

'What did Chloe say?'

'She said Joss only had herself to blame for her death and that she was asking for trouble going to live in the township. But *Chloe's* Daddy's favourite now, isn't she? That's why she doesn't want him to be told.'

'Hannah?'

Silence.

'Hannah, I need to move. The tide's getting high. The water's going to be at my neck soon.'

28

Crossing the sound in the police RIB, Helen wondered where Cal was. Night was closing in. Shouldn't he have returned? *He'll be delaying until after dark. He'll be somewhere out there. He'll be happy because he's alone.* A sinking feeling of despondency seeped into her. For a while she had thought she might be able to share that impulse in him. The day before, for example, when she'd been overwhelmed by the beauty of the landscape, she hoped she was beginning to appreciate the pull that wild and remote places had on Cal. With more time, with more familiarity, she told herself, she would love them too and, like Cal, would feel that tug at her soul.

Yet, on this short journey across the sound, she began to think the opposite. Instead of being entranced by the contrasts of a place where violent storms were followed by the stillest of days, she found they put her on edge. She looked around. Looming banks of cloud darkened the sky. The sea appeared oily and black. Priest's Island, on her right, was brooding and unwelcoming – what a change in thirty-six hours. Instead of liking its variability, as Cal would, she found it disturbing, as she might a person who altered character at the drop of a hat: now smiling, now sullen, now demented with rage. Rather than regarding dusk as exhilarating, as Cal would, she found the prospect of night threatening. Given the choice, she realized, she would rather have been in a city street. She was more comfortable in an environment like that.

The thought worked away at her as the RIB turned to

starboard along the south coast of Priest's Island, out of sight of the *Jacqueline* and Chloe. So, when she saw Cal's RIB in the bay below the shieling, she felt a jolt of resentment at his absence rather than concern for his well-being. She peered into the gathering darkness and it seemed to her like a gaping and unknowable void, one that would always separate her from Cal.

She sighed then gave the order to put ashore.

She told the younger of the two police constables – Fraser Carmichael – to head inland and to find a vantage point overlooking the north of the island with a view of the bonfire and the *Jacqueline*. He should radio back any movements. She warned him against talking too loudly. Noise travelled long distances at night when there was little wind. Handing him the night-vision binoculars, she impressed on him Beacom's warning about stumbling and damaging them against a rock. 'They're the only ones we've got.' The other constable, a taciturn, heavily built man by the name of Bob Stevenson, remained with Helen. They turned out to be kindred spirits. Carmichael was puppyish, enthusiastic and talkative. Helen wasn't in that kind of mood and neither was Stevenson. They sat quietly in the RIB and waited for Carmichael's first report in their earpieces.

It came after twenty minutes. Chloe was standing by the fire. Carmichael had seen movement inside the *Jacqueline*. He presumed that was David Wheeler.

The next report was half an hour later. Chloe had banked up the fire with driftwood and was sitting close by. Twice more Carmichael reported the same. Helen could tell he was becoming bored but she told him to stay alert. At eight thirty, Carmichael reported, 'She's putting more driftwood on the fire. It's blazing.' A few minutes later, 'I think she's on the move, heading this way. I won't report in again until she's passed by in case she hears me.'

Twenty minutes later, in a hoarse, excited whisper, he said that Chloe was descending the hill towards the island's south coast: 'Heading towards the shieling. She might spot the RIBs, because she seems to be able to see in the dark; she hasn't put a foot wrong since she started.'

Suddenly a light shone. Helen whispered to Stevenson, 'She's got a torch.' The beam jumped and flickered as she descended the hill. 'It's not very powerful,' Helen said. 'If she's going to the shieling it'll hardly reach us.' She offered up some thanks that both RIBs were black.

As a precaution Stevenson put his coat over the engine, which had a white stripe. He said under his breath to Helen, 'Be careful it doesn't pick up your face.'

She squatted beside him and watched Chloe shine the light one way and another as she negotiated the steepest part of the hill. Afterwards she seemed to veer to her left. Helen wondered where she was going. 'She's heading for the other side of the bay, not the shieling. Why?' The torch went out. 'What's she doing?' she asked Carmichael.

'She's still on her feet, still walking. She's among some rocks, going closer to the shore.'

'And now?'

'She's crouching, looks like she's waiting for something.'

'What on earth for?'

Helen asked Carmichael to tell her what time it was. She couldn't look at her phone in case Chloe saw the light. 'Just past nine,' Carmichael replied.

Chloe was still waiting in the dark thirty minutes later when Helen whispered to Stevenson, 'Oh my God, I didn't expect that. I think she's waiting for the tide to fall.'

Cal swapped hands as he'd been doing for hours. 'I won't be able to hold on much longer,' he said. As before, when he talked about moving his position, Hannah didn't answer. When he'd first climbed the chamber wall, using the old iron handholds and footholds, he'd told Hannah he would come as close to her as he had to – to keep his head and neck above water. But now he wasn't sure how much longer he could hold on even though the sea had stopped rising. His fingers ached, so did his wrists. Pain travelled from his hands up his arms. He shifted his weight from his left leg to his right and could only tell he had done so by a slight sensation of one thigh being heavier than the other. His feet, ankles and knees were numb from being submerged in the cold water. He decided he could put off the moment no longer.

'Hannah . . .' He heard her move. 'Hannah . . .' As they had agreed, he turned on his torch so she could see where he was, so she would know he wasn't using the sound of his voice to cover for moving closer to her. The light flickered and dimmed. He shook the torch and directed the light on to his waist to show her the height of the tide, how far up the wall it reached. 'It'll fall now,' he said, 'but it won't be low enough for me to climb down for two or three hours. I need to get out of the water. I have to sit down. I can't hold on any more.' Once again, he waited. 'Hannah.' He listened to the sea splash against the chamber's walls. 'Hannah, you don't have to worry. I'm not going to try anything. I give you my word.' Now he lit up his face to let her see how sincere he was.

'Stay there.' Her voice was shrill; panicked.

Cal said, 'I've got no choice. You'll have to let me sit with you.'

He heard a quick movement, as though she might be pulling back into the alcove, making room. 'I'm going to start climbing now,' he said, putting the torch into his jeans pocket. After pulling himself up to the next ring and finding the foothold, he rested. 'Hannah, you've got to believe me. I can't stay where I am. It's not a trick.' He heard a gasp, followed by another. He shone the torch on Hannah. She was sitting with her legs hanging over the edge of the alcove. She looked startled as if she was surprised by what she'd done. The knife was in her hand and crimson showed up against the white skin of her upturned arms. Her wrists were cut and bleeding. As the torch flickered and started to dim, she fell forwards into the water. 'Hannah,' Cal shouted. He watched her swim deep. The torch lit up a trail of pink staining the water before the light faded and went out.

Cal jumped after her.

Helen listened to the flop of the waves, the wet slap of water against rock, the rattle of pebbles and shells, and she wondered if it was just the shifting of the sea or whether Chloe was moving too. 'What's she doing now?' she whispered to Carmichael.

'Same as before,' he replied.

'Still crouching?' Helen stared into the dark and tried to imagine her on the other side of the bay.

'Hasn't moved a muscle,' Carmichael replied.

'Tell me when she does, even if she scratches her nose.' While she was talking, Helen heard an unfamiliar rippling sound. It was over so quickly she wondered if she had imagined it. She moved her head to the left, then back to the right, listening again.

Carmichael said, 'Something's moving in the water below Chloe. No, there's someone swimming.'

Helen heard a splash. 'Was that Chloe? What's she doing?'

'She's jumped in,' Carmichael said. 'She's helping. No. No, she's not.'

'Quick, turn on that spotlight,' Helen ordered Stevenson.

Cal was groping blindly at the bottom of the cave when he saw a glow. He wondered whether the torch had come back to life. But the light was different; bright white and further away. He swam in its direction and found he was at the exit. He propelled himself between vertical rock walls and looked up into a glare so bright it was as if the sun was shining. Cal was momentarily disorientated. Was it day or night? Kicking towards the surface, his lungs almost bursting, he registered the bottom of a boat above him and, close by, the silhouette of a body suspended in the sea. A silent, anguished shout filled Cal's head. *Hannah*.

In the RIB's spotlight, there was a tangle of arms and bodies.

'I've got her,' Stevenson said, lifting Chloe clear of the water with one heave.

She screamed, 'Get off!'

Helen grabbed Hannah and pulled her towards the RIB. She made a choking sound and Helen said, 'Thank God.'

Hannah gagged then coughed as Helen lifted her aboard. She tried to sit up and her head fell forward between her knees. She coughed some more and spat. Helen knelt in front of her and took her hands. 'You're all right now. You're safe.' A warm trickle ran across Helen's fingers. Turning over Hannah's arms, she saw the slashes. She clamped her hands tight round the girl's wrists to stop the flow. 'Bob, this one's bleeding. I need some bandages from the medical box at the back of the RIB.'

Chloe shouted, 'Get your fucking hands off me!' and Stevenson threw the box towards Helen.

'Sorry, this one's trouble.'

Cal surfaced, gasping for breath. Helen called out to him. 'Cal, are you OK?'

'Have you got Hannah?' He was dazzled by the light.

'She's here.'

'Is she all right?'

'No, she's hurt. I need your help.'

After clambering aboard, Cal bound a bandage tight round one of Hannah's wrists while Helen attended to the other. 'She cut herself,' Cal said. 'She tried to kill herself.'

'She's not the only one. Her sister attempted to drown her.' Helen looked at Hannah. 'Why would she do that? Why would Chloe want you dead?'

Hannah said nothing. She was looking at Chloe struggling with the policeman.

Cal touched her on the arm. 'Shall I tell her?'

There was a slight nod.

'Chloe was frightened of what Hannah might say,' Cal said. 'Hannah killed Max. It was an accident. Joss and Chloe knew and covered it up. Joss was going to tell their father just before she was killed. Hannah has changed her mind too – she wants their father to know. I think that's why Chloe tried to drown her, to stop her.'

'Is that right?' Helen looked from Cal to Hannah before talking into her radio. 'Carmichael, see what you can do to put out that fire. And be careful, there might be some important evidence in it.'

Then she looked at Chloe, who had fallen silent. 'Is this the first time you've wanted one of your sisters dead?'

29

Bella looked at the clock. Ten past eight in the morning. Less than two hours to opening time. Normally, she would be resting and having a cup of tea. The kitchen would be filled with the smell of baking. There would be bread and brownies cooling. Yet, this morning, she hadn't even managed to turn on the oven. She had been standing at the table since six. She'd done nothing. Nor had she been aware of the time passing. What was the matter with her?

'That doesn't sound like you,' Isobel said when she rang. 'That's not the Bella MacLeod I know, busy, busy.'

This Bella Macleod was a stranger to Bella too.

'No,' she replied uncertainly, 'I'm worn out.'

'There's so much going on it's hard to sleep,' Isobel said. 'But the main thing is that it's over. You must be relieved about that. I know I am.'

'Yes, I suppose so.' Again her reply was hesitant, as though it was simpler to agree, as though she thought something else.

'You don't sound relieved.'

'No,' Bella said. 'It's just that I can't stop thinking about that family. Did we do that to them? Was it our fault?'

'Why would you think that?'

'I don't know. I just do. I haven't been able to think of anything else since Alistair phoned last night to say the township would never have stood up to Wheeler if it hadn't been for me. He said he wanted me to know how appreciative everyone was. Without me, the township wouldn't have won.

We wouldn't have been able to get back our good name and now we can; we will.'

'I'm not sure I'd have used those words,' Isobel said. 'It doesn't feel like winning after what we've been through, being called murderers when we always said Max had died in an accident. If only Wheeler had listened. It wasn't as if he wasn't told often enough. No, it wasn't our fault.'

'I suppose not.'

Bella hurried off the phone, saying she'd better start baking if the tea room was ever to open. But the goading voice that worked on the old Bella seemed to have no effect on the new one. She continued to stand at the kitchen table, her hands clenched and her knuckles pressing so hard against the wooden top that they started to hurt. She thought of David Wheeler and of a remark Isobel had made. *I know I shouldn't think this, but doesn't it serve him right?*

'No,' Bella said, making up for being silent before. 'No one deserves that.'

The vague feeling of being to blame was so strong it felt like a weight pressing on her head and her shoulders. With sudden clarity, she saw herself as similar to Wheeler, as implacable, as possessed. With mounting dismay, she recalled her reaction when she heard about Priest's Island being sold and the grazing lease being cancelled. She'd been so upset on behalf of Donald Grant and Ewan that she'd put up a notice outside the Deep Blue barring the Wheelers from entering. She hadn't even spoken to David Wheeler. She hadn't met him or his family. If only she'd been less impulsive. Instead of encouraging Ewan's resentment, she should have urged him to be sensible, to look to the future, to go to college. She should have made him realize how lucky he was to have the prospect of Grant's Croft when he was older.

If only she had.

If she had been more level-headed, Ewan wouldn't have felt so hard done by. He wouldn't have taken out his anger on Max. Hannah would have been able to spend the night on Priest's Island without Max putting her through one of Ewan's tests. Max would still be alive. Joss wouldn't have come to live in the township. She wouldn't be dead. Hannah wouldn't be helping the police with their inquiries into Max's death. Chloe wouldn't have been charged with attempted murder, or questioned about Joss's killing.

As the day brightened outside, so it was that everything became illuminated to Bella. Instead of blaming Wheeler as she'd done these past five years and encouraging others to do the same, she should have been more critical of her own behaviour. She remembered Donald Grant coming to her and asking her to have a word with Ewan because 'you're the only one he pays any attention to'.

If only she'd been less quick to pass judgement on the Wheelers.

The phone went. Bella let it ring. It stopped and started again. Catriona appeared in the kitchen doorway, looking half asleep. 'Aren't you going to answer that?'

'I don't think I can.'

Catriona gave her aunt one of her sideways looks before picking up the phone. 'Hello . . . yes, it'll be a busy day.' Apart from the odd 'uh-huh' and 'I see', Catriona was quiet while the other person talked. After a few minutes, she said, 'I'll tell her. Yes, ring again if you hear any more.'

Catriona put down the phone. 'That was Isobel. The whole story has come out. The police have been searching the ashes of the fire on Priest's Island. They've found some buttons and the buckle of a belt. They think they're from the clothes Chloe was wearing when she killed Joss. Isobel also says traces of blood have been found under Chloe's bunk in the *Jacqueline*. They think that's where she hid the clothes until she was able to get rid of them. Joss was killed because Chloe was terrified of her telling their father about Max's death and her part in the cover-up. She used an old knife of Donald Grant's that she found lying on Priest's Island to make sure that Ewan was the obvious suspect. Later, when Hannah said she'd changed her mind about telling their father, Chloe threatened her. That's why Hannah left the *Jacqueline* in the middle of the night. She abandoned the dinghy in the sound and swam ashore so that Chloe and everyone else would think she'd fallen in. But she'd told Joss and Chloe about the cave at the time of Max's death and Chloe figured that's where she could be hiding. So Chloe waited for dark and for the tide to start falling and for everyone to be paying attention to the fire. If Hannah hadn't swum out, Chloe would have found the entrance at low tide – the next one was at three in the morning – and would have killed her. In Hannah's case, drowning was the best way – by then everyone expected Hannah to be found drowned.' Catriona shook her head in wonder. 'What a bitch!'

She looked at her aunt and a frown of worry formed. 'Are you all right?'

'No,' Bella replied, 'not really.'

'Why, what's wrong?'

Bella said, 'I'm sorry.'

'What for?'

Bella looked at the ceiling, as if she didn't know where to begin. 'For letting you think that other things or people were more important than you.' Bella continued as though listing her sins: 'The tea room, the township, Ewan, Joss, the fight with Wheeler.'

Catriona dropped her eyes.

Bella saw the hurt in her niece's gesture, how quickly she turned in on herself. 'It was never true. It isn't true.'

The phone rang again and Bella was stung by the speed with which Catriona answered, as though she was glad of an escape. Had she lost her forever?

'Hello, Isobel . . . Yes, I'll tell her . . . Yes, see you later in the tea room.'

When she turned back to Bella, she still didn't meet her eyes. 'They've found some bones under the raven's nest – they're human – and some pieces of clothing. Tests will be carried out but it's likely they're Max's. According to Isobel, every year the ravens have been adding to their nest, making it bigger. That's why Max's remains were covered up . . .'

Bella said, 'Stop, Catriona.'

'Why?'

'Because nothing, no one is more important than you. You know that, don't you?'

Catriona nodded.

Then Bella said, 'Would you mind if we didn't open the tea room today? I'd rather not have to listen to what everyone has to say. In fact, I don't think I want to again.'

Cal stood on the Priest's Island jetty. Someone watching him from the Deep Blue might have thought he was taking a last opportunity to study the sound and to fix in his mind the places where there were swirls of turbulence and sudden flares of white water, warnings to the unwary of hidden danger. In fact, he was only dimly conscious of the sea's movement, whether the tide was flowing or ebbing, which was a certain sign of there being jagged rocks beneath his own otherwise calm surface. He was standing still, and had been for the last ten minutes, because he was paralysed by indecision. An internal argument kept him rooted to the spot. Should he go on or should he go back? The flare-up of anger that had impelled him to cross the sound had grown weaker as Cal questioned his motivation for invading David Wheeler's privacy – the man was close by in the ruined chapel, taking refuge from the tragedies that had befallen him. To disturb him would require good reason and Cal wondered whether he'd crossed the sound on impulse because of his own emotional response to the aftermath of the investigation into Max Wheeler's disappearance. In other words, was he being self-indulgent?

Beacom's final attempt to dissuade Cal from going to see David Wheeler influenced him more now that he was so close. 'You'll be wasting your time, Cal. He's not going to give you the time of day. Whatever your opinion of him, don't you think the guy's had enough?'

But just as Cal was being persuaded that he'd made a mistake and should get back into his RIB, he was again overtaken by the idea that a further and avoidable injustice was about to be perpetrated, this time not against the township but against Chloe and Hannah, particularly Hannah. The feeling was strong enough to propel him from the jetty in the direction of the chapel.

Cal walked quickly, determined not to let his doubts change his mind. What he had to say was too important for that. He found Wheeler slumped on the stone bench inside the chapel. Whether he was praying or overwhelmed by despondency and grief at all the misfortunes that had overtaken him and his family, Cal couldn't guess. Nor at that moment did he care. He cleared his throat. Wheeler moved his head a fraction to the right. Cal took the gesture to indicate he had Wheeler's attention, or as much as he would ever be likely to have.

'A week ago, you asked me if I had a son. I said I hadn't and you told me that I wouldn't be able to understand what Max's disappearance, his death, meant for you. You were right. I can't imagine how awful it must be to lose a son. But I do know what it's like to lose a father. Don't abandon Chloe and Hannah. Whatever they've done, they did because they were frightened. Hannah was terrified that Max would pull her off the ledge. All three of your daughters covered up Max's death because they were frightened of you. That same fear made Chloe kill Joss and attempt to murder Hannah because she was desperate to be your favourite. Chloe will be sent to prison. Hannah might be too. Their lives aren't going to be easy. They're still very young. They need a father.'

Wheeler jerked his head back to where it had been, a movement of a centimetre or two, a gesture of dismissal.

~

Helen's eyes opened. She stared at a white ceiling. Some people were talking. She wondered where she was, who they were. Now she was wide awake, sitting upright and briefly surprised to find she was in her running clothes, lying on the sofa in the chalet's sitting room. The television was on, a man and woman arguing. She glanced at her phone. 'Oh, no!' It was almost ten. The tea room would soon be open. She hurried to the shower. 'Nobody tell her.' She said the same when she was drying, brushing her teeth, doing her hair and dressing. Before going outside, she closed her eyes, wishing she could sleep. What a long night it had been. But sleep had caused this panic. Instead of being at the Deep Blue at nine thirty when Catriona would be on her own, laying tables, Helen would have to try to talk to her when the place was mobbed.

Walking round the side of the tea room, she was non-plussed to see the lights were off and the tables empty. She checked her phone again. Ten twenty. Carrying on to the front, she saw a dozen people gathered around the door, some reporters as well as Ina and Mary-Anne. 'What's happening?' Helen asked and was relieved when both women appeared pleased to see her. If Ina and Mary-Anne hadn't heard, perhaps Catriona hadn't either.

'The tea room is shut today,' Ina announced as though another unsettling mystery, another tragedy, had befallen the township.

'There's a notice on the door,' Mary-Anne said to Helen. 'The Deep Blue will open tomorrow under new management. Catriona's taking over. Bella's only going to be doing the baking. Even Isobel didn't know. What could have happened?'

More people were arriving. Helen nodded to Grey and managed to slip away without Ina noticing. She returned to the chalet, intending to ring Catriona and ask her over for coffee. But Catriona was outside Bella's house, smoking.

'Celebrating your promotion?' Helen called over before going along the pathway to join her. Catriona smiled back and all Helen could detect – thank goodness – was a little self-consciousness. *She doesn't know*, Helen thought. Relief was replaced by apprehension. How would Catriona react?

'Well, nobody could ever accuse Eilean Dubh of being a backwater after what's happened in the last twelve hours,' Helen said brightly. 'A five-year-old mystery solved. A murderer caught, all change at the tea room and it won't be long before your Ewan is released.'

'No,' Catriona seemed suddenly thoughtful, 'I suppose it won't.'

'There's something you should know.'

'About Ewan?'

'About me. I haven't been honest with you. I told you I came to Eilean Dubh to recover from a break-up with my boyfriend.' Helen shook her head. 'I didn't have a boyfriend. I don't have a boyfriend. I came here because I'm a police officer, a detective sergeant. I work with Detective Chief Inspector Beacom. I wanted to tell you myself before you heard it from other people, because some people know I was involved in Chloe's arrest.'

Catriona dragged on her cigarette. 'So there isn't a blonde called Phoebe?'

'No.'

Catriona's face was turned slightly away so that Helen was unable to see her expression.

'My name is Helen Jamieson. That bit was right and I am thirty-two years old and I do holiday alone and like cake. That's all true. And I have enjoyed meeting you, getting to know you. It's been, well, fun. It didn't feel like work.' She touched Catriona's arm. 'I'm sorry. DCI Beacom thought there was no other way of getting anyone in the township to speak to the police because of the background of mistrust. We hoped someone would say something that would lead us to discover what happened to Max Wheeler – and you did.

'Without you, Ewan would be going to prison. We would never have discovered the truth if you hadn't told us about Max being bullied or about the way he tried to make you go on the swing at the sea cliff. If Cal hadn't found that cave by the shieling, Hannah Wheeler would be dead. Either she would have killed herself or Chloe would have drowned her. But, thanks to you, it's over.'

Catriona looked round. Helen expected her to be angry or hurt. Instead she seemed anxious.

'You won't tell anyone. Ewan won't have to know.'

'No.' Helen allowed herself a brief smile at Catriona's instinctive concern about anyone in the township finding out. 'If you'd known I was a police officer you wouldn't have spoken to me, would you? You wouldn't have agreed to meet Cal McGill?'

'No.'

'I'm glad you did but I'm sorry I had to lie.'

Catriona nodded.

'About Ewan . . .' Helen decided only to tell her the headlines. 'He'll be released this morning. He won't be charged for taking eggs from the raven's nest. It's been removed for forensic analysis along with Max's bones. The clutch would have been destroyed anyway. The money has been confiscated because it was the proceeds of criminal activity. But there won't be a further investigation.'

Helen paused, then: 'Are you angry with me?'

'No.' Catriona's eyes flicked towards Helen's before darting away.

'Sure?'

Catriona nodded.

'But something's wrong.'

'It's not that.'

Catriona turned her face towards Helen's, as if deciding whether she could trust her. 'Their aunt's car being attacked . . .'

'The night Max died?'

'That was me.' Catriona again studied Helen, this time for her reaction. 'I hated the Wheelers for stopping Donald Grant grazing his sheep, and I was angry with Ewan for sneaking off to the island whenever Max was there.' She sighed. 'I wish I hadn't done it. It complicated everything . . . the police thinking the damage to the car was linked to Max's death. I didn't own up before because I thought it might make things worse for Ewan. They already thought I knew more than I was saying – they'd just have used my admission as evidence to show that Ewan and I were working together.'

'Does Ewan know?'

'No.'

'Hasn't he asked?'

Catriona shook her head.

'He must have guessed.'

'I think he did.' Then the worry returned to her eyes. 'Will you have to report me?'

'What, for a few scratches to a BMW five years ago? I don't think so.'

A brief smile wavered on Catriona's lips. 'Thanks.'

Helen asked, 'What will you do about Ewan? Will you get back together with him?'

Catriona was thoughtful again, as though that had been on her mind too. 'I love him but he liked Joss more than me. I can't get that out of my head.'

'Oh, come here.' Helen gave her a hug.

Going along the road to the old slipway, Helen watched how Priest's Island changed with the light. One moment it was dark and obscured as clouds blotted out the sun. The next a ray would burst through and paint the land in bright pools of green and yellow. As a last impression it struck her as appropriate, a metaphor for the township which hid away in the shadows and only allowed outsiders to see occasional shafts of light. She was wondering about the connection between the weather and the inhabitants – did the former mould the characters of the latter? – when she saw Cal. He was sitting on the bonnet of his pickup, a bottle of water beside him.

He was staring at the sound. 'What are you thinking about?' she asked.

'The sea,' Cal said.

Helen laughed. 'Of course you are.' Then she became serious. 'Beacom's told me.'

'Told you what?'

'That you're refusing to be a witness against Ewan over the raven's nest.'

Cal shrugged. 'He's been under suspicion for five years for a crime he didn't commit. That's punishment enough.'

'There's no case without you,' Helen continued. 'Ewan and Bella won't talk. No one else saw him with Pinkie Pryke.'

Cal said, 'I know.'

Helen looked at the sound. 'Do you think Pinkie's under there somewhere?' Then, as if settling an argument in her head: 'Anyway, as Beacom says, there's no law against people falling off cliffs if that's what happened.'

Cal didn't reply and Helen carried on. 'Our wildlife crime people are picking up chatter about Pinkie. There's talk about him visiting the sites where his clutches of eggs are buried, a farewell tour before he joins his wife in Portugal. She flew there a few days ago and is apparently looking to buy a property with a nice garden. There's another rumour about Pinkie planning to disappear after faking an accident. But, apparently, there's always some talk or other about Pinkie.'

'Pinkie's in there somewhere.' Cal nodded towards the sound. 'I was trying to work out where he'll turn up ... if he'll turn up. If he was wearing a harness and some rope was attached, he'll probably be snagged on a rock.'

Neither spoke for a while.

Helen found herself remembering how pleasant that was. Being with a man who was accepting. *Not* feeling that nervous compulsion to talk.

Cal said, 'Are you leaving today?'

'Yes.'

'You're going back to Edinburgh?'

'Uh-huh.'

'Would you like dinner on the way back, in Fife?'

Helen delayed her answer in case she sounded excited. 'That would be nice.' She imagined a little harbour restaurant, somewhere picturesque with candles and wine.

She imagined *it*, whatever *it* was.

'With some friends of mine,' Cal said.

'That's nice.' Helen tried to hide her disappointment. 'At their house?'

'No, it's on a beach, it's a barbecue.'

Helen laughed.

'What?' Cal said.

'Cal, nobody has a barbecue on a beach in Fife in *March*.'

Epilogue

He was tall, blond, Scandinavian-looking and one of a number of kayakers to visit the Deep Blue that summer. He seemed slightly at a loss. Catriona called over from the counter, 'Sit wherever you want. What would you like to drink?' But rather than find a table or place his order, he appeared eager to talk. 'I've just been told to get off that island by a madman.' He looked across the sound towards Priest's Island and back at Catriona. 'My guidebook says it's uninhabited. That's why I went there in my kayak.'

'*Was* uninhabited,' Catriona corrected him. 'The man you met is the owner. He's called David Wheeler. He lives there now.'

'By himself?'

'It's a sad story. His wife and two of his children were killed and the other two . . . well, they've had to go away.' Catriona wondered if she should tell the man: Chloe was serving a life sentence in a women's prison on the mainland; Hannah was at a special school somewhere in England, having been released after six months.

The kayaker frowned. Instead of commiserating, he said, 'Surely, no one can live there. How can he? There isn't a proper house, only a little shed.'

Catriona laughed. 'We call that a shieling. It used to be occupied during the summer when sheep or cattle were taken over to the island for the grazing. That's where David Wheeler is living.'

The kayaker seemed almost offended at the idea. 'I

wouldn't want to spend a single night on that island. It doesn't have a good atmosphere. It's a creepy place. Look at this.' He opened his backpack and withdrew the stiff body of a small black bird. 'I found it lying by the ruined chapel. I was going to ask that madman what it was but he just shouted at me.'

'Wait there.' Catriona went to the office and rang Bella. 'Can you come over? There's something you should see.'

When Bella saw the dead bird, she exclaimed, 'Oh my goodness, it's a storm petrel.'

Catriona and her aunt exchanged glances.

'What?' the kayaker looked from one to the other. 'What?'